Warmaster 5: The Glory Games

Melissa McShane

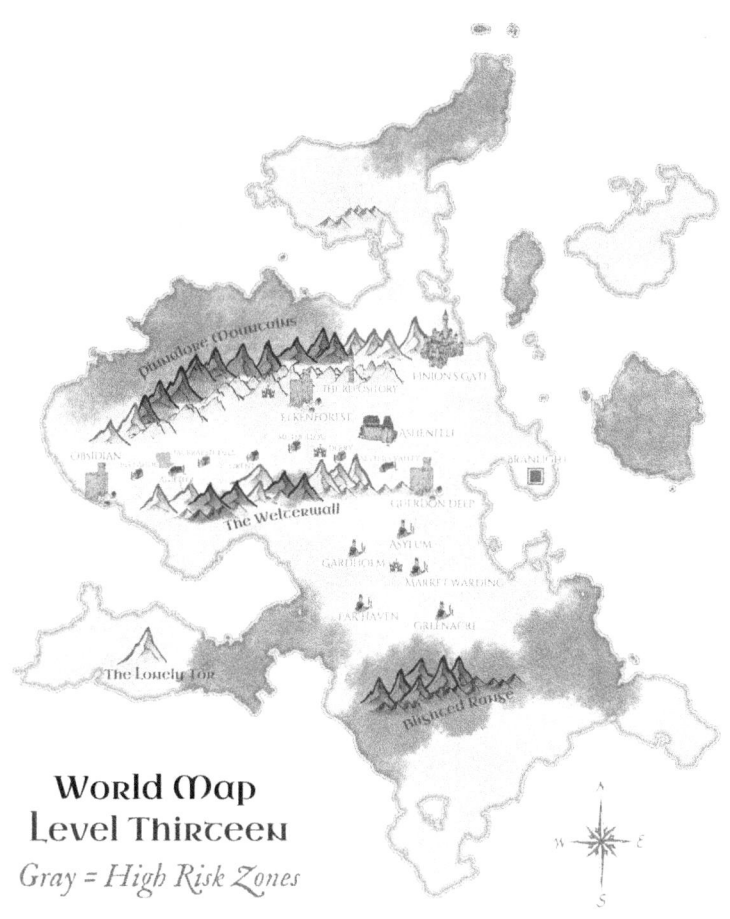

World Map
Level Thirteen

Gray = High Risk Zones

CHAPTER ONE

Aderyn still didn't like the look of Guerdon Deep. The buildings matched the mountain's stone so closely the city looked more like a pile of geometric rubble than anything built by humans. In front of it, the plains sloped down to meet the city like a funnel, giving Aderyn the illusion they were being swept along the plains, pulled toward the mountain city.

"It looks the same, and yet I feel so different coming here at level thirteen instead of level five," she said.

"Did you Assess it?" Owen asked.

"We're too far away. My range increased when we reached level thirteen, but I still have to be within three miles. In another hour, maybe."

"Remember the cat-hawks?" Weston said. "That's another difference. We'd take them out no trouble now."

Aderyn remembered all too clearly the bite of the cat-hawk's claws and the moment of terror when another cat-hawk had landed on Isold, nearly killing him. "I'm still glad we don't have to."

By the time Guerdon Deep's walls loomed over them, forty feet high and made of the same stone as everything else, it was midafternoon and Aderyn was mentally ready for a meal and a bed, even though she wasn't all that tired. When the guard demanded the entrance fee, she couldn't help remembering how desperate they'd been the first time, how twenty-five gold had nearly bankrupted them. This time, she simply dropped five largish gold coins in the basin and waited for the gate to swing open.

Even at midafternoon, the streets of Guerdon Deep were bleak and forbidding. The gate opened on a road wide enough for a couple of oxcarts to pass easily, with tall, narrow buildings of the familiar gray stone rising above it. The street wasn't very busy, but people passed in and out of doors over which hung signs advertising what could be found within. Balconies with wrought-iron railings extended from skinny doors on the second and third floors, taking advantage of the space between buildings. The overhangs made the city even darker.

Aderyn scanned the signs, looking for something that might be an inn. "We are *not* going back to the Horse and Hound," she said. "That Clerra woman was way too attentive to Owen."

"It's not like I found her attractive, sweetheart," Owen said.

"Still. It was annoying then and it's even more annoying now we're together."

"Okay," Owen said, sounding amused. "I wish Guerdon Deep had those people in the yellow tabards like in Setter's Valley. That was so useful."

They passed two inns before Weston said, "That's what we want."

"I don't see the sign," Owen said.

"It's down that side street a bit. But it has posters advertising entertainment on the walls facing the main street. That means it's well to do, but probably known more for its bar than its bedrooms. Which further means the innkeeper likely won't charge as much, because he'll be grateful for the custom."

"Good logic," Livia said. "Let's try it."

Aderyn wasn't sure about Weston's reasoning, because she heard no music coming from the inn even though the posters advertised a beautiful fiddler with large breasts probably not based in reality. Probably there weren't many patrons yet. On the other hand, she smelled fresh pies, sweet and savory, and she hadn't had a good pie since leaving home. Her father was a master of the art.

The door opened directly on the taproom, and Aderyn realized she'd been wrong about at least one thing: the room was half-full of men and women, mostly clustered around the bar, drinking and talking and laughing. Pillars held up the low roof, making the room feel cozy, though it probably would feel cramped when the place was full. A few people had platters of sliced meat and vegetables at their tables and were eating chunks of bread stuffed with the same. Aderyn had never seen that kind of food before. It looked messy.

An attractive, busty woman wearing an apron that showed off her considerable assets approached them. Her smile was friendly and not at all flirtatious. "Hey there, welcome to the Pigeon's Roost," she said. "I know, you haven't seen pigeons in Guerdon Deep. The cats take care of that. But my father liked the disgusting little creatures, and I keep the name in his memory. You want drink, or food?"

"Yes, but we're also looking for rooms," Isold said. "Three rooms, to be precise."

The woman looked their group up and down. Aderyn took the opportunity to Level Assess her.

Name: Heskia

Class: Herald (retired)

Level: 7

"You're a team?" Heskia asked.

"We are."

"Don't see a lot of teams that are paired off quite so neatly. Hope you don't feel left out, fellow Herald." Heskia's smile became mischievous.

"I assure you, I am more than happy with how things stand. So many possibilities." Isold matched her smile for mischievous smile.

"Well, you're all very welcome here," Heskia went on. "Parinna will show you upstairs. We've got enough free rooms you can be close together if you want. Then come on down and I'll feed you. You look like it's been a while since you had a good meal."

The door to the kitchen opened, sending out a whiff of pie crust and hot berries. On cue, Aderyn's stomach rumbled, and she laughed with the others.

The room Parinna showed Aderyn and Owen to was plainly furnished, just a bed and a crate for belongings that didn't even qualify as a clothespress and a single chair. But the bed's mattress was thick, it had two woven wool blankets, and the room smelled sweetly if faintly of lavender. Aderyn dropped the <**Knapsack of Plenty**> in the crate and returned with Owen to the taproom. They chose one of the empty tables and waited for the others to join them.

"This inn was a good choice," Owen said. "The price is right and the accommodations are good enough. Plus, that smell—" He drew in a deep breath through his nostrils. "I haven't had pie since I reached this world."

"I miss it. My father makes the best meat pies you can imagine."

"I don't suppose she meant she'd feed us right away?" Weston asked, drawing out a seat beside Aderyn. Livia and Isold sat as well. "Because I'm hungrier than I realized."

A young man bearing an enormous tray appeared beside Weston as if he'd just been waiting for his moment. He began setting down plates of food that looked like nothing Aderyn had seen before. There was chicken and beef and mutton, but all sliced thin and apparently cold. There were tomatoes and cucumbers, two kinds of pickles, and three kinds of cheese, all of them similarly sliced thin. Two pots of mustard and cruets of oil and vinegar joined the meat and vegetables. Finally, the young man set down a basket of bread chunks about the length of Aderyn's hand. "Enjoy," he said, and walked away with the empty tray.

The five friends stared at the plates. Aderyn prodded the corner of a slice of yellow cheese. "Enjoy... what?"

Owen started to laugh. "For once I know more than you all about your world," he said, drawing his belt knife. He sliced one of the bread chunks in half down the middle and layered slices of meat, cheese and vegetables on one half, slathered it with yellow mustard, stacked the other bread half on top, and took a bite. "It's a sandwich."

"What is a sandwich?" Weston said.

Owen waved the thing he'd made at Weston. "I'm sure it's called something else here, because in my world it's named after a nobleman called the Earl of Sandwich. The story is he loved gambling so much, he hated to leave the gaming table to eat, so he arranged for food to be brought to him in this form." He took another large bite. "I would never have guessed I could come all the way to another world and still end up with a sub sandwich."

Aderyn hesitantly followed Owen's example. The combination of having everything in one place was strange at first, but after a few bites, she decided she liked it that way. She ate one sandwich and made herself another.

The door swung open behind her, and several people entered. "Yes, something to eat," a man said.

Aderyn dropped her sandwich, which broke apart and scattered across the table. She leaped to her feet, knocking over her chair, and nearly tripped turning around. The older man was handsome in a burly way, the woman was beautiful if sharp-featured, but it was the man with the staff Aderyn couldn't take her eyes off. Her heart was trying to burst out of her chest, and she could barely breathe. She gasped, *"Borrus!"*

The man with the staff glanced her way, did a double take, and dropped his staff. In just a few strides, he'd caught Aderyn up in his arms and spun her around. "Aderyn!" he shouted. "Look at this! My little sister!"

"Little?" Aderyn exclaimed. "You're—hey, put me down!—barely fifteen months older than I am!" She threw her arms around his neck and hugged him so her legs dangled a moment when he released her.

Borrus was laughing, that delighted, deep chuckle that never failed to disconcert her, coming from the boy she remembered with his high-pitched voice. "What are the odds?" he said. "I can't believe it's you. You got your Call, and you're—" His smile fell away. "A Warmaster. That's, um, different."

"A level thirteen Warmaster," Owen said.

Borrus's gaze switched to Owen. "Who's this?"

Aderyn wanted to laugh at his clear consternation. "These are my friends. My adventuring team. Everyone, this is my brother Borrus."

Borrus said, "Wait a moment." He turned to the man and woman who'd accompanied him and spoke a few quiet words. The older man nodded and turned away in search of seats. The woman gazed at Aderyn in an indifferent way that made Aderyn stiffen up. She'd never liked being the focus of a stranger's gaze, and the woman had the look of someone who thought Aderyn beneath her.

"Can I sit here?" Borrus asked. He picked up his staff and drew up a chair between Aderyn and Owen without waiting for permission. He'd grown bigger since Aderyn had last seen him two years ago, stouter and close to fat around the middle, but the weight suited him even though it did make him look more like a Stalwart than a Staffsworn.

"Sit, please." Excitement bubbled up inside Aderyn. "I can't believe it's you."

"No reason we might not run into each other eventually," Borrus said. "And this is the finest eating establishment in Guerdon Deep. I come here every time I pass through. Still, it's some good luck, right?"

"I'm not going to question it. Borrus, I want you to meet my friends. This is Isold, and Weston, and Livia, and Owen." She had to lean past Borrus to see Owen and was disconcerted to see the tension in his shoulders that said he wasn't happy about this. Well, Borrus *had* implied that Aderyn's class was useless, but it wasn't as if everyone didn't think that way.

"It's good to meet you," Borrus said, but his attention was still on Aderyn. "How long have you been here? No—how long since you got your Call?"

"It's been—" She had to count back. "About three and a half months."

Borrus's jaw fell slack in astonishment. "You reached level thirteen in *three and a half months*? Aderyn, I've been adventuring two years and I only just got to level fourteen a month ago!"

Aderyn blushed and didn't know why. That time period hadn't seemed strange until now, but if she thought about it, it had been awfully fast. "We had some luck. And—" She didn't want to bring up the Fated One thing in the middle of a public taproom. "Anyway, I'm so glad to see you!"

"You'll have to tell me how things are going back home. Nollan and Pia aren't back, are they?"

"No. I—Borrus, I have so much to tell you! Come, eat with us, won't you?"

"Yes, sure, but—" Borrus glanced back at his companions, who were seated across the room and talking to each other. "You know what? You might be interested in this. Can I introduce you to my companions?"

"Companions?" Aderyn still felt uncomfortable about the woman, and his question made her wary.

"Yes. Javath and Kendria." Borrus examined Owen, then gave

Weston a longer look. "And it's most of what I wanted to tell you, what I've been doing for a while now."

"Now I'm curious," Aderyn said. "What have you been doing?"

Borrus leaned back in his chair. "Are you and your friends interested in fame, experience, and more money than you can count in a lifetime?"

CHAPTER TWO

"What?" Owen asked. "What does that mean?"

"Javath, Kendria's father, is a recruiter for the Glory Games in Finion's Gate," Borrus said. "He travels all over the Forsaken Lands, looking for the next big contender. He pays me a bonus for every adventurer I sign up. It's a sweet deal even before those adventurers compete in the Games. The best adventurers gain a lot of experience."

"Oh," Aderyn said. "So... how do you gain experience by doing that?"

"The Games are nonlethal," Borrus said. "Wealthy men and women support champions, and it's not much of an investment if your champion gets killed. But a defeat is still a defeat, and some of these fighters are high level, so winners get experience as well as coin from their sponsors. Coin, and the best lodgings, and benefits and all that."

"I meant you. How do you advance if you're recruiting for this fellow Javath?"

Borrus's sun-darkened skin reddened slightly. "Well, I don't exactly. But I used to be a champion before I was a recruiter. It's why

Javath hired me—I'm an example of how an ordinary adventurer can find success and wealth through the Games. I gained my last two levels by fighting."

"And you want us to talk to Javath," Weston said.

"Of course. I want your whole team to meet him, and Kendria too." Borrus gripped her hand. "Weston, you've got a good, solid build, and of course Owen as a Swordsworn is a good candidate too."

"Good... candidate? For the Games, you mean? Borrus, I'm not sure that's our thing."

"Of course it is! You all want experience, right? And no adventurer says no to money. I have connections—I could promote you for a good sponsorship."

Aderyn felt cold. "Is that all this was? A recruiting pitch?"

Borrus recoiled. "Aderyn, why would you say that? I know we haven't seen each other in two years, but how could you think I only wanted to talk to you for mercenary reasons?"

"Because it's practically all you've talked about from the moment you walked in!"

"That is so unfair. I admit I'm enthusiastic, but that's because I believe what I'm doing is good." Borrus ran a hand through his hair in a characteristically frustrated gesture. "I'm sorry. I guess my emotions are tangled because of Kendria." He blushed more hotly and lowered his gaze to look at the table.

Aderyn couldn't help herself—she whipped around to stare at Kendria again. "You're in love with Kendria? She's your sweetheart?"

"Try not to shout it to the rafters, Aderyn," Borrus said. "She's not my sweetheart. Yet. I'm working on winning her heart."

"Then—" Aderyn's head whirled. She pinned down the one thing she was certain of. "Then you hope to impress Kendria by fighting? Or by signing up combatants?"

"Kendria's a level sixteen Staffsworn. She's hard to impress that way. But she sees me working hard, and gaining her father's respect—

she's very close to him, see, and he relies on me to bring in the best. So me not advancing is just temporary while I court her."

Aderyn didn't like the sound of that. Borrus was almost plaintive, and she'd never known Borrus to be less than confident in his abilities. "I guess that makes sense."

"You'll understand better when you meet her," Borrus said, sounding more like himself.

"Will they want to meet us right now?" Isold murmured. "It's not as if they were expecting their meal to be interrupted by your family reunion."

"Javath is more avid about recruitment even than I am," Borrus said with a chuckle. "We were supposed to meet with some other potentials, but they haven't shown up, so why not you? And I'm sure he'll want to know my sister better."

"Well..."

"Let's talk to them at least," Livia said. "I'm not sure I care about fame, and we've already got plenty of money, but I never say no to experience."

Borrus led the way across the room and, when Javath and Kendria stopped pretending not to notice all of them, said, "Sorry about the disruption, Javath, but this is my sister Aderyn. We haven't seen each other in two years. This is her team."

Javath rose and extended a hand to Owen. "It's good to meet you. I'm Javath, and this is my daughter Kendria."

Aderyn felt intimidated all over again. Javath was built along the lines Weston was, but more so. He wasn't as tall as Weston, but he had the same broad chest and shoulders and the same massive arms and thighs. He was also handsome in the way some men get as they grow older—Aderyn judged him to be in his late forties—and walked with the careless assurance of someone who knew how handsome he was.

It was that attitude that intimidated Aderyn. Javath projected an aura of rock-hard confidence even Owen, who usually commanded a room just by being there, couldn't manage. It was an air that said Javath knew who he was and what he was capable of, an air of supreme self-assurance that he, Javath, was always and undeniably right and it was just a matter of time before the rest of the world agreed with him. And the fact that he'd pegged Owen as their leader said a lot about his observational skills. Aderyn was grateful he wasn't their enemy.

Kendria's features resembled her father's in a feminine way, but where he was broad, she was slim, and she was an inch taller than he. She moved with a lithe grace that Aderyn admired, carrying herself with a similar self-assurance that in her case suggested she was willing to listen to someone else's opinion so long as it wasn't total nonsense. Aderyn could see what about Kendria had appealed to Borrus; aside from her self-assurance, she held herself as if she wielded an invisible staff, ready to attack if that became necessary. Aderyn knew Borrus was attracted to powerful, dangerous women, and she had no doubt Kendria could be dangerous.

To regain her equilibrium, she Level Assessed Javath and Kendria.

Name: Javath
Class: Stalwart (retired)
Level: 17
Name: Kendria
Class: Staffsworn
Level: 16

Javath shook Owen's hand, but his attention was on Aderyn. "Borrus's sister," he said. "I can see the family resemblance, though you're a good deal prettier."

"Thank you," Aderyn said. Javath's compliment didn't fluster her, to her surprise; it sounded as if he was stating an obvious fact rather than trying to flatter her. "We all of us look like one or both of our parents."

"Yes, he said there are four of you siblings. It's unfortunate you aren't all here. You'd make an intriguing competitor for the team battles." Javath smiled. "And there I go again, talking shop when we've only just met. Sorry about that. I'm afraid I'm single-minded when it comes to this passion of mine. Please, sit." He resumed his seat next to Kendria, who hadn't moved.

"Tell me something about your team," Javath said.

"I'm Owen, and this is Isold, Weston, Livia, and of course Aderyn," Owen said.

"How long have you been together?"

"Almost since level one," Owen said. "We met Isold after reaching level two, and we've been together since then."

"And how many years has that been?" Kendria asked.

Owen glanced at Aderyn. Aderyn said, "Three and a half months."

Kendria made a choked sound. Javath's eyes widened. "Are you serious?"

"We wouldn't lie," Owen said. "I realize it's unusual."

"It's unprecedented, is what it is." Javath leaned back in his chair and surveyed Owen. "You're not exaggerating to impress me, are you?"

"I don't know you to feel I need to impress you," Owen said coolly. "No offense."

Javath's sudden grin transformed his handsome face. "Nice," he said. "I dislike pandering, and I don't respect anyone who can't stand up to me."

"Which means you like to push people's buttons to see how they react." Owen folded his arms over his chest. "Understandable, though I imagine people will call you arrogant for it."

"But not you," Javath said. "I don't understand that expression. What buttons?"

"It means find their vulnerabilities and test them," Owen said, not twitching at all at having his otherworlder phrase challenged. Aderyn was always more nervous about him saying incomprehensible things than he was. But she knew better than he the possible consequences of being identified as a demon.

"Ah." Javath's bland response made Aderyn wish, as she often did, that **[Read Body Language]** worked on people other than Owen. Javath struck her as potentially dangerous in a different way from his daughter. Kendria could handle herself in a fight, but Javath could wreck someone's future. He was definitely the one to watch.

CHAPTER THREE

"It's looking like those two candidates aren't going to show up, Javath," Borrus said. He'd positioned himself where Kendria could see him clearly, but she was watching her father.

"That's unfortunate, though it seems we've found... not replacements, of course, but a different set of possibilities?" Javath smiled. "Now, I assume Owen and Weston have an interest in becoming champions?"

"Not me," Weston said. "I'm guessing the Glory Games are more competitive than I like to be. I'm too easygoing."

"Now, that is unfortunate," Javath said. This time, he sounded sincerely regretful. "You've got the build of a Stalwart, and that would compensate for your lower fighting skills as a Moonlighter. And there aren't a lot of Moonlighters who enter the Games, so you would have an advantage, with your emphasis on stealth and misdirection. But I like a man who's self-aware enough to recognize his drives."

"You mentioned team battles. I'm not opposed to competing on a team," Weston said. "We've all learned to fight well together."

"We'll discuss that too," Javath said. "But first, let me explain how the Games work—the solo fights. Individuals battle in a competition that determines those fighters' ranks in the system. Each potential champion has a sponsor who pays his or her expenses, plus rewarding their successes with money and other benefits. The top ten ranked champions determine how many votes their sponsors have in the city government. All clear so far?" He addressed Owen directly.

"We understand," Owen said. "What I want to know is why the Games aren't swamped with contenders. It sounds like a plush deal, so I don't get why you'd need to recruit."

Javath smiled. "Good question, and not one I'm often asked. You sure you've never heard of the Games?"

"It's just common sense."

That wasn't true, but it wasn't as if Owen could say he had knowledge gained from experiences in his own world. Unexpectedly, Aderyn worried for him. Javath did not look like the sort of person who ignored a mystery, and she was sure he was smart enough to figure out something about Owen was different, especially if Owen kept betraying himself with weird metaphors and unnatural insight.

"Common sense. Sure," Javath said, in an amused tone that deepened Aderyn's concern. "Well, you're right. There are rules about who's allowed to compete. The first rule is a minimum level eligibility. Keeps the Games from being overrun by adventurers with low fighting skill ranks. Ideally, the eligibility requirement would be for a minimum skill rank, but we can't see someone's skills and there's nothing stopping a potential champion from lying about them. So instead the requirement is champions have to be level twelve or higher."

"Which Owen is," Borrus said, unnecessarily as of course Javath would have Assessed him already. Aderyn eyed her brother skeptically. He sounded eager, as if he hoped to impress someone. Aderyn quickly glanced at Kendria. She was intent on the conversation and didn't seem to have noticed Borrus's contribution.

"Right," Javath said. "Of those of the right level, we look at their adventuring history. Not literally, because I'm not a magistrate to read someone's Codex, but we ask about what kinds of battles they fought, whether they achieved their current level through questing or through fighting, how fast they leveled. The idea is to winnow out adventurers without the right kind of drive."

"And what drive is that?" Owen asked.

"Someone who gained most of his experience through fighting monsters has a different approach than someone who's done a lot of quests," Kendria said. "There's some evidence that this alters an adventurer's mindset. Since questing rewards many different skills, not just fighting, an adventurer with more quests under his belt may not be the sort of person who can succeed at the Games. We sometimes steer them toward team competition."

"On the other hand, leveling fast by any means reveals passion and drive for success," Javath said, "and that's a balancing factor." He drummed his fingers on the arm of his chair. "Very well. You've leveled fast as a team, but what does that say about you personally? You there, Earthbreaker. Livia, right? Tell me what you think of Owen."

Livia didn't startle at being so abruptly addressed. "He's a strong fighter who leads from the front. He knows our strengths, and he's good at choosing fights we can win that will also challenge us. And he's humble enough to ask for advice when he needs it."

"All of which make him a good team leader, I'm sure." Javath turned his attention on Aderyn. "Is that why you're such a high level? I've never seen a Warmaster that wasn't a useless drag on a team. What does Owen get out of your presence, aside from the obvious?"

Owen's hand curled tightly into a fist. "If you're going to sling insults, we're done here."

"Quick to defend your sweetheart, huh?" Javath's grin became nastier. "That doesn't exactly make you look good."

"Neither do cheap shots like that one," Aderyn said. "Owen and I figured out early on how to make a Warmaster useful. I pull my weight with tactical analysis. And the rest is frankly none of your business."

Javath's smile disappeared. "Tactics? Enlighten me."

Aderyn didn't really feel like giving this man any information he might use against them, but it wasn't as if her class abilities were secrets, they were just unknowns. "A Warmaster sees monster weaknesses and directs her partner and teammates to take advantage of them. But it takes a partner working together with a Warmaster to give both of them advantages."

"That's intriguing," Kendria said. "Does that mean Owen is less powerful when he doesn't have you as a companion?"

"That depends on what you mean by 'powerful.' My skills don't work against humans, and Owen's weapons skill is independent of my direction." Neither of those things were strictly true. Aderyn's skills, as far as she could tell, worked on any living creature—it was just that she rarely needed to turn them against humans. Also, Owen's weapons skill was as high as it was thanks to their partnership. But she had a sudden rash desire to prove to Javath and Kendria that Owen was worthy of their stupid Glory Games.

Javath and Kendria exchanged the kind of glances that conveyed meaning between two people who knew each other well. "Would you say you gained experience more from fighting or from quests?" Javath asked.

He hadn't addressed anyone in particular, but Owen answered. "It's been an even mix, I think. We've fought more monsters than we've had quests, but most of those quests earned us a lot of experience."

"What about the most powerful monster you've ever fought?" Kendria asked.

Owen hesitated only briefly before saying, "The Sarnok. It roams north of Obsidian."

"Never heard of it," Javath said, "but then I've never been that far west. What power level?"

"Sixteen."

Javath whistled in appreciation. "When was this? What level were you?"

"Level ten. It was an unexpected encounter, and we survived due to teamwork and luck." Owen hesitated again, then added, "We didn't rely on our weapons skills."

"Still, that's impressive." Javath straightened, then leaned forward to rest his elbows on his knees in an informal gesture that invited confidences. "Normally, the third step is to test your skills against Borrus, but I don't think that's necessary. You're an excellent candidate."

"Then I think you should convince me that this is worth it to my team," Owen said. "We're interested in gaining experience, and Borrus said this is the way to do it."

"And earning a little coin would not offend us," Weston added.

Javath pursed his lips. "Most potential champions are grateful for the opportunity."

"I'm not most champions," Owen said.

"No," Javath murmured, "no, you are not." He nodded and sat up, slowly. "Every battle you fight has the potential to earn you experience. In the first round, you fight for the privilege of entering the second round. Eight combats, eight opponents, a minimum of five wins or you're out."

"All right," Owen said. "What happens in the second round?"

"In the second round, two losses means you're out. If you win, and go on winning, you'll fight several battles intended to rank the final ten champions. You'll earn experience for defeating each one depending on that opponent's level, just as if it was a real fight. Given the average level of the potential champions, we're talking at least eleven thousand experience per battle, usually more. A lot more, in some cases. The number-one ranked champion earns an experience bonus from the system for winning the lot."

"That explains my side of things," Owen said. "What about team battles? Borrus said those weren't as prestigious."

"He's right, though I'd say they're prestigious in a different way." Javath shrugged. "Team contests are to get the crowds excited for the solo fights. But that means the crowds love them, get invested in their performance. Successful teams earn experience and money—there are prizes awarded in the team battles—but popular teams gain fame, which translates into other tangible rewards. Gifts and so forth." He eyed Weston, then the others. "You know, it's not a bad idea. You're an odd mix of classes as far as most teams go. You'd be unexpected. Certainly with a Warmaster—no offense."

"It's what everyone thinks," Aderyn said.

Owen paused for a moment, then said, "I don't think I have any other questions."

Javath raised a single eyebrow in a practiced gesture. "So you're in?"

Owen turned so he could see Aderyn and the others. "Any objections?"

Isold and Livia shook their heads. Weston said, "Is wagering allowed?"

"Try and stop it," Javath said with a chuckle. "Teams can't wager on themselves or anyone in a match they're part of, and sponsors aren't allowed to wager on their own champions. But any other wager is permitted."

"I'm satisfied," Weston said.

Owen's eyes met Aderyn's. "Still enthusiastic?" he asked.

"I think you have as good a chance as any," Aderyn said, "and for our purposes, every fight you win is an experience gain, even if you don't win the lot."

Owen nodded. "We're in," he said.

"Excellent," Javath said, slapping his knee with a sharp crack.

"We leave two days from now if you want to travel together, or you're free to start sooner. Borrus will provide you with the chits that show you're legitimate contenders." He shook Owen's hand. "I anticipate seeing great things from you."

"I'd say I hope I don't let you down, but you'd know it was pandering," Owen replied.

Javath laughed, a single short bark, and shook his head. "Definitely one to watch," he said. "I'll see you back at the inn, Borrus." He left the taproom with Kendria behind him.

"Fantastic!" Borrus said. "I knew you'd like them. Let's get some food. Something solid, none of this wedger nonsense. Making people assemble their own food—that's never going to take off." He waved a hand at one of the serving women.

Aderyn's head still whirled at how rapidly things had changed. "Can we talk about something else? What have you been doing the last two years?"

"Oh, this and that. Nothing extraordinary. I've been with two teams, one to level six and another from level eight to level ten." Borrus chuckled. "It's probably why it's taken me so long to reach this level. I prefer working alone, but it's hard to take on most monsters solo. I've done a lot of city quests and a couple of escort quests. But you—Aderyn, I still can't believe how fast you've advanced! And as a Warmaster!" He sobered. "Seriously, I'm really sorry you ended up with that class. How awful."

Aderyn suppressed her irritation. There was no reason Borrus shouldn't be like everyone else, ignorant of a Warmaster's potential. But irrationally she felt he should have more faith in her, his closest sibling.

Owen said, "Warmasters aren't useless. They just need to partner with the right person. Then their abilities are unlocked." His tone was mild, but Aderyn could tell when he was irritated at someone insulting her.

Borrus whistled, long and low. "Really? Why don't more people do it, then?"

Aderyn shrugged. "Because nobody thinks a Warmaster is worth anything. I got lucky, really, because Owen wasn't stuck-up and was willing to take a chance. We sort of fell into working together."

"Owen. You're her partner?" For once, Borrus didn't sound astonished at her revelations.

"Yes." Aderyn drew in a deep breath. "And he's my sweetheart."

Borrus's eyebrows nearly climbed off his forehead. He stared at Owen, then at Aderyn. "*You* have a sweetheart?"

Aderyn blushed. "Don't act so surprised."

Borrus sat up straight and folded his hands demurely in his lap. "'I don't need romance. It's a distraction from adventuring. I'm never going to be sidetracked from what I want,'" he said in a high-pitched, falsely prim voice.

Everyone at their table burst out laughing, Owen hardest of all.

"Borrus!" Aderyn slapped him lightly on the arm, laughing even as she blushed harder. "I can change my mind."

"Not the girl who swore a blood oath with me that we would never fall into the romance trap," Borrus said. "Seriously, you must be something to make Aderyn change, Owen."

"I don't know about that, but I know I love her, and she loves me." Owen captured Aderyn's hand and twined his fingers with hers.

Borrus mouthed the word "love" with his eyes wide. "All right, I'll stop," he said when Aderyn smacked him again. "Can I at least tell the story of how the two of us snuck into Gramps Fullis's barn and—"

"Borrus!" Aderyn's cheeks burned with remembered embarrassment. "We had a deal!"

"All right, I know, I swore I'd never tell that story again and *you* promised not to fill my pillow with slugs." Borrus gave an exaggerated shudder. "You all probably don't know how good Aderyn is at getting revenge. She'll wait until you've forgotten you pissed her off—"

"*Borrus!*"

"I'm starting to be really grateful we met," Weston said. "It's a whole new side to our companion."

"I've outgrown that stage," Aderyn said haughtily. "I no longer feel the need to avenge myself for perceived slights."

"Now you sound like Isold when he's in a mood," Owen said. He accepted a mug from the serving woman and saluted Borrus before drinking. "I'm grateful Aderyn has learned to be forgiving. I'd hate to be on the receiving end of her anger."

Borrus drank as well. "You can be grateful it was me and not Nollan you met. Nollan is great, but as the oldest, he feels he has duties toward us. He's protective of his sisters and thinks anybody who can't stand up to him isn't worthy of them. Pia got so tired of him interfering in her flirtations she stole one of Mother's truth potions and laced his beer with it."

Owen raised both eyebrows. "How did that help?"

"It meant Nollan told everyone he met what he really thought of them over the course of twenty-four hours. That kind of honesty doesn't look good on anyone, but when that includes the woman you're walking out with, a woman who doesn't take criticism well, a woman who's sensitive about the size of her nose... we were all glad, because none of us cared for her—"

"She didn't really care about Nollan, either," Aderyn put in. "He was the only one who didn't realize it."

"Right, that too. Anyway, Nollan backed off some, but he still believes he's justified in testing the serious suitors. Though I don't know that I'd be opposed to seeing the two of you fight. I bet you're good."

Owen and Aderyn exchanged glances. Owen twitched his head in a way that said *Should we tell him the whole truth about the Fated One?*

Her reluctance to share the details of their quest with her favorite brother surprised her. Two years ago, she would have told Borrus everything. Now, having seen him act like a fool in front of Kendria, she wondered if she still knew him. On the other hand, he *was* still her brother, and she loved him even if he was acting a bit strange.

"You told us what you've been up to," she said. "Let me tell you our story in return."

CHAPTER FOUR

S he didn't tell him everything. The secret that Owen was from another world was potentially dangerous, and while she trusted Borrus not to overreact, he'd always had trouble keeping secrets long-term, and he might give it away to someone less temperate in their reactions. But almost everything else, she explained in enough detail that when she finished with the explanation of how the second quest in the **[Fated One's Destiny]** quest chain wouldn't unlock until they were level fourteen, Borrus stared at her in silence. Uncomfortably, she said, "I didn't think it was enough to strike you mute."

"It's a lot," Borrus said. He surveyed Owen, blinked, and added, "How can you be so sure you're the Fated One? The real Fated One, I mean. There are dozens, maybe hundreds of pretenders to that title, and most of them only say they are so they can get laid."

"The system sets challenges in the path of the Fated Ones, even the fake ones," Owen said, "and rewards those who accept those challenges knowingly. And we're the first people in centuries to try to discover what the Fated One is meant to do. What actions he has to complete. Tarani's journal proves it."

"I don't think I'd be as certain as you, but I'm sure things look different when you've experienced them." Borrus tipped his head back to stare at the rafters. "But you're the ones pursuing it, not me, so it's your opinion that matters more."

"Thank you so much for your unqualified approval," Aderyn drawled.

Borrus nudged her with his elbow. "You know what I mean."

"Sadly, I do. I told—Borrus, I forgot to say I met our grandfather. Mother's father."

Borrus stopped. "You did what? Aderyn, how many surprises do you plan to pull out of thin air?"

"I'm sorry. I forgot in all the excitement. We met on a caravan going north. He was going to return to Far Haven—he might be there now, actually."

Borrus grabbed Aderyn by the shoulders and shook her gently. "You've changed," he said. "You were always brash, but now you're confident, and you've seen and done so much... it's strange, but it's almost like you're the older one now."

Aderyn felt uncomfortable. "I don't know if I like the sound of that."

"It's a good thing. Don't worry, I'm still your big brother, and I can still whup your ass if you get uppity." He released her with a grin. "I should get back. I want to see if I can track down those fellows who stood us up. They might just need reassurance, and I had a good feeling about them. Come with me for a second."

Borrus put his arm around her shoulders and steered her to the taproom door. In the inn's tiny front room, he said, "I'm really looking forward to you traveling to Finion's Gate with us. Who knows what other surprises you might reveal! Not to mention getting to know better the man who convinced you a life of virginal solitude was a bad idea."

"You're not bothered? I was afraid you might think it was your brotherly duty to bluster and threaten Owen with bodily harm if he hurt me."

"I could do that if you want, but if he's as good a Swordsworn as you say, that wouldn't end well for me. Besides, we could use another man in the family. Tip the balance in our favor."

Aderyn blushed. "It's not like we're married, Borrus."

"Sister mine, the one thing about you I'm sure hasn't changed is your fierce holding on to anything you deeply care about. If you love him, I doubt you'll be satisfied with anything but a lifetime commitment."

"I—" She'd forgotten how close she and Borrus had been once, how he'd known everything she wanted and everything she dreamed of. "We haven't discussed anything like that." She'd thought about it sometimes, more often recently, but preparing an elaborate proposal as was tradition seemed impossible while they were on the road, and maybe Owen wasn't interested in marriage.

"Which is why I didn't embarrass you by saying anything. I want you to be happy, however that works out. I'll see you in a few days." He hugged her, messed up her hair with one hand, and made his laughing escape while she sputtered in pretended fury.

She returned to her seat and flopped down, feeling limp from all the excitement. "I can't believe it. First Marrius, then Borrus. All this time, and we end up in the same taproom. Is that a wonderful coincidence?"

"It is, but like you say, there's no point questioning it." Owen put an arm around Aderyn's shoulders. "Though if we run across Nollan and Pia in Ashenfell, I'm going to start thinking conspiracy."

"He doesn't look much like a Staffsworn," Weston said. "But I don't look like a Moonlighter, so I'm not in a position to judge."

"He has put on weight since I saw him last," Aderyn said. "He loves to eat, and he has a taste for the best food, so I guess that's not so strange."

"It is strange to come across Aderyn's brother in a random inn in a random city," Livia said. "But isn't anyone going to address the real issue? Who realized we were leveling awfully fast?"

"I didn't think about it," Weston said. "The only other adventurers I know are ones we've met in our travels, and we never discussed leveling."

"I knew." Isold leaned forward as if imparting a great secret. "I assume it's related to Owen being the Fated One. Either we've been put in the way of gaining more experience than normal, or the system has been granting us levels faster than it does others."

"But it's not like what happened with Jessemia, because our skills are all what they should be," Owen said. "Right?"

"Well," Aderyn said, "or higher. Much higher. Most everyone I Assess has ranks in their class skills that correspond to when they got a particular skill. So anyone who's level thirteen will have map access skill ranks of three or four because they got the skill at level ten. Except for Heralds."

"Wait," Owen said. "Wait a second. You mean I'm not supposed to have—" His voice lowered so it went no farther than their table. "Twenty-one ranks in **[Advanced Weapons Proficiency]**?"

"Of course not," Aderyn said, perplexed. "I thought you knew. It's part of why you beat Araceli so thoroughly back in Obsidian even though she was five levels higher. And a lot of people have commented on your skills, like the woman who sold us the <**Twinsword**>."

Owen looked like Livia had hit him between the eyes with *drench*. "I guess I didn't put it together." He squinched one eye to bring up his Codex and said, "Advancement."

"None of us have any skills that high, though," Isold said. "I believe that's a feature of the Warmaster's relationship with her partner."

"Holy shit," Owen said, somewhat distantly. "That's unbelievable. And all the paired skills are really high, too."

"They also match, or keep in step, or something," Aderyn said.

"Our [Outflank] is always the same, and [Keep Pace] and the others. Like they're truly paired skills."

"As if I wasn't the overpowered super-special main character already," Owen said, sounding sardonic. "Guess I should go on embracing my destiny." He blinked away the Codex and picked up the remains of the meat pie Borrus had ordered for them.

"Aderyn is overpowered too, don't forget," Weston said with a grin. "So you won't be alone on your pedestal."

Owen raised his eyebrows as if acknowledging Weston's point and went on chewing.

"And Borrus is interested in that Kendria woman," Aderyn said. "I don't like it. He was never one to pine after a woman who wasn't interested in him."

"Two years is a long time," Owen said. "People change."

The idea made Aderyn uncomfortable. "I guess. But I don't want my siblings to change! *I* haven't changed!"

"You haven't?" Owen licked meat juice off his fingers. "Are you sure?"

"Well—" She thought about it. "I guess I'm more likely to speak out now. And I give you all direction, and I have a sweetheart—I never cared about romance before I left Far Haven. But those aren't big changes."

"I think you'll find they're bigger than you realize." Owen took her hand. "And yet you're still you."

The discomfort became a squirmy ball of anxiety in her stomach. Suppose she'd changed so much she couldn't relate to her siblings the way she always had? "I hope that's true," she said.

Isold stretched and pushed his chair back. "I believe I will see if Heskia wants a rest," he said, nodding at where the well-endowed Herald played her fiddle with great enthusiasm.

When he was out of earshot, Weston said, "A rest, huh? I can't tell if he's got an in with her or not."

"She's twenty years older than him!" Aderyn gasped.

"I don't think that matters to Isold. Besides, maybe she'll teach him a thing or two for a change." Weston scooted closer to Livia. "I feel like dancing."

"So dance," Livia said.

"Livia, someday you'll change your mind. I know it."

"Today is not that day, dearest." Livia kissed him soundly.

Weariness swept over Aderyn, and she rose. "I'm going upstairs for a bit. I want to wash up."

"I'll join you," Owen said.

In their room, Aderyn poured water from the flowered porcelain pitcher into the matching basin and splashed her face and the back of her neck. "All right," she said. "What's bothering you?"

"Who says something's bothering me?"

"**[Read Body Language]** does. You were clearly unhappy about something. Don't you like Borrus?"

"Of course I like Borrus. I like him about as well as I could for the dozen or so sentences we spoke." Owen shook his head. "That came out wrong. I meant I look forward to getting to know him better, and I anticipate liking him a lot once I do."

"Then why were you all stiff and standoffish at first?" She took the drying cloth from its rail and patted herself dry.

Owen sat on the edge of the bed and sighed. "It's irrational, but I didn't like him looking at me like I'm nothing to you. And yes, I know he didn't know who I was at first, so why wouldn't he look at me that way, but I—"

Aderyn hung up the cloth. "What?" she prodded him when he didn't continue immediately.

Owen rubbed his face. "I don't know. I told you it was irrational. I know a lot about him because of everything you've told me, and that makes me feel like he should know me that well, too. Like I'm not part of your life because he thought I was a stranger. But we know each other now, so this is just leftover irrationality."

Aderyn took Owen's face in her hands and kissed him. "That's right. He already wants to know you better because you're my sweetheart."

"And he reacted better than I'd feared about the Fated One stuff. I was afraid he might think you were crazy for hooking up with a wannabe Fated One who told you that so you'd sleep with him."

"Borrus would never think that. Though he'd have punched you if he really believed that nonsense."

"And I would deserve to be punched." Owen slid his arms around Aderyn's waist and drew her closer. "I'm sorry I'm being weird about your brother. I'm really happy you found him. No <**Wayfinder**> necessary."

"You're so wise. It's why I love you."

Owen stood, keeping his arms around her waist, and kissed her, slow and sweet and promising a world of delights. "Is it?"

"Well," Aderyn said, pretending shyness, "there might be other reasons, but I'm afraid I've forgotten what they are."

"Then I'd better remind you," Owen said.

CHAPTER FIVE

Aderyn's first sight of Finion's Gate took her breath away. Though it was built into the side of the easternmost peak in the Pinnalore Mountains, it looked nothing like Guerdon Deep. Guerdon Deep lay at the base of a plain, backed into its valley so no enemy could take the city from the rear. The approach to Finion's Gate was up a rise too steep to ascend directly, so the road wandered back and forth across the slope, making it easy for travelers and caravans to reach the city. That it also made it easy for the defenders of Finion's Gate to pick off attackers easily was not lost on Aderyn.

But what made the city so beautiful was its construction. Unlike sullen, blocky Guerdon Deep, Finion's Gate was a dream of white spires and arches, marble domes and alabaster towers rising higher and higher until the tallest towers clung to the mountainside in ways Aderyn would have sworn were impossible. She recalled seeing this city in a painting in Alcester. At the time, she'd believed the artist had made it up. Now she realized the painting had fallen short of reality.

"Close your mouth, little sister, you'll catch flies," Borrus said, striding along beside her. It was their turn to walk point.

Aderyn smacked his shoulder. "Cut it out with the 'little' unless you want me to salt your waterskin again."

"Sorry. I was teasing." Borrus poked her. "Fine, enough. It's a beautiful sight, isn't it?"

"Amazing. And it's the biggest city I've ever seen. Or is that an illusion thanks to distance?"

"No, it really is that big. It's the largest city in the northlands. I hear there are bigger ones in the south, but I've never gone that far." Borrus stretched. "We'll be there by midafternoon, which gives you time to find lodgings."

"I can't wait to Assess it. It must have so many benefits!"

Borrus frowned. "What do you mean, Assess a city? Is that a Warmaster thing?"

"It is. **[Improved Assess 2]** tells me what type of town it is, and how many crafters and spellslingers there are, and information about its history. Mostly it's just interesting, but sometimes the information is important." Aderyn tried Assessing, in case her range had changed in the three weeks since they'd left Guerdon Deep, but got nothing. "I have to be within three miles, though."

"I'm still getting used to what you can do, Aderyn. It's too bad we didn't fight many monsters on the trip. But with all these recruits, and Javath's caravan being what it is, we never get attacked." Borrus grinned. "Save all that fighting energy for the arena, huh?"

Aderyn turned as Owen joined them. "Can you believe how beautiful that place is?"

"It reminds me of Disney—I mean, of a castle I've seen pictures of," Owen said. "Though that wasn't dropped on the side of a mountain. That place must be defensible as hell."

"That's what I was thinking." Idly, Aderyn surveyed the city, considering how she would capture it as an invader. There were aqueducts, so there had to be water sources, and there at the base of the walls were dark spots that might be sewage or runoff ports. Those were generally weak. And she couldn't see beyond the city to the mountains on the far side, which might have more vulnerabilities. Wouldn't it be amazing if **[Improved Assess 3]** let her see those weak spots?

She blinked. She was actually considering an invasion plan for that beautiful city. She didn't know if that made her a good Warmaster or an evil person. Though, was it really evil to contemplate such a thing? Suppose she came up with a plan she then turned into strengthening those weak spots? It didn't matter, because it wasn't as if she was going to meet the city Council to give them advice. But it did give her something to think about as they walked.

Finion's Gate loomed large in the near distance when Aderyn's desultory attempts at Assessing it finally paid off.

Name: Finion's Gate

Status: Metropolis

Government: Limited-Term Council

Civilization level: 18

Resources: Spiritsmith x18, Spellcrafter x20, Tidecaller x24, Windwarden x29, Flamecrafter x27, Earthbreaker x30, Bonemender x16; Crafters level 18; Hospitality level 20; Food supply level 15

Finion's Gate was originally named Stonehaven. It grew up over the centuries from a village to a city, when it was devastated by an attacking force from Branlight. Having barely defended themselves, the citizens decided to relocate to a more defensible position in the mountains. The Moonlighter Finion was outspoken in her determination to make the new city not only safe, but beautiful, and to build with an eye to future growth. Under her direction, the city was constructed, renamed, and prospered.

Finion's Gate is probably the biggest city you'll ever see, but don't let it intimidate you. You should not act like a foreigner, because the citizens will take advantage of your ignorance, calling it a valuable lesson when they cheat you.

Find a good inn and stick with it, because the hospitality sector knows better than to cheat those it depends on.

The Glory Games are the biggest draw for outsiders, both as competitors and as observers. Their recruitment strategy means only the best fighters compete, and the battles are amazing even if they don't end in death. If you intend to compete, keep in mind that death is the only thing disallowed. Better to watch and wager. You're less likely to lose a hand that way.

"You didn't say people could be maimed, Borrus," Aderyn exclaimed.

"What?" Borrus said. "Oh, you mean the Games. Well, I suppose that's true. It's not completely safe, Aderyn. In the main events, people use real weapons, and accidents happen. But there are Bone-menders on hand—what brought this on?"

Aderyn had silently read the Assessment in snippets, not wanting to stop and maybe slow the caravan down while she read aloud. "It's what the system says about the Glory Games, that death isn't allowed but that's the only thing that isn't."

"Well, sure, but I thought that was a given. You're making it sound like I deceived you." Borrus sounded hurt.

"Not deceived. Forgot to mention, maybe."

"It's not a big deal," Owen said. "It wouldn't be exciting if there wasn't some chance of injury."

Borrus brightened. "Right. You get it."

"As long as we know what to expect, I guess it's all right," Aderyn said. Privately, she thought Owen and Borrus had a very warped idea of what constituted "exciting."

At the end of her turn at lookout, she climbed into the wagon she and her team had been assigned and continued to examine the city as they approached. The illusion of towers clinging to the mountainside disappeared once they were a mile away, when Aderyn could finally see that the mountainside was deeply terraced. Each terrace looked like a city in itself, complete with a wall guarding the edge. White marble wasn't the only building material; some of the construction was granite the same color as the mountain, particularly the terrace walls. The contrast between the marble and the granite made it look as if some of the buildings emerged from the side of the mountain, but the city wasn't as fanciful as all that.

Aderyn counted terraces, five of them, each narrower than the one beneath. Lines hung down the cliff faces, some of them strung with boxes Aderyn couldn't make sense of, tiny at this distance. She watched as one box made its slow but steady ascent and realized these were lifts like the ones she'd seen outside Obsidian. But those had moved in a jerky, hesitant fashion, and these slid smoothly up or down their ropes.

"Those elevators have got to be enormous for us to see them this far away," Owen murmured to Aderyn so the wagon driver couldn't hear. "Smart thinking, though. I bet the stairs between those shelves are long."

"Is 'elevator' your word for them?"

"It is where I come from. Other places say 'lift.'" Owen shielded his eyes, though it wasn't that bright a day. "That place may actually be bigger than my home city."

Aderyn felt obscurely comforted in knowing her world was superior to Owen's in at least one way. It was a stupid reaction, given that his world had no magic and no system, but they did have indoor plumbing, and Aderyn considered that a major point in its favor. "I'm intimidated, honestly. It's so big."

"I bet people group up by neighborhoods. There's no way to feel at home in an entire city that size, so people where I come from get to know their little part of it really well." Owen clasped her hand. "Besides, we have your Assessment to help. Did it give you hints?"

"It said don't act like foreigners and find a good inn quickly. Not exactly something we couldn't have figured out on our own, but it's a reminder to not take things for granted."

She considered going to find Borrus, who she thought had joined Javath and Kendria in the lead wagon, but decided against it. Borrus's behavior when he was around Kendria disturbed her. If Javath was there, Borrus was alert and attentive to his instructions, showing no sign of servility. But with Javath gone, Borrus's attentions to Kendria verged on pathetic. He tried to engage her in conversation on subjects she clearly didn't care about, he offered to bring her food or something to drink, he babbled like a maniac whenever she did respond to his conversational overtures... Aderyn had known her brother all her life, and she'd never seen him behave like this, not even to other women he'd been interested in.

She wished she could tell him his tactics were all wrong. It was obvious to her that Kendria didn't admire sycophancy and pandering. If Aderyn had to guess, she'd say Kendria's ideal man was someone aloof and self-assured, someone who didn't hang on her every word and who didn't feel the need to fill up silences with nonsense talk. But Borrus had never, not once, listened to Aderyn's opinion about the women he cared for. It was his one big flaw, that he was convinced he understood women better than anyone, including his own sister who happened to be a woman herself.

On the other hand, Aderyn didn't think she wanted Kendria to return Borrus's affections. Three weeks of travel had given Aderyn plenty of time to observe the Staffsworn, and she didn't like what she saw. Kendria was polite enough, but she had enough arrogance for three people bound up in one. Aderyn noticed it whenever talk came around to adventuring and people's accomplishments. It wasn't like she wanted people to fawn over her and her team for having defeated the Sarnok or destroyed an evil dungeon, but those were objectively amazing feats and it was reasonable that people should acknowledge that.

Kendria, though, always gave offhanded remarks like "Well, that's certainly something" in a tone of voice that said she wasn't impressed. Given that she was only three levels higher than Aderyn's team and hadn't actively adventured for the past two years, Aderyn thought this was a ridiculous attitude for her to have. But Borrus didn't see that behavior, either, and Aderyn felt awkward about bringing it up, like she expected praise.

She fell back on hoping Borrus would wake up to reality soon and forget about impressing Kendria. Maybe then he'd go back to adventuring, and she could suggest he take the last spot on their team. He was only a level higher. And then her old dream of teaming with her siblings wouldn't be so foolish as it once had been, back when she was level one and they were all off adventuring separately.

She glanced at Owen then, and Livia and Weston and Isold. If she'd been able to team with her brothers and sister, she never would have met her friends. She'd never really regretted that dream, but now, offered the choice, she knew she'd turn it down.

CHAPTER SIX

"I can't get over the engineering that must have gone into that city," Owen said, bringing her back to the present. "They had to cut those steps, those levels—"

"Borrus called them terraces," Aderyn said.

"That's a better word. They had to cut those terraces out of the mountain, one by one, and even if they quarried the granite so they used it for walls and stuff, that's a lot of rock to move."

"One of the wagon drivers told me the marble was hauled from many miles away," Isold said. "One block at a time, without the use of magic."

"Astonishing," Owen said. "And I think I see the arena. That big building that looks like a wall within the terrace wall, on the first level up from the ground. Is that how they count them? Or is that considered the second level?"

"The ground level is called Foundation," Weston said. "Then it's Terrace One, Terrace Two, all the way up to Terrace Five." He ran his fingers idly up and down Livia's stone arm.

"Borrus said we'll need to find a place to stay in Foundation. He lives on Terrace One in the same hostel as Javath and Kendria, but they can't show us favoritism by letting us join them. I'm just as happy to be anonymous for a while." Aderyn had felt a pang at being separated from Borrus, in part because he was her brother and in part because he knew the city and could help them avoid making stupid foreigner mistakes. But Borrus had said "We don't want any of you disqualified before things even start" and she had to admit he was right.

"I've had a recommendation of a couple of good inns," Isold said, "and directions good enough to place them on my system map."

"How does that work for you?" Livia asked. "My system map fills in as I visit places, but it never shows me details of cities the way it does you."

"A new city map starts out as a blank, and the streets become visible as we encounter them, just as your map does. But if I have enough information, other locations appear, unconnected to what I've physically passed." Isold's eyes were focused on a point a foot from his face as if he was looking at something there. "It's a pleasurable sensation, watching the details fill in. Like an invisible hand sketching a picture."

Owen sat up. "We're nearly there. I can't believe how much traffic there is. We might wait a while for our turn to enter."

Aderyn examined the mass of wagons and horse riders and people on foot, all of them funneling into a loose queue aimed at the nearest gate. This one happened to be near the center of the wall surrounding Finion's Gate's lowest level, Foundation, but there were other gates with queues as packed full of people as this one. "Good thing we're not in a hurry."

Not being in a hurry didn't mean they were patient. By Livia's pocket watch, it was one hour and seventeen minutes before the lead wagon of their caravan, Javath's wagon, reached the gate. Aderyn watched Javath talk to one of the four guards at the gate and idly made up a conversation for them, though probably it was just Javath explaining who was in their caravan, since the guard stopped talking and gazed at the other wagons intently. "That's right, we might be famous champions someday," Aderyn whispered. "You should be awed."

"What was that?" Owen asked.

She shook her head. "Nothing. Just making up stories."

Javath got back into his wagon, and their caravan lurched into motion. When they passed the guard, Aderyn saw his lips moving, like he was counting how many of them were under Javath's protection. Aderyn smiled at him, but he ignored her.

The gate doors, a handspan thick and banded and studded with iron, were swung wide to welcome visitors. Aderyn recalled how Finion's Gate, Stonehaven at the time, had been attacked by an invading force and guessed Finion had learned her lesson. The wall was even thicker, and as in Obsidian, a tunnel of stone led through the wall and into the city. Beyond the tunnel was a wide, empty expanse that Aderyn recognized immediately would allow for squads of defenders to group. She didn't think it was a great idea, because if the defenders were pushed back, that big empty space could be used by attackers to move their forces quickly into the city. Better to force that spot into a chokepoint.

The wagons collected to one side of the empty space, making room for other visitors to pass. Borrus approached Aderyn's wagon. "This is where we part ways for now," he said. "You've got your challenger's chits? How about an inn? Did you need money?"

"We're fine, Borrus, but thank you for caring," Aderyn laughed. She withdrew a large wooden token on a long string from the <**Purse of Great Capacity**> and displayed it. One side showed a crude carving of a lightning bolt, and the other side displayed a big letter T. "T for team. Owen has S for solo. And we know where we're going."

"I hate leaving you on your own in this city." Borrus did look unhappy. "It's not generous with outsiders."

"I know, and we'll be careful." She hugged her brother. "We'll see you at the start of the preliminary trials in three days."

"See you then. Love you, sis." Borrus gave her a final hug and strolled off toward the lead wagon. Aderyn watched him go and pretended her heart didn't ache a little. It was just three days, and compared to two years of absence, that was nothing.

Owen handed her the <**Knapsack of Plenty**>. "You all right?"

"Just being unnecessarily sentimental. Is it much of a walk?"

"Not far," Isold said. "Though with my map not showing the details of the city between here and the inn, we should stay alert in case the path leads through dangerous territory."

"Then stick together, and let's see what Finion's Gate can throw at us," Owen said.

They found the Alabaster Inn with no trouble, not even the kind of harassment Aderyn expected to get because they were foreign. Granted, they looked just like all the other adventurers on the street, and they didn't gawk or stand hesitantly on the corner, but superstitiously Aderyn felt someone should intuit they weren't from around here.

She wished she could gawk, because she'd never seen construction like this before, not even in Guerdon Deep. The buildings were taller than the tallest trees, as if building on granite rooted them so they could grow higher than normal, and their stonework was exquisite, not utilitarian as in Guerdon Deep. There, it had looked like the citizens deliberately chose not to make their city beautiful. Here, Aderyn couldn't look anywhere without seeing fanciful carvings or the curve of a balcony or elaborate marble porticos that would protect doors from the rain.

Despite its name, the Alabaster Inn was built of the same granite as every other building on the street. It looked narrow to Aderyn because it was five stories tall and didn't appear to have a stable yard, but it was as beautiful as everything else they'd yet seen, with sculptures of leaping fish along its roof and at the corners of its porch and elegant brass fittings on the oak door stained a rich reddish brown.

The door opened before they reached it, and a young man no

older than fourteen emerged, saying, "Hey there, welcome! Come on in. Adventurers, right? Ma likes adventurers. She says they're more appreciative of hospitality than other travelers. Don't worry, we'll take good care of you."

Aderyn Assessed him in the middle of his speech.

Name: Davith

Traits: helpful, kind, obedient, talkative

Davith swept them all into the inn's front room, which was crowded with all six of them there, and then swept them up the stairs to the fourth floor, saying, "You're all used to exertion, so a few extra flights of stairs won't be a problem. Besides, this is where the nicest rooms are. How many do you need? Three? We have three in a row, so—oh, you're together? Wow. Wonder what that's like." He stared at Aderyn for a few seconds, then blushed and looked away and added, "Sorry, I shouldn't pry. Ma always says my tongue is hinged in the middle the way I yap like it's loose on both ends."

"It's fine," Aderyn said, amused. She didn't mind being stared at by someone who was as awkward about it as Davith.

"Well, rooms are two gold per person per night," Davith said, "and two meals a day are included. You should skip the midday meal, it's mostly leftovers from yesterday's supper. Ma's the best cook in Foundation, better than some of those snobby ones on Terrace One, says Pa. First supper service is in about an hour, at seven, but you can get a meal any time until ten. Bathhouse is out back but you have to sign up for your turn, sign up sheet is by the kitchen, which is straight back from the entry."

"Thank you, Davith," Owen said.

"You're welcome, but let me think if there's anything I've forgotten. Oh, right. If you need anything, ask Pa. He knows all of Foundation like he built it himself, and you're better off if he directs you so you don't wander and maybe look like a foreigner. Plenty of Gaters will—"

"Sorry, what?" Owen asked, sounding confused.

"Gaters. Citizens of Finion's Gate. Plenty of Gaters will take advantage of anyone they know isn't from around here. Pa can either give you directions or send someone to get whatever you need, your choice." Davith smiled. "And you can ask me or Bessa, she's my sister, if you have any questions about the inn or the city or anything. All right?"

"That is extremely helpful, Davith, thank you," Isold said, since Owen looked like he was controlling a laugh.

They gathered in the middle one of their three rooms, and Aderyn said, "What is so funny?"

"It's not funny really. I just heard him say 'gators' instead of 'Gaters.'" Owen still looked like he thought it was hilarious.

"I don't hear a difference," Weston said. "What are gators?"

"Alligators. Big swamp lizards? I guess none of you have ever seen a swamp."

"Not really," Livia said. "Though it is pretty funny to think of big lizards overrunning the streets. Do they eat people?"

"Not if the people can help it," Owen said. "Never mind. I say we settle in, have supper, and enjoy beds that aren't on the ground."

"It's a shame we can't explore the city, but it sounds like that would expose us as foreigners," Isold said.

"Maybe once we're famous combatants," Weston said.

"That's optimistic even for you," Livia said.

"We've survived challenges that could have killed teams higher level than we are. I don't think it's outside the realm of possibility that we're going to rise to the top." Weston, for once, sounded serious.

"I agree," Owen said. "But I'm reserving judgment until we meet the other combatants. Gradin and Pace aren't weak, and if the other recruiters are as tough as Javath, there's no reason to believe their recruits aren't the same."

Aderyn agreed. Gradin and Pace were the Swordsworn and the Lone Wolf who had stood Borrus up the night he and Aderyn had found each other, and they'd passed the recruitment tests and joined the caravan going north. They kept to themselves so completely they didn't even have to reject overtures of friendship; they gave off a sense of "stay away" Aderyn didn't need **[Read Body Language]** to interpret. All she knew about them was they were cousins who'd adventured separately until their paths had crossed in their home town of Branlight, and then they'd teamed up.

"I'm starting to look forward to meeting our rivals," she said. "I hadn't thought about it until now, how this means we'll be pitting our skills against others, but the idea is exciting."

"You see the sense in my plan now, don't you?" Weston said. "Though let's not discuss it anywhere we can be overheard. It will ruin everything."

"I'm not sure of the sense in any plan that makes me its pawn," Owen said, grimacing in mock irritation. "But I don't think I can stop you."

"Think of it as me demonstrating my faith in your skills," Weston replied.

CHAPTER SEVEN

T he following morning, they hired Davith to guide them to the arena. Isold's map said only that it was on Terrace One, one level up from Foundation, and gave no hint as to how to get there. Aderyn worried briefly that they'd look like foreigners if they had a native guide, but realized immediately that their native guide would keep them from being cheated. She tucked the <**Purse of Great Capacity**> inside her clothes, just to be safe. Pickpockets were the same everywhere.

The morning's bustle filled the air with shouts and laughter and a thousand haggling conversations. There weren't as many carts as Aderyn expected from her times in other large cities. What carts there were seemed to be food vendors, sellers of fruits and vegetables and prepared meals like sausages or fried apples. Most of the buying and selling was happening in the shops lining the broad streets. Aderyn watched in fascination as a woman trailing two children emerged from a bakery, her arms laden with cloth bags filled with food and long, skinny loaves of bread. The children were attached to their mother with leading strings, though neither of them looked like they meant to make a break for freedom. Aderyn tried to imagine herself tethered to her mother or father as a child and came up blank.

Davith led them through a dozen turns in the streets until Aderyn was thoroughly lost, unable even to remember in what direction the city wall lay. "This lift isn't the closest, but it's less busy," Davith explained. "We'll still have to wait a bit, but only maybe fifteen minutes. You ever seen a lift before?"

"Only for cargo," Isold said. "In Obsidian."

Davith's mouth formed an O of astonishment. "You've been to Obsidian? I thought that city was a myth. Is it true it's made of black stone and people kill each other in the streets?"

"No, it's made of ordinary stone, and people don't kill each other in public." Isold answered Davith gravely, though Aderyn wanted to laugh at the young man's imaginings. It wasn't as if she hadn't had some of the same assumptions herself once.

"No, they do their killing in private," Weston rumbled.

"Wow." Davith realized he'd stopped walking and sped up. "I don't know if I'll ever see it. I like Finion's Gate and I want to stay here my whole life."

"What about when you become an adventurer?" Owen asked.

"Oh, I'm not going to. I want to run the inn when I'm grown. I don't see much point in going out and maybe getting killed before that happens." Davith stopped again. This time, he looked embarrassed. "I didn't mean insult. That was me flapping my tongue at both ends again. Sorry."

"We weren't insulted. Everybody has to make the choice that's best for them." Owen shrugged. "Besides, you look like you're good at what you do. There isn't a class for 'innkeeper,' though maybe there should be."

"With appropriate class skills," Weston said. "Cooking, Cleaning, Diplomacy. What's it called when you can find anything a customer needs?"

"Concierge," Owen said. "Though here it's more likely to be 'fixer.'"

Davith looked like he wasn't sure if he should laugh or be insulted. Aderyn said. "Don't worry, Davith, this is their way of showing respect for what the non-classed do."

Davith's face cleared. "I bet a lot more people would accept the Call if they could choose their class. Or if there were other classes than adventuring ones."

"It's an interesting thought," Owen said. "With so many people not getting assigned the classes they prepared for, it would be a huge change if that was possible."

Davith sped up again. "The lift is just over here. I was right, there's a queue, but it's not a long one. Sorry about the wait." He pitched his voice to be heard over the sound of clacking and moaning that came from nowhere Aderyn could see.

They had reached the stone wall that formed the back of Foundation's level. It rose a good forty feet to where the base of Terrace One's wall began. Davith indicated a spot where twenty or thirty people gathered in more of a clump than a queue, most of them gathered in little groups, a few standing alone. A red circle painted on the wall marked where a couple of chains thicker than Aderyn's wrist hung. The chains disappeared inside an enormous metal box, taller than Weston and painted a shiny black that was scratched and dinged near where the chains emerged.

Aderyn realized this was the source of the noise, which was almost deafening. There were actually several noises: a low bass thumping like the biggest, deepest-voiced drum in the world, a high-pitched clacking sound like short planks of wood slapping each other, and a moan like someone blowing across the mouth of a glass bottle, but rising and falling too regularly to be human.

"Up there," Isold said, speaking into her ear because hearing anything else was impossible over the noise. He pointed, and Aderyn followed the line of his arm to see a wooden box descending smoothly along the chains toward them. The closer it got, the more Aderyn had to revise her estimate of its size. It was at least as big as a caravan wagon and was open on three sides. From her position beneath, she couldn't see what was in the box, but it had to be transporting people, because otherwise, why were they there?

The box slowed as it neared the ground, though it hadn't been moving fast before—though for all Aderyn and her ignorance knew, that represented high speed travel—and gently came to a stop in front of the big metal box. Someone dressed in what looked like livery, a red smock over a white shirt with tight sleeves and black twilled trousers, stepped forward and opened a door in the front of the wooden box. Men and women emerged, walking as casually as if this was a perfectly ordinary way to travel. Aderyn counted fifteen in all.

Another person dressed in red livery called out, "Payment, please! Watch your step, and don't push."

The mob-queue moved forward. Davith stopped her when she would have joined them. "There's no room for us on this one. No point getting mashed in the crowd."

"How do they keep track of whose turn it is?" Isold asked. "Don't people try to cut in line?"

Davith looked as if this question was insane. "Why?"

"Well, so they don't have to wait."

"Nobody cuts in line. That would be inconsiderate. You wouldn't want someone to do it to you, right? So you don't do it to others, and we all keep track of who got there first."

"That's astonishingly civilized," Owen said. "Where I come from, getting on public transportation is a matter of shoving your way in. People have been killed that way."

Now Davith's expression was horrified. "Where do you come from? That's terrible."

"I, um, it's a city far away, you won't have heard of it." Owen cleared his throat. "I'm impressed at how Finion's Gate handles it."

"If someone has an emergency, they get moved to the front." Davith nodded at the diminished crowd and the full wooden box, where the red-liveried man was shutting and securely latching the door. "We can move up now. We'll get the next one."

It took about fifteen minutes for the lift to complete its journey. Aderyn paid a silver each for all of them, including Davith, and stepped into the wooden box. She looked around curiously. The lift wasn't as finely crafted as the stonework of the buildings, but it seemed sturdy enough. Probably they'd built it of wood because that was lighter than metal. There were benches across the back of the lift on either side of a second door, this one solid to match the back wall, and a number of rope loops dangled from the ceiling. Owen immediately took hold of one of these. "So you're steadied when the lift shakes," he murmured to Aderyn. Aderyn grabbed one too.

The barest lurch signaled that the lift was rising. Aderyn's grip on the rope tightened. She wasn't comfortable with heights because she was always conscious of the hard ground that lay at the bottom of them. On the other hand, the box was sturdy and barely shook at all, and from where she stood she couldn't see the ground, just the towers and roofs of Foundation. And it was a beautiful sight, though Foundation tended more toward granite than the upper terraces. The granite glittered sometimes when the sunlight lanced through the clouds. Aderyn found her nervousness evaporating.

Waiting for the lift had felt like an eternity, but it was no time at all before the walls of Terrace One rose on either side, and the lift swung to a halt and then slid backwards, inside the walls. Someone opened the back door, and everyone filed out, as orderly as before. Aderyn expected to feel the lift sway when she left it, but it was as rock solid as if it was a permanent part of the wall.

She followed Davith past the crowd of those waiting to enter the lift to the nearest street. Terrace One at first glance looked exactly like Foundation, but after a minute of walking, Aderyn noticed differences. There weren't any carts or barrows, though everyone on the street had bags or parcels that indicated they'd been shopping. There were more marble façades, not just the white marble that had so captivated Aderyn at first sight of the city, but gray and deep green and even pale pink. Letters carved into the marble indicating the names of shops were gilded, as were the edges of the porticos and the marble statuettes that decorated many of the buildings.

And the statuettes were striking. Aderyn hadn't noticed them at first, but once she did, she couldn't stop staring. Most of them were animals, cute ones like kittens or otters, sometimes fierce ones like hawks with spread wings or coiled, hooded serpents. A few were monstrous. Aderyn recognized some they'd fought, like bat-kin or cat-hawks, nothing grotesque. She didn't think she could endure entering a shop where a boggart loomed over the stoop.

She realized she was gawking like a foreigner and dragged her attention back to street level. The people were unusual, she decided. All of them dressed plainly, and some of them wore servants' uniforms. The few she Assessed were non-classed, and every one of them had the traits "loyal" and "obedient." None of them looked as wealthy as Aderyn expected people going into these fancy shops should be. Borrus had said Terrace One was where the rich of Finion's Gate lived, but Aderyn didn't know anything about rich people and hadn't expected it meant they didn't do their own shopping.

"You're going to Holder Stadium," Davith explained. "It's next to the arena, not as big but not tiny neither. It's where the champions practice for their bouts, but you go there to be assigned your matches and for the teams to register and qualify."

"You've been helpful, Davith, thank you," Owen said. "Do you know how long this will take?"

"Oh, I'll wait for you," Davith assured him. "I bet you can find your way back all right, the Herald can at least, but I want to see what happens. If you don't mind. And if I'm with you when you return, you won't face any grifters or thieves."

"What's going to happen that you want to watch?" Weston asked.

Davith grinned. "I love the team matches. I'm for the Hooligans, of course, but I bet you'll be just as good. And then I can say I knew you before you were famous!"

Livia concealed a snort of laughter. Weston clapped Davith on the shoulder, staggering the young man. "Guess you'll have to change your allegiance, because we plan to be the best."

"Maybe. The Hooligans have been top ranked for almost three years." Davith eyed the well-built Weston. "If it was a wrestling match, maybe, but agility is really important."

"I guess I'll just have to do my best," Weston said, winking at Livia over Davith's head.

CHAPTER EIGHT

Davith was right, Aderyn realized: Holder Stadium was huge by her small-town standards, but next to the arena, it looked like a puppy playing near the feet of a full-sized guard dog. The arena's vast walls were made of granite like everything else, elaborately carved and rising at least four tall stories above Aderyn's head. Holder Stadium, by contrast, was built of warm, rough sandstone whose presence in Finion's Gate Aderyn couldn't explain. She liked it better than the arena, which intimidated her. Mentally, she slapped herself. If all went well, they'd be competing in the arena, and being intimidated put them at a disadvantage.

Like the arena, the stadium was an oval, with several large, square openings in its outer wall. But Davith led them to a small door to the left of the nearest large opening. "Go on through there, you'll see where to go," he said, and hurried off through the opening like he was afraid of missing something.

The hall beyond the door was well-lit by <**Everburning Candles**> and led to an empty room that smelled of sweat and musk. Two men stood near its center, talking quietly. The shorter man glanced their way, took in Weston's appearance with wide eyes, and said, "Tokens."

Everyone handed over their tokens. The man's gaze flicked from Weston to Owen and back again. "You sure you haven't gotten these mixed up?"

"Very sure," Weston said. "I'm not into solo fighting. This is my team." They'd agreed that Weston would present himself as their team leader because Aderyn had guessed they'd get exactly this response from anyone who looked at him.

"I'm here for the fights," Owen said. "Javath recruited me."

"Did he," the short man murmured, running a finger over Owen's token in a calculating way. "Javath does know how to spot talent. Fine. You, go with Herton." He pointed at Owen and jabbed a thumb at the taller man. "The rest of you, out this way for the qualifier."

Aderyn and Owen exchanged glances. Owen shrugged and followed Herton through one of the two other doors. The short man marched over to the largest door and flung it open without waiting to see if the others would follow. Trying not to scramble to catch up, Aderyn followed, letting Weston go first.

The large door led to an equally wide ramp going up. Its surface was ridged to give wheels a good grip, though Aderyn saw no evidence of carts or trolleys. Far ahead, a square of sunlight revealed the ramp opened on the outdoors. Aderyn guessed they'd gone up at least a full story by the time they emerged onto the platform at the end of the ramp.

She looked out over the stadium floor. At first, she didn't understand what she saw: green hills and valleys, tall poles of wood or metal arranged at random, a couple of little ponds connected by a wandering river. Then it all came into focus, how everything was laid out to make a path circling the stadium's interior. "An obstacle course," she said.

"So observant," the short man said dryly. "Get that with being a Warmaster?"

Aderyn ignored the jab. "You want to time us. Do we run it together, or separately?"

"Do you want to deliver the orientation lecture, or can I get a word in?" He sounded more amused than annoyed. "The obstacle course is a timed run, averaging your individual performances. Emphasis on 'perform.' The team challenges are meant to entertain the crowd, get them excited for the main event. So I'll give you the only advice I ever give you would-be darlings of fate: make it look good, or you're out no matter how fast you run."

"What is the required path?" Isold said.

The short man pointed. "You'll start there where Lorus is standing, at the white flags. He'll give you the signal to go, and he'll mark your time. On your run, you have to remove each flag from its staff. Keep it or drop it, whatever you want, though I'll tell you it's faster to drop it. You have to take them in the right order, red, yellow, green, blue. Miss a flag and it's a fifteen-second penalty. The black flags mark the finish line. Got it?"

They all nodded.

"Does it matter how we get from one flag to another?" Livia asked.

"No flying, *transport,* or levitating allowed, but otherwise, all skills and spells are acceptable." He appraised Livia, short and compact and looking like the ideal Earthbreaker. "But if you wreck my course, you'd better be able to put it back together."

Livia shrugged. "That's acceptable."

"Down there, then." He caught Aderyn's eye and smiled, not a very nice smile. "Guess we'll find out if Warmasters are good for anything. Level thirteen, eh? Your teammates can't carry you on this."

"Imagine my disappointment," Aderyn shot back.

Steep stairs led from the platform to the ground. Aderyn looked around at the tiered seating as she descended. Rows of curved benches circled three-fourths of the stadium, giving spectators a good view of the obstacle course. There weren't more than a handful of people in the stands, and she couldn't see Davith anywhere.

Lorus was a thin man with restless eyes who barely looked at them as they approached. "Your choice who goes first," he said, fiddling with his pocket watch. It was an exact duplicate of Livia's own, an elegant piece of mechanics rather than magic that kept time down to the second.

Isold stepped forward. "I will."

Lorus quickly pointed out the four flags along the course. "Take your place here, and go when I give the word. Ready?"

Isold positioned himself at the spot between the white flags. "I'm ready."

Lorus held up the pocket watch. "Go!"

Isold took off. Aderyn admired the speed at which he took the grassy hill approaching the first obstacle. He was the fastest of them, and he had never run faster. At the top of the hill was a wooden wall pierced with holes big enough to fit a hand or a foot. Isold swarmed up the wall and snatched the red flag from where it flew from a little stick wedged into the wood. He dropped the flag and jumped the short distance from the top of the wall to the ground, which was higher on the far side.

Beyond the wall lay a gently curving path to a long, narrow pond lined with rushes, from which a river flowed. A couple of ducks floated in the pond, apparently uninterested in Isold. The pond lay next to a cliff wall, down which poured a number of tiny waterfalls. Where the path reached the pond, it became a wooden walkway that ran beside the cliff face, shiny with spray from the waterfalls. Isold's steps slowed as he started down the walkway. Aderyn guessed it was slippery. She clenched her fists tight, willing him not to slip.

Then the cliff face bulged, shooting out a fist of stone that caught Isold on the shoulder and shoved him into the pond.

Aderyn let out a startled squeak that made Lorus chuckle. Isold splashed to the surface, then stood. The pond wasn't more than thigh deep, but it still slowed him as he sloshed to the far side and climbed out. Undeterred, Isold snatched the yellow flag from its staff at the end of the walkway and raced on.

The third obstacle looked as straightforward as the others, a long horizontal metal pole from which hung loops of rope at different heights, extending over another pond. Aderyn didn't think for one second it was that innocent. Clearly, neither did Isold, because he examined the ropes for a few precious seconds before swinging himself out over the pond. Aderyn realized he wasn't committing his weight fully to each new rope when he gripped one that pulled free of its fastenings. Isold dangled one-handed as he groped for another handhold, then carefully made his way across, not going for the most obvious ropes, and snatched the green flag, tossing it over his shoulder into the pond in what looked like smug disdain.

Isold had come more than halfway around the circle, making up lost time with the speed at which he ran up and down the hills between the green and blue flags. At the top of the final hill, a thick pole, rough and ridged like a tree trunk, extended fifteen feet in the air. The blue flag waved merrily in the breeze from atop it. Short poles, scarves, and objects too small for Aderyn to see as more than dark blotches against the grass littered the ground around the pole.

Isold ignored everything except the pole. He grabbed hold of it and with some effort hitched himself to the top, where he snatched the blue flag and let the wind carry it away. Then he slid rapidly to the ground—too rapidly; he winced as he landed—shook his legs out, and ran for the black flags marking the end of the course. All that lay between him and those flags was another arm of the river, this one filled with floating logs.

Aderyn's fists clenched so hard they hurt. Isold was fast, but those logs were moving randomly, bobbing up and down and spinning gently. She held her breath as Isold neared the pond.

Isold sped up. Instead of putting a careful foot on the first log, he leaped, stretching his long legs to jump the river and bypassing every log. He didn't even stumble as he landed. Two more strides brought him between the black flags.

Isold, breathing heavily, joined the others. "That was bracing," he said. "I certainly did not expect a swim."

"Forty-eight seconds," Lorus said. "Not bad."

It had felt like much longer. Aderyn wished she knew what "not bad" meant. She was sure Lorus wouldn't give them any hints.

"I'm next," Weston said. He stretched dramatically, showing off the muscles of his arms and shoulders. Aderyn caught the dismissive look Lorus gave Weston. It was true, Weston looked like someone for whom brawn always won out over agility. Well, Lorus was in for a show.

On the man's signal, Weston sprinted up the hill and hauled himself up the wall to where the red flag had been replaced. Aderyn could tell from Lorus's smug expression that Weston hadn't been as fast as Isold. She reminded herself that it wasn't over yet and watched Weston hurry straight across the path, ignoring its curve in favor of taking the most direct route, and put his foot on the wooden walkway.

"Isn't it an unfair advantage to the rest of us that we know about the wall trick?" Aderyn couldn't help asking.

"The Earthbreaker manipulating the stone does it randomly," Lorus said. "It's not enough of an advantage to make a difference."

Weston moved carefully, one hand on the slick stone as if feeling for its movement. When the stone punched out, Weston was ready. He leaped forward, out of its way—and a section of the walkway broke free, tripping him so he fell to his knees with one hand in the pond. He got to his feet, too slowly to Aderyn's impatient eyes, and snatched the yellow flag almost as an afterthought.

Aderyn realized Livia was alternating between staring at her pocket watch and keeping an eye on Weston. Much as she wished she knew how fast Weston was going, she was superstitiously afraid if she stopped watching him, even to move to where she could see over Livia's shoulder, he would fall again.

But she needn't have worried. When Weston reached the rope loop bridge, instead of pulling himself across hand over hand, he climbed atop the pole and ran full speed across it, as if it wasn't twelve feet in the air and no more than two inches wide. Aderyn heard Lorus take in a short, sharp breath and felt vindicated on Weston's behalf.

When he reached the ridged pole, Weston didn't hesitate for more than a second. He snatched up a length of rope and flung it around the pole, using it to give himself leverage as he climbed to the blue flag. He landed more gracefully than Isold had and raced for the final obstacle.

"If that fellow leaps the river," Lorus said, but didn't complete his sentence.

"He won't," Livia said. "He's terrible at the long jump."

"Then how—"

Weston slowed nearly to a stop at the riverside. Then, as gracefully as a dancer, he leaped from log to log, setting them spinning wildly but always being gone before they could tip him into the river. Panting, he crossed the finish line and bent over to catch his breath.

"Forty-seven seconds," Lorus said. Now he sounded impressed.

"You'd better go next," Livia told Aderyn. "Who knows what I'll end up doing to the course?"

Aderyn nodded. She wiped her sweaty palms on her trousers and walked slowly to the white flags. For a moment, she reviewed the course as she'd seen it run twice and tried to come up with strategies for each section. Then she shook her head. This went too fast for conscious thought. Instinct, and her Warmaster's vision, would have to guide her.

At Lorus's signal, she took off up the hill.

CHAPTER NINE

She raced as fast as she could to the wooden wall, surveying the terrain as she ran. She saw nothing that would give her an advantage, no trick she could play, but fortunately she'd always been good at climbing trees, and these hand- and footholds almost felt like cheating. She snatched the red flag free and rushed onward.

Taking Weston's example, she ignored the curve of the path and gained a few seconds by taking the direct approach. As she neared the walkway beneath the waterfalls, she scanned its surface. Too bad **[Improved Assess 2]** didn't tell her anything about terrain. All she could tell from her frantic glance was that it wasn't as slick as it looked, the wood grainy and swollen from years of spray. So she didn't slow at all, just made for the walkway as if it was a simple path.

With **[See It Coming]**, the obstacle wasn't even a challenge. The ghostly shape of the wall punching her warned her to stop, leaning well back, before rushing past it. As if the unseen Earthbreaker resented her avoiding the first blow, the wall struck at her twice more, and Aderyn avoided the punches each time, flattening herself beneath one and leaping ahead of another. She jumped the broken section of the walkway before it fell away beneath her feet, grabbed the yellow flag, and ran on.

[See It Coming] made the rope loop bridge simple as well, though Aderyn lost time because she wasn't strong enough to propel her body quickly. She refused to think about how much time that might be. Instinct, not analysis.

She pushed herself hard going up to the pole climb, knowing she needed to make up time beforehand because this was the one that could ruin her. She had never been able to climb a pole, not with any amount of help. She scanned the ground as she approached, swiftly examining the objects. They had to be there for a reason, and Weston had used one to help his climb, so that reason was to give contestants options.

Her eye fell on a length of pole with a funny end. Threaded. Inspiration struck, and she grabbed it and immediately found another pole that was its mate. She let her hands work at joining them and cast about for more inspiration. There. A hook, also threaded at the blunt end. She attached it to her pole and swung the hook at the blue flag, snagging it neatly so it floated free. Aderyn didn't stop to watch it land. She dropped the pole and raced for the river.

As she ran, she examined the logs. She couldn't leap the river like Isold and she couldn't bound across like Weston, so fast he just wasn't there when the logs moved. She would need a different approach.

She aimed at one of the logs a little ways out in the river, one that bobbed up and down without spinning or rotating. Leaping off the bank, she hit the log and gave it exactly the right push to send it spinning, propelling her forward. Without thinking, she aimed for another log like the first and used her momentum to land on it, stretching her legs to their limit. The third log nearly dumped her in the river, but she corrected swiftly, and with another two jumps she'd reached the far bank and sprinted for the black flags.

Lorus gazed at her with narrowed eyes. "Wait here," he said, and walked with measured steps to the stairs leading to the platform where the short man still stood. Aderyn, winded and feeling she'd strained something on that last obstacle, watched him warily.

"He was not happy that you didn't get dunked," Weston said in a low voice, though there was no one to hear but the four of them. "He said something about how it was impossible."

"That man said all skills and spells were acceptable," Aderyn protested. "It's not my fault no one knows what Warmasters can do."

"I doubt it will be a problem," Livia said. "Forty-five seconds, by the way. That was clever what you did to get the blue flag."

"Why won't it be a problem?" Weston said. "If he thinks Aderyn should be disqualified—"

"That man *also* said make it a good show," Livia pointed out. "And that was amazing. You think audiences won't eat that up? If this trial course is at all like what they do in the real thing, I predict they'll have betting pools on when Aderyn finally gets dunked."

Aderyn laughed despite her anxiety. "That will be a long time coming. I can barely swim."

Lorus returned with the short man following him. "She had to have inside knowledge," Lorus said. "There's no way anyone could avoid all the traps."

The short man eyed Aderyn. "Warmaster," he said. "Is this a skill?"

"It's called **[See It Coming]**," Aderyn said. "I glimpse blows or attacks a second before they happen. And if Lorus was telling the truth about how an Earthbreaker controls that obstacle, I could hardly have inside knowledge unless I was complicit with that person."

"Good point." The short man pursed his lips in thought. "You can do that every time?"

"If I'm alert, sure."

"Good." He turned to Lorus and said, "Don't let your bloodthirstiness interfere with doing your job. One more run, is that right? I think I'll watch from down here, if you don't mind, young lady."

"You won't rattle me, if that's what you're worried about," Livia replied coolly.

She took her place at the starting flags, and when Lorus shouted "Go!" she walked rapidly, not running, to the first wall. Lorus let out a sigh of triumph. Aderyn disliked him immensely.

But Lorus's triumph didn't last long. As Livia approached the wall, she chanted something that made the earth rise beneath her, carrying her to the top where she plucked the red flag free and let it fall.

At the stone cliff, she strolled along the wooden walkway, and when the stone surged toward her, she punched back with her stone fist, shattering the wall.

When she neared the bridge of rope handholds, she raised the bed of the river and let the squelchy wet earth carry her rapidly to the far side.

She took a solid wrestler's stance at the pole, ignoring everything scattered around it, and with a heave yanked it out of the suddenly soft earth and dropped it so the blue flag wilted in acquiescence to her mastery.

And at the final river, she cast one last spell. Thick vines like tentacles rose up from beneath the water, twining around the logs until they made a solid platform Livia walked across easily.

As she passed the black flags, Lorus said, "Fifty seconds. Maybe you shouldn't have been so cocky."

"I'm not a runner," Livia said. "And I put on a show, or am I wrong and you don't care about that?"

"Ignore Lorus, he enjoys taunting the contestants," the short man said. "Average time for your team is forty-seven and a half seconds. Respectable. Not stellar, but very few of the actual dungeons are like this one."

"Dungeons?" Aderyn asked.

"The team events take place in small, single-instance dungeons, crafted specifically for the Glory Games. You'll gain experience based on defeating the dungeon."

"Meaning we're in?" Weston asked.

The short man examined each of them in turn. When his gaze fell on Aderyn, it felt like a giant thumb pressing down on her. "You are," he finally said. "What's your team name?"

"Team name?" Weston said, taken aback.

"Yes, team name, you need to have something your supporters can chant. What is it?"

Aderyn felt like every name she'd ever heard of had flown straight out of her head. "What are some of the other names?" she asked, stalling for time.

"The Hooligans, the Rowdy Ruffians, the Indomitables... come on, stop wasting time. It's not like you're choosing a life partner. Just something bold and exciting."

"Bold and exciting," Weston said. "The Cat-Hawks?"

The short man's eyes narrowed. "Maybe too exciting. The Wildcats. There, that wasn't so hard. Report back here in three days. And be dressed properly. Blue on black."

"What's wrong with how we look now?" Livia demanded.

"You're new to Finion's Gate," the short man said. "Find someone to explain how the team matches work. Then you'll know why you look all wrong." He waved them in the direction of the stairs. Aderyn was halfway up them when she realized he'd never said his name.

OWEN WASN'T IN THE ROOM THEY'D STARTED IN WHEN they returned down the ramp. "Let's find Davith and see if he knows what they want solo champions, or champion candidates, to do,"

Weston suggested. "It beats wandering around this place looking for Owen and getting lost."

"Or being yelled at by Lorus," Aderyn said. She was still smarting from his accusation that she'd cheated.

They exited to the street, but before they could explore the big square opening, Davith came running through it. "That was amazing!" he shouted, drawing a couple of stares from passersby. "You were all—and *you* ran that pole and—then you made the earth go *vroom* and it was—I've never seen anyone so fast—" He drew in a breath. "And *you* dodged everything!" he said, grabbing Aderyn's shoulder. "Everyone gets at least a little wet, everyone, and you went *whoosh* and *bam* and—it was *amazing!*"

"Thank you, Davith," Aderyn said with a laugh. "I'm glad we impressed you."

"Ready to change your allegiance?" Weston said, grinning.

Davith paused. "No," he said with a thoughtful air, "no, I don't think so. The Hooligans are *really* good. But we'll see what happens in a real dungeon. You might beat them!"

"I don't suppose you know where Owen went?" Aderyn asked.

"I don't know what they do with the solo competitors, no." Davith looked up and down the street as if Owen might pop out of the air. "But we can wait in the stands. Let him come to us. It's more fun than waiting inside."

They sat on the stands and watched two more teams go through the qualifier. The first was hopelessly slow according to Livia's watch, each member running the course in over a minute. The second was faster, though not faster than their team, but they put on a better show than the first. They had a Tidecaller who used the water features of the course to give himself an advantage that was nearly as dramatic as Livia's run. "We could take them," Livia muttered, running her fingers idly over her stone arm.

"It will depend on the dungeon," Davith said. "Some of them are where you race against an environmental challenge, timing yourself against another team doing the same. But I don't like those as much. The good ones are the head-to-head contests. Free the Prisoner, or relays, or Defend the Castle."

"That man we spoke to said we need to dress properly when we return in three days," Weston said. "What did he mean?"

"Well, matching colors, of course," Davith said. His mouth fell open in astonishment. "You don't have uniforms?"

"He said something about blue on black," Isold said.

"Wow, you really don't know anything," Davith said. "I mean, no offense, but you're so new it's kind of sad."

Davith's chagrin made it impossible for Aderyn to be insulted. "Everybody has to start somewhere, right? I bet there was a time when you didn't know any of this."

"Yes, but I was three." Davith shook his head. "Sorry. You're right. Besides, what matters is that you learn now. Blue on black means you wear black trousers and shirts with a blue jerkin or tunic over them. Boots can be whatever color you want. Shirts usually have short sleeves, but that's just for comfort. No magic gear allowed. If a dungeon requires weapons, you'll be given an assortment to choose from, and those can't be magic either."

He tapped his lips in thought. "Let's see, what else... most teams wear matching uniforms, not just any old tunics in the right colors, but it might be hard to get those made in less than three days. I'll ask Pa what he can find. What's your team name?"

"The Wildcats," Weston said.

"Oh, that's good! Sounds fierce. Anyway, if you get to be popular, you might want to have an emblem made that you can wear on your tunics. But that's a long way off." Davith blew out his breath. "I can't think of anything else. In three days, you'll see how it all works."

"Is that another qualifying round?" Isold asked.

"Oh, no! That's the beginning of this season's Glory Games. Though you might not get picked to compete right off. There are eight teams—oh, I forgot, you must have done really well, because there are only two open slots for new teams this season. All the others have at least one season behind them, and the Hooligans have been competing for six!" Davith's excitement rose again. "Anyway, there's two team dungeons before the morning fights, and two in the afternoon, so you might not compete right away. That's all right, though, because going second gives you a chance to see what it's like."

Movement off to one side caught Aderyn's eye, and she waved to attract Owen's attention. Owen made his way across the empty rows to sit beside her. "I hope you had more fun than I did. I don't think I've seen that much paperwork since the last time I applied for college financial aid."

"How strange. We just had to run that obstacle course," Aderyn said hastily, glaring at Owen and jerking her head in Davith's direction. Owen was better these days about not referring to his own world in front of strangers, but he sometimes forgot.

"That does look like fun. Why is Isold wet?"

"The obstacle course," Isold said. "Fortunately, today is sunny and warm."

"And they made it in!" Davith exclaimed. "They're the Wildcats, and they're going to be almost as great as the Hooligans!"

"Ringing endorsement," Owen said with a grin. He tapped a coin-sized enamel pin attached to his shirt near the collar. "I am officially challenger number thirty-one. I am not allowed a name until I prove myself by being one of the top ten challengers as established by honorable combat. Challengers being the newbies, by contrast with the established champions."

"Wow," Davith said, his eyes round. "Are you going to make it?"

"I sure hope so," Owen said. "There are still some challengers coming in. Herton says there's always a rush the last two days. He anticipates there being no more than forty-five fighters total."

"And you have to win eight matches to proceed," Weston said.

"I fight eight matches, and I have to win five of them or I'm disqualified. Then whoever wins the most matches is ranked first, and so forth, with tiebreaker matches if necessary. Wooden weapons, no magic armor." Owen spun the <**Ring of the Cat**> on the middle finger of his left hand. The row of three gems, red, blue, and green, glinted in the bright sunlight. "Herton said magic like this isn't illegal, but that might be because he didn't know what magic was on it aside from how it doesn't give me a boost to my abilities or skills."

"I'm just as happy if you don't take it off," Aderyn said. "Gamboling Coil said it would save your life."

"I doubt I'm in any danger here. They're very strict about the non-lethality aspect. Half the papers I filled out had to do with me swearing on the head of my firstborn I would not harm the other combatants or through inaction cause them to be harmed. Lawyers could—I mean, it was quite the example of binding agreements." Owen cleared his throat. "What about you all?"

"According to Davith, we need to acquire uniforms," Isold said. "And present ourselves here three days from now."

"Davith, there's betting on the challengers, right?" Weston asked.

"Oh, sure, but that's not interesting," Davith said. "Or I guess it could be, but I never gamble. Pa says it's a mug's game and the only ones who win are the bookkeepers."

"We'll see. I'd like to give it a try anyway." Weston looked Owen up and down. "This would be better if we knew you'd go up against some mountain of a Stalwart first."

"He still doesn't look like much, true," Livia said, appraising Owen.

Owen rolled his eyes and stood, bringing Aderyn with him. "You're both filling me with confidence. Let's get something to eat. And I'll pretend I still have my team's respect."

CHAPTER TEN

The uniform Davith's pa, Gerant, had found for her fit well enough after the seamstress, also introduced to the team by Gerant, finished her magic on it. Not literal magic, though the woman was a Windwarden as well as a seamstress. The trousers were lightweight, nothing that would interfere with agility. The short-sleeved shirt fit loosely, again giving her freedom of movement. The blue tunic wasn't more than a rectangle of fabric stitched up the sides to make armholes, with another hole cut out of the top for a head. The seamstress had said, "What color blue?" and presented them with an array of shades, more than Aderyn had believed existed. They'd picked a bright, vibrant blue the seamstress called cerulean.

Now they waited in a room packed full of people beneath the arena. Some wore clothes like theirs, but with different-colored tunics, sunset red and buttercup yellow and a warm brownish-gold, subdued by contrast to the others but still compelling. The other teams kept to themselves, though Aderyn caught some of those team members eyeing her and looking away swiftly when their eyes met.

The rest of the windowless room, which had to be a good thirty feet on a side, was packed with men and women wearing plain white shirts and gray trousers tucked into knee-high boots. Each of them wore a shining coin-sized pin near the neck of their shirt, enameled with a number Owen had said ranged from 1 to 42, the final number of challengers who'd registered.

Owen, also dressed in white and gray, didn't look nervous. Aderyn felt like her pants were permanently wrinkled and damp from how often she'd wiped her sweaty palms over them. "I don't know how you can stay calm," she told him in a low voice. "Aren't you even a little anxious?"

"Not really." Owen shrugged. "I'm sure I can take most of these colts—that's what the experienced guys call us. At worst, I'm eliminated immediately, and I get to watch the rest of you perform."

"Except the teams go before the individual combats," Livia pointed out. "So, unless we get picked—"

"Everybody listen!" The short man, whose name had turned out to be Seonn, strode forward so he was standing near the door that led to the arena. "Teams! You'll all be presented to the crowd today, but only four of you will compete this morning. The other four will get their turn this afternoon. First, it's the Indomitables, the Hooligans, the Fearsome Five, and the Trailblazers. Later, the Rowdy Ruffians, the Wildcats, the Vagabonds, and the Scrappers. Got it?"

A murmur rose from the assembled teams.

"Good. You new people, the Wildcats and the Trailblazers, you follow the others onto the arena floor when your team name is called. Do what they do. After introductions, you teams not competing, go to your seats in the covert. Enjoy the spectacle. Now get out of here while I talk to the challengers."

Relieved, Aderyn squeezed Owen's hand and followed the other teams out the door. She liked the idea of getting a feel for how the competitions went before having to compete herself. She did wonder if they weren't getting an unfair advantage, seeing the other teams perform—but they wouldn't compete against any of the morning's teams, so it wasn't that much of an advantage.

The door led to a long, low-ceilinged tunnel with a square of daylight at the far end. Behind Aderyn, just before the door shut, Seonn shouted, "Listen up, colts! When your number is called, advance—"

"This is crazy," Livia muttered.

"What is?" Weston said.

"That we can earn experience this way. We ought to be out killing monsters and beating dungeons, not pandering to a crowd. It's weird."

"It's also less deadly," Isold said. "And we only have to make it as far as level fourteen. It's not like it's a life's commitment."

"It's still weird." Livia tilted her head back to look at the tunnel's ceiling. It was worked stone, big slabs fitted together so closely they looked like a painting of a curved wall. "This arena is beautiful, though."

"You haven't seen it yet," Weston said. None of them had. The arena was closed when the Glory Games weren't in session.

"I can feel it. All that stone, all around me. Somebody who cared about stonework built this place, I can tell." Livia let out a pleased sigh. "I think I'll have an advantage here. It feels welcoming."

Aderyn didn't agree. The low, curved ceiling of the tunnel made her feel like hunching, though it wasn't all that low, just wider than it was tall. She looked ahead to the tunnel's end, where the other teams gathered. The team nearest her, backlit by the bright sunshine, wore dark tunics that were probably green in full light, with a blobby pale shape she couldn't make out stitched to their backs. She thought back over the team names. Except for their own, no representative symbols leaped to mind that any of the others might choose.

A quiet murmur filled the air, growing louder as they neared the tunnel exit. It sounded like the sea outside Obsidian until something clicked in Aderyn's head, and she realized it was the noise of thousands of people, making all the little noises that were quiet on their own but added up to a clamor when you got enough of them. Aderyn wiped her palms on her trousers again.

"Welcome to the 47th semi-annual Glory Games!" an unseen speaker boomed out, exactly as if he had **[Amplify Voice]**. The clamor surged into a roar, unnerving Aderyn further. She was just a girl from a sanctuary city that could be dropped into Finion's Gate and disappear; what was she doing here?

"Presenting... the eight team contenders!" The speaker sounded so excited Aderyn would have guessed he was announcing the arrival of some fabulously wealthy king. "Let's give a wild Glory Games welcome to... the Indomitables!"

The four men and one woman in the dark green tunics jogged out onto the arena floor, waving at people Aderyn couldn't see. She couldn't see anything, really, past the other teams and the hard-packed earth and the bright sunlight. She had an image in her head of Holder Stadium, of the arena being just like that only bigger. But maybe that was wrong, and the arena was big enough to swallow Far Haven, too. In that case, Livia was right. This was crazy.

"The Hooligans!"

The roar of the crowd became frenzied. Aderyn watched the four men and women dressed in golden-brown run from the tunnel. So this was Davith's favorite team. It sounded like he wasn't the only one who loved them. It relieved Aderyn's mind that her team wouldn't face them today. She already felt more unsettled than she expected.

"The Wildcats!"

"That's us," Weston hissed, grabbing Aderyn and startling her out of her fugue. "Come on!"

She'd expected the crowd to quiet at their appearance, since they were total unknowns, but the shouting, while not as loud as for the Hooligans, still shook her. She ran without thinking out of the tunnel and into the biggest enclosed space she'd ever seen. Low walls circled the arena floor, which was so wide she could barely see the far side. Above the walls, seats rose in tiers just like in Holder Stadium, but with enough room to seat thousands, maybe ten thousand. The outer wall of the arena rose high above the highest tier, carved and pierced with ornamental holes so its top looked like lacework.

A shimmering midnight-blue veil, too thick to see through, circled the center of the arena, rising high enough that no one who wasn't a bird or a spellslinger with *fly* could see what lay behind it. The sight made Aderyn's heart beat faster. The first dungeon. Of course they'd want to set it up in advance, and of course they wouldn't want the teams seeing it too soon. Aderyn wasn't even competing that morning and the idea still thrilled her.

Waving automatically, Aderyn turned in a slow circle. To the left of the tunnel exit and above the inner wall sat a row of what looked like giant boxes, with rectangular roofs supported by pillars at each corner. Several people sat within the nearest box, but Aderyn didn't stop to stare. To the right of the tunnel exit, a short flight of stairs led up to another box, this one larger with a lower roof. Some of the teams who'd exited before them were seated there. The covert.

Aderyn waved until the speaker bellowed, "The Fearsome Five!" Then she ran for the covert, outpacing even Isold, and climbed the stairs to where she could duck inside the covert and pretend she wasn't hiding. Behind the landing at the top of the stairs, more stairs went down, back under the arena somewhere, but she was too flustered to care about what seemed to be a second exit.

"Aderyn, we've got seats," Weston said. Dozens of wooden chairs with no cushions lined the interior of the covert, arranged in little groups of six each painted to match the teams' tunics. Aderyn dropped gratefully into one of the blue chairs. She didn't even care that it didn't have a great view of the arena floor. She was happy that she was shielded from the view of the thousands of spectators, all avidly watching her and her fellow... combatants? No, that was the fighters. Entertainers? More accurate.

"Are you all right?" Livia asked.

Aderyn nodded, then shook her head. "Overwhelmed. I guess I didn't know how it would feel to be stared at by so many people. I'll get used to it. It was just unexpected."

"I found it exhilarating," Livia said, stretching both arms over her head. Aderyn caught one of the Indomitables staring at Livia's stone arm, but the man said nothing.

"It is kind of amazing to have all those people cheering for us," Weston said. "And imagine what it'll be like when we've earned that applause."

"Hey there," a man said. It was one of the golden-brown Hooligans, a man with curly black hair and eyes so dark a brown as to be nearly black. "The Wildcats, right? I'm Jesper. The Hooligans." He extended a hand to Weston.

Weston rose and shook Jesper's hand. "Weston. This is Livia, Isold, and Aderyn. Good to meet you."

Jesper shook each hand in turn, ending with Aderyn. He held her hand a little longer than she found comfortable, but he didn't leer or examine her with his eyes, so she decided it was nothing. "Nice to meet the new teams. I have to say I'm not sad the Speedsters packed it in last season. They were obnoxious." He chuckled. "You and the Trailblazers made it through the qualifier. That's great. Competition was stiff this year."

"We're looking forward to competing," Livia said. "I hear you Hooligans are the favorites."

"We do our best," Jesper said, grinning. "All right, yes, we're the best. But nobody should ever think they're safe at the top, right? I hope you'll give us a good fight when the time comes."

"Count on it," Weston said, grinning back.

A horn sounded, loud and echoing, and the announcer's voice said, "Prepare for an incredible show today, friends! Our first dungeon is... *Escort the King!*"

Jesper glanced over his shoulder. "That's the first team challenge," he said. "Come on down here and sit in the yellow seats. The

Fearsome Five won't care so long as you move before they get back, and you'll want a good view."

Weston shrugged and led the way between other teams to sit in the yellow chairs near the front of the box. From there, the arena floor was visible, and the smell of dust and metal and warm bodies all packed together in one place unexpectedly roused Aderyn's excitement. The noise was louder now, thousands of people all shouting the same thing at once, though the echoes made it so the word they shouted might have been "Ring" or "King."

Five people in sunburst yellow and five people in purple so dark it was almost indistinguishable from their black clothing strolled toward the shimmering veil, arranging themselves in loose groups on opposite sides of the concealed space. This put the purple contenders out of sight, but the yellow team, the Fearsome Five, gathered where Aderyn could see them. They appeared to be discussing among themselves and gesturing. Finally, one woman nodded and walked back toward the tunnel entrance. A moment later, one of the purple-clad men came back around the corner and joined the yellow woman.

"Only four competitors allowed per challenge," Jesper said as if he'd noticed Aderyn's curiosity. "The teams who have more than four members have to choose each time who sits out, and there are rules about how often a team member can do that. Since there's no substituting mid-dungeon, there's not much benefit to having more than four, but some teams are like that. The Scrappers have six, the maximum allowed."

The horn blasted twice, two short honks, and the Fearsome Five —or was it Fearsome Four now?—tensed, ready to run. "Here we go," the announcer boomed.

After a couple of interminable seconds, the horn blew again, loud and long. The veil disappeared, revealing the rugged terrain of two miniature mountains and, beyond that, the waiting forms of the Trailblazers in purple. As the crowd screamed, both teams plunged forward into the dungeon.

CHAPTER ELEVEN

The dungeon looked exactly like real mountain terrain, with foothills covered in scrub and short grasses rising to bare, craggy cliffs facing each other. Aderyn looked closer, her gaze shifting from one mountain to the other and back. Surprised, she said, "The mountains are identical."

"It's so neither team has an advantage," Jesper said. "The hills match each other, too, but mirrored."

"What is the goal?" Isold asked.

Jesper leaned forward, resting his arms on the edge of the covert's box. "This dungeon is Escort the King. The goal is to take an object, the king, to the top of the mountain. The 'king' is a ball matching the team's colors, hidden somewhere in the dungeon at ground level. Yellow's mountain is the one on the left."

Aderyn leaned forward, fascinated. The Fearsome Five were easy to keep track of, their yellow tunics bright against the scrub trees and bushes. "And the other team tries to stop them, while still getting their own ball to the top?"

"Right. You've seen it before?"

"No, but we used to play a similar game back home."

"Well, the strategy varies according to a team's preference. Some teams put most of their effort into evading the 'enemy,' and some do the opposite, interfere with the other team to keep them from advancing." Jesper waved a hand at the dungeon terrain. "Those Trailblazers picked a stupid shade of purple. You want to be sure your ball or armband or whatever is readily visible. Dark purple will look like shadow in most of these terrains."

"I don't suppose you'll give us advice?" Weston said with a grin.

"What, and risk finding out the new team is a real challenge?" Jesper grinned back. "All I will say is that the secret to winning at Escort the King is to play to your strengths."

Aderyn was still watching the yellow tunics. The Fearsome Five were spread out, searching the area for their 'king.' It was harder to keep track of the Trailblazers, because what Jesper had said was true —the purple tunics made them all look like dark blotches against the green.

A shout went up from the crowd as a woman in a yellow tunic held aloft a head-sized yellow ball. Immediately, she and one of her teammates took off running for the mountain, with the other two lagging behind. "And the Fearsome Five have their king!" the announcer shouted. "That's the kind of alertness we've come to expect from team captain Nandia. Now, how will the Trailblazers react?"

Aderyn recognized the Fearsome Five's positioning as a defensive barrier, watching for an enemy attack. She didn't say anything. Jesper probably recognized the tactic, and enlightening him wasn't her business. More importantly, she didn't want him to know about her Warmaster's vision. He struck her as smart enough to figure out how to use it against her.

On a whim, she Skill Assessed him. Maybe it was overkill, but she had a feeling knowing his skills would matter to her team eventually.

Name: Jesper
Class: Deadeye

Level: 15

<u>Class Skills</u>: Advanced Weapon Proficiency (15), Advanced Armor Proficiency (13), **Knowledge: Monsters (10)**, **Dodge (15)**, Point-Blank Shot (13), **Thrown Weapon Proficiency (12)**, Sneak Attack (8), **Precise Shot (9)**, Basic Map Access (5), **Demoralize (6)**, Called Shot (4), **Shatter Confidence (3)**, Fast Draw (2), **Weapon Mastery (short bow) (4)**

A Deadeye, huh? Seonn had said combat between teams sometimes happened, but no lethal weapons were permitted, particularly ones where you couldn't pull your punches like bows and crossbows. Jesper might be at a disadvantage, but somehow, she didn't think so.

The crowd's frenzied shouting grew louder, drawing her attention back to the dungeon. Three Trailblazers had surrounded the Fearsome Five, trying to get the yellow ball. One of them, a Tidecaller Aderyn realized was the one she'd watched run the obstacle course the other day, had an enormous bubble of water suspended in front of him that he sent shooting toward the woman carrying the ball. The two yellow defenders took turns deflecting it with their hands and feet, so expertly Aderyn didn't need **[Improved Assess 2]** to know they were both Swifthands. Why the bubble didn't pop, or encompass them, Aderyn didn't know. But the Fearsome Five continued to progress, more slowly now, into the foothills and toward the base of the mountain.

"The Trailblazers still haven't found their 'king,'" Weston said. "Which is funny, because I can see it just fine."

"I can't tell if they've got a strategy or they're just desperate," Jesper said. "Fewer searchers means they're losing time, but on the other hand, if that one Trailblazer does manage to stumble across the ball, she probably thinks she could just saunter up the mountainside. Hard to tell, with the new teams."

Aderyn could see the ball too. So could a large section of the crowd on this side. She became aware that large numbers of the spectators were shouting at the searching Trailblazer. "Is that allowed?" she asked Jesper.

"The dungeons are isolated. We can hear them if the arbitrators allow it, but no sound gets in from outside unless it's one of the arbitrators announcing a rules violation. They believe it's a distraction. And, of course, it keeps outsiders from revealing information that might give a team an advantage. Once someone wins, the teams can hear the cheering." Jesper pointed. "Ah, looks like the woman with zero ranks in [Spot] finally saw the purple ball."

Just as he said this, the announcer declared, "And the Trailblazers have finally found their king! It might not be too late for them, but let's see what happens when Jena reaches the mountain. She'll be in for a surprise, won't she?"

Sure enough, the Trailblazer had snatched up the ball and was running for the mountain, not bothering to show it off to the crowd. Jesper hissed in annoyance. "Somebody forgot the first rule. Make it look good."

"We are playing to the crowd, yes?" Isold said. "Does the experience gained from defeating the dungeon vary according to how good a show it is?"

"Yes, but not by much," Jesper said. "There's a set experience amount and then a bonus for crowd-pleasing maneuvers, or a fast time, things like that. Mostly the point of putting on a good show is, to be perfectly honest, to get the fame. A popular team gets all sorts of benefits."

"And you know this from experience, I gather." Isold smiled to show it wasn't an insult.

"We've been ranked at the top for the last four seasons," Jesper said with a shrug. "I won't apologize for being the best."

"Of course not. I meant your insights are valuable because you have the experience." Isold gestured at the dungeon. "It's something we can aim for."

In the dungeon, one of the Fearsome Five, the one nearest the woman with the ball, shouted, "Back there!" and waved an arm at the Trailblazer heading up the mountain. One of the Fearsome Five defenders broke away and ran at the Trailblazer Tidecaller. With swift, acrobatic movements of hands and feet, she bore him to the ground and gave a kick to his head that made him fall in a boneless, unconscious heap. In the next second, she was racing after the Trailblazer with the ball.

"Oooh, ouch!" The announcer sounded torn between amusement and sympathy. "Nice work, Holla. Tethris is going to be sleeping this one out, what do you think?"

The other two Trailblazers hesitated, first taking a step toward their fallen partner, then apparently changing their minds and engaging the second Fearsome Five defender directly. Aderyn could have told them it was a mistake. She didn't need an Assessment to know the Trailblazers were no match for another Swifthands, even when it was two against one. The Fearsome Five Swifthands easily deflected blows from staff and wooden sword, and his teammates guarding the ball hurried away.

Aderyn turned her attention on Jena, the woman in purple carrying the ball. She had a good lead on the pursuing woman in the yellow tunic, but as she got to the first ascent of the mountain, she immediately found she needed both hands to cross some of the terrain. She shouted, "Rosvin! Hurry!"

"That's right, friends, it looks like Jena needs a pal," the announcer said with a chuckle. "What do we always say?"

"*Teamwork!*" rose the chant from the crowd, raggedly as some shouted later than others.

One of the Trailblazers fighting the Swifthands shouted, "Coming!" But that was a lie, Aderyn saw, or at least hopeless optimism, because his fight was not going well and the Swifthands wasn't letting him disengage. All the while, the Fearsome Five's second Swifthands, the woman following the purple ball, got closer and closer to her prey.

Aderyn found she was gripping the rail so hard the wood rubbed her hands painfully. She couldn't decide who to watch, the doomed Trailblazer clinging to the mountainside or the pair in yellow who were taking turns climbing the slope, tossing the ball back and forth as they slowly ascended.

A groan sounded from the crowd. Aderyn looked just in time to see the Swifthands bat the purple ball out of the Trailblazer's hands, sending it sailing away across the foothills.

"Oh, no!" the announcer moaned. "They're going to have trouble recovering from that!"

"You can't hold the other team's ball," Jesper answered the question Aderyn hadn't asked, though she'd thought it. "So there's no stealing an enemy ball and keeping them from winning that way. But that's a fairly definitive blow to the Trailblazers."

Aderyn agreed. The Trailblazer hurried down the slope, bounding rapidly toward the ball as her friend Rosvin finally escaped the other Swifthands and raced toward her. It was obviously going to be too late for that team. Aderyn turned her attention on the Fearsome Five. The one Swifthands was still holding off the Trailblazer, the Tidecaller was moving weakly like he was waking up, but the two with the ball had nearly reached the top.

Then, with three bright flashes of light and a sound of trumpets, it was over. A system message flashed above the dungeon.

Congratulations! You have defeated [Escort the King terrain variation 2].
You have earned [10,000 XP] plus a bonus of [1000 XP]

"Congratulations to the Fearsome Five!" the announcer bellowed. "Go on, everyone, show them some love!"

The yellow-clad man and woman clung to the mountaintop as it gently collapsed, bringing them back to earth. Their companions stood by to give them a hand down. With the fifth member running to join them, the Fearsome Five waved at the crowd, which went crazy with excitement. The woman still holding the yellow ball wound up and threw it into the stands, where a surge of motion like a wave of people rushed to swallow it up.

"She does that every time," Jesper said. "She's not supposed to, but it makes the crowd happy, so no one stops her." He pushed off the rail. "That's us up next. See what you think." He nodded and returned to the rest of his team, who after a moment's conference clasped hands in a four-way handshake and then walked through the crowd of other team members. As they passed, Jesper gave a clap on the shoulder to one of the men wearing green and said something too low for Aderyn to hear that made him laugh. The man said, "You wish, Jesper," and led the men in green after Jesper, trailed by the one woman in that color who caught Aderyn's eye and smiled in a friendly way.

"We should move, in case those Fearsome Five are territorial," Weston said, and they all settled into their own chairs. "The green are the Indomitables, which is a great name, though obviously not as great as the Wildcats." He tilted his chair back so it rocked on two legs, perfectly balanced.

"I want to get a good look at the other teams," Aderyn said. "I'm going to stand at the front, where Jesper was."

"Daring," Livia said. "But worth it, if you can identify his weaknesses. He had the attitude of someone who's earned the right to be arrogant, and since he wasn't..." Her voice trailed off suggestively. "This isn't a bad spot right here. Look, the concealment is up, and we can see all of it."

"Even so." Aderyn wasn't sure why she was so convinced Jesper was the one to watch. The Indomitables had moved with the same easy assurance. Maybe it was just nerves, knowing how popular the Hooligans were, but she didn't intend to give up an advantage.

The noise of people ascending the stairs drew her attention away from the shifting veil that concealed the new dungeon. The Fearsome

Five entered the covert, talking loudly and energetically to the members of the Trailblazers. It surprised Aderyn that the talk was all friendly. From what she could hear, the team in yellow was giving their defeated opponents pointers on what to do next time.

"...and that strategy looks good, but you can see how it breaks down when you get to the mountain," the female Swifthands was saying to the woman in purple who'd nearly carried the "king" up the mountain.

"We didn't realize the climb was challenging," the Trailblazer said.

"That's because you didn't take time to analyze your surroundings," the Swifthands said, not unkindly but in a straightforward way. "The dungeons' secrets aren't impossible to know, but sometimes it means taking a look around. Thing is, you won't be caught out again, right?"

The Trailblazer shook her head vigorously, making hair come loose from the ponytail tied at the nape of her neck. "No. Definitely not. But—" She smiled suddenly. "We'll probably miss other things sometimes, huh?"

"You've got it. Just remember to make it look good, do your best, and you'll be fine." The Swifthands glanced at Aderyn. "That's Jesper's seat."

"He's down there. He's not using it," Aderyn said, and hoped she sounded assertive rather than brash.

The Swifthands shrugged. "That's true enough. I'm Holla." She extended a hand for Aderyn to shake.

"I'm Aderyn. The Wildcats," Aderyn said.

"The other new team. That should give you and Jena something to talk about. Good luck this afternoon." Holla turned away to rejoin her teammates.

"Did it look like as much of a rout as it felt from inside?" Jena asked with a wry smile.

"It looked like your strategy would have succeeded, actually,"

Aderyn said. "It was bad luck you didn't have two people guarding the ball."

"Bad luck, maybe. Certainly bad analysis." Jena leaned on the rail with her back to the arena. "You're a Warmaster. I was going to say I thought Warmasters were useless, but you can't be if you're level thirteen."

"Maybe my teammates dragged me along," Aderyn said.

Jena surveyed Aderyn closely. "For a few lower levels, maybe, but you know as well as I do there's no way a team can survive past level seven with dead weight. What's your secret?"

When she put it like that, Aderyn's reluctance to tell the truth increased, as if her partnership with Owen really was a secret that could harm her. But that was wrong, dangerously wrong if concealing the truth meant more Warmasters didn't find their true potential. "Warmasters have to have a partner to unlock their skills. We're tacticians who support the party."

Jena whistled. "By thunder, now I'm scared to go up against you. You probably saw the truth about that mountain, didn't you? If you know tactics that well."

Aderyn shrugged. "I didn't think to look. It was all so exciting." Now she really wished she had [Improved Assess 3], because she was increasingly convinced it meant terrain assessment.

"Even more exciting when you're on the ground," Jena said. She swiveled around as the horn sounded. "They're coming out now. This should be interesting. I hear the Hooligans are the ones to beat."

CHAPTER TWELVE

Aderyn watched the two teams, bright green and golden-brown, advance onto the arena floor to the sound of tremendous applause. The Hooligans might be the favorite, but the Indomitables weren't far behind. Aderyn noticed the woman wasn't with them. It made her curious about the rules Jesper had alluded to, the ones governing how often someone could sit out. She wasn't sure those rules even mattered. What would be the point of having a team member who never participated?

"Sorry, what was that?" Aderyn said in response to a question from Jena.

"I said, who's your partner, then? One of your teammates?"

"Yes. I mean, no, not one of the Wildcats. We have a fifth party member, our team leader. He's competing in the solo fights as a challenger."

"Exciting. You must be really eager to gain experience if you've got both possibilities covered." Jena stood. "I'm going to sit with my team. Nice meeting you."

Aderyn nodded.

The Hooligans had moved around to the far side of the dungeon and were now out of sight. The Indomitables grouped near the shimmering dark veil, their heads together like they were planning something. Aderyn wasn't sure what, given that they didn't know what the dungeon was. Or maybe they did, in general, and the veil was to conceal the specifics? She had so many questions.

"Back again, friends, and this time we've got an old familiar rivalry, the Indomitables and the Hooligans!" The announcer sounded even more excited than before. "Get ready for Pass the Stick!"

The horn sounded again. The veil disappeared, revealing terrain that reminded Aderyn of the qualifier obstacle course, complete with hills and waterway. The crowd roared its approval. And both teams sprinted for the far end of the dungeon.

Aderyn didn't know from looking what the goal was, and the shouting had been unintelligible, but clearly the teams knew. One member from each team ran at top speed, ignoring the terrain features, to where a couple of short colored sticks, one green, one brown, were stuck into the ground. Jesper was one. The other was the man he'd spoken to in the covert. Each gripped his colored stick in one hand and, more slowly, made his way to opposite sides of the dungeon.

The other team members had spread out in ways that made no sense to Aderyn. She focused on the Hooligans. One of them was positioned some distance ahead of Jesper at the side of the dungeon nearest the covert. The other two were on the other side, nowhere near their teammates. Neither team was attacking or interfering with the other. Aderyn wished she could ask one of the experienced teams to explain, but she felt sure something was about to happen, and if she ducked away, she would miss it.

Then it happened. Jesper was about halfway to his teammate, who now appeared to be waiting for him, when a wind came out of nowhere, buffeting him so he staggered back. Aderyn noticed one of the Indomitables standing partly concealed nearby, gesturing and chanting nonsense words. Suddenly, it made sense. This was a relay race. Half the team ran; the other half interfered with the other team's runners. Aderyn held her breath in sympathy. Jesper couldn't possibly breathe properly with the Windwarden's spell stealing his air.

Jesper stopped and tucked the stick inside his tunic. From a pocket along the outer seam of his trousers, he drew something small. He cocked an arm and let the thing fly. Whatever it was struck the Windwarden, knocking him back so he staggered and fell on his posterior. The wind stopped buffeting Jesper, who shook his head and ran on.

"A fifteen-second pause for the Indomitables' Warron!" the speaker's enormous voice boomed. "That was quite a crack to the head, there—let's hope he's all right!"

Aderyn guessed that meant Warron the Windwarden had to sit out for fifteen seconds before harassing the Hooligans again. She was deeply impressed at the skill that had let Jesper fling anything with enough accuracy and force to overcome the wind's power.

Jesper made it to his teammate without any more attacks and handed off the stick. Aderyn watched him instead of the runner. He sped around the hills, leaping the small river, to get into position to receive the stick again. Nobody stopped him, but he moved like he was conscious of the possibility. So far, aside from knocking back the Windwarden, she hadn't seen anything impressive enough to justify his team's reputation. On the other hand, she couldn't watch everywhere at once.

She turned her attention to the other side of the dungeon, where the Indomitables had just passed the stick the first time. The runner took two steps and gave a shout as he slid down the slope of a pit that hadn't been there before, thanks to the chanting and gesturing of one of the Hooligans. Aderyn leaned forward to get a better look. The Hooligans' Earthbreaker had combined *create pit* with a spell Livia didn't have that created ever-moving sand at the bottom of the pit.

The Indomitable waded slowly through the sand and clambered up the side of the pit, but Jesper had received the stick from his teammate before the man made it to the top, and from there, it was all over.

After the system message had faded and the crowd's cheering had diminished enough for ordinary speech to be audible, the speaker announced, "We'll start the matches in ten minutes, once the floor has been cleared. We've got quite the batch of challengers this season, so pay attention, because who knows which of these might go on to be your next champion!"

After a pause, the announcer continued, "Oh, who am I kidding? We all know who comes out first, every time—let me hear you scream her name!"

The crowd's raucous cries turned into barely intelligible shouts of "*Kendria! Kendria! Kendria!*"

"She's more popular even than we are," Jesper said, startling Aderyn. "And you're in my seat." He was sweating from his exertions, but breathing easily.

Blushing, Aderyn moved to the side, though Jesper had sounded amused rather than angry. "That was good," she said. "Your dungeon, I mean."

"It was awful," Jesper corrected her. "I hate that variation. The relays are the worst when it's team against team. Much better when you're fighting the environment as you run. And we were sure the Indomitables knew Meara meant to lay that trap and were ready to counter it. Our victory looked too easy."

"Do you... I'm sorry, this is probably insulting. Never mind."

"Don't be afraid to ask questions, Aderyn."

Aderyn nodded. "You don't, um, arrange with the other teams who will win, right? Or how you'll approach a challenge? It doesn't seem so, but you did say the show was the important thing."

"That's a natural assumption, and believe me, people have made the accusation with much more malice," Jesper said. "No, we don't, because it's not fun if it's not a real competition. And it would be virtually impossible, too, because we don't know in advance what dungeons they've planned, and we're not allowed contact after they tell us, so we couldn't plan that well even if we wanted to. You may have noticed we're all friendly, though. Most of us have been doing this for a while, and great competition happens when you respect your opponent's skills and you're both committed to testing yourselves at your peak."

"That's what I hoped. Thanks."

"You planning to leave? The first sets of challenger fights are boring. Lots of people whacking each other with wooden swords. We usually go for drinks after our work is done."

"Oh! No, actually. We have a teammate competing in the solo trials."

"Interesting." Jesper arched one eyebrow, something Aderyn found ridiculously difficult to manage herself. "You'll have to point them out to me. But not today. I wasn't kidding about how boring the fights are—unless you have an interest, of course." He clapped her on the shoulder in a comradely fashion and rejoined his team, who made their way past the others and headed down the stairs, the ones leading deeper into the arena. That relieved Aderyn's mind. She didn't think she could endure walking out across the arena floor again when it was time to leave.

After the Hooligans left, and several other teams followed, Aderyn found herself alone in the covert with her friends and the six members of the orange team, the Scrappers, as well as the purple Trailblazers. She felt terribly conspicuous as well as concerned. Everyone had seemed so friendly, and suppose going for drinks was how they got that way? What if her team was missing out on an important activity?

She reminded herself that it was more important to watch Owen, and they'd have plenty of opportunities to make friends with the other teams. Even so, when the booming voice called out, "Let's welcome this year's Glory Games challengers!" relief filled her, and she leaned forward to watch for Owen. She didn't think it would be boring at all.

Two irregular lines of men and women dressed in gray and white entered the arena. All of them carried wooden weapons, mostly practice swords, though there were a couple of longstaffs. A handful of people wearing loose red shirts so bright they seemed to glow followed the challengers. They were more relaxed than the stiffly-moving challengers, talking to one another with the loose hand gestures of people comfortable with one another. One of them laughed. They were too far away to be heard over the noise of the crowd, but Aderyn had the impression of a bunch of people out for a pleasant stroll.

Aderyn searched the challengers for Owen, but she didn't see him. She counted quickly and came up with ten challengers. So, they had them fight a few at a time. That made sense if they wanted the spectators to be able to see more than just a few of the fights. Owen had explained that in addition to choosing the top ten challengers, these early fights let people get attached to their favorites, to boost audience engagement. Aderyn also thought it boosted the spectators' desire to wager on those favorites.

She sat back in her chair. She wished she hadn't been so cavalier about the trial matches' boringness or lack thereof. Owen was the only one who interested her.

The challengers spread out in pairs across the arena floor, each pair joined by someone in a red shirt. Aderyn watched the nearest pair idly as the red-clad woman beckoned them close and spoke to them. They both nodded, and the woman backed away and gave a shout. Swords clashed, and despite herself Aderyn was drawn in to the spectacle. She Level Assessed the two. One man was a level twelve Swordsworn, and the other was a Swifthands of level thirteen. Aderyn hadn't ever seen a Swifthands use a weapon, but the man handled his sword well. Still, the Swordsworn looked like he had the upper hand. When his sword connected with the Swifthands' shoulder, the red-clad woman shouted again, and Aderyn made out, "One!"

Owen hadn't said the rules of the challenge, but Aderyn could guess. Her father had supervised hundreds of practice bouts along these lines: three strikes to win, no hitting the head, intentional injury a forfeit. She felt drawn back through time to her father's fighting studio at the front of their house, watching him referee fights. And now here she was a thousand miles from that studio, watching the same thing.

The Swifthands tagged his opponent's knee, earning a point, and then caught him in the stomach. Aderyn's sympathies were with him, though she couldn't say why. But then the Swordsworn, in quick succession, struck the Swifthands across the shoulder and then along the thigh in a strike that would have cut deeply had the weapon been steel. "Number seven!" the referee shouted. The crowd cheered, not terribly energetically, and both men shook hands and ran back to the tunnel.

All the other fights but one were over when Aderyn stopped watching that fight, and as she turned her attention on the remaining match, the female Staffsworn disarmed the male Staffsworn and struck him in the center of his chest. "Number twenty!" their referee shouted.

The next set of challengers was already entering the arena when the two Staffsworn left. This time, Aderyn saw Owen's bright blond hair near the center of the group. "It's Owen's turn," she said over her shoulder.

The others joined her at the rail, even Weston. "I thought you were going to place a bet," Aderyn said.

"I did that during the first set of fights," Weston said. He didn't look as smug or elated as Aderyn thought he should. "They don't take large wagers on the challengers in the qualifying rounds. Too boring. I did what I could, but so much for making a killing." He folded his forearms across the rail and sighed.

"We'll just have to be satisfied with knowing our team leader is the best," Aderyn said.

"I'd rather get coin," Weston grumbled. "Owen can be the best anywhere."

Owen was paired off against a hulking Stalwart whose practice sword looked like a toothpick in his meaty hand. Next to him, Owen looked tiny, and Aderyn felt a flash of regret that they hadn't been able to fully implement Weston's plan, because Owen looked like he was going to be crushed.

The pair were on the farther side of the arena, so Aderyn couldn't hear the referee give the signal to start. So, from her perspective, Owen leaped forward unexpectedly and struck his opponent three quick blows to shoulder, arm, and belly, pausing only a few seconds between blows, then leaped back, out of range. The Stalwart, caught in the act of raising his sword, froze. The referee's mouth hung open. He stared at Owen, who wasn't even breathing hard. Then the man shouted, "Number thirty-one!"

Aderyn didn't think most of the spectators had seen that, Owen had moved so fast. "Hey, that was amazing!" she exclaimed. "They ought to cheer."

"What—it's over?" Livia said. "I was looking at those two down there. Neither of them could hit a wall."

"Yes, it's over," Weston said glumly. Then he brightened. "Though if nobody saw that, our secret is still safe. Anyway, I'm going to collect my winnings." He paused. "Hey, shouldn't we have gotten experience for that?"

"Oh, practice matches don't count as defeats," Aderyn said. "My father teaches sword fighting to adventurers and novices both, and he says the system doesn't award experience for sparring because people would otherwise be able to level up artificially fast, and then they'd be in the position Jessemia was, with skills too low for their level. So if you fight with wooden swords, the system recognizes it's not a real fight."

"Still, I can't believe I missed it," Livia said.

"It was astonishing," Isold said. "I think the referee wanted to find a reason to disallow it, because he couldn't believe his eyes."

Aderyn felt like bouncing with joy. Her sweetheart was the best, and everyone would know it soon enough.

CHAPTER THIRTEEN

The morning wore on into noon. After a while, the same numbers started returning. Aderyn heard number 7 once more, and 16 twice. She also thought she heard 27 three times, maybe four, but she never caught a glimpse of that challenger to know who it was.

Owen fought three more battles, winning all of them, though not so readily as the first. By the third battle, Aderyn could hear the crowd's interest every time he appeared. When he won his fourth battle, and the referee called out his number, there was a definite surge in the noise level.

Finally, the booming voice said, "That's it for the morning's Games, friends! We'll see you back here in two hours, when you'll witness more exciting action!"

The covert was already empty of all but their team. Aderyn made her way down the back steps, which ended at a long, curving passage. That took the decision of where to go out of her hands. She hoped it ended up somewhere near the big room beneath the arena, since that was the only place Owen would know to wait for them.

The back way was quiet except for her team's footsteps—well, hers and Isold's and Livia's, since Weston never made any more noise than a cat. None of the spectators leaving the arena had noticed them leave the covert, or maybe they weren't interested. That would change if the Wildcats became famous. It was still a weird idea, them being famous for something that wasn't adventuring.

The long passage felt mildly claustrophobic, but it was cool and didn't smell of sweat the way the tunnel had. Aderyn didn't have any sense of where it was taking them except that she felt they were even lower than the tunnel. Eventually, the passage began rising, and after another minute, they came out into the large room where they'd all waited just a few hours ago.

Some of the challengers were there, not as many as before. Surely not many would have been eliminated already? Aderyn hated the thought of someone losing too many matches in a row and being disqualified without a single win. How discouraging. She wished she had the kind of mind that could hold all that information in her head, to know how many matches had to be fought between which combatants to determine the winners.

They only waited a minute or two before Owen appeared, drying his face and wet hair with a cloth. "No point in getting totally cleaned up when I have to fight again later," he told them, "but at least now I feel a little less sweaty." He put his arm around Aderyn's waist, then released her. "You probably don't want to get too close."

Aderyn threw her arms around his neck and kissed him. "That's where you're wrong," she said. "You were amazing! That first match—"

"Yeah, that was embarrassing for everyone," Owen said, a little sheepishly. "I knew he was slow, but I didn't think he was *that* slow. I was sure he'd block my blows. You should have seen the look on the adjudicator's face. He looked like he wanted to accuse me of cheating, but they're strict about stuff like that and he knew it was legit."

"I wondered if you slowed down on purpose later," Weston said.

Owen glanced around to see who else was near enough to hear. "I did, for two of them. I didn't want to look too good, and I didn't want to humiliate anyone. One of the fights was tougher, a real challenge. I liked that one."

"Jesper said something like that, about it not being fun if it's not real," Aderyn said.

"Who's Jesper?"

"One of the Hooligans. He told us a few things about how the team matches work. I thought he was nice."

"But he's still the enemy," Weston said. "Well. Not the *enemy*, but we're not going to make things easy on his team just because he's nice."

"And you're competing in a couple of hours. Nervous?" Owen hugged Aderyn briefly and released her. He was right, he did smell like sweat and his skin was damp.

"Yes," Aderyn said, just as Livia said "Of course not" and Weston said, "Nervous? Me?"

Isold laughed. "I am nervous because I'm not sure how well my skills will aid us. If it comes down to speed, then possibly I have an advantage."

"We can't know until we see the course," Livia said. "And it won't be anything like what we saw this morning, I'm sure."

"I'm sorry I won't be able to see it," Owen said. "They keep us out of sight before our matches. What a stadium, right? It's easily as big as the Jungle—well, one we have back home. Bigger than where the Reds play."

"Who are the Reds?" Aderyn asked. "Are they a team? What game do they play?"

"Baseball," Owen said. "But I'm a Cardinals fan, so I—you know what, I'll explain it later." He clasped Aderyn's hand. "Let's get something to eat. You'll want your strength for whatever the Games throw at you."

"That could literally happen," Weston said.

TWO HOURS LATER, THEY WERE BACK IN THE ROOM beneath the arena. Aderyn wasn't sure, but she thought there were fewer gray-clad challengers than before. Not by much, but she couldn't help imagining, again, how awful it would feel to be eliminated in the first set of matches. Owen always said she was good at seeing other people's perspectives, and she wasn't sure it was a virtue. It wasn't as if those eliminated challengers were deserving of staying because they were good people. That wasn't the point of the competition. Besides, some of those eliminated had probably fought Owen, and they deserved what they got.

Seonn strode into the room, drawing everyone's gaze. "Teams!" he shouted. "Rowdy Ruffians versus the Wildcats first, Vagabonds versus Scrappers second. Everybody else, into the covert. Let's show some friendly solidarity, all right? Now, go, go!"

The other teams ran into the tunnel, this time mingling instead of grouping by color. When the only ones left were Aderyn's team and four women in red tunics, Seonn said, "Your dungeon objective is Loot the Room—watch it, Kathra, I don't care about your disappointment and you'd better not show it out there." That was directed at one of the red women, who had curly blonde hair and scowled when he addressed her. "You know full well these events are as exciting as *you* choose to make them. So none of this nonsense about which dungeon types are better or worse."

He returned his gaze to the others. "I'll review the rules, since we not only have a new team, it sounds like Kathra can use a refresher." Kathra's scowl deepened. "In Loot the Room, the dungeon contains a number of rings colored to match your teams, some red, some blue. Your goal is to collect as many of your own rings as you can and deposit them in your team's treasure chest. Once they're in the chest, they can't be removed. Otherwise, you're free to interfere with your opponents' rings in any way except flinging them out of the dungeon or stowing them in your own chest."

"What about interfering with other team members?" Isold asked.

Seonn eyed him like he thought Isold planned an immediate assault right there. "Intentional injury will mean you forfeit the game. Accidental injury is frowned on by the crowd. Anything else, skill or spell, is allowed. You get ten minutes. Remember Rule One: make it look good. Any other questions?"

Aderyn's mind went blank. Surely they needed more information! But she couldn't think of a single thing to ask. As Seonn turned away, she told herself there wasn't anything else to learn until they saw the dungeon. She wiped her sweaty palms on her trousers.

"That's it, then," Seonn said. "Wildcats to the north, Ruffians to the south. Let's have a good match."

The horn sounded, and they ran, grouped together, up the tunnel and onto the arena floor. Ahead, the shimmering blue veil, this time in the shape of an oval, obscured the dungeon. Aderyn heard chanting from the crowd that didn't at first make sense, she was so anxious. Then she realized they were saying *"Loot the Room! Loot the Room!"* Kathra might be disdainful of the dungeon type, but it sounded like the crowd loved it.

The cheering drew Aderyn on even as it unnerved her. She mentally slapped herself. This was just noise. It couldn't hurt her. And once she was in the dungeon, she wouldn't be able to hear it, anyway. She was being stupid, and that could cost her team the victory. Suddenly she felt impatient to start. She wanted the experience, yes, but even more, she wanted to win.

North was around the far side of the dungeon. Aderyn took the extra time as they walked to Assess the dungeon. It probably wouldn't work, but it was a good habit.

To her surprise, information appeared.

Name: Loot the Room terrain variation 5

Type: Variable timed instance, tiny, victory condition variant C-2

Power level: N/A

This variable dungeon seeded by the Arena Master contains [47] red rings and [47] blue rings. Teams must collect and deposit rings in designated repositories to achieve victory. Bonus XP is awarded if one team collects all [47] rings of their color. If at the end of ten minutes, no team has achieved the target number, the team with the highest number of rings is declared the victor. The red team repository is located at the top of the northern mesa, while the blue team repository hangs from the highest branch of the tallest tree in the southern copse.

She'd slowed to a walk while reading, and blinked away the words to find Weston grabbing her arm and hauling her along. "Don't go daydreaming now," he shouted over the noise of the crowd.

"I was Assessing the dungeon. It worked." Aderyn stumbled to a halt in front of the others. "And I have an idea. Actually, a couple of ideas." Her nerves had settled, and now she felt nothing but anticipation and excitement. Those Ruffians were in for a surprise.

The horn blew again, and the veil disappeared. Almost directly in front of Aderyn and her friends, a passage between two mesas of gray stone extended into the heart of the dungeon. Aderyn grabbed Livia before she could enter and explained what she had in mind. Livia grinned. "They didn't say no interfering with the chest," she agreed. She took a running start and dove into the wall of the mesa, disappearing into the tunnel she bored with *burrow*.

"Look for our rings as we go," Aderyn said, and ran for the passage. Weston and Isold swiftly outpaced her, but she didn't mind; she was looking around for the enemy team. The dungeon was carpeted with thick, dense grass cut short, and a few apple trees grew here and there, their boughs heavy with ruddy fruit. Nothing that would interfere with the spectators' view. The mesas, for there were several throughout the dungeon, looked incongruous in what was almost a pleasant valley, as if an Earthbreaker had come through raising the stone at a whim.

She saw her first blue ring before she saw anything else. It wasn't a tiny ring for one's finger, as she'd half expected despite knowing something that small wouldn't make for a good show. It was a fat torus of wood painted cerulean blue that stood out against the green grass. She snatched it up as she ran and shoved it over her hand to circle her forearm. That ought to make it harder for a Ruffian to snatch it. She briefly considered putting it in the <**Purse of Great Capacity**>, but she wasn't sure it was legal for her to have brought a magic item into the dungeon, even one that didn't give her an advantage. Since there was no way she meant to leave it and the <**Wayfinder**> behind, she just resolved not to use it and hoped that was a fair compromise.

Behind her, she heard the rumble of Livia emerging from the earth. Aderyn's first thought was hope that Livia had chosen the right mesa, but she remembered that Livia's range with *immobilize* was long enough that all that mattered was being within sight of the enemy's chest. Aderyn grinned at the image of Ruffians running up to deposit rings in their chest only to find the thing covered in tentacles of solid earth. They could break through eventually, but every minute they spent on that was a minute they weren't out hunting for rings.

"Aderyn!" Isold shouted.

Aderyn sped up. Isold and Weston had found the copse where their chest hung in the branches of the tallest tree, far above their heads. Isold had two blue rings and three red ones. Weston had two red rings and one blue one.

Aderyn rubbed her palms on her pants once more, this time in readiness for climbing rather than nerves. "Give me the blue rings, and see about hiding the red ones," she said. "Should I bring the chest down here, or leave it?"

"Down here," Weston said. "They may think to interfere with it once they see what Livia's done, but we'll save time getting rings into the chest if it's not up there."

Aderyn nodded. She shoved the other rings onto her arms and pulled herself into the tree.

She was an expert at tree-climbing, and this apple tree was easy to climb, with many wide, horizontal branches and a gnarled trunk that was better than a ladder. In no time, she was at the top and examining the chest. It looked like an ordinary chest with a rounded top, only painted blue, even the metal fittings, but it was sealed shut. There wasn't even a latch. It wasn't made to open. Instead, there was a slot in the top of the lid that was wide enough to admit one of the rings.

Aderyn swiftly slid each of the rings into the slot. As she did, a patch of black below the slot, the only thing about the chest that wasn't blue, shifted to display the number 1, then 2, then 3, then 4. And they needed forty-seven. She decided not to worry about that for now.

She examined the chest again, this time looking for how it was fastened to the tree. Ropes threaded through steel rings at each corner beneath the lid secured it to four branches. Aderyn reached for her belt knife only to remember she'd had to leave it behind—no weapons in this dungeon. She picked at one of the knots, which came loose readily, as if someone had planned on the possibility a team would try this.

The ropes had long, trailing ends, and Aderyn freed three of the corners, careful not to jog the chest so it fell sooner than she wanted. It was possible it was unbreakable, but she didn't want to risk it. She threaded one of the free ropes through the ring that was still tied to the tree and wrapped the rope around a nearby branch. Then she untied the other rope and lowered the chest through the branches.

She had to descend with it as she discovered the branches that had been so helpful in her climb were in the way now. When she reached the bottom branch, the rope slid through her sweaty palms, and the chest lurched and fell to the ground, landing heavily but not breaking. Sweating and feeling the urgency of knowing none of her teammates had returned yet, Aderyn leaped down and settled the chest securely between the tree's roots.

Running footsteps caught her attention, and she whipped around, prepared to do battle though she was completely unarmed. But it was Weston, his arms laden with red and blue rings. "The Ruffians are dealing with their *immobilized* chest," he said, grinning. "Take the blue ones. What's our count?"

Aderyn fed rings into the chest. "Eleven. How long has it been?"

"No idea. There's no point checking the time, because it slows us down. We just have to move fast, is all. I'm going to deal with these." Weston settled the captured red rings more securely and ran east.

Aderyn looked around, feeling temporarily at a loss for what to do. She didn't see any rings nearby. Well, she wouldn't find any if she stood here doing nothing. Weston had gone east; she went west.

Immediately she left the shelter of the copse and began ascending the nearest mesa. High ground was the tactician's friend. Climbing the rock face was more difficult than climbing the tree. It wasn't perfectly vertical, but the slope was still steep, and she had to focus on where she put her hands and feet.

She reached the top of the mesa and surveyed the land. Mesas, trees, a tiny pond off to the east. She counted three Rowdy Ruffians and Weston and Isold, all of them scurrying around gathering rings. That would be the strategy for the early part of the match—collect all the rings you could find, deposit your own, secure the enemy's. She didn't know where Livia was, though she might be underground again, and as for the fourth Ruffian—

In a flash, she caught the ghostly image of a glass bulb filled with a violet liquid that sloshed as the missile flew through the air, aimed at her chest.

CHAPTER FOURTEEN

Aderyn dropped to lie flat as the real potion sailed over her, impacting on the mesa and sending splashes of thick purple liquid in every direction. She scooted away from it and headed in the direction it had come from, then had to roll as **[See It Coming]** showed her a second glass bulb flying her way.

She reached the edge of the mesa and peered over it. No one. She scanned the area, wishing for Weston's ranks in **[Spot]**, and finally saw her enemy—a woman in a red tunic perched in the branches of a tree some ten yards away, gaping at Aderyn in clear consternation. Two more bulbs hovered in front of her, held by *telekinesis*. Aderyn Level Assessed her swiftly.

Name: Bethla

Class: Windwarden

Level: 14

One of the other Ruffians must be the Spiritsmith who'd brewed those potions, which by the color and thickness were meant to reduce Aderyn's strength and endurance. It didn't matter. What mattered was getting out of her range.

She scooted backward, staying low and waiting for her skill to alert her to another attack. None came. She clambered over the far edge and half-climbed, half-slid down the slope to the ground. She listened, but heard nothing that might be a woman coming after her. Circling the base of the mesa, she came out beneath the tree where Bethla had perched. The woman was gone.

Aderyn continued scouting in the direction she'd been heading, to the west, carefully searching the ground and the trees. She found two blue rings wedged into trees' branches, a red ring that blended with the apples, two more blue rings beneath a couple of shrubberies, and a clutch of five red rings where one of her friends had clearly stashed it. She began to add her red ring to the pile, but changed her mind. If the Ruffians were good, they might come close to achieving the full count of forty-seven rings, and maybe stowing this one somewhere unexpected would make a difference.

When she'd come west so far she'd begun to circle north, she ran back the way she'd come. She nearly ran into one of the Ruffians, Kathra, who'd hooked several rings over her arms the way Aderyn had. Aderyn spotted blue rings among the red ones, but decided not to attack. She was smaller than Kathra, and she didn't want to risk losing the rings she had for the possibility of gaining others.

Having found two more blue rings on her way back, she hurried to deposit her loot in the chest and met Livia returning from doing the same. "You were right," Livia said. "They about went crazy trying to get at the chest opening through *immobilize*. And in their distraction, Weston picked up some of the rings they'd collected."

Aderyn dropped blue rings into the chest, whose number now read 30. "That's good. Seventeen more."

Weston entered the copse, followed by Isold. "We think we've found all the loose ones," Weston said, "of both colors, I mean, between our two teams. Time for a new strategy."

Livia checked her pocket watch. "Five minutes."

"We need information," Aderyn said. "*Scrying* information."

Livia put away her watch and pulled out her mirror. "*Scry* for what?"

Aderyn thought. "Let's find out how many rings they have."

"Easy enough. I know that chest well now." Livia muttered a few words and passed a hand over the surface of her mirror, which gleamed brightly before darkening to show something other than Livia's face. Livia angled the mirror sharply and said, "Twenty-seven. Way closer than I like."

"All right. How about... can you back up and show us their chest's surroundings?"

Livia nodded. They all huddled around the mirror as the view expanded. "Crap," Weston said. "They're hunkered down. There's a whole pile of our rings there. Looks like their idea is to hold onto them and wait us out."

"They must assume we have fewer than they," Isold said. "And I notice that woman Kathra is not with them. She must be out searching for the ones we hid."

"They don't know how many there are," Aderyn said. "Seonn didn't tell us. He only said 'a number.' It was **[Improved Assess 2]** that told me forty-seven. What can we do with that?"

"We can hide a few of their rings where they're easily found," Weston said. "They think they have the advantage, so they might assume they've got all of theirs and won't search for more."

"I love that plan," Livia said. "But we can't do it unless we can get our rings first. They only need four more to beat us."

"There are three of them guarding the pile," Aderyn said. "What about *telekinesis? Burrow* under, grab the rings and go?"

"I can only lift one item at a time," Livia said. "Well, technically I can lift three items. The point is, I can't pick up the entire pile with *telekinesis* unless we could somehow convince them to put them all in a bag for us."

"Convince them—Isold? How many people can you use **[Charm]** on at once?"

"It would take more than **[Charm]**," Isold said. "**[Fascinate]** works on multiple targets, but it isn't very strong against higher-level adventurers. **[Hypnosis]** will do it, but unfortunately I can only use that on a single person at one time. If we could get some of them away, maybe..."

"No," Aderyn said. "I know what to do. But it will take all of us."

ADERYN DIDN'T TRY TO CONCEAL HER ASCENT FROM THE Ruffians on their mesa. She refrained from making extra noise, in case they guessed she was playing them. But she didn't try to escape when two of the women grabbed her arms and hauled her over the edge, restraining her.

The Windwarden, Bethla, stepped away from where she'd been guarding the little pile of blue rings. "What are you thinking?" she asked. "You expect to get these away from us on your own? A Warmaster?"

For once, Aderyn didn't feel insulted. Bethla hadn't sounded dismissive, more like she was genuinely puzzled and curious about what a Warmaster could do that other classes couldn't. Aderyn held up her one red ring. "I was going to trade you this for our rings," she said. Her voice echoed strangely, and she shook her head to clear her ears.

Bethla and the others laughed. Their laughter echoed the way her voice had. "You're kidding, right?" one of the other Ruffians said.

Aderyn shrugged. Behind Bethla, Weston rose silently over the edge of the mesa and tiptoed forward. "Yes, I'm kidding," she said. "I was just distracting you so my teammates could get the drop on you."

The Ruffians froze. Weston pounced, snatching Bethla up and restraining her in his massive arms. With a crack, Livia leaped from the ground and cast *immobilize* on one of the Ruffians holding Aderyn, the tentacles breaking her grip. The third released Aderyn and backed away. She held her foot poised over the pile of blue rings. "Let them go, or you'll waste the rest of your two minutes chasing these all over the dungeon."

A rattling sound behind Aderyn alerted her to Isold climbing over the edge. Even that noise echoed strangely. The Ruffian aimed a kick at the pile of rings. "I don't think so," Isold said, positioning himself in front of her and raising a hand. The woman froze again, this time wobbling slightly at being off balance. Her face slackened as if she'd fallen asleep, though her eyes were open. Isold stepped closer. "Aderyn, hurry."

Aderyn scooped up the blue rings and scurried back over the edge. As she did, she considered leaving them the one red ring she had. It would be a good, dramatic gesture. It might also mean defeat if Kathra got back with enough rings to put them over the edge.

She raced back to their chest, dropping a few rings but not stopping to pick them up because her team was following close behind. Panting, she fed rings into the slot as quickly as she could, feeling time slipping away. Isold stepped up behind her and dropped two more rings in. 45. 46.

Disappointed, Aderyn sagged to the ground. "So close," she said.

"We still win," Livia pointed out. "There's less than a minute to go. No way are those Ruffians going to make up the difference."

"Yes, but we're *so close*."

"Wait," Isold said. "Let's see if **[Find Object]** can help. The last ring might still be too far away, but it's worth trying."

He knelt and put a hand on the chest. "Blue ring," he said, as if he was addressing the chest. "The size of an armband. A torus of wood."

His head jerked back and his eyes flew open. They shimmered silver for a moment and then returned to normal. "Ah," he said. "Lift the chest."

It took them a second to comprehend this. Then Weston heaved the chest off the ground. Beneath it, pressed into the soft grass where Aderyn had dropped the chest on it, was a single blue ring.

Aderyn snatched it up and with trembling hands pushed it into the slot.

Immediately, a bright light flashed three times, and the roar of the crowd washed over them. A system message appeared in front of Aderyn's face.

Congratulations! You have defeated [Loot the Room terrain variation 5].
You have earned [10,000 XP]

Congratulations! You have achieved a perfect score in [Loot the Room terrain variation 5].
You have earned [2500 XP]

Aderyn looked up. The same messages lit up the sky above the dungeon. Then Weston grabbed her and Livia, hugging them, and Isold was pounding on Weston's back, and the crowd screamed so loudly Aderyn thought her ears might burst.

The mesas were sinking into the ground, and the apple trees vanished. Aderyn hadn't thought to ask if it was an illusion, or something else. They'd seemed so solid, and yet now they were gone. Weston steered her away from the dungeon, saying, "Not bad for our first dungeon, eh?"

"They certainly think so. Wave, Aderyn, they're cheering for us." Livia put her own advice into action, waving wildly at the spectators. Aderyn waved, first hesitantly, then with vigor. They'd won! And it had been exciting and fun and felt like much longer than ten minutes.

They climbed the stairs to the covert and were met with total silence.

Aderyn hesitated on the threshold. Nobody looked friendly.

Anxiety gripped her. They'd done something wrong. They hadn't put on a good show. They'd made the Ruffians look stupid. It could be anything.

Jesper stepped forward. "You want to explain how you got inside information?"

It was so unexpected Aderyn gaped. Weston said, "We didn't have inside information. How would we have gotten it?"

"You tell me," Jesper said flatly. "You clearly knew in advance where the Ruffians' chest was, because *you*—" He pointed at Livia— "went straight for it, no reconnaissance, no fumbling."

Livia involuntarily glanced at Aderyn. Jesper's gaze fixed on her instead. "You cheated," he said. "I'm going to see you booted for this."

"I did *not* cheat," Aderyn insisted. "Seonn said any skill and any spell. I used my Warmaster's skills."

"You have a skill that lets you cheat?" Jesper said coldly.

Anger rushed through Aderyn. She stepped closer to Jesper, feeling like the two of them were alone in the covert. "It's called **[Improved Assess 2]**. It reveals information about people's classes and city qualities. It also shows me information about dungeons. I didn't think it would work on that one, but I Assessed it out of habit and I learned some important details. And then I used them."

She drew in a breath and overrode Jesper when he would have spoken. "Maybe you'll call that cheating, since I'm the only one among these teams who can do it. Is it cheating for you to use **[Called Shot]** when you're the only Deadeye? Or for Bethla to *levitate* into a tree when none of the rest of us can?"

Jesper shut his mouth. He was still glaring, and Aderyn's heart sank. The last thing she'd expected was to find trouble because she was the only Warmaster in the Glory Games and nobody knew what Warmasters of her level could do.

The horn sounded, announcing the beginning of the next dungeon, but no one in the covert paid any attention to the two teams assembling below. One of the Indomitables, the one who'd raced against Jesper in the first leg of their race, said, "It doesn't matter if it's an allowed skill. You're going to make the rest of us look bad. Worse, you'll make the matches look too easy. No one wants to see one team walk all over another."

"We still had to work for our victory," Weston said. "I didn't think it was at all easy. All right, so we had some extra knowledge, but it didn't make us better able to find those rings or deceive our opponents."

Someone came stomping up the stairs, sending tremors through the covert. Seonn stormed in and shouted, "What in—"

The horn blasted again, drowning out the rest of his words, and the roar of the crowd surged. Seonn marched up to Weston and pitched his voice to be heard over the noise. "You'd better tell me who sold you that information. And do it quickly. For every minute you delay, that's a month I'll add to your sentence."

"Sentence?" Livia said.

"There are penalties for interfering in the Games, Earthbreaker," Seonn snarled. "Imprisonment and a heavy fine, for one. So start talking."

CHAPTER FIFTEEN

"I t wasn't—" Aderyn began.

"She says it's a Warmaster skill," Jesper overrode her. "I doubt she can prove it. It's not like anyone can see anyone else's skills."

Aderyn sighed. "I can. Which does me no good now, I know."

Seonn focused on her. "What in thunder are you talking about? See people's skills? What does that have to do with you buying inside information?"

Something clicked in Aderyn's head. "You're the Arena Master, aren't you? You didn't say, but that's your title, right?"

"Don't act stupid. Everyone knows I'm the Arena Master. And you just added a month to your sentence." Seonn eyed her as if he really did believe she was mentally deficient.

"Then who would I have bought information from? You're the one who seeds the dungeons. The only ones who know the details are you and whoever you told, if anyone." Aderyn's thoughts were humming along lightning-fast. "So what you're really wondering is if you can trust that person. Or pcople."

Seonn's eyes narrowed. "Don't think you can deflect blame."

"I'm not. I want to prove I learned that information through my skill." Aderyn glanced out of the covert at the dungeon where orange and light green tunics scampered around the newly-revealed terrain. "And I just figured out how. Does it matter if everyone here knows the details of that dungeon? Since they're not going to compete in it?"

"The details? Young woman—"

Aderyn Assessed the dungeon and read off what she saw. "Name, Capture the Flag terrain variation 14. Type, variable instance, tiny, victory condition variant B-6. Power level not applicable. This variable dungeon seeded by the Arena Master is zoned for two teams whose goal is to capture the other team's flag and hold it prisoner for five consecutive minutes. Bonus XP is granted—"

"Stop. Stop! What are you doing?" Seonn's face was red. "How do you know that? That is privileged information!"

"It's [Improved Assess 2]. I use it when we're out adventuring, any time we encounter a city or a dungeon." Aderyn chose not to remind everyone that it worked on people, too. "I used it on our dungeon instance, but I didn't expect it to work because these aren't regular dungeons. But when it *did* work, I thought it was fairly gained information, because you said all skills—"

"I didn't know there was a skill that would let someone cheat!" Seonn shouted.

"And *I* didn't know you'd think it was cheating!" Aderyn shouted back. "If you don't want me to use it in future, fine. That Indomitable there—"

"Martis," Jesper said.

"Thanks. Martis made a point that it's important not to unbalance the Games, because people come to see a good competition. I can see how in some of these dungeon instances, [Improved Assess 2] would give a really big advantage to our team and it wouldn't be a fun challenge. So, like I said, I can stop using it if you judge that's necessary. But I acted in good faith, because I'm no cheat. And I think you know that."

Seonn's high color was fading. "I can't believe it," he said. "Since when can Warmasters do anything like that?"

"Since, um, level eight, I think," Aderyn said.

"By thunder," Seonn said, his voice quiet. "The only people who know the details of the Games dungeons are me, Lorus, and the spellslingers who create the terrain. If any of them sold information, it would break the Games."

"I can see how you would have worried," Isold said. "But I assure you none of us bought information. You saw what Aderyn did. What more proof do you need?"

Seonn's lips pursed in thought. "Don't use it again," he said. "It's like you said, we can't have an imbalance so great the Games aren't fun. I don't suppose you have any other game-altering skills I need to know about?"

"That's the only one that provides me with knowledge no one else can gain," Aderyn said, madly reviewing her skills and hoping she wasn't lying to Seonn. "I promise I won't Assess any more of the Games dungeons."

"I should revoke that extra experience for clearing the dungeon," Seonn said, musing. "Your skill told you the total number of rings, didn't it?"

"Yes," Aderyn said, feeling guilty again.

"The only advantage that gave them was knowing to look for one final ring," Jesper said, startling Aderyn. "It didn't show her where it was. That was the Herald."

"Good point. All right. The experience stands." Seonn clapped his hands and rubbed them together vigorously. "Besides, I doubt any of the spectators knew there was something fiddly going on. That *burrow* spell made for a dramatic entrance, Earthbreaker. Not to mention those tentacle things." He nodded at Livia in approval, then waved in the general direction of the covert. "No more secret game-breaking skills, understood?" he said, and stomped back down the stairs.

"You sure had us cursing your name, Livia," Kathra said with an unexpected grin. Aderyn, who'd pegged her as antagonistic, couldn't believe the difference in her appearance.

"I should have told you how many rings there were," she said. "It would have given us both an even chance."

"It's nothing." Kathra waved her words away. "We ended up with only forty-four, so you would have beaten us even if you hadn't got the final ring. No worries. And that last encounter—did you all hear that?" She laughed and grabbed Bethla around the shoulders, shaking her. "We gave the crowd a real show—you people basically popping out of thin air. Excellent teamwork. I was almost distracted from searching."

Aderyn recalled Kathra hadn't been there on the mesa for that confrontation. "How do you know?"

Bethla extricated herself from Kathra's grip and stretched. "The spellslingers monitor the dungeon and amplify our talk anytime something interesting but non-physical happens, so the spectators can hear what it is. It makes things dramatic. 'I was just distracting you so my teammates could get the drop on you,' that was great!"

Aderyn blushed. "I'm glad my skill didn't ruin anything."

"It could have been bad, but it wasn't, and I choose to move on," Kathra said. "Right? Now, let's see how things are—"

The light flashed three times, and the speaker's booming voice said, "Let's hear it for our victors, the Vagabonds! We'll be back soon with the rest of the qualifying trials for this year's challengers!"

"Oh, well," Kathra said with a smile. "I hear you've got a friend among the challengers. Hope he places well. We'll see you around."

Aderyn sat and waited while the other teams left. Jesper and Martis remained behind. Jesper still looked annoyed, but less so than before. "You could have used common sense," he said to Aderyn. "Knowing more about the dungeon gives you a great advantage."

"I'm used to doing it in the Forsaken Lands, where that advantage has saved our lives more than once," Aderyn said. "I'm not used to thinking in terms of competing with other humans."

"Let it go, Jesper," Martis said. "She gets it. You're just browbeating now."

Jesper looked startled. "I didn't mean to. I was just thinking about—well, you're right, it doesn't matter." He smiled. "That really is remarkable. I wish we'd had a Warmaster on our team a few levels ago, before we came to Finion's Gate for the Games. And that is a sentence I never thought I'd say. How did you make it work?"

"I have a partner. He and I share skills and boost each other."

Jesper looked at Aderyn's friends. "A team member? One of you?"

Aderyn leaned forward over the covert rail and pointed. "Yes," she said, her heart swelling. "Him."

Owen was just exiting the tunnel, not looking around at the spectators even though the noise of the crowd had grown louder as he appeared. Aderyn was sure that was no coincidence. Among the general clamor, she heard chants of "*Thirty-one!*" Owen didn't seem to notice, though he might just be good at pretending.

She watched him pair off against a Deadeye who wielded a sword more competently than she would have guessed someone of his class could manage. He and Owen circled each other, feinting and parrying, testing each other. Aderyn watched the Deadeye's stance, observing how he favored his right side and had a habit of letting his sword gradually lower when he hadn't struck for a while. If this was a real fight, the <Twinsword> would carry those observations to Owen for him to take advantage of. Now Owen was on his own... all right, Owen and twenty-one ranks in [**Advanced Weapon Proficiency**]. She Assessed him out of habit. Make that twenty-two ranks. He ought to walk all over these challengers.

Sure enough, it took less than a minute for Owen to stop circling and go on the attack. He took one blow before delivering his third strike, winning the match. This time, the adjudicator's cry of *"Thirty-one!"* was taken up by many voices. Owen stepped back as if startled and raised a hand to shield his eyes as he looked into the stands. The cries grew louder. Owen lowered his hand and stood still for a moment. Then he saluted the crowd, whose shouting grew frenzied. Owen walked back to the tunnel, trailed by the noise of the spectators shouting his number.

"That's unexpected," Livia said. "He's already a favorite. I mean, not that he wouldn't be a favorite, just that it happened so soon. I thought that sort of thing didn't start until the actual matches."

"Any of the challengers who makes a dramatic showing gets noticed," Isold said. "Numbers twenty-seven and sixteen, for example. They are undefeated like Owen, and the crowd appreciates that."

"Well, he won't be disqualified," Weston said. "Three more matches. Crap, I should have wagered on him sweeping the competition." He began to rise and was pulled down by Livia.

"It's too late now," she said. "Let's cheer him on. Does anyone know what happens if he's undefeated in all eight matches?"

"They rank the top ten challengers according to how many victories they have," Isold said. "I think with as many challengers as there are, it's possible for more than one person to win eight matches. If that happens, those undefeated challengers fight each other to see who takes the top rank. The same can happen in the lower positions. That allows them to determine the top ten. Then those ten challengers go on to face one another and the ten champions. Owen called the second set of fights 'double-elimination rounds.' I'm afraid I failed to follow his explanation about something called seeds and brackets. Not dungeon seeds, is all I know."

"Twenty-seven!"

Aderyn leaned forward, searching for challenger number 27. Almost directly beneath them stood a pair of women, one a sturdily-built Stalwart bearing a longstaff, the other a petite Swordsworn with long, dark hair pulled back from her face. Aderyn was reminded of

Owen facing off against his first opponent, the enormous Stalwart. This woman wasn't as big as that, but next to the Swordsworn she looked like a giant. Aderyn assumed it was the Stalwart who'd won.

Then the Swordsworn raised her wooden sword and pointed it at the crowd, who all started chanting *"Twenty-seven! Twenty-seven!"* over and over until the arena echoed. The Swordsworn woman tilted her head back and laughed in delight. Her eye caught Aderyn's, and she smiled, a proud, knowing expression that said she knew she was amazing and she didn't think much of Aderyn by comparison. Aderyn sat back, breaking their contact.

"So that's number twenty-seven," she said, mostly to herself.

"She'll be the one to beat," Weston said. "Which means Owen will look even better once he's trounced her."

"He hasn't fought her yet," Aderyn warned. Superstitiously, she felt celebrating Owen's victory prematurely would mean it wouldn't happen.

A few rounds later, Owen returned. This time, he was matched against the big Stalwart woman number 27 had defeated. The Stalwart moved lightly for someone her size, almost as easily as Weston always did. When the adjudicator signaled, she stepped in and tapped Owen lightly on his shoulder almost before he'd begun to move. Aderyn let out her breath in a hiss of concern. **[Read Body Language]** told her Owen wasn't worried, but this was his sixth fight, and the competitors he faced from here were the best of the lot.

She shouldn't have worried. Owen blocked a few more strikes of her longstaff, then went on the attack, swiftly hitting her upper arm, her thigh, and her belly before she could react. The crowd roared its approval. Owen clasped the woman's hand and held it for a few moments as the woman spoke. Then he laughed and nodded. He saluted the crowd once and then followed the Stalwart back to the tunnel, trailed by the sound of cheering.

CHAPTER SIXTEEN

Aderyn found her palms were sweating again. She really needed to find some way of expressing emotion that didn't leave her trousers wrinkled and damp. She wiped her hands on her trousers anyway and leaned back. "This is too much tension."

"You could go down there to wait," Livia said.

"That would be worse. I wouldn't be able to see anything." She sighed. "I don't know why it matters. It's not like we care who the top champion is. We just want Owen to get into the real Games so he can earn experience."

"It is natural to want victory when the opportunity comes," Isold said. "Weren't you the one who was so eager to get all forty-seven rings? Humans are made to love winning."

"I guess you're right. I'll be happier when it's over, though." Aderyn put her feet up on the covert rail. "And we do have a good seat, though it's getting chilly. Think how those people in the stands must feel when the wind blows." Clouds had rolled in to obscure the sun, and the temperature had dropped by several degrees.

Another round passed, and then the cheering grew so loud it

caught Aderyn's attention. She sat up. Owen had entered the arena, followed by number 27. They stopped near the center of the arena, and Aderyn had only just realized they were the only ones fighting when the adjudicator gave the command to start. Owen and the woman didn't move at first, though they were poised like coiled springs waiting for a nudge. Then they sprang at each other, wooden swords flying furiously as each sought a gap in the other's defenses.

Owen got the first hit, a blow to the woman's upper arm. They separated as the adjudicator called out "One to number thirty-one!" and again fell to circling, feinting without committing to anything.

The woman struck, fast as a snake, and Owen rubbed his arm briefly. His lips moved. The woman just smiled. Her next blow struck his hip, not as hard as the first because Owen barely reacted. With every confirmed hit, the crowd screamed its approval.

"Go on, Owen, hit her," Aderyn murmured. "You can do this."

Again, the two came at each other in furious attacks. Owen dodged two blows, spun past her guard, and struck her stomach in the same finishing move he'd used on the Stalwart woman. The crowd screamed just as loudly for Owen as for his opponent. Aderyn couldn't tell which of them was the favorite. Maybe both, at this stage of the Games.

The next hit would be the winning one. Aderyn's hands were clasped so tightly her knuckles were white. Owen and the woman slowly circled each other. The woman struck, but Aderyn already knew it was a clever feint. She bit back a warning cry. Owen wouldn't hear her, and if he did, her words would only distract him.

But Owen saw it too. He dodged and thrust as she converted the feint to a real attack. Both blows landed at the same time, or looked like they did.

Aderyn held her breath. She hadn't seen who had hit first, but the adjudicator would have. The crowd fell silent for the first time all afternoon, waiting. It felt like forever before the adjudicator shouted, "*Number Twenty-seven!*"

The mingled noises of cheering and groans made the crowd sound like an injured animal crying for help. Owen turned sharply on the adjudicator. His lips moved. The adjudicator shook his head and said something in return. Owen's whole body tensed, but he nodded and turned back to the woman, who was pointing her wooden sword at the crowd and laughing that triumphant laugh.

"He's angry," Aderyn said, responding to what [**Read Body Language**] told her, though she thought his anger was obvious to anyone.

Owen said something to the woman. She stopped laughing, though she still saluted the cheering crowds with her sword, and replied, not looking his way. Owen's shoulders tensed as his anger redoubled. He made his usual salute to the crowd, then walked back to the tunnel, his stride covering the ground in seconds.

"Something's really wrong," Aderyn said, turning to face her friends. "I think the adjudicator made the wrong decision."

"I couldn't tell who struck first," Livia said. "Maybe the adjudicator couldn't either."

"But in that case, he should have disallowed the hits and made them continue," Weston said.

"My guess is that the adjudicator's decision is final," Isold said, "and if he saw something the rest of us didn't—"

"But Owen wouldn't be angry if the adjudicator got it right, and *he* ought to know which of them hit first." Aderyn's anger was rising to match Owen's. "This is so unfair."

"We don't know what happened yet, Aderyn," Isold reminded her. "It's one loss. Even if he has a second loss, he's still solidly in the top ten, and that's all that matters."

"Now I'm glad I didn't wager on him sweeping," Weston rumbled. Livia elbowed him in the ribs. "Ow!"

"I'm glad half the crowd was disappointed," Livia said, ignoring Weston's pained muttering. "That means he made an impression, and he's going to carry that into the Games."

Aderyn exhaled deeply, willing her breath to carry away her tense anger. "You're right. The important thing is that he makes it into the Games. Whether he's top rank or second doesn't matter."

But she watched the next couple of matches sullenly, her anger rising again when number 27 fought her eighth match and won. Her earlier dislike of the woman flowered into sharp hatred. She was arrogant and smug and she'd probably cheated, and Aderyn resented the crowd for being so stupid as to like her.

Owen's final match was, to her surprise, against someone she knew: Pace, the Lone Wolf who'd traveled with them to Finion's Gate. The match cheered her, because both Owen and Pace fought well, and she could tell from Owen's body language that he felt confident as well as respectful of his opponent. Though Pace only landed one hit to Owen's three, it was a clever strike, and Owen had had to work hard to prevent him making any other hits. The adjudicator declared Owen's victory, and he and Pace shook hands, with Pace clapping Owen on the shoulder. Owen, in turn, raised both their hands in salute to the crowd, which Aderyn thought was a nice touch.

She rose to go down to meet Owen, but Isold said, "Wait. The crowd's not leaving. I think it's not over."

Aderyn sat impatiently through three more matches, the last of which was Pace fighting the woman Stalwart Owen had defeated earlier. Pace won that one. "I've lost track," Aderyn complained. "That number twenty-seven woman is first, and I think Owen is second, but I don't know where anyone else stands."

"I've been counting," Isold said. "If I'm correct, that last fight was between the two third-place challengers to determine third and fourth place, which means Pace is in third and the Stalwart is fourth."

"Then can we—"

"Thank you all for waiting!" the speaker boomed. "It's been a great day, hasn't it, friends?"

The noise of cheering grew louder until the unseen speaker's voice drowned it out. "Well, I won't keep you waiting any longer. Presenting the challengers for the 47th semi-annual Glory Games! In tenth place—number five, Horgeth the Swordsworn!"

A man Aderyn remembered noticing before because he was easily the tallest person among the challengers ran into the arena to loud, excited cheers. She leaned forward, eager again. These were the ones whose defeats or victories mattered. Idly, she Assessed Horgeth for his level—thirteen. He'd be worth a lot of experience when Owen defeated him. Then the next one—

"Wait," she said. "Look there. The ninth-place challenger, Caprissa. She's familiar."

The others all leaned out over the rail. "By thunder," Weston said. "We defeated her outside Dungeon Spiteful, months ago. Her and her companions. What are the odds?"

"I love the idea of getting experience twice for the same victim. I mean opponent." Livia's vulpine grin amused Aderyn.

Aderyn continued to Level Assess the challengers as the speaker announced them. "Denae, level fourteen Staffsworn... Asantis, level fifteen Lone Wolf... Farron, level thirteen Swifthands... look, it's Gradin!" Pace's cousin had come in fifth. The level thirteen Swordsworn looked cheerful and excited by the attention of the crowd.

"And in fourth place—number sixteen, Eirian the Stalwart!"

The Stalwart woman didn't smile at the crowd as she ran to join the other challengers, but Aderyn liked the stern set of her jaw, like she took all of this so seriously and with such respect there wasn't room for humor. She might have finished fourth, but Aderyn felt she was one to watch.

"Third place—number thirty-three, Pace the Lone Wolf!"

Pace jogged into the arena, casually waving at the crowd on both sides. He was lean and rangy the way Lone Wolves were traditionally held to be, but he had a friendly smile and Aderyn could see why Owen had enjoyed sparring with him.

There was a longer pause this time. "Now, in second place," the speaker announced, "number thirty-one, Owen the Swordsworn!"

The roar of the crowd deafened Aderyn, who clapped her hands over her ears for a moment before realizing that made her look stupid. She gripped the rail so her hands wouldn't do anything else ridiculous and leaned far forward to watch Owen make his run. It didn't matter that he hadn't won first place, because everyone in the arena knew how good he was. Her heart swelled with joy at her sweetheart's success.

"And in first place—" The speaker hesitated so briefly Aderyn wasn't sure she'd heard it. "Number twenty-seven, Jael the Swordsworn!"

The cheering was as loud for Jael as it had been for Owen, which annoyed Aderyn even as she tried to be fair-minded. She was a good fighter, and it was just bad luck Owen had lost to her.

"That's strange," Weston said. "People are booing her."

"What?" Aderyn dropped back into her seat and stared at Weston.

"It's hard to hear, even for me," Weston said, "but some people aren't thrilled about her as their first-place challenger. I think maybe they saw what happened in her match with Owen and don't agree with the adjudicator's call."

"Looks like they're leaving," Livia said, nodding at the arena floor where the challengers had begun to walk, some alone, some in little groupings of two or even three, back to the tunnel. "Let's go. I'm dying to know what really happened."

At the foot of the steps, they met Seonn. "Took your sweet time about leaving," he said. "Aren't you eager to collect your reward?"

"Wasn't that the experience?" Weston said.

Seonn rolled his eyes. "Sure, experience. Every team would fight for free if it meant getting experience. No." He handed Weston a leather purse that by the look of it was heavy. "Five hundred gold to the winner, half that to the loser. Don't spend it all in one place."

Weston tucked the purse away beneath his tunic without opening it. "Thanks," he said, as casually as if Seonn had handed over a handful of coppers instead.

When Seonn was gone, Livia said, "*Five hundred—*"

"Let's not shout it where everyone can hear," Weston said. "I didn't expect nearly this much. I was thinking about what Borrus said about gifts and special treatment, not a payout."

"I admit I'm more determined to win now," Isold said with a smile.

Owen wasn't there when they reached the room under the arena. Pace and Gradin were standing near the tunnel entrance, talking quietly. They noticed the friends and walked over to join them.

"Congratulations," Weston said. "Good thing you both made it, right?"

"We actually were counting on only one of us getting in," Pace said. "It's why we both tried for it. It's a promise we made to our uncle on his deathbed. He was a competitor, years ago, but he didn't make it to the final ten. He wanted one of us to do what he couldn't."

"I'm not sure what I'm doing here," Gradin said with his slow, easy smile. "I know I'm a plodder. Not fast like Owen or that Jael."

"You're methodical," Pace corrected his cousin. "And it paid off."

"You both have to be good to rank so high," Aderyn said. "I really didn't know which of you would win, Pace, you or Owen. It was a good match."

"Oh, Owen had my number all right," Pace said without rancor. "Though he hesitates sometimes, which is how I landed even one hit. Like he's waiting for direction from whatever mental link he has to the system that grants him that uncanny speed." He laughed to show it was a joke.

Aderyn didn't think it was funny. It hadn't occurred to her that his experience with the <**Twinsword**> might be a disadvantage when he fought without it. She suppressed a twinge of guilt. There was no reason to blame herself for inadvertently hampering him, and besides, it couldn't be much of a disadvantage or he wouldn't have won so many matches.

Pace looked past Aderyn's shoulder, and his cheerful expression faded to neutral so fast Aderyn turned to see what had disturbed him. Behind her, approaching them slowly, was Jael.

CHAPTER SEVENTEEN

"Congratulations," Jael said, smiling that same annoying, self-satisfied smile. She reached past Aderyn to offer Pace her hand. "You fought well."

"Thanks," Pace said without a trace of a smile. Aderyn liked him even more knowing he found Jael distasteful.

Gradin shook her hand with more enthusiasm. "I've never seen anyone fight like you," he said in an admiring tone. "Well, except Owen. I can't wait to see the two of you fight again."

Jael's smile didn't waver. "Owen's a formidable opponent. I look forward to seeing more of him." She drawled those last four words just enough to make Aderyn want to laugh. So, Jael was attracted to Owen, was she? Aderyn hoped she was in a position to see him rebuff her.

"And you Wildcats," Jael said. "I hear you beat your dungeon spectacularly. What a way to start your Games career. Too bad we couldn't see it, but I'm sure there will be other chances." She glanced briefly at Aderyn, then at Weston. "Did you come to congratulate us? That's nice of you."

"They came to meet me," Owen said, approaching rapidly. His

hair was damp again, but this time he'd washed completely and put on his normal clothes. "We're a team."

Jael's eyes widened. "A team? But you're a challenger."

"An adventuring team," Owen said curtly. "And we're leaving. Congratulations, Pace and Gradin. I look forward to testing myself against you in the Games."

"Be seeing you, Owen," Gradin said.

"And me?" Jael said. "Are you ready for a rematch?"

Owen looked her up and down with such disdain it should have set Jael on fire. "Not unless you've discovered a sense of honor in the changing room," he said, and walked away. Aderyn hurried after him, torn between admiring his method of leaving a conversation on his terms and being deeply curious about what he'd meant.

They were on the street, and [Keep Pace] was straining Aderyn's calves, when Weston said, "If you don't slow down, we'll leave Livia behind, and you know she's no runner."

Owen stopped and blew out his breath. "Sorry. I'm still angry, I guess. I thought I was over it, but I hate injustice. Let's get out of this wind and get something to eat."

The sky to the west was still pink and orange with the light of the setting sun, but the sun's disk itself had disappeared, and the evening air was chilly with night breezes that felt like they were shaping up to be sharp winds. As if Owen's words had drawn her attention to the temperature, Aderyn shivered. Owen looked at her, and his features relaxed. He put an arm around her shoulders and hugged her. "I wish I'd seen you all today. Everyone was talking about the Warmaster who ducked every attack by Bethla the Windwarden. Apparently Bethla is a crack shot with *telekinesis*."

Aderyn blushed. "We'll have to tell you how the Warmaster nearly got everyone on her team imprisoned. I bet that's not common knowledge."

They found a tavern on the next street and took seats at a table far from the fireplace, not because they didn't like the heat but because it was the last table available. While they waited for food to be brought, Aderyn said, "I'm not saying anything until you explain what happened in the fight with Jael. I could tell you were furious."

Owen's jaw clenched. "In that last exchange, I hit first. It was a close call, like maybe a second's difference between my blow and Jael's, and the adjudicator decided for Jael. Which is fine. Referees make mistakes all the time. But Jael knew who'd hit first, and she refused to correct the call."

Aderyn sucked in an astonished breath. "She didn't. How could she bear to win with a lie?"

Owen let out a short, sharp bark of a laugh. "Hah. I told her to admit the truth, and she said winning was what mattered, and I'd better learn that lesson fast. So, yeah, I was furious." The serving man set down mugs in front of them at that moment, and Owen took a long drink and set his mug down hard enough to rattle the others. "I can't believe she thinks I'm at all interested in friendly competition after that. Or friendly anything."

"She's attracted to you," Aderyn said. "Can I watch you tell her to screw herself? Because I would enjoy that."

Owen laughed, a more natural sound than before. "I got the impression that she wants *me* to be attracted to *her* so she can toy with my emotions. Didn't you say men are supposed to approach women, and not the other way around?"

"That's true, but a woman can send signals that she'll be receptive to a man's advances," Aderyn said. "The ones who are overt about it are considered sad and desperate."

"That fits," Owen said. "I don't know what about me told her I would ever be interested. She may be an excellent fighter, but she's sure clueless about men."

"Well, she is pretty in a sort of scrawny, underfed way," Livia said. "Probably she's used to getting men to do her bidding."

"Not this man," Owen said firmly. "And I'm done talking about her. What happened that you all nearly went to prison? Wait, don't tell me, I have a guess. **[Improved Assess 2]** got you in trouble."

"You're insightful," Aderyn said.

Between the four of them, they told the story of their dungeon battle and the aftermath. Owen laughed when they described Livia's clever use of *immobilize* and laughed harder when they revealed where they'd found the final ring. He was less amused by Jesper's accusations and Seonn's readiness to assume the worst. "Seonn should have been more worried about who in his organization was selling secrets," he said. "I think he saw you as a better scapegoat. It makes for a dramatic story, new team comes in and blows the competition away with inside information."

"At least **[Improved Assess 2]** got us out of trouble too," Aderyn said. "I should have considered what using the information would look like, but I was so surprised when it worked on that dungeon I didn't think. At the very least I could have told the other team the target number. That would have made the challenge more exciting."

"Stop blaming yourself," Livia said. "Everything worked out, and we won't use that skill again. We can win without it. After all, they didn't say no using the Warmaster's vision, and nobody could object to **[Secret Message]**."

"Which I didn't tell them about," Aderyn said. "I feel no obligation to reveal all my secrets. I promised I wouldn't use the skills that unbalance the game, and I won't, because I do have a sense of honor."

"And we're back to that Jael woman," Weston groaned. "It would be easier if she was actually awful at fighting."

"She's a good fighter with the heart of a snake, which is an insult to decent snakes everywhere." Owen drained his mug and waved for another drink. "I'm starving. Even with rests between matches, that was a long day."

"I would have thought rests were not enough, not if you had to fight eight times," Isold said.

Owen leaned back for the server to set a plate of deep-fried chicken and mashed potatoes in front of him. "They had a <**Rejuvenation Wand**> they used if we didn't have enough rest time between matches. All of us needed it at least twice. It resets your stamina to full, is all, no repairing strained muscles or restoring health. And the Bonemender who used it told me it delays weariness, but doesn't remove it, so I'll sleep soundly tonight." He bit into a chicken leg and let out a muffled moan of pleasure. "Forget KFC and Chick-Fil-A," he said indistinctly. "This is the best chicken ever."

Aderyn refrained from asking him what those things were. Sometimes he referred to his world just to make her ask questions. Well, she loved him, but she wouldn't give him the satisfaction. And the chicken was delicious, with seasoned crispy deep-fried skin and juicy meat. The potatoes were just as mouthwatering, loaded with cream, butter, and melted cheese. She ate, and felt content. The day's near-catastrophe faded in memory until she thought she might someday be able to laugh at the other teams' consternation over her skills.

"Miss?"

Aderyn choked briefly on a bite of chicken, swallowed hastily, and said, "Yes?"

The speaker was a young woman, too young to have gotten her Call. She wore her dark blonde hair in two braids down her back and had freckles sprinkled generously across her nose and cheeks, all of which made her look even younger than Aderyn judged her to be.

"You're the Wildcats, right?" she said, sounding nervous.

Aderyn was stunned at being recognized outside the arena. Then she remembered they were all still wearing their bright blue uniforms. "Yes, we are."

The girl's nervousness vanished as a blinding smile spread across her face. "I saw you today in the arena, me and Lorcan and Pa. You were amazing! How did you know to look for that last ring? We all saw the chest land on it, and we were sure it was lost for good."

"My Herald's skills include one called **[Find Object]**," Isold said, smoothly cutting Aderyn off before she could say anything incriminating. "We didn't actually expect to find anything. It was simply a way of using all our resources."

"Well, it was amazing. I never saw anything like it, how you all worked as a team." The girl blushed, dimming her freckles. "Burrowing through solid rock, and balancing on those skinny little branches, and—" She nodded at Aderyn. "Bethla's never missed anyone these last four seasons, and you dodged her potions like they were nothing!"

Owen took Aderyn's hand. "Swifter than lightning."

"Oh, I like that, I'll—" The girl's mouth fell open. "You're Owen the challenger. I didn't even see you there, sorry!"

"It's fine, don't worry about it."

"But what are you—" She noticed their clasped hands and blushed brighter. "I see now. Are you sweethearts? That's beautiful, both of you competing in the Games—though of course you couldn't compete against each other in the teams, it's against the rules—oh, but I'm rattling on, aren't I? Pa says I don't think before I talk."

"We know someone you should meet," murmured Weston. Livia nudged him with her elbow.

The girl hadn't heard him. "I'm sorry to have kept you, I just wanted to say how much I liked how you won. All of you. And good luck, sir," she said to Owen before hurrying away.

"I didn't think about us being recognized," Aderyn said, "mainly because I forgot how conspicuous these make us." She plucked at her tunic, feeling self-conscious.

"I like it," Livia said. "We don't get recognition for killing monsters and defeating dungeons, even when it's things like the Sarnok and Sorrowvale."

"The system thanked us for Sorrowvale," Aderyn pointed out.

"All right, yes, and that was rewarding, but it's not the same as getting respect from our fellow humans." Livia picked up another chicken wing and tore into it. "I like the idea of people telling us we're great."

"You had better not turn into an entitled snob like Jael," Weston said.

Owen groaned. "I'm never going to be able to stop hearing her name, am I?"

CHAPTER EIGHTEEN

Aderyn woke to the first light of dawn and lay still for a few minutes. She enjoyed this time of day, when everything was peaceful and the air was new and fresh. She liked it even more when she was in her warm bed with the covers drawn up against the cool autumn morning air.

Beside her, Owen breathed quietly in sleep. She rolled onto her side and propped herself on one elbow, watching him. He needed a haircut so he didn't look quite so shaggy, though the truth was she loved how he looked regardless of the length of his hair. But now he was a challenger, he needed to look good for the crowds, not to mention long hair would obscure his vision.

She ran a hand lightly over his bare chest, waking him just enough that he clasped her wrist to still her movements. Without opening his eyes, he mumbled, "It's too early. Go back to sleep."

"I'm fully awake."

"Are you?" He smiled, a lazy, provocative smile. "How awake?"

"Really? Again, after last night?"

His eyes opened. "What do you mean, last night?"

Aderyn put on a sorrowful face. "I can't believe our glorious night wasn't memorable."

Puzzlement gave way to understanding. "You're hilarious," he said, and grabbed her to roll her beneath him. "I fell asleep two seconds after hitting this bed and you know it."

With a laugh, Aderyn said, "But the moment when you were afraid you'd forgotten was priceless."

Owen lowered his head to brush her lips with a kiss. "I will never forget a single time with you," he whispered before kissing her more deeply.

Aderyn freed her wrists from his grip and put her arms around his neck, pulling him close so his body was pressed against hers. He shifted his weight so he could slide a hand beneath her, caressing her lower back and her bottom, and she gave a little moan of pleasure. She wanted to have this forever. Maybe—

Someone pounded on the door. "Aderyn! Owen! Borrus is here," Weston called out.

"Damn," Owen muttered, dropping his head to rest on Aderyn's shoulder. "I'm starting to wish I hadn't fallen so deeply asleep last night."

Aderyn stroked his cheek. "We have plenty of time. And Borrus is not usually an early riser, so if he's here at the break of day, it must be important."

"Important to him. I have other priorities." Owen kissed her again and rolled out of bed.

Fully dressed, they went downstairs to the Alabaster Inn's taproom, where they found Borrus seated with Weston at a table near the fireplace, in which a fire burned brightly against the morning's chill. Sliced ham, bowls of peeled hardboiled eggs, a tureen of steaming porridge, rashers of bacon, heaps of buttered hashed potatoes, and piles of glistening sausages covered the table, more food than Aderyn could imagine any one person eating.

Borrus and Weston had plates piled high with food and were

eating steadily in the manner of two men who weren't confident about where their next meal was coming from. Aderyn said, "This isn't a competition, is it?"

"Of course not," Borrus said, his words muffled. "I like to eat, you know that. And Weston feels the same. Mistress Arlia is the best cook in Foundation, possibly in all of Finion's Gate, though if you tell Chef Gorban I said that I'll deny it."

"We don't know Chef Gorban, so you're safe," Owen said. He sat opposite Borrus and accepted a plate from an unusually quiet Davith. Aderyn expected him to ask why Borrus was here so early, but he simply helped himself to sausage and potatoes and dug in. Since Aderyn was sure Borrus's appearance here had to do with the excellence of Davith's mother's cooking, she decided questions could wait until she was full.

They ate, only speaking to ask for someone to pass a dish, until the sausages were gone and they'd made serious inroads on all the other foods. Borrus leaned back in his seat and let out a belch. "Sorry," he said, not sounding very sorry.

"Better out than in, Mother always says," Aderyn replied, making Borrus chuckle.

"Your *mother* says that?" Owen said. "My mother would tell me if I can't remember my manners I can eat in the shed with the pigs. Though we don't have pigs, so I think that was something *her* mother always told her."

"Mother has a rather earthy sense of humor," Borrus said. "I think it amuses Father because Spiritsmiths have a reputation for being highly educated and therefore elevated in their tastes and language. Mother says that's bullshit, in that exact word."

"I'm looking forward to meeting your mother someday," Owen said. "Or, meeting her again, when I'm less disoriented and can appreciate it."

"What do you mean, disoriented?" Borrus leaned forward. "Where did you and Aderyn meet, anyway?"

Owen glanced at Aderyn for guidance. Aderyn hesitated, then shook her head minutely. "Owen is from beyond Greenacre, and he and I were attacked by monsters outside Far Haven when we were both only level one," she told Borrus, madly editing the truth as she went. "That's when we became teammates, and partners. He met Mother and Father before we set out."

"I remember you said you became partners early on, but I guess I never heard the story of how you met." Borrus's calm acceptance of Aderyn's lie made her feel guilty about it. She wanted Borrus to know the truth, always—wanted him to know about Owen's true origins as someone from another human world beyond their own— but she was too aware of Borrus's inability to remember what he was supposed to keep secret. He never intentionally gave anything away, but even being reminded multiple times wasn't enough to keep him from slipping.

"Anyway, it means I met your parents before I knew what Aderyn would eventually mean to me, so knowing them matters more now than it did when I thought I was leaving them behind forever." Owen clasped Aderyn's hand casually, but **[Read Body Language]** sent the clear message that he, too, wasn't comfortable about lying to her brother.

Borrus flicked a glance at Aderyn before focusing on Owen again. "That makes sense."

Aderyn could guess what he was thinking without benefit of a Warmaster skill: what were Aderyn's intentions toward Owen? As she had that morning, she considered the future. She couldn't imagine leaving Owen, which meant, as Borrus had said before, that she wanted a lifetime commitment. But that meant marriage, and she wasn't sure she was ready for that. *But* that was what a lifetime commitment meant, and her parents had married while they were still adventuring, so it wasn't that unheard of—

"I know Aderyn is wondering what gets me out of bed when the sun's barely up," Borrus said, interrupting her train of thought.

"It does have me thinking about what Herald altered your behavior," she joked, grateful for a distraction.

"I'm here to help you choose a sponsor," Borrus went on. "The offers will start arriving this morning, and you're not, forgive me, in a good position to choose well. If you want, I can winnow them down for you."

"I would appreciate that," Owen said. "I'd mostly forgotten what comes after placement in the qualifying matches. Too busy focusing on winning."

"I was there once, so I remember." Borrus glanced up as Livia slouched to the table and sank down on a chair next to Weston. "Is she all right?"

"Coffee," Livia muttered.

"I'll get it," Davith said, hurrying away before Weston could do more than start rising from his seat.

"Where's Isold?" Aderyn asked.

"He spent the night elsewhere," Weston said with a grin. "I'd call it 'fraternizing with the enemy' except he said explicitly he wasn't going to get involved with the other teams. Too much opportunity for misunderstandings. So really it's 'fraternizing with Owen's former opponents.' Of whom there are many."

Owen rolled his eyes. "So Isold is off being Isold. Borrus, what should I expect about the sponsors?"

Borrus watched Davith push platters aside to make room for a tray with a coffee pot, a cream pitcher, and a handful of mugs. "In some ways, it's straightforward. Anyone who wants to sponsor you will send an invitation for you to join them for a meal, or coffee, or drinks—something that will give them the opportunity to sell their many virtues and explain what they'll do for you. They might offer a nice residence, or good weapons and armor, or expensive jewelry. Less often they'll throw money your way—it's considered crass on their part, but not on yours if you accept. They'll tell you all about the social cachet you'll gain by being affiliated with them."

"And the less straightforward ways?"

Borrus took a mug from the tray and reached for the coffee pot only to have Livia snatch it away and pour a second cup for herself. "The invitations convey hidden meanings you won't recognize if you're not a Gater. Some of them hint at sexual favors, for example, either from the sponsors themselves or from them on behalf of another. Some of them indicate that the sponsor is interested in a challenger who will be active in pushing that sponsor's political agenda. You don't want to be mixed up in either of those things."

"No." Owen picked up a stray sausage left on the tray and bit into it. "I want nothing to do with Finion's Gate politics, and I'm definitely not interested in sex with strangers."

"Right. The other issue is knowing which sponsors to meet with. Your choices send messages to others. The way you turn down an offer, or accept, will be seen as meaningful by all those scrambling to sponsor a challenger this season."

"And I have no idea about any of that," Owen said. "But you do."

"And I'm happy to help, even before I consider how my sister feels about you. I watched you fight. That Jael woman lost that match, didn't she?"

"The adjudicator's call is final," Owen said flatly. "And... yes."

"That kind of behavior will bite her on the ass someday." Borrus looked dangerously competent, not at all the easygoing brother Aderyn remembered. "Believe me, I'm not the only one who saw what happened, and everyone saw how you behaved. You earned yourself a lot of credit with the spectators, and with the sponsors. I predict you'll have at least thirteen, maybe fifteen offers today."

"That's a lot, right?" Aderyn said. "Will he have time to meet with each of them?"

"No," Borrus said. "But it doesn't matter. There's only one sponsor you'll accept."

"I was about to get annoyed at your highhandedness before I

remembered I want you to make that decision for me," Owen said with a grin. "Who will be sponsoring me?"

"You'll choose Raynir." Borrus finally retrieved the coffee pot from Livia and poured himself a mug of coffee laced with cream. "He's the second-ranked Councilor going into this season. He used to be first, but Raewyn had some bad luck last season and dropped to number eight in the rankings. He sponsors two champions right now, but I've heard he's looking to hedge his bets against his other champion, Gabryl, ending up like Raewyn."

"If he's got two he's supporting now, can he afford a third?" Owen asked.

"Raynir's fortune is vast enough he could support five champions if he wanted. Honestly, I'm not sure why he doesn't. I know he hates Balan, though I don't know why. Balan is the Chief Councilor right now, thanks to him sponsoring Kendria." Borrus frowned. "I wish Kendria hadn't chosen him. I think he's using her as a figurehead, someone who wins him social points. But she always says he provides for her better than anyone else could."

"Raynir and Balan," Weston said. "Who are the other councilors?"

"Camlon, Brisa, Sabetta, and Emmalia. Camlon and Brisa have two champions each, and Sabetta and Emmalia each have one." Borrus made a face. "Sabetta won't approach you despite how good-looking you are. She only ever has one champion at a time, he's always male, and he's always attractive. The rumor is that she sleeps with them, but it's not true."

"How do you know?" Livia asked.

"Because she was my sponsor back when I was a champion," Borrus said. "She just likes to look at attractive men and use them as escorts to social functions. I got tired of being her lapdog about the time I got tired of fighting." He cleared his throat. "Anyway. I've heard Camlon is looking for someone new to sponsor now that Quillon seems to have lost his edge, but Brisa is too conservative to gamble on a newcomer and Emmalia isn't wealthy enough to afford more than one champion. Most of your offers will come from non-Councilors, which of course you can't accept."

"Because that would send the signal that I'm interested in Finion's Gate politics, wanting to elevate a new person to the Council," Owen said.

"You catch on quick," Borrus said. "To answer Aderyn's earlier question, you'll have plenty of time to meet with sponsors because Raynir's is the only invitation you'll accept. You'll send a polite note declining any councilor's request and ignore those who aren't councilors. And I estimate Raynir's message will arrive sometime midmorning, inviting you to lunch."

A bell rang from the front of the inn, and Davith hurried away to the door. He returned almost immediately with two folded papers, one white, one pale blue, each sealed shut with wax imprinted with images too blurry to make out. He handed them both to Owen. "They said, 'for the challenger,' but they didn't say your name, so they were trying to pretend you're not important enough for them to remember it," he said.

"That's right. Clever of you to realize that," Borrus said, sounding impressed.

Davith shrugged. "We deal with the wealthy sometimes, and Pa says to pay attention to what they and their servants don't say, because that's where the information is."

Owen cracked the seal on one paper, read the contents, and passed it to Borrus while he opened the other. "No names you mentioned."

"These are nobodies," Borrus said. "Though you might keep track of how many offers you get. If you can drop that casually into conversation, it might impress some."

Owen nodded slowly. "It's going to be a long morning."

CHAPTER NINETEEN

The Alabaster Inn had a pretty little sitting room for the use of its guests on the opposite side from the taproom. It was comfortable and elegant without being pretentious, and Aderyn enjoyed sitting in it and daydreaming about maybe having a room like this in her own house someday. A nice sitting room, and a bathing room with a giant tub equipped with its own heated water tank like the one she'd seen in Elkenforest... her imagination stopped there, but she thought back over all the houses and inns she'd seen since leaving Far Haven. Surely there were more establishments she could draw on in creating her imaginary home?

Across from her, Isold idly tapped his drum, more to test the sound than to make music, Aderyn thought. With his head down, he seemed lost in a reverie just the way she was. Livia and Weston sat close together on a nearby couch, reading the same book at the same time. Aderyn had no idea how they managed that, especially since Livia was a faster reader.

They were waiting for Owen to return from his visit with Councilor Raynir. The invitation, Borrus had explained, was for Owen alone, even though it wasn't uncommon for challengers to take advocates along to negotiate the terms of the sponsorship. "It looks crass, though," Borrus had said. "For one thing, it suggests that the deal is already made, and for another, it implies the challenger doesn't trust the sponsor to act in his or her best interests. And Owen's smart enough not to need that."

The front door opened, making Aderyn sit up. Footsteps sounded, and then Owen appeared in the doorway. "I'm extremely full and slightly drunk," he announced. "And I could be fuller and drunker because Councilman Raynir lays on quite the spread. I'm not used to hard liquor, especially in the middle of the day."

Aderyn hurried to his side and led him to sit where they could all see one another comfortably. "Did he try to get you drunk on purpose?"

"Yes, and no." Owen sprawled in his seat with his head tilted back. "That is, I think he was testing me to see how much self-control I have. I must have passed, because he extended his sponsorship and I accepted."

"That's not enough detail," Weston said. "What's he like?"

"Sharp. Clever. Urbane, even, though as I'm an otherworlder, the specifics of his high-class manners were lost on me." Owen raised his head, which wobbled slightly. "He was straightforward about the details of the contract, didn't dance around at all. He'll supply me with my choice of equipment, with assistance in choosing from his experts if I desire. Ditto new clothes, new shoes, accessories, the lot. He offered a choice of residences, and when I said I'd have to think about it, converted it into an offer of a daily stipend for housing and expenses."

"That's unexpected," Isold said. "I would have guessed he'd want you where he can find you."

"I didn't think I could bring the lot of you along to any residence he gave me, since that would look like he's supporting the Wildcats, and the hints he let fall like stones into a pool let me know that would be against the rules without him coming out and saying it.

That was the only time he was less than direct." Owen clasped Aderyn's hand and raised it to his lips. "He'd done his homework, though. He knew all about our team and who the Wildcats are, and he even knew I have a sweetheart. It was unsettling. Though not unexpected. Like I said, he's sharp."

"So, what did he want from you?" Livia asked.

Owen gave her a slightly tipsy smile. "Appearances at a number of social events chosen by him. My presence in his box when I'm not fighting. And a promise that I will conduct myself honorably. With a wink and a nudge to say he knew what happened with Jael. Damn, but there are a lot of people who saw it. At least three of the invitations I got today said it right out, no dancing around the issue, and another five hinted at it."

"It's too bad those people weren't there to lay witness at the time," Weston said. "Still, it seems to have done you good. How many invitations was it? Sixteen?"

"Eighteen," Aderyn said. "Two more came while you were gone."

"I am so glad I don't have to go to all these lunches and dinners and teas and drink parties. My liver would shrivel and die." Owen tipped his head back again. "I need a nap that I'm not going to get. I have to go to Raynir's tailor to be fitted for a wardrobe appropriate to my station as his sponsoree. Or whatever I'm called now. The first of those social events happens tomorrow night."

"I'll join you," Aderyn said. "If that's all right. Is it a problem for us to be seen together now?"

Owen let his head flop from side to side in an exaggerated gesture. "Raynir can't look like he's supporting a team, but the public likes it when champions and challengers have relationships with prominent citizens. Which includes the members of the Games competitors. Which goes double for the newcomers on the scene who swept their dungeon to great acclaim." He grinned at Aderyn. "Wonder which of us will be more famous?"

Aderyn blushed. "You, obviously. I'm just one of four."

"Possibly not," Isold said. "I went for a walk, incognito, last night before bed, and listened to the talk. There is a great deal of excitement over the coming Games, and a great deal of speculation on how the team competitions will play out. And it seems our performance is being discussed everywhere. Aderyn's skills in particular. You already have admirers."

"Admirers?" Aderyn buried her face in her hands. "Should I be grateful they don't know where we're staying?"

"Oh, embrace it," Livia said. "How often are you going to have the chance to be famous? It's not like it will last. Once we're gone, some other team will be popular."

"You make a striking couple, too," Isold said, "when Owen isn't drunk, that is."

"Hey! I am not drunk. I am a little tipsy." Owen tried to stand and managed it on the third try. "Let's go get me some fancy clothes, o famous swifter than lightning Wildcat."

Aderyn scowled. "Do I need Borrus to remind you of the consequences of pissing me off? There are a lot of slugs in Arlia's garden this time of year."

"Famous swifter than lightning Wildcat, ma'am," Owen amended.

ADERYN BRUSHED HER HAIR A FINAL TIME AND considered putting it up. She knew nothing about formal events except for what she'd read in some of her parents' books, fanciful stories of dances and receptions and coronations. In those, the woodcut illustrations showed women in elegant gowns with their hair piled high on their heads. Aderyn's hair was long enough she could maybe get it into a bun or something, but it might look silly when she wasn't wearing an elegant gown.

"I wish our uniforms were fancier," she complained again as she set down her hairbrush. "I can see the importance of the teams being visibly different from the other guests, but it's not like *you* have to wear a uniform."

Owen sighed. "Come here," he said, crooking a finger at her. Aderyn sulkily walked toward him and let him embrace her. "You like the idea of dressing up, don't you?"

"I didn't think I would until we were at the clothier's and I saw all those dresses. They were so beautiful." She sighed and draped her arms around his neck. "But instead I have to wear this tunic that looks like someone cut a couple of holes in a blue potato sack."

"That's not true. It fits you very well. And you know you're beautiful no matter what you wear." Owen ran a hand from the nape of her neck to her bottom. "I guarantee you'll have the attention of everyone at that party, even dressed plainly like this."

Aderyn rested her forehead against his shoulder. "I was more thinking how much I'd like you to see me in something that isn't adventurer clothes."

"Oh, I see." Owen chuckled. "Someday, sweetheart." He put a finger beneath her chin and tilted her head back to meet her gaze. "Maybe there will be dances we can attend."

"You don't know how to dance."

"I'd love for you to teach me. Or I'll teach you some of mine." He put his hands low on her hips and began moving rhythmically in an extremely provocative manner. Aderyn laughed.

"I think we'd get in trouble for outraging public decency with that one," she said. "All right. Someday."

Owen did look good. He wore a full-sleeved white silk shirt beneath a fitted vest of heavy blue and gold brocade, with narrow-waisted trousers that tapered close around his ankles. Aderyn had never seen shoes like the ones the tailor had sent for; they were leather, but black and hard and so shiny she could see her wavery reflection in them. Dressed like that, with his blond hair neatly trimmed, Owen looked the ideal image of a Swordsworn challenger.

Owen checked the fall of his trousers in the mirror once more and sighed. "I wish we knew more about what to expect. Borrus said this was as much political as social. I hate going into a situation with no more information than that."

"Borrus also said it's acceptable for us to decline to comment any time we think the conversation is headed somewhere heavy." Aderyn hooked her arm through his. "It's going to be fine. And if it goes bad, I'll use [Secret Message] to get us all out of there. All right?"

"That reassures me more than you know," Owen said.

The weather that day had been warm for autumn, but the temperature had fallen as the sun set, and now Aderyn felt chilled. She wished she had her nice warm coat, bought months ago in antici-pation of visiting this city, but she'd felt she shouldn't cover up her uniform. Still, goose pimples rose on her bare arms, and she walked closer to Owen, grateful for his body heat.

The five friends walked through Foundation to a lift farther away from the one they'd been using since arriving in Finion's Gate. This one had more attendants, all wearing dark blue tunics more elabo-rately sewn than the Wildcats', but the space around it was empty, with no one waiting in a queue for their turn. Instead, the one woman attendant bowed at Owen's approach, and her companions opened the lift door and bowed in turn. Aderyn followed Owen into the lift and tried not to meet anyone's gaze, for fear she might offend them by laughing. This was the kind of treatment royalty got, and she was just Aderyn of Far Haven... it was ridiculous if you thought about it.

The lift took them as far as Terrace One, where they were met by a carriage shaped like a golden pumpkin that took them to a second lift that brought them to Terrace Two. Terrace Two looked exactly like Terrace One, though it was after sunset and Aderyn might be missing details in the dimness. Another identical carriage waited for them there. This time, Aderyn saw a golden emblem impressed on the carriage door. It looked the way she imagined a summer wind would, carefree and tangled in lines of gold. Its casual beauty comforted her.

When the carriage stopped, she got out—and stared. The building before her was much smaller than the arena, and shorter than most of the buildings in either Finion's Gate or Guerdon Deep. But it radiated light from every window like the sun burned within, illuminating the many carvings and statues decorating it. It was also surrounded by shrubs that made a dark border even in all the light, shrubs Aderyn would have mistaken for stone if not for their strong, rich, resiny scent.

Broad stairs led up to the front door, with uniformed guards armed with swords standing opposite each other on every other step. They were completely motionless even when Weston got right up in front of one of them and waved. "I think they're conscious," he said.

"They're like the guards in front of Westminster Palace—that's in a country in my world," Owen said. "You shouldn't taunt them because they aren't allowed to react."

"I wasn't taunting, I was genuinely curious about whether they were alive." Weston rejoined the others, and they continued up the stairs and through the open door.

Ahead, the low murmur of conversation and the sound of string instruments made Aderyn slow her steps. Then she stiffened her spine and hurried after Owen. This was nothing. She was a popular member of a popular team, and everyone there wanted to meet them. There was no reason to be nervous.

Owen paused as she neared him. He smiled and offered her his arm. Aderyn took it, and together the five friends walked through another wide doorway and into the colorful whirl of the most exclusive party in Finion's Gate.

CHAPTER TWENTY

The warmth of the room hit Aderyn like a wall, easing the chill immediately, though she suspected she'd be too warm before long. Big metal hoops holding dozens of <**Everburning Candles**> hung from the ceiling, with larger versions of those magic items in sconces on the walls. The smell of lavender that scented the candles was so strong it wrinkled Aderyn's nose. It would certainly cover any body odors, assuming wealthy people sweated. Aderyn couldn't think why they wouldn't, but she wasn't going to rule it out.

She walked forward with Owen and didn't bother to pretend not to gape in wonder at the beautiful paintings hanging between the sconces and the small statues of nude human figures displayed on pedestals here and there. All the statues looked like they were dancing, as if they only needed the right signal to leap down and frolic among the guests. She looked like a yokel from Far Haven, probably, but she didn't see the point in pretending she knew what she was doing in this gathering.

Owen gently steered her toward a large man dressed much as

Owen was, though his vest of brocaded silk strained over his stomach and his face was fleshy and pink from heat. His longish brown hair, swept back from his face, was threaded with silver, and Aderyn guessed him to be in his fifties. Before she had time to Assess him, they were standing in front of him and Aderyn was afraid of saying the wrong thing in her distraction over reading his Assessment.

"Councilor Raynir," Owen said, "thank you for the invitation. May I introduce Aderyn of the Wildcats, my sweetheart."

Hearing him say the word so casually made Aderyn tingle all over with pleasure and a peculiar longing. She smiled politely and said, "It's nice to meet you, sir. Is that the right form of address?" Some of the storybooks in her parents' small library told tales of rich and noble people, and many of them had titles, but she couldn't begin to guess at Raynir's and hoped he would understand.

"'Sir' is acceptable, young lady," Raynir said. "I saw your competition the other day. Most remarkable. If I were thirty years younger, I'd pay you my respects more directly."

"Thank you for the compliment, sir, I'm honored," Aderyn said. Owen's arm tensed beneath her hand, and she tightened her grip. Owen still didn't understand all the nuances of courtship in her world, and [Read Body Language] told her he considered Raynir's traditional compliment from an older man to a woman too young for him insulting. She needed to explain to him that those compliments meant nothing. "And thank you for sponsoring Owen."

"The benefits are mostly mine. I anticipate Owen placing highly in the Games, and at the risk of speaking too plainly, my status in the Council is linked to that of my champions. Come, I'd like to introduce you to your fellows, my other champions."

Raynir had addressed Owen, but he didn't seem to mind Aderyn tagging along. He led them through the crowd to where a man and a woman stood together, apparently ignoring each other despite how close they were. But Aderyn had noticed them before, and then their heads had been close together in intense conversation. Her immediate guess was that they were a couple and didn't want anyone to know. Again, she started to Assess them, but changed her mind at once. Too many people, too close together—she could use [Improved Assess 2] if she didn't mind potentially being rude by inadvertently ignoring someone who addressed her while she was preoccupied. She couldn't imagine needing that skill's edge in this gathering.

"Owen, this is Gabryl the Swordsworn and Raewyn the Swifthands," Raynir said. "Gabryl is ranked second and Raewyn is eighth among the champions. Gabryl, Raewyn, you've seen Owen fight, and you may recall Aderyn's performance in the team battles. Why don't you get to know each other? I see someone I should speak to."

"Of course," Raewyn said as Raynir moved away. "It's a shame about that one match, Owen, but seven out of eight is a remarkable record anyway."

"All that matters is how you perform in the real Games," Gabryl said. He was taller than Owen and more heavily built, but still muscled like a Swordsworn. His gruffness put Aderyn on edge, though she knew he wasn't likely to attack her or Owen or anyone in the middle of this party. He gave off a low-grade sense of menace, though, and if she'd been able to use [Read Body Language] on him, she was sure she'd have seen he felt threatened by Owen.

"I hope to do well," Owen said. "Raewyn, do you use a weapon in the fights, or do you do unarmed combat? I've been wondering how Swifthands compete."

Raewyn stiffened, and Gabryl's glare intensified. "I prefer short-staffs," Raewyn said tersely. "Though it's hardly impossible for a skilled Swifthands to wipe the floor with a Swordsworn using nothing but her hands and feet. But I find the shortstaffs are a crowd pleaser, which is an important part of any match."

"I'm sorry, I didn't mean insult," Owen said calmly. "I agree those weapons are dramatic. I suppose that means I'll be allowed to compete with sword and dagger, if a pair of shortstaffs is legal?"

"If you want," Gabryl said, his voice gruff. "As long as they're not magic weapons, any melee weapon is permitted. No bows, obviously, no whips, but almost anything else."

"There aren't a lot of fighters who take advantage of the [Two-Weapon Fighting] skill," Raewyn said. She sounded calmer now. "And you, Aderyn. I'm afraid I wasn't in the arena for your team battle, but I heard about it later. How many of Bethla's strikes did you dodge? Five?"

"Just two. She stopped flinging potions after that."

"Even one would be remarkable," Gabryl said, sounding less angry. "*Telekinesis* is Bethla's specialty, that and *levitate* and *fly*—anything that allows for rapid movement. Of course, *fly* is only allowed in certain dungeons, when it won't give one team a huge advantage that wouldn't be fun for spectators. Was that a Warmaster trick?"

Aderyn nodded. "It's called [See It Coming]."

"Well, I was impressed," Gabryl said. "Listen, let me give you some advice." His voice lowered. "Get acquainted with as many champions and challengers as you can, swift Aderyn. If you single anyone out, they'll use that as evidence of a special connection with you and your team, and most of these colts, you don't want that. If you spread your interest around, nobody will be able to pull that stunt. Understand?"

"I... think so. Special connection—do you mean romantic interest?"

"That, but also favoring them in the matches. Teams are more popular than fighters when it comes to the Games, and their popularity spills over onto whoever they single out. Some colts turn that into support from the populace, and challengers in particular have been known to manipulate the betting odds in their favor. Not betting on themselves, of course, but there's nothing stopping them boosting the reputation of a fellow challenger or champion and wagering heavily on his opponent."

"Don't worry about the details," Raewyn said, in a gentle way that made Aderyn suspect her growing distress was obvious. "Think of it as being friendly with everyone. And it helps that you're attached to Owen." She laughed. "Not that that will stop men from approaching you. It's a pity you're not married."

"Thanks for the advice," Aderyn said. "I'll do that now. Owen?"

As they strolled away, Owen said in a low voice, "What did she mean about men approaching you? Isn't it obvious we're together?"

"Well, yes, but it's not—"

"Excuse me," a woman said. She spoke in a low, sultry voice that made Aderyn think of the kind of rich desserts that tasted good with the first bite and left you feeling sick at the last. "Owen, right?"

"I am," Owen said. "I'm afraid we haven't been introduced."

The woman laughed. She was beautiful, though not young, and her dress was exactly the kind Aderyn had salivated over at the clothiers, flowing amber silk pinned at the shoulders with sparkling sapphires set in gold bezels. Beside her loomed a handsome, muscular man who was almost certainly a Stalwart. "Councilor Sabetta," the woman said, extending her hand to clasp Owen's. Her eyes lingered on his shoulders and well-muscled chest highlighted by his elegant vest. "I wanted to see the one everyone's talking about. That was quite the show you put on. Why didn't you push the adjudicator to nullify his call in that woman's favor?"

"The adjudicator's call is final," Owen said politely. "I'll have plenty of opportunities to prove my skills in the Games."

Sabetta laughed again. "You're so honorable. I admire that." Her gaze told Aderyn honor wasn't all she admired. "This is my champion, Rhidius. Rhidius, you'll have to be in top form if you want to defeat this one."

Rhidius nodded, a ponderous action that made Aderyn question whether he'd be fast enough to beat Owen. Then she caught the alert, intrigued look in his eye and knew he was putting on an act.

"I look forward to testing my skills against yours, Rhidius," Owen said. "It was nice meeting you, Councilor Sabetta."

Sabetta glanced without interest at Aderyn and then smiled at Owen. "Very nice indeed."

When she and Rhidius had disappeared into the crowd, Aderyn said, "So that's Borrus's former sponsor. She certainly does have a type." She wanted to ask Owen why it was all right for him to be leered at by appreciative women, but not for her to receive perfectly innocent compliments from men, but she was sure that would start an argument.

"Yes, and her type is Chris Hemsworth," Owen muttered. "I guess Rhidius and I should both be grateful I'm not the highly muscular type."

"You think she'd dump a successful champion in favor of someone more handsome?"

"I have no idea. I think it's possible." Owen clasped her hand briefly. "I need a drink. Just one, because I feel I should keep my wits sharp here, but I'm thirsty. And hot. Wish there were windows to open."

Among the guests were slender men dressed all in white bearing trays of glasses. Owen and Aderyn secured drinks and moved through the crowd at random. Other teams, visible by their colored tunics, nodded and waved but didn't approach. Aderyn wasn't sure if that was on purpose as a social expectation, or if they didn't feel the need to chat with their fellow competitors after spending all day together. She was overwhelmed enough that she didn't feel like figuring out the mystery.

They occasionally saw Weston and Livia, who looked like they were enjoying themselves, telling stories that had their listeners laughing like mad. Isold, on the other hand, was surrounded by young women, listening to them talk. He always claimed to be bad at romantic talk, which Aderyn had once considered essential to courtship, but he never had a shortage of admirers and potential bedpartners.

She didn't know how to follow Gabryl's advice, since she barely remembered any of the challengers apart from the awful Jael, but Owen knew them all and steered her from one to the next. With Owen starting conversations that showed he was interested in his fellow fighters, Aderyn found it easy to join in.

They encountered Gradin and Pace in company with their sponsor, Kesslon. Kesslon was boisterously loud and prone to slapping his combatants on the back, but Aderyn's instincts were that it was a show he was putting on, the way Rhidius had acted like an over-muscled idiot. This left her feeling confident in her ability to maneuver in this social situation, after all. Then someone bumped into her. "Excuse me," she said automatically, though she hadn't been the offender.

"Oh, it's you," the woman said. She sounded weary, as if Aderyn was an old acquaintance she didn't look forward to seeing again.

Aderyn turned. The woman was tall, with long blonde hair beautifully arranged high on her head. Despite her beautiful gown, which was a blue almost the same shade as Aderyn's tunic, she looked more like a warrior than a socialite, her arms smoothly muscled and her stance solid. After a second glance, Aderyn recognized her. Her mouth fell open.

"So you do remember me," Caprissa the Swordsworn said. "Should I be grateful you don't have a lantern on you?"

Aderyn reddened. "That was a fair fight."

"I know," Caprissa said. "I was joking. It's remarkable we should end up here, don't you think? After what was just a random encounter outside Dungeon Spiteful?"

"It was a real surprise," Owen said. "Congratulations on making the final ten."

"Thanks. You, too. You've improved dramatically since we last met." Caprissa shook her head admiringly. "You weren't bad then, but you're amazing now."

"Thank you." Owen clasped her outstretched hand. "What happened to the team you were with?"

Caprissa shrugged. "We split up after we reached level eight. Amicably, just a matter of different goals. I teamed up with a couple of spellslingers and a Deadeye for a few levels, and then I heard about the Glory Games and decided it might be fun to gain experience this way, plus test myself against the best."

As she spoke, Aderyn Assessed her, interested in her level, which turned out to be twelve. She'd been higher than their team back at Dungeon Spiteful, and now Aderyn and Owen had surpassed her. But that was still reasonably fast leveling.

"That's what brings us here, too." Owen sipped from his glass. "Aderyn and our friends are competing in the team Games, if you haven't heard. The Wildcats."

Caprissa nearly choked on her wine. "*You're* the Wildcats? I didn't put it together that that team's Warmaster was you. The Wildcats were all anyone could talk about yesterday evening. I got the impression that the new teams usually take a while to get their stride when it comes to competing against the experienced ones, and your performance excited a lot of attention. Was it a fluke?"

"I hope not," Aderyn said. "We worked hard for our victory."

"Sorry, no offense meant. It's just that about half the people consider you likely to be the next big winners, and the other half claimed you wouldn't be able to repeat that victory. And all of them thought I was crazy for suggesting a Warmaster might have any advantage in the dungeons." Caprissa smiled and set her half-empty glass on a passing tray. "Sorry. I don't drink much."

"What made you think my being a Warmaster matters?" Aderyn asked.

"Like I said, I didn't know that was you, but the skills you have impressed me. You saw the true door to Dungeon Spiteful and you made a clever attack against me. I figure there must be something to your class that makes a difference." Caprissa inclined her head in salute to Aderyn. "I'm heading out now. This place is too stuffy and I'm getting hot. But I hope I get to see you compete sometime." She saluted Owen, one Swordsworn to another, and made her way through the crowd to the exit.

CHAPTER TWENTY-ONE

"That was unexpected," Aderyn said.

"Now we really have to get to know everyone," Owen replied. "Though I didn't get the feeling that Caprissa meant to use our connection to benefit herself."

"Me neither." Gradin and Pace were gone, and Aderyn didn't see anyone she knew. "She's right about how warm it is in here. Maybe we should see if there's a back door, or a patio, or something."

"I keep seeing people go through that door to the left. Let's see what's there." Owen took Aderyn's arm again.

The door led to a short hallway that was blessedly cool with night breezes. The hallway was open to the outdoors at the far end, and Aderyn and Owen emerged into a small courtyard encircled by trellises bearing night-blooming jasmine vines. The small white flowers gleamed in the light of torches on long poles set up all around the courtyard, their hot scent obscuring the smell of jasmine. Beyond the courtyard, a path extended through a garden Aderyn could only see the beginnings of because it wasn't well lit. A man and a woman holding hands walked into the dim garden, close enough together that it was obvious they were looking for privacy. Aderyn couldn't imagine doing that at a stranger's house in the middle of a party.

Three people stood close together near the garden path, talking too low for Aderyn to hear, not that she wanted to eavesdrop. One of the women was older than her companions, with graying black hair cut short to frame her face and faint lines across her forehead and at the corners of her eyes. The younger woman and the man were muscled like Swordsworn and looked like twins, almost: both were the same height, both had brown hair of the same shade, both had blue eyes that almost matched. They even held themselves with the same alertness that said they anticipated an attack here in this fancy house at a social gathering.

The older woman glanced their way. Her gaze moved on for a few seconds before jerking back to Owen. Her lips paled as they tightened briefly. Then she approached Owen and Aderyn, trailing her younger companions. "The second-ranked challenger," she said. Her voice was creaky and sounded older than she looked, but she didn't sound like she meant an insult. "Owen. Your refusal was extremely polite. Who coached you?"

"Borrus advised me on how to respond," Owen said. "You must be Brisa."

Brisa inclined her head. "I can't hope to outbid Raynir, of course, and I hold no ill feelings toward you. It's business, after all. And this is one of the Wildcats. The Warmaster. I admired your team's performance, though in general I don't care for those competitions. So showy—that's a criticism of the system, not of you, dear." She patted Aderyn's hand in an extremely patronizing way.

Aderyn didn't jerk away. "I understand. Everyone's tastes are different."

"Naturally. Let me introduce my champions, Nator and Evalyn." She gestured at the pair. "They're not twins, not even related, but it's what everyone assumes."

"It's good to meet you," Owen said, extending a hand. Nator and Evalyn ignored it.

"You'll have quite a job ahead of you, defeating these two," Brisa said. "I hope you don't regret not taking my offer."

"I'd still have to defeat them, wouldn't I?" Owen sounded calm enough Aderyn was sure none of the three could tell he found them all distasteful. "You just wouldn't benefit. No offense meant."

Brisa's lips tightened again. "None taken." She again glanced at Aderyn, dismissing her. "Please excuse us."

When Brisa and her champions had disappeared into the house, Owen said, "I wasn't going to accept her regardless, but now I'm really grateful for Borrus's counsel."

As if his name was a spell for summoning, Aderyn heard her brother's laugh raised above the other voices. "He's here. Let's go talk to him."

They found Borrus with Kendria, Javath, and the Stalwart woman, Eirian, as well as a handful of well-dressed people Aderyn didn't recognize. Borrus looked good in his formal clothes, but Kendria was stunning in a red silk gown slit up the sides to reveal shapely, powerful legs. With her hair swept off her neck, the long white line of a scar extending from the base of her left ear down across her collarbone was visible, but the mark made her look dangerous and beautiful.

Borrus stood close beside her, not speaking, but laughing too loudly whenever Kendria told a joke. A lump of ice settled in Aderyn's stomach. She'd never seen her brother play up to anyone like that, and she certainly never would have expected he would make a fool of himself over a woman, even a woman like Kendria. She watched Javath every time Borrus laughed too loud, but Javath's attention was on his daughter and he didn't seem to notice Borrus's pandering behavior.

Eirian, unlike the other women, wasn't dressed in fine silks or satins; she wore a wool dress that was probably overwarm in this room but would feel comfortable on the way back to her inn. The dress suited her stocky frame, and she held herself as though she didn't feel at all awkward about not looking like everyone else. Aderyn decided she liked her.

Borrus saw Aderyn, and his face brightened. "You are here," he exclaimed. "I figured you would be visible in that blue, but I didn't see you anywhere." He clasped Owen's hand and then hugged Aderyn around her shoulders. "My sister Aderyn, everyone. Member of the Wildcats."

Most of the unfamiliar people wore the glassy-eyed look of someone Assessing someone else. "A Warmaster," an elderly man said. "How interesting."

"And what is it you bring to your team, young lady?" another man, this one even older than the first, said.

"Warmasters are tacticians," Aderyn said. "We perceive things others don't and pass that information to our teammates."

"Well, well," the first man said. "And such a pretty young lady, too. Wish I was fifty years younger!"

The others laughed. Kendria didn't. Neither did Eirian. Javath chuckled, but in an absent way that suggested he didn't actually find the comment funny. Aderyn smiled politely and wished Owen hadn't tensed up just then. She really didn't understand why men complimenting her bothered him, particularly men as old as these were.

Borrus glanced at Kendria and said, "And Owen is one of the challengers. He and Kendria are sure to give us a good show!"

"You know I don't like referring to it as a show, Borrus," Kendria said, not sharply, but still with enough force that Borrus blushed and subsided.

Aderyn, furious, drew in a breath to say something cutting, but Owen clamped down hard on her arm and said, "Isn't it, though, at least in part? If it was nothing but combat, there would be no point in fighting before the crowds."

"That's a good point," Eirian said. Her voice was sweet, though deep, and she spoke like someone who'd given the matter serious thought. "I suppose it depends on what you mean by a show. We don't arrange with our opponents who's going to win to make it more dramatic, for one."

"I believe in taking the Games seriously," Kendria said. "I hope you do too, Owen."

"I agree," Owen said. "I look forward to seeing you fight. Borrus says you're the best."

Kendria shrugged. "Every season is another chance to prove myself. I—"

"*Kendria!*"

The call came from a willowy man waving at the champion. Kendria said, "Excuse me, that's my sponsor," and walked to the man's side, the crowd parting before her like wheat before the harvester. Everyone in their little group except Borrus and Eirian trailed after her. Javath nodded politely to Aderyn before heading in a different direction.

"Balan," Borrus murmured. "I hate how he acts like he owns her."

"Well, *I* hate—" Aderyn began hotly.

"There sure are a lot of people here," Owen said, overriding her. "You'd have to speak loudly to be heard, wouldn't you?"

"Well, yes," Borrus said, sounding slightly confused. "Who have you met? And is Isold planning to sleep with all three of Master Warriner's daughters?"

Aderyn glanced to where Isold sat surrounded by three beautiful young women. "Not all at once," she guessed.

Borrus shook his head ruefully. "I wish I had half his personality. Sometimes I think my courtship isn't going very well."

"Borrus, she—" Aderyn heard how shrill her voice was and lowered it. "I don't think she respects you."

"Of course she does. She knows what I'm capable of and she sees me helping her father every day."

"Then why does she speak so dismissively to you?"

Borrus frowned. "She's forthright and she speaks her mind. That's not dismissive."

"All right, but she doesn't act at all as if she cares for you. How can you not see that?"

"Shut up, Aderyn, you don't know what you're talking about." Borrus's voice was cold. "I know what I'm doing. Don't think you can make decisions for me."

It felt like being slapped. "That's not—"

"Watch it, Borrus," Owen said, sounding every bit as cold as Borrus had. "Aderyn cares about you. She wants you to be happy. Don't repay that with hostility."

"If she wants me to be happy, she shouldn't talk that way about the woman I love." Borrus pushed past them and headed toward Kendria and Balan.

Owen clasped Aderyn's hand and, with a nod to Eirian, who was pretending she hadn't heard that, pulled her in the opposite direction. "He didn't mean it," Owen said.

"He's so blinded by what he thinks is love he doesn't see that she is never going to care for him." Aderyn swiped a hand across her eyes. "I hate seeing him diminished like that. Like he's a puppy instead of a grown man. An unwanted puppy, too."

"You want to leave?"

Aderyn looked around. "Can we? I don't know where Livia and Weston went."

"Let's find them and see how they feel. It's not like we can't all find our way back to the inn. Besides, who knows where Isold's sleeping tonight?"

They hadn't taken four steps before a deep voice stopped them. "Owen. You've done well."

"Thank you, Javath," Owen said.

Javath held a wine glass whose delicacy seemed out of place between his big Stalwart's fingers. "So, you nearly swept the trials. Congratulations. Any thoughts on why you failed?"

Aderyn stiffened in outrage, but Owen didn't react. "The adjudicator's call is final."

"So you're claiming it was bad luck."

"I'm not claiming anything. I fought my best, and it wasn't enough. Now, if you'll excuse us..."

Javath didn't move. "A word of advice. Don't expect to beat Kendria."

Owen raised his eyebrows. "You want me to sabotage myself before we've even clashed?"

"Just a friendly comment. Kendria is the best, and I don't want someone as good as you blaming yourself for that failure, too." He raised his glass to Owen and drank.

"Thank you for the advice," Owen said. "Forgive me if I decide not to take it."

Javath shrugged. "That's up to you."

Owen's hand closed painfully tightly on Aderyn's arm. He tugged her away from Javath, muttering, "Sorry. He—"

"I understand. He made me angry, too," Aderyn said. "Let's see about leaving."

They found Isold still surrounded by beautiful women on a sofa beneath one of the big ceiling lights. He had the look of someone who'd drunk just enough wine to be relaxed. "Ah, my friends," he said. "Enjoying yourselves?"

"Very much so, yes/*Do you want us to leave without you?*" Aderyn said with **[Secret Message]**. She didn't want to make Isold feel obligated to decide one way or the other because they had an audience.

Isold nodded in acceptance of her second meaning. "So am I. In fact, I've accepted an offer to perform here tonight. Don't feel you should wait on me." His eyes widened, and he said in a lower voice, "'Ware Jael, coming up behind you."

Owen stiffened. Aderyn, torn between pretending the woman wasn't in the room and wishing to act on Isold's warning, ended up saying, "I hope your performance goes well, and Owen and I were just leaving—"

"Not without a few words with me, surely," Jael said. In her black satin dress that bared one shoulder, with a bracelet of polished onyx stones clasped around her wrist, she looked elegant and beautiful and made Aderyn in her suddenly awkward blue tunic and rough black shirt and trousers feel gawky and hideous.

"I'm not sure what we have to say to each other," Owen said. "Excuse us."

"How about 'Stop lying about me,' eh?" Jael's tone was light, but her eyes were hard and cold.

"I haven't said anything about you, lies or truth," Owen replied.

Jael stepped closer and lowered her voice. "You've been telling people lies about what happened during our fight. You need to give up on trying to blacken my name. What matters is who won. That was me. You're just making yourself look jealous and bitter."

Owen raised both eyebrows. "The adjudicator's call is final. That's the extent of what I've said. It's not my fault other people saw what really happened. And I disagree with you. It doesn't matter who won. It matters who's going to win next. Don't think you'll get away with that stunt twice."

Jael's jaw hardened. "I don't have to—"

"*Jael!*"

Aderyn, astonished, heard Balan's voice calling Jael's name. Jael's expression smoothed into a smile. "That's right," she said. "The Chief Councilor is my sponsor. Not something you could achieve, is it, Owen?" She smoothly walked away, but stopped after a few paces and said over her shoulder, "And I don't need a stunt to beat you."

"That's not what those rumors say," Owen retorted.

Jael's smile wavered. Then she continued toward Balan and Kendria, her gait smooth and rippling like a snake.

"All right," Owen said quietly. "I need to get out of here. I've exhausted my supply of friendly conversation."

"I'll tell Weston and Livia," Isold said. "Go."

Outside, waiting for Raynir's pumpkin carriage to take them back to the lift, Aderyn breathed in the cold air. Owen had sounded more like himself talking to Jael, not angry over men who approached Aderyn in perfect innocence. Her earlier thoughts about asking him to marry her seemed stupid now. She certainly couldn't propose while he might think she'd done it to deflect his anger.

Owen said, "I don't hate a lot of people, but I hate Jael."

Aderyn suppressed her discouragement and smiled. "Me too. Did you see how she shook her ass when she walked away? She wanted you to see what you were missing."

Owen laughed bitterly. "Can't miss what you never wanted. Let's go back and get out of these clothes."

"Mmm. And warm each other up. It's so cold tonight."

Owen wrapped his arms around her. "What I saw," he murmured in her ear, "was how much more beautiful you are than Jael, even in your blue potato sack."

Aderyn gasped. "You said it fit me well!"

"That was so you'd feel confident. Now I'm telling you otherwise so you'll let me take it off you."

Aderyn tried to summon more outrage, but with his warm breath tickling her ear, all she could come up with was, "You're awfully sure of yourself. I might need more convincing."

"Challenge accepted," Owen replied.

CHAPTER TWENTY-TWO

When the Wildcats entered the big room beneath the arena the following morning, Seonn wasn't there. The Indomitables in their green tunics and the Fearsome Five in their yellow ones crowded around a sheet of paper nailed to the wall. They turned away as Aderyn and her friends approached. "Good luck today," Martis was saying to the Fearsome Five's captain, Nandia. "You'll need it."

"No need for luck when we have skill," Nandia said with a grin. "Or did you hope we'd go easy on you this time?"

"Rule number one: make it look good," Martis said in a fair approximation of Seonn's blustering voice, and they both laughed.

"Aderyn, look at this," Weston said.

Aderyn turned her attention from the two team captains to the paper—except it wasn't regular paper, it was thick and creamy with a rough texture, the sort of thing Aderyn would have thought too expensive for casual use. It was hooked over the nails by two metal-reinforced holes rather than being nailed through. On it were written, in beautiful but blunt handwriting, a few short lines:

Morning bout 1: Scrappers v. Wildcats

Morning bout 2: Indomitables v. Fearsome Five
Afternoon bout 1: Vagabonds v. Trailblazers
Afternoon bout 2: Hooligans v. Ruffians

"Guess we don't have to sit around being nervous," Weston said. His grin clearly showed he wasn't the least bit nervous.

"So, do we wait here for instructions, or what?" Livia asked.

Another team entered the room, talking loudly and laughing as they pulled golden-brown tunics over their heads and belted them snugly. Jesper caught Aderyn's eye and joined her at the schedule paper. "Looks like we won't face each other today," he said. "You get the unenviable task of warming up the crowd."

"Isn't that what we all do, to get people excited for the solo combats?" Aderyn asked.

"Yes, but the first bout of the day is the hardest in that respect. You get people coming in late, and some spectators are still waking up—"

"I can relate to that," Livia said. She was alert, but it had taken a lot of coffee to get her that way.

"So between that and the fact that nobody's excited yet, the first teams don't get as much attention. But don't worry about it. You won't hear the response of the crowd through the noise suppression field, so just do your best to win and make it look good. The good news is you aren't likely to compete first again, not for a while anyway." Jesper clapped Aderyn on the shoulder in a friendly way. "Wait here for Seonn. He'll give you and the Scrappers your instructions."

"And have fun!" one of the other Hooligans said. "The crowd can sense it when you're having a good time."

Jesper leaned in closer to Aderyn. "Between us," he said in a low voice, "the Scrappers take things too seriously. If you end up going head to head, keep that in mind." With that, he and his team exited the room through the side door that led to the back way to the covert.

"That's ominous," Weston said.

Aderyn didn't bother exclaiming at how he'd heard that. Weston's Moonlighter's hearing was acute. "I wish I knew what kinds of dungeons were possible."

"At least they give instructions instead of assuming we'll know the rules," Livia said.

They moved away from the schedule so the Vagabonds in their green tunics could get a look at it. The room was full now of men and women passing through the back door, talking quietly and occasionally laughing. None of them acknowledged Aderyn's team, which made her feel uncomfortable, like they were invisible—or worse, outcasts.

Then a group of four men and two women in orange tunics entered. The Scrappers' tunics looked even less elegant than the Wildcats' potato sacks, as Aderyn couldn't help but think of them now, and the team was perfectly silent even when they looked at the schedule. Aderyn's discomfort increased. They all looked so competent, so ready for a contest—

Then one of the men glanced at her, his gaze flicking from her head to her feet with a total lack of interest. Suddenly Aderyn's insecurity vanished like water on a hot stove top, sizzling into irritation. How dare he think she was nothing? They'd won their first match, and, as she recalled, the Scrappers hadn't. He was arrogant and snobbish, and she and her friends were going to beat their team no matter what the Arena Master threw at them.

"Scrappers! Wildcats! Listen up!"

Aderyn turned with the others to face Seonn, who was trailed by Lorus today. Seonn looked cranky, but Aderyn thought he always looked cranky in the morning. Maybe he needed a coffee habit like Livia.

"Your dungeon for this match is Pass the Stick, environmental challenge. As always, all four team members must run one leg each of the relay, and you choose who runs which one. You'll have one minute before the second horn blows to survey the course and call the number of your chosen leg. No leaving your starting point to reach your teammate who's bringing you the stick. There's also no interfering with members of the other team. If you do, you'll incur a five-second penalty. Getting wet also means a five-second penalty. No *fly* or *transport* allowed. Any questions?"

"What about *earth glide*?" Livia asked.

Seonn surveyed her. "How fast?"

"At my level, faster than a running man but not faster than a horse."

"Hmmm." Seonn chewed his lip in thought. "I'll allow it."

One of the Scrappers made a noise of protest. Seonn glared at him, and he shut up. Seonn then turned his glare on Aderyn. "I have your word you won't use that skill of yours?"

"I said I wouldn't," Aderyn replied, irritated at having her honor questioned.

"Fair enough. Wildcats on the north, Scrappers on the south. Scrappers, choose who won't be running. You've got five minutes before the horn sounds. Make it a good show." Seonn headed for the tunnel, followed by Lorus.

"You'd better not cheat," the shorter of the women told Aderyn. "The crowd hates a cheat."

"I don't cheat," Aderyn retorted, "and you'd better take your own advice."

"We don't have magic items," another Scrapper protested. "That would be against the rules."

"Yes," the woman said with a nasty smile. "Just our skills."

"Ignore them, Aderyn," Weston said, drawing her away to the far side of the room. In a low voice, he said, "Did you see if they have skills they can use against us?"

Aderyn hadn't Assessed the opposition yet, and now she hesitated. "What if that's a cheat as well? Knowing what skills they have?" She almost put a hand on the <**Purse of Great Capacity**>

concealed beneath her tunic. Seonn probably wouldn't care that she didn't intend to use it or any of its contents, but she was superstitious about it vanishing if she left it behind.

"I say use it," Livia said. "They haven't earned any consideration."

"Aderyn has a good point," Isold said. "If Assessing a dungeon gives us an unfair advantage, so might knowing their skills, given that only a Warmaster can perceive them."

"But we aren't going head to head against them, remember?" Weston glanced over his shoulder, but the Scrappers were in their own huddle and not paying them any attention. "So it's not an unfair advantage, not to mention Aderyn might discover their skills at any time outside the match. I think it has to be up to her."

Aderyn nodded. "Let's see who we're up against first."

Two of the Scrappers, both men, had left the huddle and were on their way to the back door to the covert. Aderyn ignored them and Level Assessed the other four, starting with the obnoxious woman.

Name: Kaida
Class: Spellcrafter
Level: 14
Name: Jorek
Class: Moonlighter
Level: 13
Name: Ravin
Class: Stalwart
Level: 14
Name: Teena
Class: Lightfingers
Level: 13

She relayed the information to her team, saying, "Two stealthy classes. They must want to optimize for speed and trickery over these obstacles."

"But, a Spellcrafter?" Weston said. "What good is that? She can't use anything she's created, and there'd be no time for her to enchant anything in the dungeon to help her."

Aderyn nodded. "I think I need a closer look."

She Assessed Kaida again, this time with Skill Assess.

Name: Kaida

Class: Spellcrafter

Level: 14

Class Skills: **Knowledge: Magic (14); Imbue Common Item (14); Scribe Scroll, Basic (6); Create Common Item (12); Analyze Enchantment (12); Imbue Weapon/Armor, Lesser (10); Disenchant 1 (13); Imbue Uncommon Item (10); Create Uncommon Item (10); Imbue Weapon/Armor, Standard (6); Disenchant 2 (10); Basic Map Access (3); Scribe Scroll, Intermediate (4); Imbue Rare Item (4); Create Rare Item (2); Disenchant 3 (2); Imbue Weapon/Armor, Greater (0)**

Skill Alert: **Analyze Enchantment, Disenchant 1**

Disenchant? She didn't know it and couldn't guess what it was, so she Assessed it as well.

[Disenchant 1]: Removes one or more magic effects from an enchanted object. Higher ranks in this skill increase the number of effects that can be removed.

[Disenchant 2]: Allows the skill to affect one person under an enchantment effect. Higher ranks in this skill increase the number of effects that can be removed.

[Disenchant 3]: Allows the skill to affect multiple people under a single enchantment effect. Higher ranks in this skill increase the number of effects that can be removed.

"I get it," Aderyn said. "It's [**Disenchant 1**]. If there are magic effects on the terrain, that skill will neutralize them. I think. [**Improved Assess 2**] says 'objects,' but parts of a terrain might qualify. And I'm certain Kaida at least believes it."

"If she's done it before, and Seonn didn't tell her not to, it must be legitimate," Weston said. "But that means we're free to use our other skills as well."

The horn blasted, startling them all. "That's it," Weston said. "Let's give it our best shot."

"And make those Scrappers eat their words," Livia said.

Aderyn wasn't sure, but when she and her friends ran out of the tunnel onto the arena floor, she thought the crowd wasn't as excited as it had been the last time. Jesper was right, though he hadn't said how discouraging it was to hear such a lackluster response to their entry. She told herself to ignore it. So what if there weren't many people there yet, and they weren't enthusiastic? She was there to beat the Scrappers and earn experience and money. And have fun. What was it Jesper had said about great competition, that testing yourself against a worthy opponent made it more exciting? She wasn't sure she considered the Scrappers a worthy opponent, but at the very least she could push herself to her limit.

Weston led the way to the north side of the shimmering veil, where this time they found a square ten feet on a side marked out on the hard earth. "Seonn didn't mention this," he said, gingerly putting a foot inside the outline.

"He probably forgot we don't know everything about the Games," Livia said. She stepped all the way inside. "Guess this is the starting point. I wonder—"

Her voice cut off as Aderyn, who'd lagged behind Isold and Weston in entering, stepped over the outline. Immediately, the walls of a cage rose up around them, stopping at waist height. The cage shuddered, making them all grab the rail to stay standing, and then they were being lifted into the air, higher and higher until they were just below the top of the obscuring barrier. Now they were level with the second tier of seats.

Livia turned around and waved at the people sitting there. They waved back, more enthusiastically than the cheering had been. "See? They just need encouragement."

The veil was close enough to touch, though Aderyn didn't try to. "Pay attention, Livia, the horn could blow at any moment," she said.

Livia shrugged. "There's no point in being alert too soon," she said, but she turned back around. Aderyn gripped the rail tightly. Her heart was thudding painfully, and her skin felt tight and tingling in anticipation. She wished she'd thought to see where Owen was, or rather where Raynir's box was, but it wasn't as if knowing that would make things easier.

Two short blasts of the horn startled Aderyn into letting go of the rail. "Goooooood morning, friends!" the announcer boomed. "Let's start things off with a bang, shall we? First off today we have... *the Scrappers!* Let me hear you say it!"

Cheers burst out, definitely not as enthusiastically as before. Aderyn couldn't see through the shifting veil, but she could picture the Scrappers waving to the crowd.

"And here to give them a good match are... *the Wildcats!*"

The noise of the crowd grew perceptibly, and Aderyn could hear shouts of *"Wildcats!"* here and there. The sound boosted her spirits. All right, it didn't matter whether the crowd loved them, and they'd do their best regardless—no, who was she kidding? It mattered *tremendously* that people were cheering them on. Aderyn waved to the crowd, and imagined the noise increased again.

"Today's dungeon is Pass the Stick!" the announcer cried. "Let's see which of these valiant competitors can make it across the finish line first. Good luck to both of you!"

With that, the horn blew one long, loud blast, and the shimmering veil dropped as if it was a real curtain. Aderyn gasped. Below them were the ruins of an ancient city, or part of one. Broken walls and upended paving stones gave the landscape an irregular, patchwork appearance. Four brightly glowing discs numbered 1 through 4 lay evenly spaced from one end of the long dungeon to another, at different levels of the destroyed city. Another set of identical discs lay along the southern side of the dungeon.

Aderyn had to resist the urge to Assess the city, telling herself **[Improved Assess 2]** didn't work on terrain anyway. "Number one at the left," she said. "That's a climbing section."

"Two is a maze," Weston said. "Three—"

They all watched for a few seconds as pillars of stone shot up and down at random across a vast plain. "Three is for Aderyn," Weston said, sounding amused. "And four... there's the pond Seonn alluded to that we can't fall into." The pond was dotted with islets ranging in size from three feet across to someone's bare foot.

"I'll climb," Isold said. "Aderyn takes the third position. Weston runs the maze?"

"I'll take the maze," Livia said. "*Earth glide* won't help, but I have another idea. And Weston is more agile, anyway."

"Then—let's go!" Aderyn shouted, "Three!"

As the others called out their numbers, an invisible fist closed around Aderyn, lifting her off the platform and carrying her swiftly over the race course to deposit her on the glowing disc. The moment her foot touched it, the glow dimmed and went out. The noise of the crowd had vanished, and all she could hear was an eerie wind blowing through the ruins, whistling and howling by turns.

The horn sounded, and the race was on.

CHAPTER TWENTY-THREE

Aderyn immediately searched for Isold but couldn't see him. She was perched near the top of one of the buildings, at one side of a stone courtyard. The building's roof was long gone, and the sky was a brilliant blue, unhindered by the tiers of the arena, which had also vanished. The courtyard sloped visibly downward, but the pillars that shot up and down at random were perfectly vertical, not perpendicular to the sloping ground. She knew Weston was on the far side somewhere, but she couldn't see him either.

Poised to run, across the courtyard from her, was Ravin the Stalwart. He ignored her and everything around him except the pillars. She suspected he was trying to memorize the nonexistent pattern. Well, good luck to him.

She looked eastward, away from the pillars and across the maze. It, too, wasn't completely horizontal; it rose in terraced steps from a lower level of the city to an exit near where Aderyn stood. At the bottom of the maze, Livia had her back to Aderyn and was shielding her eyes against the sun, watching something. Aderyn hoped Isold was giving the spectators a good show. Too bad she couldn't see it.

Seconds passed, so slowly Aderyn was sure they had been minutes. She wished she had Livia's pocket watch, since Livia wasn't looking at it. Of course Livia could no doubt see Isold, which would mean she was even tenser than Aderyn, watching him make his way up walls with increasingly hard-to-find handholds and across mostly fallen roofs. Aderyn tried to recall what she'd seen of the first section, but all she could remember was the final wall, smooth and slick and with the barest of gaps between stones for climbing. No point worrying now that the race had started. Isold would make it.

Just as she thought this, Isold lunged over the top of the wall near where Livia stood and stumbled forward, thrusting out the blue-painted stick. Livia grabbed it and jogged to the maze entrance—the closest one; there were five that Aderyn could see.

From her position, Aderyn had a clear view of the maze. It was a true maze, not one with a detectable pattern, with dead ends and switchbacks, and Aderyn's heart sank. Livia didn't have nearly the experience with solving puzzles that Weston or Isold had.

Movement caught her eye, off to the side where Teena the Lightfingers had just scrambled over the edge of the wall and handed off her orange stick to her teammate Jorek. The Moonlighter tucked the stick into his belt and tried to haul himself up onto the maze wall. Aderyn sucked in an outraged breath. Walking over the top had to be against the rules!

But Jorek almost immediately dropped back down, dusting off his gloved hands, and headed for the nearest maze entrance. Aderyn took a better look at the tops of the walls, which glinted in the sunlight. She'd assumed it was mica reflecting the sun that made them glitter, but a closer look revealed they were covered in large shards of broken glass. Aderyn grinned. So much for that strategy.

When she looked back at Livia, Livia was gone.

Startled, Aderyn surveyed the maze and discovered Livia was nowhere near her original spot—in fact, she was in a passage she couldn't have reached from where she'd been. Puzzled, Aderyn leaned closer to look down the slope.

Livia had stopped and was facing one of the uphill walls, a tall one that bordered the next terrace of the maze. She placed both palms against the wall and drew them apart like parting a curtain.

And the stones of the wall shifted to let her pass.

Aderyn let out a whoop of excitement that caught Ravin's attention. He scowled at her, but said nothing. Aderyn thought about making a rude gesture she'd learned from Owen, but it didn't mean anything in her world and it would be wasted on the Stalwart.

Slowly, Livia made her way straight uphill, *passwall* opening walls for her and closing them after she'd gone by. She was making headway, but Jorek was fast, and worse, he was good at identifying false trails. Aderyn had to stop watching him, his progress was making her so tense. Instead she kept her eyes on Livia until she was high enough on the slope that Aderyn couldn't see past the walls.

Just as she realized she was hearing stone grate on stone, the wall in front of her parted, and Livia burst through. She looked exhausted, but she hurried to where Aderyn stood, the stick in her outthrust hand. Aderyn snatched it and ran.

She was aware peripherally of Ravin making his steady way through the pillars just ahead of her, and then **[See It Coming]** took over. The ghostly images of pillars filled her vision, and she strode forward, dodging, sidling past, pausing for a pillar to shoot up in front of her. Keeping her balance while moving downhill was the hard part, as her growing momentum carried her farther along the sloping pavement than she at first expected. She saw a pillar shoot out of the ground just half a second before she stopped her slide, then paused for the briefest moment to regain her balance. Hoping that moment wouldn't cost them the race, she pushed herself harder.

By the time she was halfway across the courtyard, she'd regained her confidence. With every step, she sped up until she was running across the courtyard, her hair lifting as the pillars sent up stone-smelling gusts of air.

She dodged one final pillar and skidded to a halt in front of Weston, slapping the stick into his palm and then crouching to catch her breath. When she felt less dizzy, she watched Weston descend the slope toward the pool. When he'd almost reached it, Kaida emerged from the courtyard, stick in hand, and raced down the slope after Weston.

Weston stood at the bank of the pool, not moving. Aderyn, her nerves keyed to the breaking point, stuffed a fist into her mouth to keep herself from shrieking at Weston and distracting him. Then she did let out a little shriek as someone touched her shoulder. Isold and Livia stood behind her. "What in thunder is he doing?" Livia muttered. "That Kaida is almost there."

"I see it," Isold said. "The islets are moving. Putting weight on them submerges them, more deeply the smaller they are."

Aderyn focused on the pond rather than on Weston. "And the easiest path is along the smallest islets. Weston's good, but he's big."

Weston put a foot on the nearest mound of earth, which bobbed slightly but didn't submerge. Cautiously, he began making his way across the field of tiny islands, never stopping, but not moving very fast.

Livia said, "Well, crap. *That's* what [Disenchant 1] is for." She gestured at Kaida, who stood at the edge of the pond and gestured at the nearest floating islet. It shivered like a horse shaking off a fly and then sank about an inch lower in the water. When Kaida stepped on it, it didn't bob or shift at all.

"She will have to use the skill on each islet in her path," Isold said. "She can't neutralize the entire pond at once. That will slow her down."

"But slower than Weston?" Aderyn said.

They stood close together, tense and alert, watching the snail's-pace race. Aderyn couldn't help picturing how this looked from the outside, whether the crowds were bored because the ending was so slow. Weston was taking larger leaps now, skipping the tiny islets altogether, but the longer the leap, the more time he needed to recover his balance. Aderyn realized she was gripping the edge of her tunic and wrinkling it with her sweaty palms.

Weston was almost at the edge of the pond. Ahead, up a short rise, stood the glass vase the final runner had to drop the stick into. Just ten more steps. Eight. Kaida was gaining on Weston, taking a straight route where he had to veer around unstable ground.

Weston reached the second to last islet. He didn't seem aware of Kaida, coming up behind him, but then he stopped and backed up. In the next instant, he ran across the mound of earth and leaped, bypassing the final islet and hitting the ground well beyond the edge of the water. He staggered briefly, got his feet under him, and ran the last few steps, dropping the stick into the vase before Kaida touched solid ground.

Sound rushed back into the world, the cries of thousands of people cheering and screaming "*Wildcats!*" The dungeon walls sank into the ground, and as the pond dissolved into the arena floor, a system message appeared.

Congratulations! You have defeated [Pass the Stick terrain variation 7].
You have earned [10,000 XP] plus a bonus of [2000 XP]

Weston bounded to join them and swept all three into his powerful embrace. "See? They love us," he said, releasing them. "Everybody wave!"

Aderyn waved with both hands, secretly relieved that she could dry her sweaty palms without anyone realizing that was what she was doing. She gradually became aware that at least one section of the crowd was shouting the same thing, one word: "*Swift! Swift! Swift!*"

"That's you," Livia said, elbowing her.

"Me?"

"You obviously don't appreciate what [See It Coming] looks like from the outside." Livia grabbed Aderyn around the waist, and with a lurch, the earth around them rose just like the stone pillars until they were level with the first tier of seats. The entire crowd in that section surged forward, waving like mad or jumping up and down with excitement. Aderyn, taken aback, managed to smile and keep waving until Livia brought them back to earth.

With the sound of the announcer's voice proclaiming the next match ringing in her ears, she ran with her friends to the covert stairs and fell into her seat. All around them, the other teams were talking and laughing, but when the Wildcats appeared, the talk hushed. Aderyn braced herself for criticism again and possibly accusations of cheating. Then Jesper said, "That was incredible. I don't think that dungeon has ever been so exciting. Nice work, both teams."

Aderyn realized the Scrappers had followed them up the stairs. They didn't seem happy. "We lost," Kaida said. "That's not good work."

"Sure it was. It was a close race, and it looked good," Kathra of the Rowdy Ruffians said. "That's what matters."

"Experience and money are what matter," Jorek said, like he was speaking to a stupid child. "Who cares what the audience thinks?"

In the silence that fell, the horn gave a long blast, announcing the competitors for the next dungeon. Kathra's face reddened, and a muscle jumped in her cheek like she was holding back an angry retort. Finally, she said, "You want to hold that opinion, that's your business. But it's just going to make you miserable."

"We wouldn't have lost if they hadn't cheated," Kaida said. "Who did you buy the pattern from?"

Aderyn, startled at how Kaida had gotten right up in her face, said, "What are you talking about? What pattern?"

"Spare me," Kaida said. "You bought the pattern of the moving pillars off someone so you could make yourself look good. Look. I don't care. Seriously, you want to win by cheating—"

"I didn't cheat," Aderyn retorted. "And even someone as stupid as you should have seen those pillars moved at random. There's no pattern for anyone to buy. Ask your teammate."

Everyone stared at Ravin, whose enormous Stalwart bulk seemed to curl in on itself. "I didn't see a pattern," he mumbled.

"Shut up. Just because you didn't see it doesn't mean she didn't cheat. Nobody moves like that naturally."

Aderyn wanted to laugh at how her fears had come true in such a ludicrous way. "You," she began, shook her head, and said instead, "Warmaster skills are a total unknown, I agree. But if it's fair for you to use **[Disenchant 1]** to stop the islets from moving, it's fair for me to use **[See It Coming]** to avoid the pillars. And it was a fair run."

Kaida glared at Aderyn. Then she stomped down the back stairs, trailed belatedly by her team.

A hand fell on Aderyn's shoulder. "Ignore her," Jesper said. "She's always bitter when she loses, which is often because she's a terrible team captain. We're all hoping they'll pack it in after this season."

"That was pretty unbelievable, though," Kathra said. "Got any other secret skills we should know about?"

"You'll find out as soon as I use them against you," Aderyn said, making the others laugh.

CHAPTER TWENTY-FOUR

This time, when the second dungeon match was over, Aderyn and her friends joined the other teams at a nearby tavern for drinks and lunch. The Scrappers didn't show up, which was fine by Aderyn. She ate, and had a couple of beers, and laughed and joked and felt cheerful all over again. She even got used to the others calling her "the Swift." "You know, like the bird," one of the Vagabonds said. He'd drunk more than she had and was so relaxed he was almost a puddle. "Swifter than lightning."

"Is that normal? Being given a nickname?" Aderyn asked.

She'd addressed the Vagabond, but it was Jesper who answered. "Sometimes. Usually when a player has a unique trait or tactic they use often. Also if their name is too awkward to chant easily. Syssela gets called Red because of her hair and because she's a Flamecrafter." He nodded at the redhead in a yellow tunic. "And I heard some people talking about 'Livia Stonefist.' That and Swift are pretty good as nicknames go."

"Swift like the bird," the Vagabond said. "I think I drank too much. Are we competing next?"

"You are, and someday you won't recover fast enough," Jesper said in amusement.

The Vagabond sat up and patted himself down. "Ah." He took a vial shaped like a glass corkscrew that was filled with a nauseatingly green liquid. It shimmered in the tavern's low light with an effect that made Aderyn feel a familiar queasiness. Her mother made that stuff by the gallon, because antitoxins worked just as well on alcohol as they did on more deadly poisons. The Vagabond uncorked the vial and drank down the contents with a shudder. When he opened his eyes, they were not at all clouded by the ale he'd been consuming so rapidly.

"I'm heading back now," he said, rising from his chair and gesturing to his teammates. "Good luck to you, Swift, and let's hope we don't meet any time soon. I have a feeling you'd mop the floor with us."

When he was gone, Jesper said, "Don't let it go to your head."

"I won't. I wouldn't." Aderyn waved away the bartender's offer of another mug of beer. "I still feel like it's luck that's gotten us this far."

"Don't start thinking like that, either." Jesper downed the last of his drink and stood. "Try to find balance—do your best, but don't anticipate winning or losing."

"Then I hope we face you eventually," Aderyn said, "because it will be a fantastic fight."

Jesper smiled. "I agree."

They all returned to the covert for the afternoon's games. This time, Aderyn realized the teams didn't cheer on their fellow competitors, and they didn't boo them, either. Instead, when the teams finished their dungeon and returned to the covert, there were general congratulations and some friendly ribbing, as well as tips on future performances. She found she liked the camaraderie even better than she enjoyed the applause of the crowd.

The Hooligans and the Rowdy Ruffians were the final match

before the afternoon combats. Aderyn watched Jesper carefully, learning his tactics. It was hard to know from just two matches what kind of captain he was, or even what kind of player he was. She also wasn't sure yet how much of his tactics were situational. Today's final dungeon was Loot the Room, and maybe he planned differently for other dungeons. But she made note of how efficiently he divided their team, sending one person to scout out the Ruffians while the others searched for rings, then using the team's Spiritsmith's concoctions to render the Ruffians temporarily unconscious while he retrieved his team's rings from the Ruffians' stash.

She also found it curious that he hadn't done that trick before the Ruffians deposited their rings into their chest. He could have stolen and hidden the enemy's rings and given himself an advantage. But he hadn't. That might be a matter of not making it look too easy, or it could be because he didn't think of it in time. Aderyn felt certain that wasn't the answer.

For fun, she Assessed the dungeon to see how many rings were hidden. Fifty-two this time. There was a hazy image above the dungeon that showed a red circle and a golden-brown circle, on which were displayed the number of rings each team had found. Red had forty-four, and brown had fifty. In between the two circles was a clock with hands ticking off the seconds. One minute and fifty-four seconds to go. Both teams were actively searching now, but Aderyn had a feeling this was going to be the final count.

When the final horn blew one minute and fifty-five seconds later, the count hadn't changed. The cheering for the Hooligans was earsplitting, and Aderyn couldn't help thinking about whether the Wildcats might eventually get that kind of reaction.

She congratulated Jesper and was sympathetic to Kathra, but when Kathra asked if she was coming to celebrate today's games, she said, "Our team leader is fighting this afternoon."

"Oh, yes, Owen, right?" Kathra grinned. "He's good-looking as well as being a great fighter, but you already know that, don't you?"

Aderyn wasn't sure why she blushed, given that her relationship with Owen was no secret, but she smiled and said, "He's *much* more than good-looking."

Kathra laughed. "Hope he's confident, because I anticipate a lot of men are going to start sending their regards your way." She clapped Aderyn on the shoulder and drew her teammates along after her, out of the covert.

Aderyn changed seats to Jesper's front-row one and leaned forward on the rail. She didn't know much about courtship, because she hadn't cared about romance before meeting Owen, and the few young men in Far Haven who'd approached her hadn't been serious. She'd easily deflected their advances without anyone's feelings being hurt. Now, though, she was older and, she admitted, more approachable, and while she wasn't sure if Finion's Gate had its own etiquette for rejecting men who paid her their compliments by way of song or poem or gift, she was confident in her ability to be kind to those men even as she turned them down.

She remembered now that Owen had been surprised that men might approach Aderyn if they knew she was attached to someone. That struck her as odd, that in Owen's world women weren't free to accept some man's romantic overtures in the spirit they were given. Aderyn knew—all right, mostly she knew from reading romantic stories, but even so, she knew men honored women they found attractive through compliments and gifts, and how else was a woman supposed to know a man was interested if not for a declaration of love? And how cruel to callously spurn someone just because you were in love with someone else!

At any rate, *she* understood the intent, and she'd explain it to Owen. He was good about learning the ways in which their worlds differed, and he'd probably find it interesting once he realized those men weren't a threat to him. And then maybe she could gather her courage for a proposal. Something bold and public that would show him how she wanted the world to know she loved him. Something original, not anything she'd read in a book.

Weston joined her at the rail, though he stood rather than sitting. Aderyn looked up at him. "Did you place another bet?"

Weston shrugged. "I did. Word's gotten around. I couldn't get good odds." He blew out his breath in frustration. "Too bad we couldn't fix any of these matches."

"Don't say that, even joking," Livia warned. "These people have no sense of humor where wagering on the Games is concerned. I said something at that party about whether one of these challengers might take a fall, and you'd think I'd suggested something lewd about their mothers."

"True. I've never seen such serious bettors in all my life. You'd think they were wagering on the outcome of a world-altering quest." Weston withdrew a purse from his belt and tossed it a few times. "Our winnings from the quest, speaking of things that aren't actually world-altering. You didn't bring the <**Purse of Great Capacity**>, did you?"

"I did, but I don't want anyone to know. I'm afraid they'd consider it a cheat, given how many things I could potentially smuggle into the dungeon." Aderyn caught the little bag Weston tossed at her and surreptitiously slipped it inside the <**Purse of Great Capacity**>. She sat up as the horn blew. "Does anyone know who's fighting first?"

"I was thinking it was too bad we missed the first matches," Isold said. "Pace and Gradin both fought this morning."

"Sorry about the delay, folks!" the announcer boomed. "Let's give a rousing Glory Games welcome to the first fighters of this afternoon! It's a couple of champions, so this should be a stunner—welcome to Raewyn the Swifthands and Quillon the Lone Wolf!"

Cheers erupted all around as Raewyn entered the arena, side by side with a man shorter and thinner than she. The man was armored with a hardened leather cuirass and vambraces, but Raewyn wore only a shirt fitted snugly to her arms and torso and a pair of trousers of a similarly lightweight fabric, and in contrast to the man's heavy boots, Raewyn's shoes were soft and flexible.

The man's sword drew Aderyn's notice immediately. It was long and broad, with a hilt big enough for a two-handed grip, and the man —Quillon—had a hand on the hilt, pushing down so the tip of the scabbarded blade wouldn't drag on the ground.

"Well," Livia said, sounding amused. "I can't tell what he's compensating for. There are so many options."

"I wonder if his name influenced his choice of weapon at all," said Aderyn. "Quillons are those short lengths of metal that make up a sword's crossguard."

"Maybe, but that sword is bigger than he is," Livia replied.

"He's got to be stronger than he looks," Weston said. "Anyone who's just a poser wouldn't have made it into the ranks of the champions."

"Quillon is ranked ninth, and Raewyn is eighth," Isold said. "Though I understand Raewyn was ranked higher last season, and I would not underestimate her."

Raewyn, by contrast, didn't look like she was armed at all. Then she turned to salute the crowd, and Aderyn saw she had a couple of sticks tucked under one arm. They looked like they were almost two feet long, and each had a short handle attached about two-thirds of the way down perpendicular to the main stick. Aderyn couldn't imagine how they could possibly defend against Quillon's absurdly huge sword.

Two red-suited adjudicators followed the champions at a respectful distance and took up positions on either side as Raewyn and Quillon stopped near the center of the arena. Quillon drew his sword and saluted Raewyn before taking a stance, waiting for the signal to begin. Raewyn bowed to Quillon and gripped the handles of her shortstaffs, but instead of aiming the lengths of wood at Quillon, she held the weapons so the shafts fit along her forearms. Now Aderyn was truly confused.

"How can she—" she began.

The blast of the horn signaled the start of the match, cutting her off. Quillon immediately went on the attack, leaping forward and swinging his sword like it weighed nothing. Raewyn brought up both arms and caught the blow. Aderyn winced. That should have broken her arms. But Raewyn shoved Quillon back with no sign of pain. She pressed her attack, using both shortstaffs to block Quillon's strikes so they never had any of the sword's full weight behind them. Then, so fast Aderyn almost missed it, Raewyn spun one of the shortstaffs away from her arm and thwacked Quillon on his shoulder below the cuirass.

The crowd screamed. One of the adjudicators shouted, "One to Raewyn!" in a voice that echoed like the announcer's. Aderyn quickly Assessed the man, in case he was a Warmaster with **[Amplify Voice]**, but he didn't have a class at all.

The two combatants separated, but immediately closed with each other again. Quillon seemed to have learned from the previous exchange, because he held Raewyn at a distance with his sword's longer reach. Raewyn continued to block his swings, never attacking directly.

"She's testing him," Aderyn said, seeing the pattern to Raewyn's movements. "Watch. She's going to get inside his guard any second now."

"She looks like she's afraid to get within a foot—" Weston began.

Raewyn darted forward, catching the blade on her left shortstaff and shoving it out of the way in one fluid circular movement. At the same time, she spun the right shortstaff out the way she had before, catching Quillon right below his throat with a hard *tock* against the cuirass Aderyn imagined she could hear over the noise of the spectators.

"Two to Raewyn!"

Raewyn backed away, spinning both shortstaffs in a complicated pattern too fast to follow. Aderyn found she was leaning almost out of her seat and made herself sit back, though her heart was racing as if she was the one down there fighting.

Quillon backed off and began circling, never getting within reach of Raewyn. He was waiting for her to go on the attack, Aderyn realized, in the hope that he could hit her before she got within the range of her shortstaffs. Raewyn looked like she knew this by the way she paced Quillon exactly. But Aderyn could hear the shift in the crowd's mood. They weren't going to be happy with this game for long. If the combatants got the same advice the teams did—make it look good—Raewyn and Quillon were going to be a disappointment.

Then Raewyn ran at Quillon, both shortstaffs folded along her arms. Quillon swung. Raewyn leaped high, somersaulted in midair, and landed *behind* Quillon. She spun around and hit him squarely in the back and then held her position, one shortstaff flung out behind her for balance, the other's tip resting against Quillon's cuirass.

The crowd screamed its approval. Raewyn stayed that way for a second longer, then straightened and accepted Quillon's hand. "And the winner is... *Raewyn!*" the announcer said. "That was astonishing! Raewyn proves once again what a master of the shortstaffs can do!"

"He's holding that sword one-handed," Livia murmured. "Guess he's not a total loss."

"Except he lost," Weston said.

"Now here's a match you've been waiting to see!" The announcer's voice was more excited than before, if that was possible. "Your fifth-ranked champion, Sethys, versus a challenger who nearly swept the trials—let's hear it for Sethys and Owen!"

CHAPTER TWENTY-FIVE

Owen and a tall woman entered the arena. Sethys waved enthusiastically at the crowd, dramatically flourishing her arms and even blowing kisses. Owen, by contrast, held one hand up in salute, turning so he could see most of the crowd as he walked to the center of the arena. Aderyn liked the look of his new brigandine and boots. Raynir had been generous.

"They love him," Weston said. "The side of the arena where Owen is is louder than this one."

"I don't know how even you can tell that," Livia said.

"Why is he facing a champion?" Aderyn asked. "Shouldn't he go up against another challenger?"

"It's the way this kind of tournament works," Isold said. "The matches are arranged so the first battles are fought between competitors of similar skill level. At least, it's assumed that placing as the challengers did in the trials represents their skill levels."

"It's not like Owen is going to have any trouble with that woman," Livia said. "Look at how she's posturing. So dramatic."

"Don't underestimate her," Aderyn said. She was watching how Sethys moved, how light-footed she was as she skipped to the arena's center, how her hand caressed the hilt of her sword. "She's a level fourteen Lone Wolf. Deception is part of her skill set, not to mention [Shatter Confidence]. I wish I could warn Owen."

"He'll be fine," Livia repeated. "Look, he's standing ready."

The horn sounded, and Sethys went on the attack, faster than Aderyn would have guessed possible even knowing the woman's class. Owen got his sword up in time to block her first strike, then parried a blow from a knife Sethys pulled out of a thigh sheath with his own second weapon. For a few seconds, their weapons flashed furiously, neither of them able to land a blow. Then Owen caught both Sethys's sword and her knife with his longsword and drove home a strike to her belly with his dagger, pulling his blow so it struck her leather brigandine lightly. "One to Owen!" the adjudicator said, and the two disengaged. Both were visibly breathing, though neither looked tired.

Again, Sethys didn't wait more than a second or two before attacking. This time, Owen backed away, then backed away again, deflecting her blows but giving up ground. A few boos rose above the general clamor. Aderyn scowled. "He's getting her measure," she shouted before remembering no one could hear her over the noise. Sethys was more competent and calculating than her grand gestures suggested, but her attacks were still wider than they needed to be, and she didn't use her knife for defense, just for the occasional attempt at a stealth blow.

Sethys raised her sword for another attack, her knife almost forgotten in her other hand for all she wasn't using it. Quick as a snake, Owen thrust at her chest beneath her raised sword, striking solidly. "Two to Owen!" the announcer shouted. "He's proving to be a deadly opponent. Imagine if this was a real battle!"

Again, the fighters separated, and this time Owen went on the attack. It was Sethys's turn to retreat, barely blocking Owen's blows with sword and knife. Then Sethys stumbled, her foot coming down at a wrong angle, and Aderyn held her breath, waiting for Owen to finish her. Instead, Owen stepped back, lowering his weapons. Aderyn saw his lips move. Sethys got her balance and rotated her ankle before putting her weight on it again.

"Why didn't he go for it?" Livia demanded. "He had her fairly."

"And the crowd is going to adore him for being so honorable," Isold said. Sure enough, the roar of the crowd had heightened, and Aderyn could hear Owen's name being chanted here and there.

Owen drew back and gestured with his dagger hand. Sethys attacked, and this time her strike was tight and contained, giving Owen no room to get past her guard for another blow to the chest.

Owen parried the sword blow with his dagger, driving it aside with some effort. He caught her knife on the guard of his sword and twisted, yanking it out of her hand. Sethys took a step back in surprise, but she caught Owen's return strike with her blade before it could connect with her shoulder. For a few exchanges, it was sword against sword. Aderyn held her breath again. She knew Owen hadn't forgotten his knife, so he had a plan, but she didn't know what it was.

Then she saw it. Owen pressed Sethys hard with the sword, hard enough that even though he hadn't forgotten the dagger, Sethys had. And in the instant Aderyn saw the tactic, Owen brought the dagger up and around, thrusting for Sethys's stomach. It struck her brigandine hard enough to startle her into freezing. Owen lowered his weapons and took a step back.

A system message appeared.

**Congratulations! You have defeated [Sethys the Swordsworn].
You have earned [13,000 XP]**

There was a moment of perfect silence. Then the announcer shouted, "The winner is... *Owen!*" and it felt like sound flowed back into the world, with the crowd screaming in delight and shouting Owen's name.

Owen sheathed his sword and dagger and bent to pick up Sethys's knife. He extended it to her, hilt first, and his lips moved. Sethys smiled and accepted the blade, and the two of them saluted the stands together.

Aderyn flexed feeling back into her fingers. "Imagine how that will sound when he's the top champion."

"Let's go congratulate him and see about getting drinks," Livia said.

"And here's another match I know you've been dying to see," the announcer boomed. "Your sixth-ranked champion, the Terrible Twin, Nator, fighting none other than the number one challenger, Jael!"

Aderyn stopped at the top of the stairs. "I want to see this," she said.

"What, that horrible skinny cheater?" Livia said. "Why in thunder do we care?"

"Because I want to know her tactics. Owen can use all the help he can get against her." Aderyn took the nearest seat. "You all can go ahead. This won't take long."

"We're not going to leave you behind," Weston said, sitting next to her. "And this will give us something to criticize."

Jael definitely looked scrawny beside the well-built Nator. She wore well-fitting black leather armor and hardened vambraces that made her look like a girl playing dress-up, though no girl would have a sword as deadly as the one that swung at Jael's hip. The sword annoyed Aderyn because it was beautiful and well-balanced and the pinnacle of the swordsmith's art, and Jael didn't deserve it.

Nator waved perfunctorily to the crowd and drew his own sword, not a big, heavy one like Quillon's, but not ornamented and elegant like Jael's. It was beautiful in its plainness, a working fighter's sword, and Aderyn felt a rush of sympathy for Nator, who she hadn't liked but who now she hoped would win this fight. Well, she would have felt that way about anyone fighting against Jael, but now she was even more interested in the outcome.

The signal horn blew, and Jael leaped forward and tagged Nator in the middle of his armored chest. Startled, Nator took a step back, and Jael, after a pause barely long enough to meet the fight's rules, pressed the attack and struck Nator again in what Aderyn thought might have been the exact same spot.

Nator backed up again and got his sword into a defensive position in time to block Jael's next attack. The crowd had quieted, though this only meant a dull roar rather than the fevered shouting that had sounded after Owen's match. Nator's greater weight gave him an advantage as he forced Jael back. He bore down on her, and Aderyn's heart soared at the realization that Jael was going to lose.

Then Jael gave a deft twist of her blade, and suddenly Nator's sword was on the ground, and Jael's sword connected with his upper arm. Again, silence reigned for the space of two seconds, and then the crowd came alive with cheering and shouting and... "Are they *booing?*" Aderyn exclaimed. "I hate her, but that was a clever move."

"Look at Nator's arm," Weston said. "She didn't pull that last punch. She cut him."

Sure enough, blood darkened Nator's sleeve, and the adjudicators were beckoning to someone waiting by the tunnel mouth. Nator had a hand clapped over his wounded arm, but gave way to the Bonemender.

"And she doesn't even care," Livia said. "I hate her."

Jael had turned her back on Nator and was pointing her sword at the crowd, throwing her head back and laughing as she had during the trials. Aderyn stood. "I've seen enough. Let's find Owen."

Owen waited for them beneath the arena. He had removed his armor and changed into clean clothes. "Let's go back to the inn. I'd rather not be recognized today, and you four are extremely recognizable. Including 'the Swift.'" He slung his arm around Aderyn's waist and pulled her close for a kiss. "I've never felt so smug in my entire life, listening to all the men around me going absolutely nuts over you and knowing who you'd be going home with."

Aderyn managed a laugh. "You keep that in mind, all right?" Owen's reaction worried her, that he seemed to think she should be dismissive of those men whose only crime was finding Aderyn as attractive as Owen himself did. The idea of proposing marriage felt uncomfortable now. With him being as vocally sensitive about her admirers as he was, suppose he thought she was only doing it so those men would stop pursuing her?

"Hey, Aderyn!"

Aderyn turned. "Borrus!" She hadn't seen him since the night of the pre-Games party, when they'd parted with such awful words between them. But Borrus's wave and smile were cheerful, and he didn't look like he'd held onto his anger long. Aderyn decided to take the same route.

"What did you have planned for the evening?" Borrus asked. "Going out to celebrate your victory? Mind if I come along?"

"I'd love that," Aderyn said, meaning it wholeheartedly.

By the time they returned to the Alabaster Inn and changed into less conspicuous clothing, it was still too early for dinner, and Weston suggested they go into the city for drinks and entertainment. Foundation was just coming alive as the sun set behind the distant mountains, and while none of them were recognized as famous Games competitors, everyone they met seemed to know they were strangers. To Aderyn's surprise, they weren't treated as unwelcome outsiders.

"It's the Games, see?" one very talkative woman told them. "Everyone who comes here for the Games is like family, because we're all here for the same thing. Did you see that Owen today? He's going to go far. Not to first place, of course, but almost certainly second."

"Why not first place?" Weston asked, ignoring Livia's elbow in his ribs.

"Well, nobody can beat Kendria," the woman said, like this was the most obvious thing in the world. "But he'll give her a good fight, and that's what matters."

"That will be a fight to watch," Borrus said.

Aderyn tensed, wishing the woman hadn't brought Kendria's name up. But Borrus didn't act defensive. It gave Aderyn hope that he might still be himself despite Kendria's influence.

When they'd left that woman behind, Owen said, "They're all psyching me out now. I'm almost convinced I don't stand a chance."

"What is 'psyching you out'?" Borrus asked. "Is it some kind of mental attack?"

"Almost," Owen said. "Hey, that's Pace and Gradin going into that tavern there."

They caught up to the cousins at the tavern's bar. Aderyn, about to greet them, heard the sound of an argument and hesitated.

"...don't know why it matters," Gradin was saying. "I don't care all that much."

"That's not what you were saying earlier," Pace said. "It doesn't matter at all that she just walked away?" He noticed the others and said, "Oh, hey there. Nice match today, Owen. You looked good."

"I was about to say the same about you and Gradin," Owen said. "Can I buy the next round?"

"We'll take turns," Pace said. "Unless Gradin has a problem with that."

"I told you, I don't care." Gradin shrugged and dropped heavily onto a bar stool.

"He's disappointed because a woman stood him up," Pace said, "and he won't admit it."

Gradin rolled his eyes. "It's no big deal. Just drinks. And she didn't stand me up. She left and didn't come back."

"And that doesn't bother you?" Borrus said. "I'd be pissed off if it was me."

"Yes," Isold said, drawing the word out a little too long. "Yes, you should be upset."

"Isold, you know I like you, but you don't know anything about how I feel," Gradin said. He didn't sound angry or hostile despite his words. If anything, Aderyn thought he sounded the way someone did when they were too tired to manage an emotional reaction.

"No, I don't," Isold said. He grabbed Gradin's chin and turned his head so their eyes met.

"Hey, stop," Gradin said in that same affectless voice. He didn't try to pull away.

Isold released him swiftly, like the contact burned. "I do not know how you feel," he said. "I do, however, know how to recognize [Beguilement] when I see it."

CHAPTER TWENTY-SIX

"What's [Beguilement]?" Aderyn asked. "I've never heard of that skill."

Isold stared at Gradin with narrowed eyes and rubbed his chin with one long-fingered hand. "You know Heralds have skills to manipulate the minds and emotions of others," he said. "Heralds who choose to use those skills against other humans for evil purposes become Beguilers. Chief among their skills is [Beguilement]. It allows a Beguiler to alter the emotions of others, making them hate, or love, or fear—or feel indifference." He gestured at Gradin. "A Beguiler has influenced Gradin to feel apathy about the young woman he was entertaining."

"That's impossible," Pace said. "We were together—I mean, not *together*, I was having a drink with a different woman, but we were in the same room, and nobody approached him."

"Beguilers are still Heralds in terms of most of their skills." Isold continued to stare at Gradin. "It might have been a musician, or someone who spoke to Gradin in passing at another time. This apathy seems to have spread from not caring about the woman to not caring about much of anything. We could slap him and he wouldn't react. Though we won't do that," he warned Pace, who looked about to implement the suggestion.

"Can you remove it?" Aderyn asked. "He's not going to be stuck like this forever, is he?"

"I can try. At worst, we find a Spellcrafter with enough ranks in **[Disenchant 2]** to overcome the Beguiler's effect." Isold placed his hands on either side of Gradin's face and began humming. The music was low, barely audible over the sound of the general hubbub, but it filled Aderyn with a sense of desire—not desire for anything in particular, just a low-grade yearning for something unattainable.

Gradin blinked.

The humming stopped, and Isold removed his hands. "Gradin?"

"I remember," Gradin said. "Denae got up and left the table to relieve herself, and I saw—" He shot off the stool. "Those men took her. I saw her struggle, and I didn't care. Why didn't I care? We have to find her!"

"Denae? The challenger Denae?" Borrus demanded. Suddenly he was sharp and focused, his easygoing attitude vanished.

"Where was this? When?" Owen asked.

Gradin was shaking, so Pace answered. "Half an hour ago, at the Salt Mines. It's a tavern near our inn—"

"Let's go," Owen said.

They ran, pushing through the growing crowds in the streets, to where several taverns lined the busy road, the music of six different players in six different keys mingling discordantly and putting Aderyn's teeth on edge. Gradin led the way to the largest of these taverns and shoved the door open. When Aderyn entered, the music had stopped, and Gradin had the violinist by the throat and shoved him up against the wall. "What did you do to me?"

The violinist looked terrified. His mouth opened and closed, but no words emerged.

"Wait, Gradin," Aderyn said. She Assessed the musician, carefully examining his skills.

Name: Belvir
Class: Herald
Level: 8
<u>Class Skills</u>: **Perform (violin) (8); Knowledge: Magic (7); Knowledge: Monsters (3); Knowledge: History (4); Knowledge: Social (8); Knowledge: World Lore (4); Identify Magic Items (5); Charm (6); Distraction (5); Map Access (4); Inspire Courage (4); Fascination (3); Persuasion (2); Perform (guitar) (2)**

None of the class skills were at odds with the Herald class. Aderyn focused harder on that. Nothing happened to the display; no words showed corrupted symbols, and the class didn't change to Beguiler. "Let him go, Gradin. He's not the one."

Pace pulled Gradin off the Herald, who gasped and clutched his throat. "How dare you," he rasped. "You think because you're a challenger you can attack people and get away with it? I'll have the law on you!"

"Calm down," Isold said. Aderyn couldn't hear any of the subtle harmonics that would mean he was using his skills on his fellow Herald. "Were there any other musicians here tonight?"

"What do you mean, other musicians?" Belvir cleared his throat and massaged it ostentatiously. "I'm the one contracted to play here. Which is what I told the flute player." A distant look crossed his face. "And yet she played here anyway. I don't know why I let her. She was beautiful, but I've never been swayed by beauty."

"She?" Owen said

"Yes, she," Belvir said irritably. "She was fair enough with the flute, though I've never understood why people find that instrument appealing. Strings are where it's at."

"Where did she go?" Borrus asked.

"It doesn't matter," Gradin said. "We have to find Denae. Anything might have happened." He pushed his way through the crowd of drinkers to the bar, all of whom had stopped their conversations to stare at what was going on with the Herald.

Belvir shook his head. "I forgot about her until just now. I don't remember her leaving."

"She might be anywhere by now," Weston said.

Owen surveyed the crowd. "Hey, did any of you see where the flute player went? The other Herald?"

Muttering began, and one or two people pointed at the door they'd just entered by. One woman said, "She left a while ago, after playing a couple of songs. I know you! Owen the challenger. Why are you harassing that Herald?"

Owen swore under his breath. "It's not—"

"It was a misunderstanding," Isold said smoothly, though again he didn't use a Herald skill. "A matter of promises made and not kept. Please, return to your business." He caught Aderyn's eye and nodded in Belvir's direction. "We apologize, but we believed you were someone else."

Aderyn caught his meaning and slipped a couple of coins into her hand. "Yes, we're sorry," she said, smiling and clasping his hand to deposit the coins into it. "Please go back to your playing. It's really beautiful."

Belvir gaped at Aderyn, then closed his hand on hers when she would have withdrawn it. "The Swift," he said, his own smile becoming meaningful. "It's good to meet you. Your beauty surpasses anything I might have imagined."

"Um, thank you," Aderyn said, jerking her hand free. "I know you won't hold our impatience against us."

"Of course not. Why don't you stay and have a drink with me? It's time for me to take a break."

"Maybe some other time," Aderyn said, feeling extremely uncomfortable. Letting men down politely was one thing, but this Herald's regard made her feel like spiders were crawling over her scalp. She hurried away, not caring that she'd left her friends behind, just needing to get away.

She met Gradin halfway to the bar. His distraught expression prompted her to exclaim, "What did you learn?"

"Nobody saw what happened," Gradin said. "The barman remembered us sitting at that table." He pointed with a shaking hand. "And he did see Denae get up and walk to the door that leads to the refresher—you know, how they have outhouses inside here? And he said the next time he looked, I was gone too."

The others had joined them, and Owen said, "But you said you saw her taken by some men."

"I remember it now. She was halfway down the hall, and some man had followed like he was going to the refresher too. Then he grabbed her wrist and dragged her away. There was another man, too —he came out of the refresher and grabbed her other hand." Gradin's voice was shaking now. "I saw it, and it was like it didn't matter. I didn't care. And now—" He made a choked sound.

"We should go that way, see what we can find. Maybe someone out back saw something." Owen sounded calm, though Aderyn thought his optimism was misplaced.

They hurried down the hall to the back door, passing the three refreshers and emerging in an alley behind the Salt Mines. No one was there. The alley extended east and west, running behind more taverns, and at the eastern end, the one nearest them, people strolling along the main street were visible.

A door opened to the left, and a man carrying a bucket emerged. He stared at them, clearly confused. Owen strode over to him. "Excuse me, but did you see a couple of men with a young woman come through here about half an hour ago?"

"This is the first time I've come out here since sunset," the man said. He dumped the contents of his bucket atop a smelly pile to the side of the door and went back inside, though not before giving the companions a skeptical look.

"We've got no Pathseer," Owen said.

"I can't track anything over these stones," Weston said. "I'm sorry."

Gradin looked desolate. Pace put an arm around his shoulders. "It's not your fault."

"Was she your sweetheart?" Aderyn asked, feeling awkward.

Gradin shook his head. "She was a challenger. We fought today, and we hit it off—I defeated her, so we figured it was unlikely we'd face each other again and it wouldn't hurt anyone if we got to know each other better." He shook his head again, more vehemently this time. "But I let her go off to who knows what kind of danger. I can't forgive myself."

"The Beguiler is to blame, Gradin," Isold said. His beautiful voice was tight and harsh with anger. "[Beguilement] is a powerful effect. If a Beguiler is successful in using it, the victim is completely unaware that anything is strange about their own behavior, and may go on feeling the false emotions for days before the effect wears off, if no one removes it. You are not at fault."

"What, not at fault for not being able to resist?" Gradin shouted.

"Laying blame has to wait," Owen said. "We need to find Denae. Aderyn?"

Aderyn had already fished out the <**Wayfinder**> from her purse. "What does she look like, Gradin? It might help."

"Help what? What are you talking about? You're not a Pathseer." Gradin's voice was hoarse, like he was nearing his breaking point.

"Just describe her." Aderyn cradled the metal sphere in both hands with the larger spike pointed away from her.

Gradin released a deep breath. "Blonde hair, blue eyes, taller than the average woman but not by much. She's Staffsworn, strongly built —it would have taken at least two men to overpower her, and even then I'm sure she gave them a fight. She has a dimple on her left cheek when she smiles."

Aderyn listened to the description with half her attention. The other half focused on willing herself to be aware of Denae. Gradin's description triggered a faint memory, someone she'd spoken to at the big party, though she was sure she wouldn't have remembered the woman without Gradin's help. Finding things she'd seen only at a glance was more difficult than tracking down a familiar person or place, but she'd done it before. All that mattered was her heart's desire, and at the moment, she wanted to find Denae more than anything else.

A rosy glow suffused the spike, and Aderyn swiveled to point first at one end of the alley and then the other. "East," she said, and hurried in that direction.

She needed Owen's hand on her elbow to keep her from tripping as she strode rapidly, almost running, down the alley and out into the street. Casting about for a new direction, she followed the <Wayfinder's> guidance left, down the street. The others formed up around her, breaking a path through the growing throng. Aderyn soon stopped hearing the sounds of merriment as the sphere's glow brightened and led her through turn after turn.

When it finally pulsed one hot, deep red burst of light and then dimmed, Aderyn's back and shoulders ached. She lowered the sphere and blinked to moisten her eyes. At first, she couldn't make sense of what she saw. They were in another alley, though this one was wider than the first. The alley made a right turn just ahead, and in the corner, garbage was piled higher than Aderyn's head, broken crates and glass bottles and the stink of human and animal waste.

Sprawled across the pile was what looked like a giant doll, its arms and legs bent at unnatural angles. Aderyn blinked again, and the scene came into focus. It wasn't a doll, it was a woman, her blonde hair tangled across her face, obscuring it. But nothing could obscure the gash across her throat or the blood soaking her shirt front.

Borrus knelt beside her and gently pushed the hair away from her face. His shoulders sagged as if he'd hoped against hope he was wrong. "It's Denae."

Chapter Twenty-Seven

No one spoke. Aderyn's heart thudded dully, hard, terrible beats like the pulse of an angry drummer. This made no sense. Denae was supposed to be alive. They were supposed to find her in time. She couldn't remember the <**Wayfinder**> ever leading her to someone who was dead before.

Gradin grabbed Aderyn's hand. "Do your magic again," he demanded. "Find that Beguiler so I can kill her." Gone was the easy-going man she remembered. She had no trouble believing this Gradin could kill in revenge.

"I don't know if I can," she said. "I don't know her name, don't know anything about her—"

"Try, blast you!" Gradin shouted. "It can't end this way."

Well, she'd found people and things she'd never seen in the past, so it was worth a try. Aderyn cupped the <**Wayfinder**> in both hands and let her desire to find the Beguiler fill her. The orb remained cool and dark. She tried focusing on her memory of the Salt Mines, the Herald Belvir—except he hadn't described the woman who'd Beguiled him into letting her play her flute over his objections. No one they'd spoken to had seen her. She squeezed the <**Wayfinder**> tightly, ignoring how the many small, dull spikes pressed into her flesh, and tried to imagine someone who could so callously arrange for a woman's death.

Nothing happened.

Aderyn's shoulders sagged. "I'm sorry. I don't know enough."

"It might not be you," Isold said. "A Beguiler has skills like [Obscure] that make them hard to be found by magical means. We're not the only ones in Finion's Gate who have a <**Wayfinder**>."

"Then the killers," Owen said. "Assuming the men who abducted Denae did so at the Beguiler's orders. Gradin saw those men."

"They, too, might have been Beguiled," Isold warned. "A clever Beguiler would make sure to cover her tracks."

"It's worth trying," Pace said. He had a hand on Gradin's shoulder. "Gradin?"

"I'm trying to remember," Gradin said. His voice was distant and hollow, the voice of someone who'd given up. "They're just a blur in memory. Like my not caring about Denae being taken extended to not caring who the men were. I can't tell you anything except they were both male, and they had dark hair."

"That's not enough, no," Aderyn said gently. "I'm really sorry, Gradin."

Gradin nodded. "At least we found her body. I think I might have gone crazy trying to find her, knowing this was my fault—I mean, I know I'm not actually to blame, but it feels like I could have done more. Like I *should* have done more."

"Does anyone know what Finion's Gate does about murders, or bodies?" Owen said. "We're all strangers here—I would hate for anyone in authority to assume we're responsible, but we can't leave Denae's body here, abandoned."

"The magistrates employ enforcement, men and women to help

them keep the peace," Borrus said. "Constables do most of the legwork when a crime is reported, take the accused into custody, that sort of thing. Then there are inquirers, or Eyes. They investigate crimes in more depth. They'll look into Denae's murder, but for right now, we need a constable."

"We'll go," Owen said. "Pace, you and Gradin should stay with the body. If you think you can bear it," he said to Gradin. Gradin nodded again.

Owen led the way out of the alley. "I have no idea where to look," he said. "Short of committing a minor crime and hoping someone reports it, which would suck."

"There are constable posts all over the place," Borrus said. "Should be something close."

"There is a constable post back the way we came," Isold said. "I noticed it because a constable was leaving as we passed and he looked as if he wanted to stop us. We did look odd, I'm sure."

The constable post wasn't much more than a hut in a space between a tavern and a clothier's shop, closed for the night. Lights burned behind its one window and through the crack where the door stood ajar. Aderyn waited with Weston, Isold, and Livia outside while Owen and Borrus went in to talk to the constables. No one else on the street paid them any attention, though Aderyn felt irrationally like the knowledge of what they'd seen was written on their faces.

She felt, again irrationally, like she'd failed Denae in not knowing her. It wasn't as if Aderyn was expected to know all the challengers, but she could barely remember meeting Denae at the big party, and she was sure Owen had introduced her to all of them. And now Denae was dead and Aderyn knowing her, or not, didn't matter. Who had she been meant to fight next? Would that match have to be cancelled, or did it mean an automatic win for the other challenger?

"What happens," she began.

The post door swung open, and Owen and Borrus emerged,

followed by a stocky middle-aged woman and two younger, thinner men. All three were dressed entirely in dark green that looked black where the light didn't hit it. The taller of the men carried a bundle of canvas. "There's a lot of you," the female constable said in a cheery voice Aderyn thought was inappropriate given the circumstances. "Let's go see this deader."

"The 'deader' was someone we knew," Borrus said coldly. "Please show some compassion."

To Aderyn's surprise, the woman cast her gaze down. "Come along," she said, which Aderyn figured was as close to an apology as they were going to get.

When they reached Denae's body, the woman constable glanced briefly at Pace and Gradin before kneeling beside the body. "You saw her be taken, and you did nothing to stop it?" she asked. "Which of you was that?"

"Our companion was Beguiled," Isold said.

"So you say. That's a nice excuse." The woman rose. "Does she have family here?"

"She's from Obsidian. Came here to compete in the Glory Games," Gradin said dully. "That's where her family is. I don't know more than that."

"Verus, Ithalin, take care of the body," the woman said. "All of you, come with me. You'll need to make statements to prove you weren't responsible."

"How are we supposed to do that?" Pace demanded. "Nobody saw her killers. If Isold hadn't recognized the [Beguilement] skill, Denae would have disappeared completely. You can't know we didn't do it."

"We'll send for an inquirer who can cast *truthspeak*." The woman looked grim. "It shouldn't take long. None of you sound like the type of idiots who would kill a woman and try to bluff your way out of being found guilty."

Aderyn had never seen the *truthspeak* spell cast before. Her only knowledge of it came from some of her parents' books, sensational stories about murder and searching for killers. But the Bonemender inquirer who cast it on her only asked a few basic questions about what she'd seen and whether she had a grudge against Denae. Every time Aderyn answered, her hands glowed blue with truthfulness. She'd expected the Bonemender to at least have her lie once to prove the spell worked, but the Bonemender had the look of someone who was doing a tedious, routine task and who would rather be out drinking with friends.

Finally, the woman constable whose name they never did learn said, "You're free to go. Any of you want to lay claim to the body?"

They all looked at Gradin. "I barely knew her," he said miserably. "But she shouldn't be left to be buried like a stranger."

"We'll see about contacting her family in Obsidian," Pace said.

Out on the street again, Pace turned to Aderyn. "Thanks for your help. I wish things had turned out differently, but at least we know."

"Yes," Gradin added. "Thank you. We'll see you around."

"Will he be all right?" Owen asked Pace in a low voice as Gradin walked away.

"He's not grieving over a personal loss, so as callous as this sounds, I think he'll get over her death quickly," Pace replied. "If anything, he's dealing with guilt. Gradin's always had a strong sense of duty toward those he cares about. He needs time." He nodded and hurried to catch up to Gradin.

"Back to the inn?" Weston said. "I don't know about you, but my desire for fun has disappeared."

"It's already been twice as long a night as it should be," Owen said. He took Aderyn's hand. "I declare it to be over."

"It's not how I expected the night to go, for sure," Borrus said. "I'll see you around. Good luck in tomorrow's dungeon battle." He hugged Aderyn and strolled away in the other direction.

They walked through the streets of Foundation, ignoring the revelers for whom the night was just starting. Aderyn couldn't stop going over the events in her head. If they'd found Pace and Gradin sooner, or if she'd thought to use the <**Wayfinder**> immediately…

"Aderyn, what's wrong? You're crushing my hand," Owen exclaimed.

"Oh, I'm sorry!" She tried to let go, but he held onto her.

"Are you all right? Did using the <**Wayfinder**> tire you? It didn't take all that long to find Denae."

"I'm not tired. Just mentally trying to make things work out differently. Poor Denae."

"Yes." Owen sounded unexpectedly distant. "Yes. Why Denae, I wonder?"

"Do you mean, why was she killed?"

"Yes. This was far too complex a plot to be coincidence. Gradin was Beguiled, Denae's attackers were either Beguiled or hired, so why would the Beguiler go to so much trouble to kill Denae?"

"Because she—no, that's not it. I was going to say, because she's a challenger, but she lost her fight with Gradin, so it's not like she mattered as far as the Glory Games go."

Owen was shaking his head as she spoke. "That's not how a double elimination tournament works. Denae got one more chance at staying in. One more fight." He tugged on Aderyn's hand. "Come on. I need to figure something out."

Back at the Alabaster Inn, Owen said, "Hang on a sec, I need some paper," and ran through the door leading to the taproom. The others waited in the entrance chamber, listening to the murmured conversations and the sounds of a drum and a fiddle. The inn was much quieter than the taverns they'd left behind.

Owen slammed through the door, holding a ragged sheaf of paper in one hand and some charcoal pencils in the other. "Upstairs," he said, not waiting for them to acknowledge him. Aderyn hurried after him, followed by the others.

They all crowded into Aderyn and Owen's room, which wasn't all that small but felt positively cramped with all five of them present.

Owen grabbed the table that sat beneath the room's one window and dragged it to the center of the room, knocking over the single chair that had been pushed up to it. He spread the blank papers on the table and shook his head when Weston offered him the chair. "I'm too restless to sit."

Aderyn watched Owen sketch out a number of short horizontal lines at the left side of the top paper, the upper group separated from the lower by some white space. "This is the schedule for the fights. The losers from these fights—" He tapped a finger, rapidly ticking off pairs of lines—"drop down to *here* and fight a second time. Or more, if they win and go on winning. It's not unheard of for a loser in the top bracket to make it all the way to the finals."

He quickly wrote names on most of the lines on the top half of the page. "This is the opening position. All the fights scheduled between all the competitors, before anyone's lost."

"How do you know all that?" Livia said. "That's twenty people."

"March Madness has three times this many teams, and I'm pretty good at keeping track of my bracket. Except last year, when everyone's bracket was busted right at the start. Though that's just a single-elimination competition." Owen seemed to become conscious of how they were all staring uncomprehendingly and cleared his throat. "Let's just say I remember the details. They post the results in the changing room, anyway."

"All right, so this is the way everyone's matched up." Aderyn touched the pair of lines showing Gradin and Denae's match. "I don't know much about this stuff, but I can see that Gradin's win puts him *here*. So where does Denae's name go, if she gets another chance?"

Owen wrote Denae's name on a line in the lower group. Then he wrote three other names on lines near hers. "These are all the losers from matches one through eight. But—damn. Denae's next opponent hasn't been decided yet. That match will be fought tomorrow."

"You mean someone might have killed Denae to give her opponent a better chance," Isold said.

"But nobody knows who that will be yet," Aderyn said. "Which match is it?"

Owen's finger landed on a pair of names. "Challenger Asantis versus—huh."

Aderyn read the name he was pointing at. "Kendria!"

Chapter Twenty-Eight

"Kendria," Owen confirmed.

"I can't imagine anyone thinking Kendria needed to resort to murder to win," Isold said. "Unless her mystique is all bluster, and she isn't as good as they say."

"No, you're right. And I didn't fight Asantis in the trials, but I doubt he's as good as Kendria. So maybe someone made assumptions, and did a little preemptive murder." Owen's expression was hard and cold. "Someone knew Denae would fight Asantis, and got rid of her so Asantis got a free pass on that fight."

"Is that what happens if some contender doesn't fight?" Livia asked. "If they're sick, or they forget and miss the schedule? Their opponent advances?"

"Yeah. They were sure to warn us about being there on time and the consequences of lateness." Owen tapped the paper idly, smearing the charcoal just enough to make the last letters of Kendria's name illegible. "But I have no idea how we could prove this theory. Any one of a million people in Finion's Gate might try this stunt. The Beguiler might be in someone else's employ rather than acting on her own. All we know is someone went to a lot of trouble to kill Denae, and her death had to have something to do with the Games. Nothing else makes sense."

Aderyn sat heavily on the bed. "I'm worried. That Beguiler might be anywhere. And if she, or maybe whoever hired her, isn't done attacking competitors, Owen might be on her list."

"There's nothing we can do about that either," Livia said. "Nothing but stay alert for the sound of a flute."

Weston took Livia's hand. "Let's sleep on it," he suggested, "and maybe something will become obvious—what are you writing now, Owen?"

"Just filling in the rest of the bracket." Owen paused with the pencil held above the paper. "Huh. Depending on who wins this match, Pace might be my next opponent."

Aderyn stood up and peered at the paper. "He has to beat Basel. He's a champion, right?"

"The fourth-ranked champion," Owen said. "That will be a match to watch."

"When do you fight next?" Weston asked.

"Not for a while. The last four openers have to be decided, and then the losers' bracket games determine the first round of eliminations." Owen grinned and put an arm around Aderyn's waist. "That means I'll have nothing distracting me while I watch my favorite team sweep its way to victory."

"Oh, don't jinx us," Aderyn said. "Some of these teams are really good. And even those awful Scrappers came close to beating us."

"It wasn't all that close. That woman was still working her way across the floating islands when Weston crossed the finish line."

"Well, I'm ready for bed, where I'll probably dream about bouncing across an endless row of floating islands," Weston said, opening the door for Livia and Isold to exit. "Good night."

Owen steered Aderyn around the table to shut the door behind their friends. Then he turned her in his arms to hold her closer. "My *actual* favorite part," he whispered, "is hearing those men talk about how they plan to approach the Swift for her favor. I hope you'll reject them where I can see."

"That's so cruel, Owen. They mean it as a compliment."

Owen released her. "You mean you like having those men fawn all over you?"

"Nobody has done any fawning yet, and it's not about liking. Those men take a risk in approaching me, because I might not accept their gifts—"

"*Might* not?"

Aderyn's heart sank. She was saying this all wrong. "Owen, this world isn't like yours."

"I'll say. Women in my world don't lead men on."

Stung, Aderyn said, "That's not how it works at all, and you're being unfair."

Owen sighed. "Yeah. You're right, that was a stupid thing to say. I'm sorry." He began taking off his clothes. "Let's get some sleep. We'll need to be at the arena early."

Aderyn, who'd been about to explain her world's courtship customs in more detail, didn't want to return to the topic when Owen clearly wasn't interested. So she stripped down to the shift and drawers she wore to sleep in and climbed into bed. Normally Owen put his arms around her so they could cuddle together. Tonight, he rolled onto his side to face away from her. It felt like a slap, like he was angrier than she'd realized. She didn't know what to do about it. Finally, she lay on her back staring at the ceiling and told herself things would look better in the morning.

"INDOMITABLES AND WILDCATS, YOU'RE UP NEXT," SEONN said the following morning. "Your dungeon is Castle Defense. Wildcats, that means a literal castle. Defenders have a marker that radiates an aura. This marker, specifically." He held up what Aderyn recognized as a coffee can, but painted bright gold and sealed on both ends.

"Defenders get two minutes to plant their marker, and then the attackers have ten minutes to reach the marker. They need at least one team member to step inside the aura to win. Defenders are allowed to set any traps they choose, using whatever skills and spells they have access to, though obviously they can't be lethal. No direct interference with the attackers. Attackers are free to progress through the castle as they choose, but *fly* and *transport* as well as *levitation* of team members are all forbidden. Any questions?"

"Who's on offense and defense?" Weston asked.

"For that, we flip a coin. Winner gets to choose." Seonn brought out a silver coin and showed it to the teams, proving it didn't have two heads. "Heads green, tails blue." With a practiced flick of his thumb, he sent the coin spinning into the air, caught it, and slapped his other hand over it. When he revealed the coin, the profile of a woman's head, worn almost to nothing, gleamed up at him.

"We'll take defense," Martis of the Indomitables said. "Sorry, but after seeing what you did to the Scrappers, I'm not going to go easy on you."

"He's apologizing because defense is considered to have the advantage," Seonn said. "I keep telling you lot it's all in how you play, but superstition will have its way..." He shrugged and walked away.

"We'll be fine," Weston said. "I take it we don't get to watch you place all those traps?"

"You're kept secluded during those two minutes, but we're allowed to go on setting traps if we can get away with it." Martis was grinning and didn't look at all apologetic. "It's a fun challenge!"

"For you," Livia said.

"For everyone, really. This is the one most like a real dungeon, and the crowd loves it—they feel like they're adventurers themselves. So let's make it a good show, all right?"

The horn blew, and both teams ran up the tunnel to the arena floor. This time, Aderyn clearly heard chants of "Wildcats!" and "The Swift!" and tried to let it cheer her rather than make her nervous. She had the irrational feeling that her performance, if you could call it that, was a kind of gift she owed the spectators, and she'd be letting them down if she lost. Which was stupid. She reminded herself that they were here for the experience and smiled and waved at the crowd.

The Indomitables vanished around the far side of the shrouded dungeon, and Aderyn gathered with her team on a square similar to the one that had been a rising platform yesterday. This one was right up next to the shimmering veil of the dungeon. As soon as all of them stood within it, a gray curtain of fog rose up along each of the square's sides, twice as tall as Weston's head. Light still shone down through the open top, but the thick fog dimmed their surroundings and made Aderyn feel slightly claustrophobic.

"I wish I had my watch," Livia complained. "We could at least keep track of how much time is left before they let us in."

"Tell us about the Indomitables, Aderyn," Isold said. "Who are we facing?"

"Their captain, Martis, is a Swordsworn," Aderyn said. "From asking around I learned that he entered the Games a few seasons back as a solo fighter, but didn't make it to the final ten. Based on his skill ranks, I'd say he's not driven to succeed, and I think it's someone else on his team who is the motivating force."

"Why isn't that person captain?" Livia asked.

"No idea. My guess is that it's Darelin the Spellcrafter. He has a passion for inventions and his ranks in [Imbue Item] are high for his level. We should watch for enchantment traps—stones made to move underfoot, or walls that close off our retreat. They also have a Spider named Gilia who has decent ranks in [Disable Traps] and might be able to create magic traps herself."

"And the last one?" Weston asked.

"They picked Warron the Windwarden over Kavan the Stalwart.

From watching Warron compete, I've concluded he's the weak link. He usually uses his wind spells in a direct attack against his opponents, and that's illegal in this dungeon. But they wouldn't have picked him over Kavan if they didn't think he was useful, so I don't want to underestimate him."

"All right," Weston said. "We stick together for this. I'll walk point, searching for traps, with Livia at the rear and Aderyn and Isold in the middle. Seonn said a literal castle, which means stone, and Livia can take advantage of that. Ready?"

The others nodded.

Nothing happened. They all watched the foggy walls for signs of movement. "Well, that would have been the perfect moment for us," Weston began, and the walls disappeared and they found themselves facing a stone arch set in the wall of a castle.

Weston signaled, and they moved forward.

The sound of cheering cut off the instant they passed through the arch, which led directly to a stone staircase going up. Aderyn examined her surroundings while Weston checked the stairs for a trap. The walls looked solid, and she didn't know how this dungeon could possibly be a crowd favorite if nobody could see through the stones.

"We're safe for now," Weston said. "But everyone stay alert."

The castle wasn't the ruin they'd encountered in their last dungeon, but it showed signs of disrepair, places where the stone was cracked or worn down. When they reached the top of the stairs, they found themselves in a long, open gallery, pierced on both sides by window holes with no glass. A brisk wind blew through the windows, whipping Aderyn's ponytail around her face. She looked through the nearest window and saw nothing but roofs lower down and another stone structure at their level ahead and around the corner from the gallery.

"It's time," Weston said. "Isold?"

Isold rested his hand on the stone casement of a window and

closed his eyes. "The marker," he said in a conversational tone as if he was talking to some unseen person on the other side. "Golden canister sealed on both ends. It emits an aura expanding its presence." His voice echoed with the strange effect that said their conversation was being shared with the crowd.

His eyes flew open and shimmered silver for a flash of a second. "I know which way to go, and I can keep us headed in the right direction. But I assume the Indomitables will have trapped the most likely path."

"They can't know which path we'll take," Weston said. "So they'll have trapped places closer to their marker because they can't afford to waste energy and supplies guessing. That means we're probably safe for a while, though I won't stop watching for traps."

"I'm sure Darelin would think of setting up something that lets him see where we are, which will give them the opportunity to set more traps as we get closer," Aderyn said.

"Let's keep moving," Livia said. "Which way, Isold?"

"Down this gallery and across to the next hall," Isold said.

They moved quickly but carefully through the gallery. Aderyn glanced out each window as they passed, on the chance she might see one of their opponents. Nothing moved beyond the windows, not even the shadows cast by clouds overhead; the sky was clear and blue and still.

The next hall ended in stairs going down. Weston gestured to them to stop. He knelt at the top of the stairs, then froze. "Trap," he said curtly. "And the mechanism is at the bottom."

"We could go around," Aderyn suggested.

"We can't waste time. I think..." Weston worked a small piece of stone loose from where something had cracked the pavement and tossed it down the stairs. It bounced once. Fast as a snake striking, something shot out of the side of the stairs, smacking into the piece of stone and crushing it against the far wall.

The four friends stared at the powdered stone scattered over a couple of steps. "What was that?" Weston said.

"The sides of the stairwell are rigged to slam sideways when something touches the steps," Aderyn said. She'd seen the ghostly image of the slab of stone an instant before it smashed the wall.

"I can tell you how to disable the trap if you want to go down there," Weston said.

Aderyn shook her head. "Even **[See It Coming]** isn't fast enough—or, rather, I can't react fast enough to avoid it."

"Is it a trap, or an enchantment?" Isold asked.

"It's both," Weston replied. "The enchantment is on the stairs, and the trap is so someone who isn't a Spellcrafter can disable it."

Isold smiled. "A Spellcrafter... or a Herald with **[Break Enchantment]**." He knelt and seemed to do nothing for a few seconds, holding his position as Aderyn shifted nervously. Finally, Isold picked another piece of shattered rock from the pavement and tossed it onto the stairs. Nothing happened. "We have to move quickly," he said. "It's a strong enchantment. I suppressed it, but couldn't eliminate it."

Livia was already halfway down the stairs. "Hurry!"

Aderyn ran after the others, leaping two stairs at a time, just in case.

CHAPTER TWENTY-NINE

At the base of the stairs, Weston paused only briefly to yank the insides out of a copper box nestled against the wall and toss them aside. "Isold?"

Isold pointed. "Straight ahead and to the left."

They were once more in a gallery, but this one had no windows and was unlit. "This has to be trapped," Weston said. "They'd count on us not being able to see."

"Bad assumption," Livia said. With a graceful gesture, she sent walnut-sized balls of light flying down the passage, where they clung to the ceiling and walls and shed a strong, bright light over the hall—and over two more copper boxes, facing each other on opposite sides of the hall.

"Not a tripwire," Weston said. He crouched beside the right-hand box and examined it, running his fingers gently over its surface and edges. Then, with a suddenness that surprised Aderyn, he smashed the thing with one blow of his enormous fist. It let out a sad little squawk like a dying duck. Across the hall, a hiss and a jet of steam erupted from the other box. Weston was already moving.

The hall split into three a few feet further on, extending right and left as well as continuing forward. "Left," Isold said, but Weston grabbed his arm and stopped him.

"Can you find a route to this thing from anywhere?" he asked.

Isold nodded. "You think we should try a different path?"

"We've run into a few pitfalls, which tells me they found the likeliest path and trapped it. We can keep going, but those traps will slow us down. If we take a back way—"

"Let's go," Isold agreed.

They moved faster now, with Weston and Isold leading the way. No more traps interfered with their progress. Up and down stairs, through vast, unoccupied rooms, outside beneath columned and roofed patios and back indoors again, they worked their way steadily through the castle. Isold reassured them occasionally that they were on the right path. "*A* right path, at any rate," he said.

Weston slowed and came to a stop. "I can hear someone ahead. Just one person. They're breathing heavily."

Aderyn gasped. "I saw Warron. He ducked out of sight, but I think he knows he was spotted."

"Another trap," Weston said. "I wish I knew how close we are, or how much time is left."

"That's a distraction," Livia said. "Keep going."

Around the next corner, the hall opened up into one of those vast rooms Aderyn found so depressing, with a floor like a giant checkerboard with most of its paint stripped away. She reminded herself this was a dungeon and not a real castle, but she had trouble not imagining people having once lived here and feeling sad about how ruined and desolate it was now.

She began to step into the room and hesitated before her foot could touch the floor. "The floor's moving."

"I see it," Weston said. "Try putting one foot on that square there."

Carefully, Aderyn rested a foot against the square, then gradually put more of her weight on it. With a snap, the square cracked in half and fell into the empty space beneath. A gust of wind rushed out of the hole, making the nearby squares tremble.

"That Windwarden," Livia growled. "He's cast *levitate* on the squares. I bet that hole isn't very deep."

"No, but it's wide, and it will slow us down," Isold said.

"I can get across," Weston said, "but—"

"We are *all* going," Livia said. "Move back."

She stepped to the edge of the trapped room and took a solid wrestler's stance. With a grunt, she spat out several nonsense syllables. Rumbling struck the room, the floor shuddered, and with a surge of energy, the ground beneath the room rose ten feet, pushing the floor squares up so they rested on the heap of earth.

Aderyn ran with the others across the uneven floor. Warron was gone when they reached the other side and began crossing the next room. "Do you think—" she began, then shrieked and ducked as something flew at her face, its ghostly double warning her just seconds before it struck.

Isold picked the missile up. "This is stuffed with goose down and pebbles," he said in some irritation. "Heavy enough to sting if it hits, but otherwise not dangerous. What are they thinking?"

"We're close," Weston said. "And time is running out."

"I thought they couldn't interfere with us directly," Aderyn said.

"They're not. It's a couple of slingshots, enchanted to track movement," Livia said, pointing at the end of the passage.

Aderyn took the missile from Isold. "This is ridiculous," she said, flinging it away. Then she sprinted for the far doorway.

It was almost too easy. The slingshots flung their missiles frequently enough that she couldn't just run straight through the room, but they didn't fly fast, and dodging them was simple. Conscious of the need to put on a good show, she darted back and forth a couple of times before remembering she didn't know how long they had left and she might be wasting time. Then she just ran, twisting and ducking, listening to the shouts of her friends as they cheered her on—no, that was wrong, they were shouting something else. *Keep going*, it sounded like.

So instead of stopping to figure out how to disable the slingshots, she kept running, down a short passage and into a round, high-walled chamber filled with a purple glow. She had a glimpse of the Indomitables gathered around the coffee can, looking up in bewilderment, and then she was inside the glow and the lights were flashing brightly.

Congratulations! You have defeated [Castle Defense terrain variation 3].
You have earned [10,000 XP] plus [10 XP] per second before [10 minutes], for a total of [790 XP] bonus.

Panting, Aderyn bent over as the walls sank into the ground and the stone floor beneath her feet vanished. Someone walked to her side, and she stared at his feet for a few seconds, catching her breath.

"That was unexpected," Martis said. "We thought you'd waste time disabling the pillow shooters." He looked strange, and it took Aderyn a moment to realize he was missing his tunic. So were all the Indomitables.

Aderyn straightened and drew in another deep breath. "It just takes one of us," she said, pretending she'd remembered this and hadn't been prompted to run by her teammates.

"It does indeed." Martis extended his hand. "Nice work. We haven't lost at Castle Defense as the defenders in the last two seasons."

"It was hard," Aderyn said. "Where did you get the materials for the pillow shooters?"

Martis gestured at his torso. "Our tunics, plus Darelin's magical duplicator. We didn't actually think you'd come that way. You bypassed all our best traps."

"Forgive me for not being sorry," Weston said from behind Aderyn. "Come on, Swift, you need to greet your admirers."

Livia grabbed Aderyn around the waist, and in seconds they were balanced atop a pillar of earth, level with the first tier of screaming spectators. Aderyn waved, then ducked as long-stemmed flowers began falling from the stands, showering her. Laughing, she caught one and clutched it to her heart. The screams and shouts grew so loud she heard Livia's voice only as a rising and falling mumble. "What?"

"I said they're going to throw themselves next!" Livia shouted in her ear. Slowly, she brought them back to earth, and the four of them ran for the covert stairs.

"And another success for the Wildcats," Jesper said with a grin. "Martis was so proud of his record at Castle Defense, too."

"They did what you couldn't, Jesper," Martis said amiably.

"True. That was our only loss last season." Jesper clapped Weston on the back. "But don't think this changes anything. We're still going to mop the floor with you Wildcats."

"Whose flower is that, Aderyn?" the Indomitables' Spider, Gilia, asked.

Aderyn had forgotten she was still holding it. "I have no idea. I hope whoever threw it doesn't get the wrong impression."

"Hardly," Kathra said. "A random flower, that's nothing. Just wait 'til you get back to your inn. By this time, someone will have learned where the Swift is staying, and you'll be drowned in poems and gifts and inappropriate declarations of love."

Aderyn recalled how angry Owen had been the previous night. He'd been back to normal this morning, but she was sure their difference of opinion hadn't resolved itself. The idea of having to explain why all those men weren't a threat to him made her feel sick and cold inside. "That sounds dreadful."

"I'll keep the gifts you don't want," Livia said.

"You'll probably get gifts too, Livia Stonefist," Aderyn said.

"Not as many as you. Still, it's fun being appreciated."

Aderyn glanced at Weston. "You don't mind?"

"Mind what?" Weston shrugged. "So long as I get my choice of the discards, Livia can entertain as many admirers as she chooses."

For the briefest moment, Aderyn wished she'd fallen in love with someone from her own world. Then she was horrified at herself. She loved Owen, and it didn't matter that he was an otherworlder. She'd explain, and he would finally understand.

Theirs had been the second dungeon of the morning, so all the teams filed out of the covert and down the back stairs, with Aderyn trailing behind. She finally looked fully at the flower she'd snatched out of the air. It was a sad little daisy missing a third of its petals. She didn't like daisies all that much. With a sigh, she tossed it over the front rail of the covert and didn't stay to see it land.

THAT EVENING, SHE CHANGED OUT OF HER UNIFORM AS Owen scribbled on the paper showing the fight bracket, as he called it. She hadn't been there for Kendria's fight with Asantis, which had been the first fight after their dungeon win, but Owen had said it was anticlimactic. "She toyed with him," he'd said, sounding disapproving, and Aderyn had agreed, though that behavior fit with what she'd observed of Kendria.

"That's a lot of people we know going to the losers' bracket today," Owen said as he added a final name to the page. "Gabryl beat Gradin, Caprissa lost to that Stalwart Rhidius. Eirian lost to Caprissa yesterday, so she's there too. But Pace won against Basel, so he and I are facing off in two days. I'm looking forward to it."

"Did they say anything about Denae? Like, make an announcement?"

Owen set down the pencil and rubbed gray charcoal off his fingers. "Just that she had withdrawn. I think the Games organizers didn't want to start a panic. I'm not sure how announcing her death would do that, unless they were stupid enough to say a Beguiler was involved and Denae was targeted for being a challenger."

"That's sad. It's like they've made her disappear. When really she was good enough to make the top ten." Aderyn straightened her shirt. "Where are we going tonight? Up to Terrace One?"

"Did you want to go there? Foundation has enough taverns for two lifetimes of carousing." Owen sounded surprised.

"Oh, no, I wasn't thinking of any place in particular. Just that Terrace One would be different. But it's probably too high-class for ordinary people like us."

"That was my thought." Owen put his arms around her waist and pulled her close for a kiss. "Though I hope we don't encounter any of your admirers tonight. Maybe Terrace One is a better idea, after all."

Aderyn didn't like the edge to his voice, but she didn't know what to say to counter it. She settled on, "I hope we don't, too."

"Good. Let's go find some fun," Owen said.

They were on their own that night, Livia and Weston having opted to stay in and Isold going back to Terrace One for a night with one of those three daughters he'd flirted with at the big party. They strolled hand in hand down the street, for the moment just an anonymous couple, and Aderyn relaxed. She wasn't likely to be recognized without her uniform and the other Wildcats.

Owen chose a tavern at random, a large building on a corner with many well-lit windows on both sides facing the streets. Aderyn didn't see a sign, but music filled the air, and a tipsy couple exited the building as Owen and Aderyn approached the door. The couple stopped in the doorway to kiss passionately, which amused Aderyn enough that she didn't mind waiting for them to finish.

Crowds filled the tavern, and Aderyn didn't see any free tables anywhere, but Owen made straight for the bar and commandeered the last two empty stools. Aderyn sat with her back to the bar and tapped her toe to the music. No flute, thankfully, but a couple of fiddles playing in harmony and a drum that didn't sound as confident as Isold's.

Her eye was caught by a woman climbing onto a nearby table. She held a foaming tankard whose contents sloshed over the rim onto her hand, but she was laughing and either didn't notice or didn't care. She took a long drink from the tankard and let out a belch that started her and her companions laughing again. Aderyn focused on her face and realized she knew the woman.

"It's Caprissa," she said.

"What?"

"Owen, it's Caprissa," Aderyn repeated, nodding in the woman's direction. Caprissa took another long drink and tossed the empty tankard to a man standing nearby.

"It is," Owen said. "Huh. I wouldn't have pegged her as the social drinker type."

"I don't—" Memory struck. "Owen. She said she didn't drink much."

"When was this?"

"At the party. Don't you remember? She had maybe half a glass of wine and then she said she doesn't drink much." Another man handed Caprissa a second mug of ale, and she drank down most of it in a series of uninterrupted swallows.

"I guess that wasn't true." Owen signaled the barman for two drinks.

Aderyn watched Caprissa drunkenly laugh as she finished her ale, and a chill ran through her. "Or something else is wrong," she said. "She's behaving out of character. What if that's on purpose?"

Owen stilled. "You mean she's been Beguiled."

Aderyn nodded. "And the Beguiler might still be here."

CHAPTER THIRTY

Owen shoved off his stool. "Wait here," he said, and pushed through the crowd toward the musicians. Aderyn closed her hand around the mug of ale the barman set before her and watched Owen's blond head progress through the crowd. When he reached the fiddlers, she turned her attention back to Caprissa. Caprissa was dancing drunkenly on the table, laughing and pushing men away gently with her foot as they tried to climb up next to her.

The music stopped as the song came to an end and the musicians didn't strike up a new one. Owen was talking to the fiddlers, both of whom were listening to him intently. When Aderyn looked back at Caprissa, she was climbing off the table with the help of a couple of men. Then, to Aderyn's horror, Caprissa headed for the door.

Aderyn was off her stool and shoving past merrymakers before she knew what she was doing. Caprissa's drunken progress was slow, and Aderyn was able to get in front of her and bring her and the men flanking her to a stop.

"Caprissa!" she said. "You're not leaving, are you?"

"We're going on for some more fun elsewhere," one of Caprissa's two companions said.

"You want to join us, pretty lady?" the other slurred.

Caprissa focused on Aderyn and clearly didn't recognize her. "Who are you? You coming along?"

"I don't think you should leave," Aderyn said, terrifyingly aware that she didn't know what the Beguiler looked like and had no idea if the woman needed her flute to use her **[Beguilement]** skill. All she could picture was Denae's dead body and the scene her imagination presented her with of Denae being hauled struggling out of the Salt Mines tavern. She glanced at both men, but neither seemed to be faking how drunk he was.

Caprissa tossed back her head and laughed. "What, you like this place better? 'S too crowded. And there's no music. I want to dance."

Inspired, Aderyn said, "Have you been here long? Did you listen to the music before? There was a flute, wasn't there?"

Caprissa's head wobbled as she again focused on Aderyn with some effort. "Flute," she said, drawing the word out like she was thinking about it. "Pretty flute. Pretty fiddles. Don't like drums, they make my head pound." She began walking forward again, not seeming to care that Aderyn was in the way. Aderyn took an involuntary step backward and then stood firm.

"Listen, pretty lady, if you wanna come, you can come, but don't just stand there," the man on the right said.

"I'm not letting you take her anywhere," Aderyn declared.

"What's all that about taking her?" the man on the left said. "*She's* taking *us*."

"It's good advice," Owen said, making Aderyn's heart jump in surprise. "Caprissa, come over here so we can talk."

Caprissa glared at Owen. "Who are you? You gonna stop me drinking more? What are you, my mother? Get out of my way."

"You're not well, Caprissa," Owen said steadily. "But I've got another drink over here for you. Then you can go wherever you want."

"Yes, a special drink," Aderyn put in, though she had no idea what Owen planned. "We'll all have one."

Caprissa suddenly smiled a lazy, drunken smile. "You're my friend," she said. "I remember. The Swift."

The two men immediately let go of Caprissa's elbows, which they'd been guiding her with, and stared at Aderyn. "The Swift?" the one on the right said. "Really the Swift?"

"Um. Yes," Aderyn said, her cheeks burning hotly.

"You never get hit," the other man said. "I bet if I punched you, it would miss."

"Don't try it," Owen said, his voice dangerously calm.

The effect was like a gallon of ice water to both men's faces. They stiffened, and glanced at one another, then at Caprissa, then at Aderyn. "We have to go," the man on the right said, and he and his friend brushed past Aderyn and headed for the door.

"Don't go!" Caprissa called out, but her words slurred so badly it sounded like *Doango*. "Hey, we were going to get more drinks!"

"This way," Owen said, steering Caprissa by the elbow as the men had done. Aderyn followed them back to the bar, where miraculously their stools were still unoccupied. Owen didn't sit, though. He handed Caprissa a shot glass filled with a familiar poisonously green liquid that moved in a nauseating way. "Drink it all."

Caprissa lifted it to her lips and then recoiled. "It smells like year-old piss."

"If you drink it, I'll buy you three of any other drink you want," Owen said.

Caprissa eyed him suspiciously. Then she pinched her nose shut and poured the liquid down her throat.

"Where did you get that?" Aderyn whispered to Owen.

"The barman keeps a supply of antitoxin for emergencies," Owen replied. "I had to argue with him and then pay all the spare coin I had on me to get him to hand it over. They consider it unethical to sober up a patron who's then going to drink more, but I convinced him this was an emergency. Damn, I wish Isold were here. He'd have no doubt gotten it for free."

Caprissa's eyes came back into focus, and she stopped weaving gently where she stood. "That tasted terrible."

"Can you think clearly now?" Owen asked.

Caprissa nodded. "Owen. And Aderyn. What's going on? Was I drunk? I remember—well, I don't remember being drunk, but everything was hazy for a while. I think I danced on a table." Her eyes narrowed. "Did someone play a trick on me? Because I never drink enough to get drunk. I—" Her face paled. "Was that antitoxin?"

"We had to clean out your system," Owen said.

"Shit." Caprissa touched her throat. "I never get drunk because I'm allergic to antitoxin."

"No," Aderyn gasped. "Deathly allergic?"

Caprissa shook her head. "But—" Her eyes rolled back in her head, and she began convulsing. Owen caught her before she could crack her head on the bar.

"Help!" Aderyn shouted. "We need a Bonemender *now!*"

Owen lowered Caprissa to the ground and knelt supporting her head as she thrashed. The music had stopped again, and a hush fell over the crowd, murmuring rather than shouts and laughter. Aderyn knelt beside Owen and gripped Caprissa's hand, though the woman clearly wasn't aware of her presence.

Someone else crouched beside Aderyn and gently removed Caprissa's hand from hers. "It will be all right," the man said. He was elderly, and his skin was wrinkled and fine as old parchment, but his voice was strong. Aderyn Assessed him quickly and drew in a relieved breath. What a level nineteen Bonemender was doing in a raucous tavern in Foundation instead of making a fortune caring for the wealthy, she had no idea, and she didn't waste time inquiring. She scooted out of the way so the Bonemender, Erwon, could get close.

Caprissa's seizure began to ebb when Erwon touched her, and after another thirty seconds, she lay limp and unmoving on the floor with her head still on Owen's knees. Erwon thumbed up her eyelids, one at a time, then brought her hand to rest on his wrinkled cheek. "She will recover," he said. "With time and bed rest, she should be fine."

"You can't do anything more for her?" Owen said.

Erwon looked at him sharply. "I stopped the seizure from doing permanent damage. What more do you want?"

"I'm sorry, I misspoke," Owen said. "I meant, isn't there anything that will get her back on her feet immediately? She's a challenger in the Games and she's scheduled to fight tomorrow."

"Well, that's not going to happen." Erwon still sounded testy, but not as angry as before. "Boosting her recovery would mean altering her body's self-repair systems, which is unethical because it can cause long-term health problems. And I can't say I think the Glory Games are worth this young woman crippling herself."

"I understand. Thank you for explaining." Owen was good at sounding humble when the situation called for it, and Aderyn agreed pissing off the Bonemender was a bad idea.

Caprissa's legs and arms shifted, and she opened her eyes. "See," she mumbled, "I said it wouldn't kill me."

"Someone call for a carriage to take her home," Erwon said. He rose easily despite his frail appearance. "And I am sorry this is the end of the Games for her this season. Fortunately, she can try again later."

Caprissa blinked. "What does he mean?"

"He says you're going to need bed rest. You won't be up again until after your match," Owen said. "I hate to be the one to tell you this."

Caprissa nodded. "I guessed. I just hoped... no, it's stupid. There will be other Games. And now that I've proved myself once, I can do it again." She tried to stand and couldn't.

Aderyn took her hand again. "Stay still. Someone's called for a carriage."

She and Owen waited with Caprissa until they heard a carriage pull up outside the tavern door. Then Owen lifted her and carried her easily outside, where Aderyn opened the carriage door and climbed in after Owen and Caprissa. She and Owen didn't speak, but she knew he was thinking, as she was, that they couldn't leave Caprissa to travel alone.

The inn Caprissa was staying at was half a mile down the street from the tavern. By the time they reached it, Caprissa had better control of her limbs and was able to step out of the carriage under her own power, though she still needed Owen's support to walk. While Owen got her to her room, Aderyn found the innkeeper and explained that Caprissa was ill and would need looking after. The innkeeper, a motherly middle-aged woman, assured Aderyn that she would give Caprissa the best of care.

A few minutes after the innkeeper went upstairs to see to Caprissa, Owen descended. "She's worse off than she seemed, very weak," he said, "but she's mentally clear. I think she'll be all right."

Aderyn opened the front door and stepped back in surprise as someone came through it at the same time. "Oh!" She'd met the elderly woman at the big party, and remembered she was Caprissa's sponsor, but it took her a moment to recall the woman's name. "Yvona!"

"Erwon sent word that Caprissa was ill," Yvona said. "I came to see for myself. Erwon said she would make a full recovery, but I was concerned."

"She'll appreciate a visit, I'm sure," Aderyn said. Inside, she was torn. Caprissa's seizure meant the end not only of her Games hopes, but of Yvona's political aspirations. If Yvona was here to tell Caprissa her sponsorship was over, what a blow that would be to the Swordsworn woman. Aderyn hated the unknown Beguiler even more.

"You know Caprissa can't compete tomorrow, don't you," Owen said, putting Aderyn's thoughts into words.

Yvona regarded him coolly. "I do," she said. "I don't see that this changes anything. There will be other Games. And I will continue to sponsor Caprissa, now and in future."

Owen nodded. "Some people will call that a foolish expense."

"You don't get to be as old and wealthy as I am through foolishness. I don't much care for what people say." Yvona smiled. "Thank you for caring for her. I'd offer you a reward, but I'm sure that's not why you did it."

"No," Owen said. "And thank you for seeing that."

The carriage was still there when they finished settling Caprissa. Owen and Aderyn rode in it back to the Alabaster Inn. Aderyn said only, "I like her."

"She's not what I expected a politician to be," Owen replied. "It's too bad she won't be a Councilor this year."

Aderyn nodded and yawned. She was weary and ready for bed, and more conversation was beyond her.

But when they were in their own room, Owen didn't undress. Instead, he sat at the table and stared at the paper with the bracket written on it. Aderyn read over his shoulder. "You think she was targeted for the same reason Denae was?"

"Caprissa was scheduled to fight Nator tomorrow," Owen said. "The last round before the quarterfinals. Now Nator is going to advance unchallenged."

"But that doesn't make any sense," Aderyn said. "Denae's death helped Asantis. Asantis and Nator, according to your bracket, won't encounter each other unless both of them win every match between now and the finals. Hurting Caprissa doesn't help Asantis at all."

Owen nodded slowly. "I asked Caprissa about that allergic reaction of hers. She says she hasn't mentioned it to anyone. Which means getting her drunk so she'd take the antitoxin and have a debilitating seizure wasn't the plan. If they wanted her too hungover to fight—no, because if she wasn't allergic, she'd have taken the antitoxin and been just fine."

Aderyn sat on the end of the bed. "Then I really don't under stand what's going on. It has to be the Beguiler, right? That's the only reason Caprissa would get drunk. But does that mean this mystery woman is just messing with the Games at random? Or is there something else Caprissa and Denae have in common?"

"I don't know," Owen said, running his hands through his hair and scratching his scalp the way he often did when he was balked. "I don't know, Aderyn. Something is wrong, but I don't have enough information, damn it." He rose from the table and took off his shirt. "In the morning, I'll tell Seonn what happened to Caprissa and what we suspect about the Beguiler. Maybe he knows something we don't."

Aderyn removed her clothes and climbed into bed, watching Owen undress and then stand by the window. That he hadn't come to her hurt. "Owen," she said.

"Hmm?"

She considered her options. She could ask him why he was upset —and sound whiny and petulant and put him off further. She could tell him she loved him—and have him act like he didn't care. She could yell at him—and make things ten times worse. "It's not important," she said. "Good night."

"Good night, Aderyn."

She lay awake for several minutes, waiting for him to come to bed, and fell asleep while he still stood at the window, gazing out into the night.

CHAPTER THIRTY-ONE

"It's coming back!" Aderyn screamed.

She threw herself flat on the grassy hill and covered her head with her arms as the tornado blew past, almost on top of her. When the roaring passed, she raised her head. Weston and Isold were already scrambling to their feet. Aderyn rose as fast as she could and took off running for the distant line that was the end of the dungeon's third elemental zone.

They'd done well so far. The Raging Elements dungeon was divided into four zones with different threats. Livia had neutralized the lava in the fire zone and sensed the pattern of earthquakes in the earth zone—and then one of the many tornadoes in the zone of air had snatched her up and carried her away, out of the dungeon. Aderyn was trying to be grateful they only needed one member to cross the finish line, but every time the wind battered her, stealing her breath, her stores of gratitude dwindled.

She ran with Weston and Isold up and over the many low hills the tornadoes roamed across, dodging their attacks. At least they didn't seem conscious of the teammates. Aderyn knew the pattern to their movement now. But they still unnerved her.

She'd stopped looking for the Fearsome Five back when they were facing the lava monsters. It was clear they couldn't do anything about their opponents; all they could do was move quickly and avoid getting picked up by a tornado.

"Duck!" she screamed. Over the noise of the winds, she heard someone shout in dismay, and when she looked up, Isold was tumbling past overhead, caught by the wind. Aderyn and Weston exchanged quick glances. Then they ran.

They felt it when they crossed the border to the final zone: the air became still and damp and smelled of swamp. Ahead, the grassy hills came to a stop at the banks of a marsh. Fat reeds and cattails swayed slowly in the movement of the water, back and forth. There were no trees, just little islands of mud and dirty grass.

Weston gingerly put a foot on the nearest island. "Solid ground. There could still be fake islands."

"I don't think so," Aderyn said. "This is the water zone, right? So any trap or hazard is going to be water based."

"Well, we need to move. Let's see what's out there." Weston leaped onto the first island and kept going. Aderyn followed him. The spaces between the islands weren't too wide for her to jump, though her feet slipped occasionally on the muddy grass.

Muddy grass.

Aderyn shouted, "Stop a minute." She bent and fingered the grass. The mud was thin and wet, not thick, like—

"Oh, crap," she whispered. In the distance she heard rumbling. "Weston, get down low and hold onto something!" she shouted, and put her own advice into action without waiting to see if he obeyed.

She listened again. The rumbling sound came from the end of the dungeon, their ultimate goal. She turned so she was facing that way and knelt, gripping the edge of the little island.

A white cloud low on the horizon tumbled rapidly toward them, its roar getting louder as it approached. In seconds, it became clear it wasn't a cloud, it was a foam-topped wave at least six feet high.

Aderyn ducked her head as the muddy water swept over her, buffeting her and trying to tear her grip loose from the island. Then it was past. Aderyn swept filthy hair out of her face and vainly wiped her hands on her soaking wet tunic.

She looked up. Weston was still there, looking wet and astonished. "Come on!" he said, and began running, leaping from island to island and not waiting for Aderyn.

For about half a second, Aderyn considered letting him go. He was outpacing her in any case, and that water had felt like being pummeled by stones wrapped in blankets. But suppose he was swept away? Somebody needed to reach the finish line.

She ran, not as fast as Weston—the gaps might not be impossible, but they were still a stretch—and hunkered down again the moment she heard the rumble of the wave. Twice more she was battered, twice more she got up and ran, until—

Congratulations! You have defeated [Raging Elements terrain variation 11].
You have earned [10,000 XP]

With a sigh, she bounded the last few steps to where Weston stood, out of breath and filthy with silt and swamp muck. The marsh was draining away like someone had unplugged a bathtub, and she and Weston stood together and dripped onto the hard-packed earth of the arena floor.

"That's my least favorite," Aderyn gasped. She wrung water out of her hair and gave a perfunctory wave at the crowd.

"Agreed," Weston said. "Good thing we were last to compete today, or I'd have suggested leaving early."

"I don't think they can expect us to sit in the covert in soaking wet clothes. Not on a day like this, anyway." The clouds were rolling in, promising a rainstorm that so far had held off, and the temperature had dropped enough Aderyn was shivering now and then.

Livia and Isold ran to join them. Isold still looked windblown. "That was an adventure," he said sourly.

"Back to the inn," Livia said.

"We should wait for Owen," Aderyn protested.

"He knows where the inn is. Besides, we were watching Raynir's box, and it looked like the Councilor wanted to show off his champions to some friends." Livia scowled as deeply as Isold. "I thought Sabetta was the one who treated her champion like a pet."

Aderyn's shivering was getting worse. "I don't want to wait on that event being over."

"That's it for today's Games, friends!" the announcer said. "There'll be a rest day tomorrow, give our fighters some time to recover before the quarterfinals begin, so we'll see you in two days!"

Aderyn, who'd been marching across the arena floor with her arms wrapped around her, stopped. "A rest day? Is that normal?"

"No idea," Livia said. "Keep walking before you catch hypothermia. Nobody wants the Swift to get sick."

"It's not like I did anything with **[See It Coming]** today," Aderyn groused. Owen hadn't been any less distant that morning, and his mood had infected her. In the face of his obvious anger, she hadn't been able to enjoy the gifts and poems that had begun arriving at the Alabaster Inn, and it had been difficult to compose genuinely regretful replies.

"I got the impression from the other teams that part of the appeal of Raging Elements—for the crowd, that is—is seeing the competitors battered by the environmental challenges," Isold said.

"Then they got their money's worth today," Weston said. His feet made a squelching sound with every step. "I'd have worn boots I don't care about if I'd known what was up."

"Gerant can find someone to clean them, and if not, I can cast *repair*. Though that's sort of overkill." Livia made as if to hug Weston, then thought better of it.

Back at the inn, Aderyn made use of the bathhouse out back,

feeling grateful that no one else was in line for it. She scrubbed and dried in record time and made way for Weston, who'd stripped out of his tunic, shirt, and boots in clear disregard for what anyone else might say about modesty.

She was still cold when she returned to her room, so she started a fire in the tiny fireplace and then dragged the blanket off the bed and wrapped it around herself. Sitting in front of the fire, she leaned against the room's one chair and finally relaxed. Too bad she couldn't manage to get the mattress off the bed, or she could lie in front of the fire and take a much-needed nap.

The sound of the door opening woke her fully. She sat up and wiped a spot of drool off her cheek. "What time is it?" she asked Owen.

"A little after seven. Why are you sleeping on the floor?" Owen deposited an armful of small packages on the table and set a handful of envelopes next to the pile.

"I was cold, so I sat by the fire, and I guess I was more tired than I imagined." She carefully didn't look at the table. "What did Raynir want? Livia said it looked like he had guests."

Owen shrugged. "There were people who wanted to meet us, Gabryl and Raewyn and me. Mostly me, since I'm new. Aren't you going to open those?"

"Maybe later." A now-familiar tension gripped her chest. "I was thinking we should get something to eat."

"If you want. Raynir served food in his box, so I'm not that hungry."

Aderyn managed a smile. "I'd love it if you'd sit with me, then."

Owen smiled back, and if it didn't seem wholehearted, at least it was a smile.

Seated at one of the tables in the Alabaster Inn's taproom, Aderyn ate Arlia's special dish, fat noodles in a sauce whose recipe was so secret Arlia would pretend not to know what people meant if they asked her about it, and had a glass of wine and began to feel better. The quiet sound of music, of fiddles playing so softly they were barely audible, filled the air. "Do you know what's up with the rest day?"

Owen leaned closer and lowered his voice. "Seonn wasn't happy to learn about the attack on Caprissa. That and Denae's murder have him worried about the safety of the competitors. So they're shutting down for a day to investigate. Personally, I don't think one day is enough, but any more than that will make people start to talk."

"What can they do, though? **[Beguilement]** seems almost impossible to resist. Wouldn't the Beguiler use it on anyone who comes after her?"

"Isold told me **[Beguilement]** is easier to resist the higher level you are, and the more in control of your emotions. And that once you've experienced it, you're close to immune. It also is less effective the more people a Beguiler tries to affect at once. So it's not a superpower."

Aderyn could guess that word from context. "That's something, anyway."

"Yeah. Though I wish I could predict where she'll strike next. I'm convinced that one of those attacks was a decoy to confuse us, which means we won't know more until she attacks a third time. Which sucks, because that could mean death for someone."

Aderyn drank the last of her wine, wishing the bitter taste his words left in her mouth was something real that wine could wash away. "It might not be anything we witness. It was just dumb luck we were there for both attacks. I mean, the aftermath of Denae's, not the attack—you know what I mean."

"If the Beguiler is going after challengers rather than champions, it might be me she attacks next." Owen toyed with his own wine glass, but didn't drink.

"That's terrifying."

"As far as that Beguiler knows, I'm no more special than any other challenger. It's not like anyone knows about the Fated One thing."

Aderyn didn't like how bitter he sounded, but she couldn't understand what was bothering him. She glanced away, trying to come up with the right words, and caught the eye of a man just entering the taproom. He'd been scanning the room, looking for someone, but when their eyes met, he focused on her. She had a sudden dread suspicion that was confirmed when he began to cross the taproom toward her.

She pushed her mostly empty plate away and said, "Let's get out of here."

Owen said, "I'm not really in the mood for—"

"Then we'll go upstairs. We haven't spent much time together this week." The man had almost reached their table. She rose and said, "Come on, let's—"

"You're the Swift," the man said as he approached. "Aderyn the Swift." He was older than she, maybe in his thirties, and very attractive, with dark hair and vivid green eyes.

Aderyn's heart sank, and she considered lying. But Owen, without rising, said, "Why do you ask?"

The man ignored Owen. "Your performance is extraordinary," he said with a smile as attractive as the rest of him. "Tell me, do all Warmasters secretly have your gifts?"

"Any Warmaster with a good partner," Aderyn said. "This is my partner, Owen."

Immediately she knew introducing Owen was a mistake. Owen tensed all over in what **[Read Body Language]** told her was intense anger. Quickly, she said, "I'm afraid we were just leaving, but it was nice to meet you."

"Please, allow me to show you how much I admire you," the man said. "I've composed a poem—"

"She's not interested in your crappy poem," Owen said. He pushed back his chair and stood. "Or in you."

The man regarded Owen in bewilderment. "That's up to the lady," he said, sounding like Owen was mentally deficient not to understand this basic fact.

"Owen, please," Aderyn said, feeling the situation slipping out of her control. "There's nothing to worry about."

"You told him we're going," Owen said. "He needs to respect that."

"I hoped to recite it for you myself," the man said, ignoring the lunatic challenging him, "but of course, if you're on your way out..." He slipped a hand inside his coat and withdrew a pale blue envelope that smelled of violets.

Aderyn managed to smile politely. "Thank you, that's—it's kind of you, and I respect your—"

Owen snatched the envelope from the man's hand. "Leave her alone," he said. "I won't tell you twice."

The man's smile disappeared. "I don't know what you think you're doing, interfering like this, but if you want a fight, we can go out back and I'll give it to you."

"That sounds great," Owen said. "After you."

Two men fighting over her. It was the stuff of nightmares. Aderyn felt like laughing. Then she wanted to cry. Then she grew angry. "That's *enough*," she said, so forcefully both men froze. "Sir, I appreciate the gesture. Thank you for thinking so highly of me. But if you fight my partner, I will never speak to you again. Owen, I'm going upstairs. When you pull your head out of your ass, you can join me." She snatched the scented envelope out of his hand and marched out of the taproom, pretending no one was staring at her. She was barely aware that the music of fiddle and flute played on despite the scene they'd made.

In their room, she tossed the envelope at the pile on the table, where to her faint surprise it landed perfectly. She stared at it until Owen opened the door. He shut it behind him and said, "Aderyn—"

"Don't," Aderyn said. "I've tried to explain things to you, and you have ignored me and treated me disrespectfully and acted like you're justified in your anger. Well, I'm done. That little scene down there showed me how you actually feel. Have you always believed I'm your property, or is that a new development?"

"Property? Aderyn, why would you think that?"

He sounded so confused it made her angrier. "And here I thought this fight of ours was my fault," she went on. "I blamed myself for not doing the right thing, when... no, it doesn't matter anymore. I'm done." She drew in a deep breath. "No. We're done."

She took in Owen's stunned expression, his growing fear, and felt nothing but emptiness. Owen took a step toward her. "No, Aderyn," he said hoarsely. "That's not—no. Please."

She snatched up her coat and headed for the door. "Don't follow me," she said. "I mean it. We're over. You should get used to it."

She slammed the door shut behind her. It didn't open again.

Chapter Thirty-Two

She put on her coat as she went down the stairs, then bypassed the taproom and exited into the cold night. The chill in the air hadn't stopped the ongoing revelry, and the street was crowded with merrymakers in pairs or small groups, laughing and talking loudly. It all seemed to be happening very far away. Aderyn recalled what she'd said to Owen, but the memory didn't make her sad or happy, just indifferent.

She walked down the street, feeling she must stand out by a mile as the only solitary person in Foundation that night. *That* thought depressed her. She needed a drink. She picked the next tavern she came to that wasn't bursting at the seams with drinkers and pushed through the door into a bubble of light and warmth.

Not wanting to share a table with strangers, and unwilling to occupy a whole table just by herself, she sat at the bar and asked for brandy. She didn't usually like hard liquor, but she wanted to feel something other than indifference, and brandy would get her there faster than beer.

She sipped her drink and thought about taking off her coat, except she'd just have to hold it, and hanging it up felt like a commit ment to this place she didn't want to make. She took another sip. She didn't like the taste all that much, but it did light a fire inside her. Maybe she'd have one more.

Someone sat on the stool beside hers. "Hey there," the man said in a casual, offhanded way. Then he looked at her more closely, Assessing her. "Aren't you the Swift?"

Aderyn felt like screaming. "I am," she said instead, as politely and with as much of a rebuff as she could manage.

"Well, what do you know," the man said. "Never would have guessed when I sat down next to a pretty lady tonight, it would be a famous one. Can I buy you a drink?"

Aderyn thought about it. "Sure."

The man waved to get the barman's attention. "I'm Tiergan. Your actual name is Aderyn, right?"

"That's right." Aderyn downed the last of her drink in one fiery gulp and picked up the new glass. Over the noise of the crowd, she heard the musicians begin playing a popular song, "Pass the Jug." That suited her mood. A flute carried the high, lilting melody, and she tried to remember why that was important.

Tiergan clinked his glass against hers and drank. "I should thank you. I've won a goodly pile of coin thanks to the Wildcats."

His smile was so mischievous she laughed. When had she last laughed? "Then I guess you owe me a drink."

"I guess I do."

He was handsome, she realized, and his smile made her heart flutter, and she liked the way he looked at her, like he was interested in seeing more of her. The idea warmed her all over. "Tiergan," she said, and when he looked at her, she leaned in and kissed him.

He responded eagerly, kissing her in return like they were the only two people in the tavern. When they broke apart, she said, "Can we go someplace a little more private?"

He looked surprised, but then he smiled again, and desire rushed through her when he said, "My room's just upstairs."

She slipped her hand into his and let him lead her out of the taproom to the stairs leading to the third floor. Outside the door to his room, she kissed him again, pulling him close to feel the heat of his body against hers, and he fumbled at the latch and let them both in.

The room was dark, though the curtains were open, revealing the clouds that still hadn't dropped their rainy burden. Tiergan lit a lamp beside the door. "Well," he said. "I certainly wasn't expecting this."

"Shut up," Aderyn said, and grabbed the front of his shirt and pulled him close for a hard, breathless kiss.

They kissed wildly, fumbling toward the bed and then lying together. Aderyn hadn't wanted anything so badly as she wanted him, not for a very long time. Owen's memory was distant and pale compared to Tiergan's body in her arms. She felt for her shirt hem and began to draw it over her head.

The door slammed open with a crack as the latch shattered, and figures poured into the room. Aderyn shrieked in surprise, then gasped when she recognized Livia and Weston, Isold and Owen. She scrambled away from Tiergan as Tiergan rolled off the bed and assumed a fighter's crouch. Then he froze as Owen's sword point touched his throat.

"Hold her," Isold said, his voice emotionless.

Caught off guard, Aderyn didn't struggle until Weston had her in his massive grip. Then she fought, kicking and shouting and trying to wriggle free. Weston reacted no more than if she'd been an angry kitten.

Isold came to stand in front of her, setting his hands on either side of her face, and now Aderyn fought with everything she had in her, because it was what she'd always feared, that Isold would use his Herald's skills on her, changing her to feel what she didn't feel. "Stop!" she screamed. "Don't do this!"

Isold ignored her. "The Beguiler hit her twice," he said in that same emotionless voice.

"Can you remove it?" Owen said.

"What is going on?" Tiergan shouted.

"Shut up," Owen said, pressing harder with his sword's point. Tiergan fell silent, but he was breathing heavily and he watched Aderyn rather than Owen.

"I will try," Isold said. "The effects are intertwined, so I can't remove one and then the other. My skill at **[Break Enchantment]** might not be enough. But I will try."

Aderyn sobbed. "No. Please. Leave me alone, Isold."

"You'll thank us later," Livia said.

Aderyn sagged in Weston's grip, hoping he might loosen his hold if he thought she'd given up, but he didn't flinch. A strange pressure built behind her eyes, like her skull was shrinking in on her brain. After a few seconds, the pressure became painful, and Aderyn's sobs increased. Then she screamed as a sharp pain like a hot needle stabbed into her forehead.

Her vision went *pop*.

She'd had a terrible dream once, where she'd believed she was awake and had heard someone enter her bedroom. Then the stranger laid a hand on her, heavy and warm, and she'd tried to scream for help or roll away or fight or anything, but she couldn't move. All she could do was stare at the wall and will someone to come in and find her. Then she'd woken for real, and she was looking at the exact spot on the wall she'd seen in her dream, but the hand was gone and she could move easily, and although she remembered the dream vividly, she also knew the difference between it and wakefulness.

That was how she felt now. The world came into clarity, as if she'd opened her eyes from a dream landscape to reality. Her feverish passion was gone, replaced by a cold ache she remembered too well from fighting with Owen—except that hadn't been real, either, not the anger the encounter with her admirer had inspired in her. She knew now exactly the moment when her genuine distress had become an imposed anger.

Imposed by the Beguiler.

She realized she was breathing heavily and said, "I'm fine now. Let go."

"She is free of [**Beguilement**]," Isold confirmed.

Weston released her, and Aderyn fell to her knees, feeling incapable of supporting herself. Livia crouched beside her with an arm around her shoulders, but said nothing.

"Who did you pay?" Owen was saying.

"Pay? I don't know what you're talking about," Tiergan said.

"Who did you pay to Beguile her?"

Tiergan shook his head. "I don't know what that means. Look, *she* came on to *me*. I'm not going to disregard good luck if a beautiful woman wants to—aargh!"

"Don't," Aderyn said hoarsely. "He's right. I approached him."

"Because he paid that Beguiler to make you attracted to him," Owen said, not letting up on the pressure where the sword dimpled Tiergan's throat.

"I don't think it was him. I heard—"

Memory rushed back. Aderyn shot to her feet, staggered, and ran for the door. "I heard the sound of the flute downstairs. She might still be here."

She needed the wall to keep herself from tumbling to the foot of the stairs, but when she reached the ground floor, she stumbled into the taproom and headed for the musicians, slowing as she realized none of them held a flute. Cursing mentally, she grabbed the nearest fiddler and said, "Where's the woman who played the flute? Where?"

The music came to a ragged halt. "Who, Damaris?" the fiddler said. "She left ten minutes ago."

"You know her?" Aderyn demanded.

The fiddler chuckled. "She's a myth," he said, pulling away from Aderyn's grip.

"More like a legend," the other fiddler said.

"Stop talking nonsense. Who is she?" Aderyn said.

"Hey, calm down. Damaris is a Herald, so she's real enough. The legend is that she'll walk in out of nowhere to sit in on a set. She plays a song or two and then she's gone again. It's supposed to be good luck to have her join your group." The fiddler looked more closely at her. "Hey, aren't you—"

"No," Aderyn said. "You don't know where this Damaris goes?"

"No, and we wouldn't try to find her. Supposed to break the good luck if you follow her home." The fiddler looked puzzled. "I'm sure I recognize you. Aderyn. You're familiar somehow."

"I've got one of those faces," Aderyn said. "Thanks anyway."

She turned to discover her friends gathered nearby, watching her like she might explode. "Her name is Damaris," she said, feeling wearier than ever. "She was here. And then she left. She must have followed me from the Alabaster Inn. But I don't understand why."

"We should discuss this privately," Isold said.

They walked back to the inn in silence. Owen walked a few feet ahead of Aderyn. She stared at his back and felt sick. She'd said all those awful things—she'd told him their relationship was over—and then she'd fallen into another man's arms, all of it because of the evil whim of that Beguiler. Owen knew she'd been Beguiled, and he blamed her anyway, because how else could she explain his cold refusal to even look at her, let alone touch her?

They ended up in Owen and Aderyn's room, all of them standing because the only sitting options were the chair, the bed, and the floor, and Aderyn felt her friends might be as uncomfortable as she was. Owen dug the paper displaying the bracket out from under the pile of packages, scattering a few of the envelopes accidentally. "So, that's the third attack," he said. "Which leaves us as clueless as before."

"Yes, because I'm not a challenger," Aderyn said.

"You weren't the only one targeted," Isold said. "The Beguiler went after Owen as well. She made you, well, hostile, and she made

Owen emotionally vulnerable to your hostility. In effect, she attacked you to get at Owen."

Rage suffused Aderyn, but distantly, like a pin poking skin through a dozen layers of cloth. She was too tired to properly experience it. "She used me," she said dully. "Then why make me attracted to Tiergan?"

"To be sure the attack hit home," Weston said. "How better to convince Owen than—" He fell silent.

Aderyn swallowed. "She wanted Owen too overwrought to fight well," she said. "Who does that benefit?"

Owen flicked the paper with his finger. "Pace, if he could defeat me," he said. "Then I'd be the one facing Nator, who advanced when Caprissa couldn't fight." He swore viciously and threw the paper edge-on so it spun across the room. "And none of it makes any sense."

"Or it does," Livia said. "You're the one who reported both Denae and Caprissa's attacks, and you were the one who told Seonn he's looking for a Beguiler. Maybe this isn't about the Games. Maybe the Beguiler wanted you out of the way."

Owen paused in his pacing. "That's true. If I was distracted, I might stop interfering with her plan." He deliberately didn't look at Aderyn.

"That fits better than thinking your attack is part of the pattern, because it doesn't seem to be." Weston picked up the paper and held it out to Owen. "There's no point going over this again tonight. Let's all go talk to Seonn in the morning. We can tell him you were attacked and see if he knows anything relevant."

"And we have a name now," Livia said. "Damaris."

Owen nodded. "Sounds good. Good night, everyone."

Weston's gaze flicked from Aderyn to Owen. He looked like he wanted to say something, but instead he waited for Isold and Livia to exit before shutting the door, leaving Owen and Aderyn alone.

CHAPTER THIRTY-THREE

Owen tried to set the paper on the table, but it was crowded with packages and stupid love poems. "That fellow," he said. "What was his name?"

"Tiergan." The word burned in her chest. She'd never felt so low and humiliated in her life.

Owen gave up on the paper and started pacing. "We explained to Tiergan as best we could, but he might still spread rumors about the Swift's, um, ardent behavior. I didn't know what else to do short of killing him, and you said he wasn't at fault."

The humiliated feeling spread. "I don't know what's worse, having it known there's a Beguiler loose in Finion's Gate or having a reputation as a nymphomaniac. It's all right. It's not like we'll be here forever."

"That's true."

Aderyn watched Owen as he returned to stand by the window. He still hadn't looked at her, but he also hadn't left. Maybe he was ready for her apology. "Owen, I'm sorry," she began.

"Do *not* apologize," Owen said in a low, harsh voice. "You've done nothing wrong."

"Then why won't you look at me?" Aderyn pleaded, wiping tears from her eyes.

Owen tilted his head back and let out a deep breath. "You were so angry, and you told me we were done, that you wanted nothing to do with me—"

"Why are you throwing this in my face?" Aderyn cried.

"Because I believed you!" Owen shouted. He drew in another breath, calming himself, and said, "You said all those things, and I didn't drag you to Isold that instant to remove the Beguilement. I should have known you were under an influence, because you are the kindest, most compassionate person I know, and no matter how angry you get, no matter how upset you are, you would never speak to me like that."

Stunned, Aderyn searched for a response and came up empty. She felt even sicker and colder than before.

Owen faced the window again. "I let you down so completely I keep waiting for you to tell me we really are done," he said quietly. "I let you go, and that damn Beguiler followed you and made you a pawn in her sick game again. You would have slept with that guy, someone you don't care anything for, and at some point you'd wake up from being Beguiled and realize what happened—you can't tell me that wouldn't have devastated you. I know you too well." He laughed, a bitter, self-mocking sound. "Or at least I thought I did."

"Stop," Aderyn said. She felt the word had been wrung out of her by force. "Stop. She Beguiled you, too. She made you believe I meant those things. You were her victim as much as I. You can't keep beating yourself up."

"Can't I?" He laughed again. "She didn't have to work hard to convince me. Aderyn, I've been crazed with jealousy for days, imagining you welcoming one of your admirers into your heart, spurning me—I know your world is different, but it makes no sense to me that you could let those men believe they have a chance with you and not on some level mean it."

She stared at him in disbelief. "Owen," she breathed. Then she shouted, "Have you completely lost your mind?"

Finally, he looked at her, but she was too far gone in anger and confusion to care. "Is that what you've been thinking, all this time? How could you—" Words sputtered out of her. "Let's forget for the moment that you just accused me of being fickle and a tease. I love you, Owen. You and I have been through things together that I'll never share with another man, and that's not even counting what we are to each other as partners. You've seen me at my worst and it hasn't made you run screaming. You've supported me, laughed with me, and loved me more than I ever imagined possible. Did you seriously believe I would *ever* throw that away for some stranger whose only appealing qualities are his attraction to who he thinks I am and some half-assed poetry?"

Owen stared at her, blinking in the onslaught. "Oh," he said. Then, with feeling, "Oh, Aderyn. How stupid was I?"

"Very," Aderyn snapped. "And if you had let me explain—"

"I don't know if that would have helped. I was deeply caught up in jealousy and fear." He shook his head slowly. "I didn't realize I was so insecure, but all those men—no. No, I'm not going to make excuses. Aderyn, I'm sorry I let my insecurities take over. I should never have believed so poorly of you. You are the one I love, and I—" He let out a short, mirthless laugh. "Listen to me. I told you I was bad at speeches."

"Why do you feel you need to make a speech?"

"I don't know." Owen let out a sharp, harsh breath. "I don't know. I guess now that I see clearly what a jackass I've been, I don't believe I deserve your forgiveness. And I'm terrified I'm right about that."

"Owen." Aderyn's heart broke for a different reason. "Oh, love. Do you really think I'd let you go so easily?"

He shrugged. "It's the worst thing I can imagine, losing you. It's really the only thing I fear."

Aderyn took a step toward him. "I felt I was losing you, too. Every time you turned away from me, every time we argued, it was like you'd forgotten who I was to you, or you remembered but didn't care."

Owen flinched. He turned his head away, as if gazing out the window, but the convulsive movement of his throat told Aderyn he was swallowing a powerful emotion. "I guess I deserve that."

"That wasn't meant as an attack! I just—I wanted you to know I feel the same. That losing you would devastate me." She blinked away tears. "I can't bear not to forgive you. Maybe that makes me weak, because what if you were a horrible person and I kept coming back to you no matter how you hurt me? But, Owen—" She took his unresisting hand in hers. "You're not a horrible person. You're wonderful, and kind, and I love you more than I can say."

Owen's hand closed on hers, tightly enough it hurt, but that small pain was nothing to the ache in Aderyn's heart. "I don't feel worthy of that—"

"Stop. Stop beating yourself up. You made a mistake, but so did I in not confronting you. What do you want? For us to fall into despair and abandon each other because we screwed up? Wouldn't it be better if we forgave, and went back to being two people who love each other? Or, better, moved forward to being two people who love each other more than before?"

Owen bowed his head. "I am sorry, Aderyn," he said. "I love you, and I apologize for hurting you. Do you think you can forgive me?"

"Oh, Owen. Of course I forgive you. I hope you can forgive me for not realizing what you were going through." A great weight freed itself from Aderyn's chest. "You must have been in a lot of pain, worrying I was going to leave you. I can imagine now how this must have looked to you." She gestured at the pile of packages. "I'm sorry I wasn't more understanding."

Owen chuckled. "You really are the most compassionate woman I've ever known, caring more about my pain than your own." He squeezed her hand, this time lightly. "I love you. I couldn't bear it if you were gone."

"I wish I didn't have the memory of talking to you like that. I know it wasn't real, and I know *you* know that, but it was still me speaking." She walked into the circle of his arms, and they held each other, not speaking, listening to the night's silence and the distant murmur of men and women on the street.

"I missed this," Owen murmured. "This closeness."

"So did I." She snuggled more deeply into his embrace.

"You know, that was our first real fight."

"It was! We're either really good at fighting or really bad at it."

Owen laughed and ran a hand down her spine. "I'd like to think we'll never fight again and have the opportunity to find out which is true, but I'm sure there will be other moments, because I'm never going to leave you."

"Me neither." She tilted her head to look up at him. "So, you fear losing me more than you fear monsters?"

"Absolutely."

"All monsters? What about the Sarnok? That was terrifying."

"Not at all. It was just a giant lizard." Owen ran a finger across the line of her eyebrow.

"Clapperclaw had that fear aura. She must have scared you."

"What, a big bug? Never."

Aderyn smiled. "What if we fought a giant spider?"

Owen shuddered. "All right, you got me there. Spiders freak me out. I'd probably run screaming and leave you in my wake if we met a giant spider."

"Owen! You would not!"

"No," Owen said, "I definitely would not," and kissed her, his lips warm and insistent on hers. Aderyn put her arms around his neck and returned his kiss. She was aware of the heat of his body against hers in a way she hadn't since their first kiss back in Elkenforest, the shape of him pressed against her.

Owen whispered between kisses, "Do you know what is the best thing about fighting? Making up afterward."

Aderyn giggled. "I'd like to think we could do the making-up activities without having the fighting as well."

"The making-up activities are supposed to be amazing after a fight. Even better than usual."

"I'm not sure I believe that," Aderyn murmured against his mouth. "You'll have to convince me—ohhhh. That works, too."

"We're just getting started," Owen said.

THEY LAY TOGETHER AFTERWARDS, HANDS CLASPED, NOT speaking as their breathing and heart rates returned to normal. Aderyn ran her finger over Owen's hand, feeling the familiar contours, the calluses from sword fighting, the warmth of his skin. She'd never felt so perfectly content.

"You were right," she said.

"Was I? I guess it had to happen sometime."

She chuckled. "About sex being better after a fight. I feel healed."

"Yeah, that's it exactly. Like we're back to being one."

She hesitated. There was something she wanted to say, but it was so close to what they'd fought about, she didn't know if she should bring it up and maybe ruin this beautiful accord they'd found. On the other hand, she was done dancing around things that might upset Owen. "You know," she said, "there's a reason women in my world treat the men who approach them with kindness."

Owen rolled over to face her. "I do want to know this, now that I've got my head on straight. Where I come from, men would take that kind of reaction as encouragement to go further."

"Here, since men are the ones who have to approach women, they do what they can to show their interest. And women choose their partners from the men who express an interest. But we are always conscious of how much men risk, emotionally, by taking that chance."

"That seems extreme. I know a lot of guys who are willing to get shot down a hundred times on the chance of getting a girl's number the hundred and first. Their hearts aren't strongly engaged."

"That's true, but men who feel that way—I'll get to that in a bit. The point is that for the men who are serious, women recognize that courage, and we treat the honorable men with courtesy even when we turn them down."

"Honorable men. I was wondering if that meant you had to put up with jerks."

"No. But that doesn't happen as often as you think." Aderyn rolled onto her side. "Anyway, it's come to be a mark of admiration, men giving women they think are beautiful or admirable gifts. All those presents, all those poems—well, not all, but most—those aren't serious expressions of interest. They know it, and I know it. Those would be like your friends who—what is a girl's number, anyway? Do I have a number?"

"Don't worry about it. Go on."

"Anyway, the few that are serious, well, it's important to me that I show I respect their courtesy and their interest. And then I turn them down."

"So it doesn't matter that you're already attached to someone," Owen said. "I don't get why that wouldn't put a guy off."

"Well, it's not uncommon for women who aren't deeply attached to their sweethearts to change their minds. I've never understood that, myself, but I have a wonderful sweetheart and I don't think anyone is superior to him." She leaned forward and kissed him lightly, trying to control her nerves. "There's only one condition where that attachment would prevent men from approaching a woman."

"Really? What's that?"

She drew in a deep breath. "If we were married."

Owen said nothing.

All in a rush, Aderyn said, "I didn't want to ask you to marry me just to make you feel better or to make those men stop approaching me. I don't have any proposal planned, either, nothing big and dramatic like a proposal should be. Though that's probably not your tradition, the elaborate proposal. Maybe in your world it's the man who proposes." She laughed nervously. "Then I'd have put all that effort in just to confuse you, and if you turned me down in public, we'd both look stupid."

Still, Owen was silent, though his hand closed over hers firmly. She forged onward, wishing she could remember anything she'd just said.

"We could go on like this for as long as you want, because I'm not going anywhere. But what I know now—what I am absolutely certain of—is when you introduced me to Raynir as your sweetheart, I wished with everything in me that you'd been able to say I was your wife instead."

Owen let out a deep breath. "I didn't know women did the proposing here, though it fits with everything else you've told me. *Was* that a proposal just now?"

Aderyn closed her eyes. "I guess it was. But if you—"

Owen rested two fingers against her lips, silencing her. "You're right about one thing. I definitely don't want you to feel pressured, like you only want to marry me because that will stop those men I'm jealous of from coming on to you. But—what does it mean to be married, here? Is there some—I don't know—some benefit from the system, or is it a recognition of a lifetime's commitment, or what?"

"Oh. Well, yes, it's a promise to stay faithful to each other for the rest of your lives, to support each other and your children, if you have any. But it's also something that registers with the system. I don't know if you've noticed that when you Assess someone who's married, there's a symbol in the Assessment next to the name of their spouse. That shows up in both classed and non-classed Assessments.

Some people say the system gives them benefits for being married, like a sense of where your spouse is or if they're in danger, but that might be superstition."

"I just want to make sure I'm not committing to anything weird or unpleasant, like obeying you without question."

She laughed. "That's ridiculous."

"Sometime I'll tell you what marriage used to include in my world, but now it would ruin the mood." Owen scooted closer and took Aderyn in his arms. "Say it again. Your proposal."

"I can't remember what I said. I was too nervous."

"It really doesn't take much, you know. In my world, it's a simple question."

"Then let's do it your way." She brushed his hair back from his face. "Will you marry me?"

"I will. No question. I love you, Aderyn. Let's make our union official."

She rested her forehead gently against his, then rolled to lie on her back. "All right. Open your Advancement in the Codex."

"What, we can do this right now? Isn't there someone who has to officiate?"

"Um, no, of course not. This is private and personal, just the two of us. Do as I do." She brought the Codex up and whispered, "Advancement."

Immediately, the display lit up, but she didn't read her class and level and skills. Instead, she said, "Unite."

You have chosen to activate the Unite effect. Please state the name of the person you wish to join with.

Beside her, Owen said, "Aderyn."

"Owen," Aderyn said.

There is no one by that name registered with the system. Please choose another person to join with.

A chill passed through Aderyn. Then she laughed in realization. "Jacob Owen Lindberg."

Is [Jacob Owen Lindberg] present?: Select Y / N

Aderyn touched the softly glowing letter Y and saw Owen make a similar gesture.

The system display rippled, then settled back to its solid silver glow. This time, it was centered between them, and Aderyn was sure the message that appeared was visible to both of them.

Do [Aderyn] and [Jacob Owen Lindberg] choose to Unite in marriage?
Select Y / N

They both touched the Y at the same time.

Warning: This commitment is binding on [Aderyn] and [Jacob Owen Lindberg]. Dissolution of this commitment may be performed only under certain limited circumstances. You may view this list of circumstances at any time by selecting [Dissolution]. Do you wish to continue?
Select Y / N

"That's intimidating," Owen said.

"Marriage is serious business," Aderyn said, "as my parents always told us."

"They got married while they adventured, right?"

"Yes. A few years before they reached level twenty." Aderyn drew in a deep breath and released it. "Now's your time to back out—"

Owen grabbed her hand and guided her to touch the Y along with him. "Sorry, you were dithering," he said with a grin.

Aderyn laughed and shifted her hand to clasp his.

To perform the Unite action, select Y from the options below. Accept? Y / N

Together, they touched the letter Y.

The system message vanished.

Aderyn and Owen looked at each other. "Is that it?" Owen asked.

"I guess. I always thought—"

Congratulations! You have agreed to Unite in marriage. You have been awarded a one-time bonus of [1000 XP]. You have gained the [Unite] skill

"[Unite]?" Aderyn called up Advancement and Assessed her newest skill.

[Unite]: Creates a connection between married partners. Paired individuals with [Unite] have access to the skills [Read Body Language] and [Secret Message] in times of distress. You could consider what it means that you and Owen already share this, Aderyn.

Aderyn gasped.

"Is something wrong?" Owen asked.

"Listen to this." She began to read the Assessment of **[Unite]** and got another shock: the final sentence had disappeared. "I think the system spoke to me. Just a second ago the message said something about it being meaningful that we already share those skills. And it called you Owen instead of by your full name."

"Do you have any idea what it means?"

"None." She checked her Advancement again. There, beneath

her name, was the ∞ symbol and "Jacob Owen Lindberg" beside it. She couldn't stop smiling. "And I don't care. We're married!"

She rolled onto her side again. Owen lay on his back, gazing at the middle distance as he read the Codex. "This beats a wedding ring all to hell," he murmured.

"What is that?"

"Just something from my world." He focused on her and smiled. "Is it weird that I'm not eager for sex after that? I would like to hold you, and sleep, and wake beside my wife."

Aderyn snuggled close. "Your wife. That's not going to get old any time soon."

CHAPTER THIRTY-FOUR

Aderyn felt odd, going downstairs for breakfast the following morning, that she and Owen had taken such a big step and nobody knew it. True, if they Assessed her, they would see the new line in her Codex display, but unless they were actively adventuring, people didn't generally use Assess all that often. And yet she felt even stranger at the thought of telling people, particularly out of the blue. Nobody was likely to discover the truth until men began Assessing the Swift before approaching her.

Owen caught her hand before they entered the taproom. "You're nervous."

"Does it show?"

"Only to me. This isn't you having second thoughts about uniting in marriage with someone like me, is it?"

Aderyn's eyes narrowed. "Someone like you?"

Owen struck a noble pose. "Handsome, a proficient fighter, soon to be top champion of the Glory Games—"

Aderyn laughed, and her nervousness dissolved. "All right. You have an excellent point. Let's tell our friends."

"Are there any other marriage traditions I should know about?"

Owen asked as they crossed the taproom to where Weston and Isold
were sitting. "Bachelor parties... though I guess we're a little late for
those. Receptions? Gifts?"

"Are we talking about Aderyn's admirers?" Weston asked. "Do you
have more gifts than you know what to do with? Because I'd be happy
to take them off your hands." He spoke with the determined lightness
of someone pretending last night's unpleasantness hadn't happened.

"Owen wants to know about marriage traditions," Aderyn said.

"Well, where I come from—" Weston began.

Isold elbowed him in the ribs to shut him up. "Do you have any
particular reason for asking?" he said, arching his eyebrows.

Owen put his arm around Aderyn's shoulders. "Just the one
you've guessed."

Isold leaped to his feet. "Congratulations, both of you. What
beautiful news."

"Wait, seriously?" Weston rose as well and thumped both Owen
and Aderyn on the back. "Aderyn, how did you keep your proposal
plan a secret? When was this? Last night?"

"She proposed the otherworlder way, which was to ask a simple
question." Owen grinned. "Though now I feel cheated, if your way is
as exciting as all that."

"I would have sworn Aderyn was the type to enlist a hundred
people. Maybe right after we had a dungeon victory so the entire
arena could be in on it." Weston waved at Livia. "Livia, come here,
you're missing out!"

"Unless you're talking about an endless pot of coffee, I doubt
that." Livia's eyes were barely open, and she slouched into a seat and
fumbled with the nearest mug.

"Livia, Aderyn and Owen are married," Isold said.

Livia dropped her mug, which fortunately didn't fall farther than
the tabletop. "No. Aderyn, how did you propose? I need details."

"Looking for ideas, sweetheart?" Weston said.

"You already know I can't propose to you until you've met my family." Livia righted the mug and filled it. "Was it beautiful? I was sure you'd want a big public proposal."

"Why does everyone think that?" Aderyn demanded. "I don't really care about those things."

"Because you're an unabashed romantic," Livia said. "All right, I'm sure it was perfect however you did it. And you picked a good day, because it's a rest day for the Games and we'll have all day to plan your bash for tonight."

"Oh, right," Weston said. "You wanted to know about traditions. You're supposed to pay for an enormous party, you and your wife, which by tradition usually means drinking until you pass out. Your guests, I mean, not you personally."

"Oh. That's intimidating," Owen said.

Weston waved that off. "You can talk to Gerant and Arlia. I'm sure they'd be happy to host it here. And Gerant can handle all the details. You just have to toss him a nice, fat purse."

"It's really fun," Aderyn assured Owen. "There's music—" She remembered the flute-playing Beguiler and fell silent.

Owen hugged her. "No flutes. I guarantee it. Here, sit down and let's talk."

"Talk? About what?"

"About what we're doing to find Damaris the Beguiler," Owen said.

The name dampened everyone's spirits. Aderyn sat and looked at her hands. The memory of being Beguiled made her feel sick. She glanced at Owen, who seemed lost in painful thought, and suddenly she wasn't afraid and ashamed, she was angry.

"I'm not going to let her win," she declared. "I am going to eat a delicious breakfast with my friends and my husband, and then I am going to use the <**Wayfinder**> to track that bitch down and make her eat her flute."

Owen had brightened at the word "husband." "You're right. We aren't her victims. We can stop her."

"Don't get excited too soon," Isold warned. "Remember a Beguiler's skill at confusing and altering people's minds and emotions can extend to obfuscating the Beguiler's trail."

"That's a good warning. All right, I will *attempt* to find the bitch. And with luck, even if we can't find her directly, we'll learn something from how she misdirects us."

"An excellent idea," Isold said, raising a mug to salute Aderyn.

By four o'clock that afternoon, the <Wayfinder> had led Aderyn all over Finion's Gate, from Foundation up to Terrace Three and everywhere in between, without finding a trace of Damaris. When the magic orb finally failed to glow at all, Aderyn lowered it and said, "I'm too tired to go on. I hope we learned something."

"Sit," Owen said, guiding her to a nearby iron bench in what he referred to as a park, one of many large areas of grass and trees that Finion's Gate inexplicably encouraged. Gardens, Aderyn had seen, but those were always attached to houses and these parks didn't seem to belong to anyone. It was beautiful, even though it confused her.

"We have learned something," Isold said. "Every place the <Wayfinder> took us to had not only never heard of Damaris, it was not a place at which Heralds play. Private houses, shops, even a couple of government offices."

"I noticed that, but I don't know what it means," Livia said.

"It means Damaris overplayed her hand," Weston said. "Her— what did you call the skill, Isold?"

"[Obscure]," Isold said. "In the sense of fogging or concealing a path."

"Her [Obscure] skill directed us to places she would never be,"

Weston said. "It would have been more clever to send searchers to taverns or playhouses, especially ones she *had* been at recently. Her mistake means we've narrowed down where to look without us having to use the <**Wayfinder**> further, and it tells us wherever she lives, it's in an inn or tavern."

"I get it," Livia said. "But there must be hundreds of taverns in Finion's Gate, so what do we do now?"

"Unfortunately, we'll have to turn the search over to Seonn," Owen said. "Hundreds of taverns means it will take a lot more people than the five of us to cover all that ground. So we're back to figuring out where she will strike next."

"I think we should look closely at Nator," Aderyn said. "He benefitted from one assault and might have benefited from the attack on Owen."

"That's true, but we might want to think bigger," Owen said. "What about his sponsor?"

"You mean Brisa might be behind the attacks?" Livia said.

"She'd benefit politically if she could boost her Terrible Twins in the rankings." Owen sat beside Aderyn and absently took the <**Wayfinder**> out of her hand.

"Too bad we don't have the bracket to see who's fighting Evalyn next," Weston said.

"Don't worry. At this point, it's imprinted on the backs of my eyelids." Owen closed his eyes as if in emphasis. "Evalyn is set to fight Gabryl, right after my bout with Pace."

"Which means Gabryl could be in danger," Aderyn said. "Can we warn him?"

"I sent him and Raewyn messages about the party tonight." Owen grimaced. "I don't know that I like either of them much, and Gabryl, for one, is deeply jealous of me, but we share a sponsor, so I thought it was the polite thing to do."

"Well, I'm no runner, and I'm not interested in chasing him all over town," Livia said. "We can talk to him if he comes to the party.

Which, by the way, we should get back to the inn for. I want some solid food in me before I carouse."

"I can't argue with that." Owen handed the <**Wayfinder**> to Aderyn and helped her stand. "You're all right?"

"Just achy. It goes away after I walk normally instead of being hunched over." Aderyn tucked the orb away in her <**Purse of Great Capacity**> and rotated her shoulders. "But I'm not planning to drink much tonight. It's more fun to watch everyone else slide into inebriation."

"I never thought watching people drink was all that fun," Owen said.

Aderyn smiled. "Just wait until the singing begins. You'll change your mind."

FOUR HOURS LATER, ADERYN SAT AT THE BAR, LEANING against Owen, and tapped her toe to the bright melody of fiddle and drum. "I told you it was fun," she said.

"You were right." Owen tipped back the last of his beer and set the mug behind him. All around them, men and women drank, and sang, and shouted for more beer, and drank again. Borrus whirled past, stopped, and backtracked to come to a panting halt in front of them.

"Welcome to the family," he slurred. "In case I didn't say it before."

"You did. Three times," Owen said with a grin.

"Always did say we could use another man in the family. Tip the balance." Borrus's face was flushed, and he sounded as drunk as practically every other person present was, which meant Aderyn had a private wager with herself on how long he'd manage to stay upright and conscious.

"So will your parents be upset at all that they barely know me?"

Owen gripped Borrus's shoulder to steady him. "I mean, in my w—where I come from, families expect to get to know their kids' spouses long before they get married."

"Some parents might. Not ours," Aderyn said. "They always say how they raised us to make our own choices, which means trusting those choices are good."

"Plus they'll be too shocked at Aderyn getting married at all to worry about what kind of man you are," Borrus said with an exaggerated wink.

"Borrus!"

"I kid, I kid. You said they met you already, so you're not a total stranger." Borrus covered his mouth as he hiccupped, which told Aderyn he wasn't as drunk as he seemed. "Don't worry about it. I'll vouch for you." He winked again and was pulled back into the dance.

"See? Nothing to worry about," Aderyn said.

"Just so he doesn't vouch for me in that condition. I'm not sure it would benefit me." Owen put an arm around her shoulders. "I do feel a little detached from our own party. You want to teach me how to dance?"

"What, here? Now?"

"Why not? Everyone's too drunk to care if I look stupid, or too much like an otherworlder." He slid off his stool and offered her his hand. "Let's do it."

Smiling, Aderyn led him to where the musicians played, red-faced and glowing with perspiration in the warmth of the taproom. "Isold, Owen and I are going to dance. Can you play 'Merry-O'?"

"Of course." Isold signaled to the fiddlers, one of them a stranger, the other the Stalwart challenger Eirian. They listened to his quiet words, and Eirian glanced at Owen with a smile so cheerful it transformed her normally serious face. Then they went into a song whose bright melody filled Aderyn with a desire to move.

The other merrymakers picked up the beat and began dancing, some in little groups, others by themselves. "You leap on the downbeat, and go tap-tap-tap at the top of the measure... oh, I should have asked if you know music at all, shouldn't I?"

"I played the trumpet when I was in fifth grade, so yeah." He took Aderyn's hand again, and followed her footsteps, hesitantly at first.

Aderyn nudged him. "Let yourself feel the music. This isn't about being perfect, it's dancing!" She released his hand and flung her arms high in the air as she leaped and was mirrored by a dozen men and women.

Owen stepped rapidly and jumped, his face red and smiling, then did it again, looser and more relaxed. "I think I get it!"

They danced, circling each other, as others whirled around them and the music built to a fever pitch. Finally, Isold hit a few last beats, and they came to earth and hugged each other, breathing heavily. "That was amazing," Owen said. "Let's keep going."

"I need some air first," Aderyn said. "You could try it by yourself."

"You know, I think I will?" Owen kissed her. "But don't be gone too long. I do want to dance with you again."

"It's our party. I think we should expect that."

She slipped out through the kitchen, not wanting to be mobbed by latecomers, and shut the back door behind her. The night was cold, but in her overheated state, it felt pleasantly cool. She drew in a deep breath and immediately regretted it when the stench of rotting food piled a short distance down the alley stung her nostrils. Gerant always said Finion's Gate was good at waste disposal, but he meant "thorough" rather than "quick."

Distantly, she heard the sounds of something scraping across stone, and then grunts. The sounds of a fight. Impulsively, she hurried toward the noise, then stopped. She was unarmed, and she wasn't big enough to intervene physically in a fight, especially if it was a couple of men larger than she.

A man came running around the corner of the alley ahead, past the pile of rotting food, pursued by another figure. Aderyn flattened herself against the wall and hoped whoever was the aggressor wouldn't stop to attack her as well.

The person following was female, Aderyn realized, and as the woman neared her, Aderyn recognized her despite how her face was contorted in anger. Raewyn. Aderyn immediately cast about for a weapon and found nothing but a couple of half-bricks wedged beneath a tilting table where Arlia took deliveries. Aderyn tugged one free and threw it at the fleeing man. Owen always said how good her fastball was, not that she knew what that meant.

The half-brick took the man in the back of the skull. He jerked, took a few steps more, and dropped to the ground. Raewyn stopped running and stared at Aderyn. "Why—oh, Aderyn. That was impressive."

"It's **[Improvised Distraction]**, but Owen taught me to throw, so it's an attack as much as a diversion. Why were you chasing him?" Aderyn wiped brick dust off on her trousers and approached the fallen man as Raewyn knelt over him.

"He's alive." Raewyn jerked upright. "Gabryl. He was fighting —" She took off running back the way she'd come. Aderyn, with a glance at the fallen man, ran after her. It hadn't occurred to her that she might have killed him with that missile, and although he probably wasn't a good person, she was grateful for his life anyway.

She came around the corner to find Raewyn kneeling over someone again, pressing down on the man's chest with both hands like she wanted to keep him from rising. "Help me," she said hoarsely. "Gabryl's dying."

CHAPTER THIRTY-FIVE

Aderyn ran immediately into the Alabaster Inn and bounced off Owen, who'd been about to open the front door. "I was coming to look for you," he said. "What's wrong? You look distressed."

"Gabryl and Raewyn were attacked outside the inn. Gabryl's wounded. We need a Bonemender, fast."

Owen half-turned to Assess the room over his shoulder. "No one here is a Bonemender. Go tell Borrus—no, he's too drunk. Tell Gerant, he'll know who to send for." He pushed his way past Aderyn and let the door slam shut.

Aderyn rushed through hall that skirted the taproom and led to the kitchen. Gerant was there, hoisting a crate of wine bottles to carry it to the bar. "Aderyn. You need something?"

Aderyn gasped out her news, and Gerant set the crate down gently and said, "It will be all right. I'll be back soon." He left the kitchen. Arlia, standing next to the enormous soup pot from which she would feed her employees that busy night, gaped in amazement.

"Attacked? Outside our inn? That's impossible. This is a good neighborhood." She discovered she'd let the long-handled wooden spoon fall out of her hand into the pot and used a couple of other spoons to fish it out.

"I know. I can't explain it." Except she could, if she was willing to reveal the existence of a Beguiler loose in Finion's Gate. Seonn, when they'd spoken to him earlier, had told them explicitly to say nothing about it. On the other hand...

"Arlia, have you heard of a Herald named Damaris?" Aderyn asked.

Arlia didn't look suspicious of this change of subject. "She's played here once or twice. I've never seen her, but the serving men and women talk about it when she visits." She laughed. "You'd think she was visiting royalty or something with the way they chatter."

"Was she here last night?"

"I don't know. Last night was so busy. You could ask Meris or Kamron." She returned to stirring her pot. "Not to shoo you away, but you ought to return to your guests if you don't want them asking questions. Was the victim someone you know?"

Aderyn nodded. "Thank you."

The party was still going strong when she returned. No one seemed to have noticed her absence, nor that Owen was also gone. Aderyn sat at the bar and smiled tightly at anyone who approached her for a dance. None of them minded when she turned them down. Finally, she couldn't stand the suspense any longer, and she left the inn with as little fuss as she could manage.

A small group of people had gathered where Gabryl had fallen, and Aderyn saw Owen among them. "Is he—" she asked.

Owen shook his head. "I mean, no, he's not dead. The Bone-mender got here a minute ago and she's working on him. This is really bad."

"You mean because we were right about Gabryl being in danger? I feel terrible that we didn't try to warn him sooner. But I wouldn't have guessed someone would attack him openly on the street." She gasped. "Did anyone capture that man I hit?"

"Who?"

She ran instead of responding, down the alley and around the corner, but came to a halt only a few steps in. The man was gone. "Damn it," she said. "I should have done something about him."

"Aderyn, what are you talking about?" Owen had followed her and was looking down the alley toward its far end, in the direction Aderyn faced.

"Raewyn was chasing Gabryl's attacker, and I knocked him out with a brick. Then we went back to help Gabryl, and in the hurry to find a Bonemender I forgot nobody else knew about him." She let out a frustrated breath. "And now we lost a source of information."

"There were two attackers," Owen said. "Raewyn chased one. She said Gabryl was holding the other off just fine when she left, but he was badly wounded when she returned and his attacker had vanished. Let's go see if he's recovered."

Gabryl, his front gory with blood, was sitting up when they returned. "I'm fine," he insisted irritably. "Get off me. I'm leaving."

"There might be other attackers," Owen said. "You should come inside."

Gabryl laughed. "Looking like this? Not that I care how it affects your party, because I'm sure you don't either, but I hate fuss. Sorry to miss out." He didn't sound sorry.

"But—" Aderyn began, then couldn't think what to say next. There were four other people, plus the Bonemender and Gerant, hovering around Gabryl, and Seonn's warning still rang in her ears. She Assessed the Bonemender quickly, reaching for the woman's name, and said, "Look, everyone, Gabryl's fine now. Mistress Liah, thank you for your quick response. Can I reimburse you for your time?"

"I can pay for my own healing, thanks." Gabryl dug in his belt pouch, then froze for the briefest moment, such a small hesitation Aderyn wasn't sure anyone else had noticed. He handed over a number of large gold coins. "Thank you, Mistress Liah. Racwyn,

I'm headed back, but you shouldn't feel you need to accompany me."

Visions of Gabryl being alone and attacked a second time filled Aderyn's head. "No, we really do want you to stay," she gabbled. "I mean, it's not like I get married every day, and having you as a guest is... is an honor. And there's so much to talk about. Like that lovely belt pouch. I'd love to know where you got it. I'm amazed you don't worry about *thieves.*"

Gabryl looked at her like she was crazy. So did everyone except Gerant, who was scanning the surroundings alertly, and the Bone-mender Liah, who was preoccupied with the contents of her purse. Aderyn widened her eyes in mute appeal for Gabryl to get the hint. His hand drifted to his belt pouch, and again he hesitated. Finally, he said, "I'll go through to the back and have a drink with you. Raewyn, no need to stay."

"I'll have a drink, too, but I'll sit in the taproom." Raewyn sounded off-handed, but Aderyn had seen them look at each other and was convinced her guess the night they'd all met was correct, and Raewyn and Gabryl were secretly sweethearts.

Owen stayed with Aderyn and Gabryl as they filed into the back hallway. Gabryl didn't go any farther. "What in thunder is this about? Has marriage made you crazy?"

"You were attacked to keep you from competing tomorrow," Owen said. "Whether the attacker wanted you dead or just incapacitated, we don't know."

"That's ridiculous." Gabryl didn't sound as outraged as Aderyn thought he should have.

"We have proof." Aderyn decided not to dance around the issue. Seonn would have to deal with it. "There's a Beguiler in Finion's Gate who's interfering with Games competitors. We think she's working for Brisa so Evalyn and Nator will advance in the rankings."

"Are you joking? Those were just random attackers tonight. They didn't act Beguiled."

Owen shrugged. "They're both gone. We can't prove they were. But if they weren't, that was some coincidence."

"They didn't take your purse," Aderyn reminded Gabryl. "You know that's strange."

"But how—" Gabryl's mouth snapped shut. He looked like he was going over something mentally. "Evalyn would advance without challenge if I couldn't fight. But Raewyn isn't fighting Nator."

"Not yet," Owen said. "Depending on how her fight against Kendria falls out, she could come up against him in a day or two."

Gabryl laughed harshly. "She's good, but Kendria will win. Raewyn knows it, too. But her getting scratched before losing to Kendria doesn't benefit anyone but Kendria. So your theory is weak."

"Unless she wasn't the one attacked. It's more likely she was a secondary target because she was with you," Owen said.

"Yes, terrible coincidence that we came together," Gabryl said roughly.

"It's all right, we won't tell," Aderyn said. "But you need to talk to Seonn. He knows about the Beguiler and he might be able to find your attackers."

"I'm not talking to Seonn. I can't do anything that might lead to suspicion about me and... anyone I might be involved with." Gabryl's mouth was set in a stubborn line.

"But you came here tonight together," Owen said. "Isn't that suspicious behavior?"

"We were walking separately when I was set upon," Gabryl said. "She came to my rescue. There's nothing more to say."

"Gabryl, other people might be in danger. Don't you want to do something about that?" Aderyn exclaimed.

"The attackers ran. There's no way anyone can find them now." Gabryl walked away. "Tell Seonn if you want to, but it won't do any good."

When Gabryl was gone, Aderyn said, "Shouldn't we stop him? He might still be in danger."

"There's only so much we can do, and Gabryl is a grown man who makes his own decisions." Owen hugged Aderyn quickly. "We should talk to Raewyn. Maybe she can convince him."

But when they returned to the taproom, Raewyn was gone. Frustrated, Aderyn accepted a glass of wine and drank half of it in one gulp. At the other end of the bar, Borrus snored with his head pillowed on his arms resting on the oak slab. "I feel sorry for them," she told Owen quietly. "It must be so hard for them to have to pretend not to care for each other."

"Someday one will retire, or both, and they'll be able to be open about their relationship." Owen had a mug of ale, but he wasn't drinking it, just running a finger around the lip of the mug. "What concerns me is we now have a strong connection to Brisa, but I'm guessing accusing one of the ruling Councilors of complicity with a Beguiler to rig the Games is something you don't do lightly."

"Seonn will know. Tomorrow." Aderyn drank the rest of her wine and set the glass down. "Let's dance again. We can pretend nothing is wrong in Finion's Gate."

Owen took her hand. "Maybe we should be grateful that the Beguiler's attack on us wasn't physical."

Aderyn made a face. "Let's pretend that didn't happen, too."

"Aaaaaaaand... welcome to today's quarterfinal matches!" The announcer sounded as cheerful as if he didn't know about all the attacks that put the Games in jeopardy. "We've got a great matchup for you, right off the starting block, and I know you know it—let's hear it for Raewyn and Kendria!"

The covert was packed today despite the Scrappers and the Fearsome Five having completed their dungeon. Nobody wanted to go for drinks when Kendria was fighting. Aderyn stood on her chair to get a better look over the heads of the others. Kendria and Raewyn strode into the arena like predators sizing the place up. Both wore well-fitted shirts and trousers, and Raewyn wore the same soft shoes she had before, while Kendria wore ankle boots. Neither looked at the spectators or each other. When they reached the center of the arena, they tapped their staffs together like this was any other sparring match. But both of them had too much at stake to take this casually.

The signal sounded, and immediately they leaped at each other, Raewyn blocking Kendria's longstaff and flicking her second shortstaff around to tag Kendria's arm. Kendria blocked just in time and swept her longstaff at Raewyn's legs. Raewyn leaped effortlessly and extended one foot in a kick that struck Kendria's midsection.

"One to Raewyn!" shouted the adjudicator.

"And Raewyn is coming out strong!" the announcer boomed. "She had some bad luck last season, but she's a strong competitor. Kendria will have to work hard today!"

The announcer irritated Aderyn. He sounded partial to Kendria, and he ought to be even-handed in his commentary.

But Kendria and Raewyn didn't look like they heard him. Kendria's staff swept around again, and this time she struck Raewyn's shoulder. "One to Kendria!"

The crowd was shouting so loudly Aderyn could feel the chair shake. She jumped down, just to be safe, and missed the next blow. "Two to Kendria!"

Aderyn stood on tiptoes to see past one of the Vagabonds, a tall man standing next to Jesper. She'd never felt short in her life before being surrounded by all these absurdly tall team members. "Was it a good blow?" she asked.

Jesper turned his head and then tugged on her arm so she could stand in front of him. "Kendria almost didn't counter Raewyn's last strike. I think it's good for her to have to work hard for victory."

Again, irritation flowered within Aderyn. "You're that sure she'll win?"

"Wish I wasn't," Jesper said.

Kendria blocked Raewyn's spinning shortstaffs, dodged a kick, and stepped back out of Raewyn's range. Switching her grip, she swung with her staff, whirling past her opponent and bringing the weapon around to strike Raewyn across the back. "Three to Kendria!" the adjudicator screamed, his voice barely audible over the noise of the crowd despite whatever magic item increased its volume.

Raewyn and Kendria saluted the spectators, though Raewyn walked away before Kendria did. Kendria bowed, saluted again, and finally turned toward one of the Councilors' boxes to salute Balan. Then she walked out of the arena with her head held high. It was all very stately and respectful. Aderyn still didn't like her.

"That was *amazing*, friends!" the announcer shouted. "Once again we see why Kendria is the best!"

"The best at posturing," Jesper said in a low voice. Aderyn giggled. That Jesper shared in her dislike for the champion cheered her.

"Up next is another match I'm sure you've all been waiting for," the announcer said. "Let's give a warm Glory Games welcome to... Pace and *Owen!*"

CHAPTER THIRTY-SIX

Aderyn gripped the rail tightly and leaned out, though thanks to Jesper she had an excellent view of the tunnel and Owen and Pace emerging from it. Owen turned in the direction of the covert and caught Aderyn's eye. With a smile, he saluted her, and Aderyn waved back frantically. It was probably just her imagination that the cheering grew louder as some of the spectators Assessed them and discovered their new connection.

"You didn't do that on purpose, did you?" Jesper shook his head. "No, of course not. I'm sorry I suggested it."

"What, got married to make everyone excited at how romantic it is, a challenger and a Wildcat together? No." Owen had moved on to wave at the rest of the crowd, making a wide arc that took him to the center of the arena where Pace was. "It's not like the crowd's approval makes Owen more likely to win."

"Right."

Pace and Owen drew their swords. Owen was more heavily armored than his opponent, who wore a lighter leather jerkin reinforced with metal plates, and his sword was longer and looked like it weighed more. Aderyn saw Owen's lips move, and Pace smiled and nodded. They tapped their swords together and stepped back, waiting for the signal.

When the horn blew, Owen leaped, meeting Pace halfway as the Lone Wolf did the same. Swords clashed, and the two men disengaged, Pace drawing his dagger half a breath before Owen did the same. Owen caught the downward stroke of Pace's sword on his dagger's crossguard, stepped inside Pace's guard and thumped his sword blade against Pace's jerkin.

"One to Owen!" the adjudicator shouted.

Pace and Owen separated, but not very far. Both balanced lightly on the balls of their feet, slowly circling, looking for an opening. Pace feinted, but Owen wasn't drawn. Pace feinted again, and then he lunged at Owen for real. As if Owen had **[See It Coming]**, he ducked to one side so Pace ran past him. Pace tried to recover, but not soon enough, and Owen thwacked the back of the man's jerkin. As the adjudicator announced the hit, Owen and Pace closed again, and now they were fighting in earnest, the sound of metal ringing against metal echoing over the noise of the crowd.

It was so fast Aderyn didn't see it, only heard the adjudicator shout, "One to Pace!" She let out a hiss of frustration.

"That was impressive," Jesper said. "Did you see it? Pace took advantage of the barest opening to tag Owen's knee."

"He's not hurt," Aderyn said, willing it to be true. She watched Owen, who'd gone back to circling, but he seemed to be moving easily.

"I don't think so. And I'm betting that's the only opening Pace will get."

Aderyn's hands hurt from gripping the rough wooden railing, but she felt superstitiously like it was Owen's lifeline, like he would win if she held on. Which, given his skill, was stupidly unlikely. She held on anyway.

It was Owen's turn to feint, but when he did it a second time, Pace took the bait, aiming a powerful blow at Owen's armored shoulder. Owen deflected the blow with his sword, catching Pace's blade and bringing both sword blades around in a skreeing arc of clashing metal. He caught Pace's dagger with the dagger in his off hand. For a terrible taut moment, the two combatants stilled, their bodies trembling with tension. Then Owen visibly gathered himself and shoved Pace away, disengaging both his weapons. Pace stumbled, the barest hiccup in his stride, but Owen was on him in that instant. Pace parried Owen's sword, but he was too slow with his dagger, and in the next instant, Owen's dagger thudded against Pace's chest.

Congratulations! You have defeated [Pace the Lone Wolf]. You have earned [14,000 XP]

Aderyn jumped up and down and screamed Owen's name a couple of times before she felt stupid and settled down. She peeled her aching hands away from the rail and watched Owen and Pace shake hands before saluting the crowd together. The noise of cheering was so loud it was palpable, pressing against her eardrums and making her skin feel tight.

"Your husband is a good winner," Jesper commented. "The crowd likes that. Not like that Jael. Any victory of hers leaves a bad taste in my mouth."

"I'm looking forward to Owen fighting her again. And beating her soundly." She loved the sound of "husband." Maybe she was an unabashed romantic, after all.

She watched the remaining two matches with interest. Gabryl showed no sign that he'd been seriously wounded and defeated Evalyn easily. That could mean he was still in danger, since killing him would advance Evalyn... but that didn't make any sense. Attacking Gabryl last night, before he fought, would just have meant Evalyn had to fight—oh, she didn't have the stupid bracket in her head like Owen did, but it would be whoever Gabryl had defeated to get to this point. So either Brisa and her pet Beguiler thought Evalyn would have had a better chance against that person, or they'd made a mistake.

The final match of the morning was the handsome Stalwart Rhidius and the awful Jael. Rhidius fought well, but he was no match for the petite Swordsworn, much to Aderyn's disgust. Well, the one good thing about Jael continuing to win was that Owen would eventually fight her and show the world which of them was actually better.

When the fight was over, Jesper clapped Aderyn companionably on the shoulder. "Hope you're not worried about our dungeon battle today."

"Who, me?" Aderyn tried to raise one eyebrow but had to settle for raising both in what she hoped was a carefree expression. "Shouldn't *you* be worried that the plucky underdogs are going to defeat you?"

"Surprisingly, I am, a little." Jesper laughed. "I mean, not *much*, but you Wildcats have done well so far. And I think I've told you that I'm not so cocky as to assume we've won before we have."

"That's how I feel. I'm excited to see how it goes!" For once, it was true—she wasn't worried about losing to the Hooligans, and she also didn't feel the Wildcats' victory was a given. She knew they would all perform to the best of their abilities, and it would be fun. She was starting to understand why Jesper had the attitude he did about competition.

Owen didn't join them for lunch, and Aderyn guessed he was with Raynir, being on display with Gabryl as important winners. Did Raewyn still qualify as successful, given that she'd lost her bout? Aderyn suspected that losing to Kendria was considered a typical outcome, and nobody held it against Kendria's opponents. At least, Aderyn hoped that was the case. She barely knew either woman, but she still resented Kendria for her treatment of Borrus.

The four friends ate lightly and drank no alcohol, and returned to the room under the arena well before the dungeon battle was scheduled to start. With the beginning of the quarterfinals, the Games offered a single dungeon before the fights instead of two. Aderyn's feeling of excitement had faded to nervousness, but it was her typical anticipatory nervousness and nothing that would interfere with her performance.

Gradually, the Hooligans trickled in, with Jesper entering last. "Wildcats!" he called out. "Are you ready for a real challenge?"

"What, are you talking about yourselves?" Weston said with a grin. "And here we thought you Hooligans were scared to face us."

"Hooligans fear nothing except a fast victory," one of the other Hooligans, Serrin, said. He was bouncing a thick glass vial filled with a thin yellow liquid that let out bubbles every time the vial hit his hand. "It makes us look mean if we trounce you too easily."

"Well, that's not going to happen," Livia said.

"Gather up, teams!" Seonn said. He sounded as cranky as ever, not at all as if he was worried about a Beguiler wandering free, attacking challengers and champions. "Today's dungeon is Escort the King. And before you say anything, Jesper, the dungeons are chosen at random."

"You know we're good at that one," Jesper said. "It's not exactly a fair match."

"One, get over yourself. You're not that great. And two, to balance things out a bit, we're going to outlaw magic items of any kind. Including potions. So empty your pockets, Serrin, and you're on your honor not to brew anything while you're in there."

Serrin gave him a haughty look and began pulling potions out of pockets all over his uniform and handing them to Seonn. A twinge of guilt flashed through Aderyn, and she imagined the <**Purse of Great Capacity**> glowing bright red with magical energy anyone could see. Maybe she should leave it behind. On the other hand, Seonn meant they weren't allowed to *use* magic items, and she intended to abide by that rule. Just having the purse and the <**Wayfinder**> didn't count, and she was convinced the <**Wayfinder**> was one of those things that ruined the dungeon experience for everyone. Besides, she sure as thunder wasn't leaving it where it could be lost or stolen.

"That's better. All right, here are the rules. Each of you must find your 'king' and take it to the marked zone. First one there wins. You get bonus experience for doing it in under five minutes—you know the drill, the faster you go, the more experience you get. You are free to interfere with the opposition with any skill or spell you have, but you can't hold onto the other team's king and you can't boot it out of the dungeon. Wildcats start on the south, Hooligans on the north. Any questions?"

"Does interfere mean incapacitate?" Weston asked. "I know, no injury, but what about knocking someone out?"

"You're welcome to try. All right, let's look good out there." Seonn juggled the many potions he held and carefully walked to the door leading to his private office.

"I want those back later," Serrin called after him. Seonn didn't respond. "He's going to steal at least one of them," Serrin groused. "He always does because he thinks it's funny to give me back the empty vial."

"Well, this is it," Jesper said. "Good luck."

Aderyn wiped her hands on her trousers and ran up the tunnel with the others when the signal came. The familiar shimmering veil defined a circle this time, so Weston positioned them along the arc that qualified as south, and they waited.

It felt like forever before the horn sounded and the veil vanished. Aderyn gasped. Before them lay a forest of trees like nothing Aderyn had ever seen before, not familiar oaks or maples but tall, broad-leaved monsters with trunks as big around as Aderyn's arms could fit. The smell of wet greenery and moss and loam rose from the forest, and brightly-colored birds soared overhead, calling to each other in hoarse, painful cries.

At the east and west ends of the circle, tangles of vines made mesh walls that rose high above the forest canopy. To the east, the vines divided to leave a round gap whose rim was painted blue; a similar hole painted golden brown appeared to the west.

"That's our goal," Weston said, pointing east. "Isold?"

Isold's eyes shimmered silver briefly. "Follow me."

They ran, dodging the enormous tree trunks, into the forest. The smell of wet earth and green growing things was even stronger inside the dungeon, and the noise the birds made was almost as loud as the spectators' cries had been. But the ground was clear of undergrowth, probably because the canopy was so thick no sun penetrated it. Aderyn reminded herself this was a dungeon, not a naturally-occurring environment, but still, it had to be modeled on something real.

Isold led them straight to where their "king" lay, thirty feet off the ground in the crook of a tree branch. "Well?"

"These are too smooth for me to climb," Aderyn said, picking at the tree's bark, which was slippery and damp.

"Hang on," Livia said. She chanted a few nonsense words and let out a grunt of effort, and the earth hunched beneath her and carried her aloft to where she could snatch the blue ball from its resting place. She waved it at the crowd for a couple of seconds and then was about to reverse the earth's movement when Aderyn said, "No, wait."

"Do you have a plan?" Weston asked.

"Maybe." Aderyn looked eastward, but the leaves were too thick for her to see the blue-rimmed goal. "I think we need to separate. Isold, you use [Locate Object] to find the Hooligans' ball, okay? And you and Livia do what you can to slow them down. Weston and I will take the ball to our goal. But we need to be in the treetops. That will give us a clear line of sight."

Livia said, "Good idea. Weston, you and Aderyn get close together." She descended as she raised the earth where Weston and Aderyn stood, until she was back on the ground and the other two could climb into the treetops. "Good luck."

Aderyn was already climbing through the canopy. At the top, the tree branches all grew close together, and her guess was right: she and Weston would be able to make their way across the forest to the vine wall with ease. She reminded herself the race wasn't won yet and tucked the "king" inside her tunic.

She reached for the next branch, and a muffled voice inside her tunic said, "What are you doing? How dare you treat me with such disrespect? Remove me from this place immediately—I am your *king!*"

CHAPTER THIRTY-SEVEN

Aderyn gasped. She fumbled inside her tunic and tugged the ball free. It looked no different than it had before. Then the same voice, clearer now, said, "That's better. I am not accustomed to being treated in such a careless way, peasant."

"Peasant?" Aderyn turned the ball around, searching for the source of the voice, though a disembodied voice was much less unsettling than a ball that sprouted a mouth.

Weston gestured to her to hand it over. "Where are the words coming from?" He checked the ball over its whole surface, then shook it next to his ear. "Is this something the Hooligans did?"

"Stop that. Stop it! I'll have your head if you don't stop shaking me immediately!" The voice definitely came from the ball. Weston recoiled, juggled the ball briefly as he nearly lost hold of it, and handed it back to Aderyn.

"Meara is an Earthbreaker, but I don't think she has any spells that could animate an object." Aderyn held the ball level with her face and said, "Um. Excuse me. Are you a magic effect?"

"I am your king, peasant. You will carry me to my destination with respect." The voice sounded smug and self-satisfied, as if it had arranged things to its liking.

Aderyn and Weston stared at each other. "What are we supposed to do?" Weston said. "Seonn didn't say anything about the ball having opinions."

"We go on," Aderyn said. She tucked the ball under her arm and clambered over a couple of branches only to have the "king" say, in a shrill, petulant way, "That's enough! I will not be subjected to your armpit, peasant."

"I can't climb well with only one hand," Aderyn told it, then felt stupid about speaking to what wasn't more than a painted, inflated leather sack.

"That's not my problem," the king said. "Handle me gently, or I'll have you imprisoned."

"Imprisoned?"

"It's a ball," Weston said. "It can't have you imprisoned. Ignore it and let's go."

"What if this is part of the challenge?"

"It probably is. We're being judged by how well we ignore this thing. Come on!" Weston headed toward the distant vine wall. Aderyn hesitated for a moment. Then she again put the ball securely under her arm and followed Weston.

She hoped the king's protests would diminish once it realized she wasn't paying attention to its demands. Instead, the volume at which it shouted orders increased until Aderyn couldn't hear Weston unless he was right next to her. Aderyn's jaw hurt from grinding her teeth in frustration.

"...and hang you by your figgin!" the king screamed. "Your *figgin*, I say!"

Aderyn was curious about what a figgin was, but she had stopped speaking to the stupid thing minutes before. Weston had reached the vine wall and was testing his weight against it. He turned and shouted, "I think it will hold both of us, but we'll—*watch out!*"

Aderyn swiveled, one arm holding the king, the other hand gripping a steadying branch, and dropped as something round and dark flew at her head. One of the Hooligans, Galadia, had emerged from the branches about fifteen feet away. Her tunic bulged in an odd, lumpy way, and from her position flattened across a leafy branch, she saw Galadia reach into it and pull out a green, irregularly round fruit slightly smaller than the king. Aderyn shoved the king into her tunic and scrambled across the branches, leaping to the next tree.

With her back turned to Galadia, she didn't think **[See It Coming]** would be any use, so she weaved from side to side, grabbing branches and swinging herself along so her ducking and weaving made her a difficult target. More of the strange green fruits whizzed past her body. She caught sight of another golden-brown tunic ahead—Serrin, also armed with fruit missiles.

"Shut up!" she screamed at the king, whose demands had reached new heights of annoying. "Weston!"

Weston clung to the vine wall one-handed. "Throw it!"

Aderyn came to a stop and hurled the ball. It was bigger than she was used to throwing, but it flew directly to Weston, who palmed it like it was nothing and tucked it into the crook of his arm. "We'll need—hey!" A green fruit rebounded off his chest.

Aderyn glanced around. Serrin and Galadia had come closer and were now ducked partly beneath the foliage, rising out of cover long enough to throw a fruit and then retreating. Aderyn had no idea what they were thinking. It wasn't like Aderyn or Weston could do anything to them. Aderyn was suddenly aware of what a long fall it would be from this height. She definitely wasn't going to stop them by pushing them off their branches.

"We'll need to do like the Fearsome Five did climbing the mountain," she called to Weston, who nodded. Aderyn dodged a couple of fruits and scampered across the branches to the vine wall. The vines were stretchy and loose, and at first Aderyn bounced helplessly on the one she put her foot on. Then she discovered the vines only stretched so far before becoming firm. So the challenge was figuring out how to move quickly along the elastic vines.

Slowly, swaying and bouncing with every step, Aderyn climbed the vines. No more missiles shot past, and she didn't dare waste time looking to see if the Hooligans were still below her. She passed Weston, who hung with one arm wrapped around a vine and the other cradling the shouting king. "...and you can be sure you will not be permitted to continue with this chicanery, peasant! I will have your gaskin slit from top to bottom and your welchet sundered from..." Aderyn reached for another vine. They were still at least twenty feet away from the goal.

She came to a stop about five feet above Weston and shouted, "Pass it!"

Weston tossed the ball. **[See It Coming]** showed Aderyn its trajectory, and she caught it with ease. She waited anxiously as Weston climbed toward her, his weight making the vines shake.

Then a powerful shudder struck the net of vines, and Aderyn juggled the protesting king, very nearly losing her grip on it. "If you drop me, I will see you drawn and quartered, peasant!" the king shouted. "Do *not* think to—I said do not put me under your stinking arm!"

Aderyn ignored it. She was looking down to where Galadia and Serrin were jerking on the vines, sending great waves of movement through the stretchy net. Then she shrieked as Weston's foot slipped, and he hung by one hand, kicking his feet in search of the net. Aderyn could do nothing but watch, her heart pounding and her ears ringing from the shrill screaming of the king.

Finally, Weston got his feet wedged back into the rungs of the net, and he continued climbing, slowly now thanks to the constant motion of the vines. Aderyn waited for him to ascend a good five feet beyond her, maneuver his legs so the vines wrapped them securely, and hold out his hand. She tossed the ball just as one of the Hooligans jerked on the vines supporting her. She wobbled, and her throw went wide.

Weston let go of the vines with both hands and arced backward, his arms spread wide, and caught the ball in both his massive hands.

Aderyn let out a relieved breath. Weston was hanging nearly upside down, but he had the ball securely in his grip. Slowly, he flexed his thighs and brought himself upright by sheer strength. That would look good to the crowd, Aderyn thought. Belatedly she started climbing again. She was wasting time staring at her teammate and thinking stupid, irrelevant thoughts.

But she hadn't pulled herself up more than another three feet when the horn sounded, startling her. She looked up and saw the system notice hovering over the dungeon. At first, she was confused. Weston still had the king, so why was the dungeon congratulating them?

Then she realized they'd lost.

The vine walls were already sinking into the ground, so Aderyn wrapped her arm around a vine and let the wall carry her down with it. Weston was bouncing the king in his hand. It had mercifully gone silent. "Well, crap," he said.

"We did our best," Aderyn said. "And we did get close."

Serrin and Galadia walked over to join them. "That was more than close," Serrin said. "I don't think any team has held us off that long. We're not getting any extra experience this time."

"I admit I threw a lot of fruit at you to see if I could hit the Swift," Galadia said with a grin. "I swear you're magic."

Aderyn decided not to explain that it had been mostly luck that time. "It was tough. Does the ball always shout at you?"

Serrin and Galadia laughed. "Oh, no, nobody mentioned it to you," Serrin said. "Sorry about that. I bet it was a shock. I always use **[Disenchant 1]** to shut it up right away, so I forgot how annoying it is."

"If I had realized, I could have used **[Break Enchantment]**,"

Isold said. He and Livia approached, followed by the other two Hooligans. "I hope it was not the reason for our defeat."

"It was just incredibly annoying," Weston said. "Nice work, Hooligans."

Jesper waved to the crowd. "Go on, let them see you appreciate their support," he told the Wildcats. "No one's ever come that close to beating us at Escort the King."

Aderyn waved, and heard the chant of "*Swift! Swift! Swift!*" grow louder. She followed the others out of the arena and up the stairs to the covert. "They're still cheering. I guess we gave them a good show."

"Earthbreaker versus Earthbreaker," Meara said, punching Livia on the arm. "Jesper was on his own to get up the vine wall—and what in thunder was that song, Herald?"

"[**Suggestion**]," Isold said. "Jesper was smart not to let me catch his eye, or I would have used [**Coercion**] and it would have been all over for you."

"Let's get out of here," Jesper suggested. "The afternoon fights are for those who were defeated this morning. Boring, usually."

"That means Pace and Gradin are both fighting," Weston said. "We should stay for those two, at least."

"We'll see you around, then," Jesper said.

Aderyn settled into Jesper's seat once he was gone and leaned back. "That was exhausting. And, do you know, I don't even feel discouraged? We did the best we could, and it was a good challenge. A good competition. I think I get why Jesper is always so eager to match himself against the best."

"I'd rather have won," Livia said.

"We earned two hundred and fifty gold, at least," Weston said. "I wonder how close we are to level fourteen? Owen hasn't fought nearly as often as I expected."

"My analysis of the bracket shows that it's the losers who fight the most often," Isold said. "Owen's wins are good, but if he'd lost to, say, Pace, he'd have two more fights than he does as a winner."

"Well, for once I wish Owen wasn't as great a fighter as he is. Fourteen thousand experience for defeating Pace!" Livia sat beside Aderyn and sighed. "You want to bet we're the only ones who feel that way?"

"Probably," Aderyn said. In her heart, though, she imagined Owen winning every fight, defeating that awful Jael, defeating Kendria, who was... well, not as awful as Jael, but not a good person, either. He'd get a bonus for being top champion, too.

"What if we make it to level fourteen before the Games are over?" Isold said.

That brought Aderyn out of her daydream. "Well, I guess..."

"We wouldn't need to stay," Weston said, "but it feels wrong to back out in the middle. Like Owen would be letting down everyone who wants to see him win."

"Do we care, though?" Livia asked. "The Fated One quest is our real goal."

"We'd be disappointing everyone who's supporting the Wildcats, too," Weston pointed out.

"Let's not worry about it until it happens, all right?" Aderyn said. "We don't have any idea how close we are to leveling. It might not matter."

Weston leaned on the rail. "That's true. And there's Gradin. He's fighting Raewyn. Is it bad that I'd put my money on her?"

"We can like Gradin and still be realistic about his chances," Isold said. "And Raewyn has been fighting like someone who has something to prove."

As Gradin and Raewyn saluted each other, Aderyn said, "Does anyone know what the rankings are right now? For the final ten, I mean. Or is that not decided until the very end?"

"I'm sure someone knows what everyone's standings are," Isold said. "Do you think that might matter to Brisa? If her goal is to improve Nator and Evalyn's position so they're worth more votes, she might be satisfied with getting them to, for example, fourth and fifth place rather than trying to boost one of them into the top position."

"I bet Owen knows," Weston said. He winced. "Ouch. That was a hard strike Raewyn made. Gradin's going to be feeling that tonight."

Aderyn watched Raewyn handily defeat Gradin, who saluted the crowd in his usual cheery way. "So Gradin's out now," she said as Pace and Nator entered the arena. Then she sat up. "Pace is fighting Nator?"

They all watched in silence as Pace got three hits to Nator's one. Weston muttered a curse under his breath. "Now Pace is in danger, if it's true that Beguiler is knocking off Nator's competitors. We'd better warn him."

"At least he knows something is wrong," Livia said. "Easier than trying to convince that Gabryl that he's in danger."

Aderyn rose and hurried out of the covert. "Let's catch him now."

Chapter Thirty-Eight

When they rushed through the door into the room below the arena, Pace was just entering. Nator was nowhere to be seen. Pace hailed the friends with a cheery smile more suited to his affable cousin. "Don't tell Gradin, but I'm glad he lost. I'd have fought him next otherwise, and that wouldn't be comfortable for anyone."

"We need to talk to you privately," Aderyn said.

Pace's smile fell away. "Something wrong?"

At that moment, Nator came out of the changing room. He eyed the Wildcats suspiciously, then offered his hand to Pace. "Good match."

"Thanks. It was a real workout," Pace said, shaking his hand.

Nator again glanced over the Wildcats as if wondering what business they had with a challenger. He nodded to Pace and exited the room by the passage that led to the sponsors' boxes.

"Can it wait until I'm cleaned up?" Pace said as if they hadn't been interrupted.

A few more competitors came out of the changing room. They

didn't pay any attention to the little group, but Aderyn felt uncomfortable anyway.

"It can wait," Weston said. "Where can we meet later?"

"Gradin and I were planning to eat at the Boar's Head Inn tonight, up on Terrace One. You want to join us?"

"We'll be there at seven," Weston said. "Don't go anywhere alone, all right? Stay with Gradin if you can."

Pace gave him a narrow-eyed look, but nodded and hurried into the changing room.

"Why Gradin?" Livia asked.

"Because of what Isold said about [Beguilement] not working well on anyone who's shook it off, or had it dispelled," Weston replied. "Gradin will be aware if anything happens to Pace."

"I don't know exactly what protection Gradin has against another [Beguilement]," Isold warned. "It is a resistance rather than an immunity, and if he fails to resist again, the Beguiler may take advantage of that weakness to work on his emotions more than once. Aderyn—forgive me—was Beguiled twice, the second time when the first effect was still active, because an active [Beguilement] renders the victim more vulnerable. But we don't have any choice, unless we're willing to follow Pace around and watch him for suspicious behavior."

"We have to take a chance sometime," Aderyn said, wishing Isold hadn't brought up her violation. "Owen will be free to leave soon. We'll meet Pace and warn him."

"Let's hope those aren't the kind of optimistic hopes that lead to his untimely death," Livia said darkly.

"THIS PLACE LOOKS LIKE A WESTERN-THEMED TRENDY gastropub," Owen whispered to Aderyn as they entered the Boar's Head Inn.

"I don't know what that is, and I'm not going to lower myself to ask," Aderyn said haughtily. "But it sounds as if it's not a good thing, whatever it is, and this place looks perfectly nice." She took a seat at a table and surreptitiously gazed at the room, trying to figure out what about it had prompted Owen to produce more of his incomprehensible words. "Gastropub" sounded like some awful intestinal disorder.

"Aderyn, there are mounted animal heads on the walls."

"True, but there aren't many of them."

"Because the rest of the space is taken up by cowboy gear. I didn't think you had cowboys in this world."

Aderyn struggled briefly with herself. "I give up. Cowboys? Part cow, part boy? Or young male cows? I thought cows were girls."

Owen snorted with laughter. "I swear I'm not laughing at you, you know that, right? It's just that your literal interpretations of words and phrases from my world make me see how absurd some of them are. Cowboys are men—I guess women too—who wrangle herds of cows and steers. They watch over them and sometimes move them from one place to another."

"Oh. We call those steersmen. That's pretty close."

"It's the 'trendy' part that's not good. It means, well, trying to look interesting and popular in the newest fashion. And I've always thought trendy things were trying too hard. This place isn't bad." Owen switched seats to sit on Aderyn's other side. "Though I draw the line at having a dead deer stare at me over my meal."

Weston waved. "Pace! Over here."

Pace and Gradin approached and took the last two seats at their end of the long table. "This place serves the best wedgers," Gradin said. "Or so the challengers from Guerdon Deep say. I didn't think wedgers had come this far north, but I guess the Boar's Head is up on the latest fashion."

Owen concealed another snort of laughter. Aderyn kicked him lightly under the table.

Once platters of thin-sliced meats and vegetables and chunks of bread had been set before them, Gradin set to assembling his wedger/sandwich, but Pace ignored the food and said, "So what's so urgent and so private you couldn't tell me at the arena?"

"More specifically, we couldn't tell you in front of Nator," Weston said.

Pace raised both eyebrows. "Nator? Is something wrong with him? He's not the friendliest fellow, but he took losing gracefully."

"We don't know if he's involved or if it's just his sponsor," Owen said, "but we have a suspicion that Brisa is working with the Beguiler who attacked Gradin. Brisa's scheme is to boost her champions in the rankings so she'll gain more votes."

Gradin, who'd been about to bite into his wedger, lowered it and stared at Owen. "The Beguiler? You mean, the one who arranged to kill Denae? But that couldn't benefit Brisa at all. Denae wasn't set to fight either Nator or Evalyn, and there's no way to predict if she ever would have."

Owen's lips tightened. "I think Denae was a test. That the Beguiler was experimenting with her skill before beginning the real attack. I'm sorry, Gradin."

Gradin's face reddened. "That bitch," he said in a hard, flat voice. "That evil bitch. You mean Denae's death was a *mistake?*"

"An intentional experiment," Isold said. "Which is every bit as bad."

"How did she do it?" Gradin demanded. "Did she Beguile those attackers? Or was I the only one?"

"We don't know," Owen said. "There was another attack that might have involved the same men who killed Denae, but for all we know they were completely different people."

"But the odds are good that they, too, were controlled," Isold said. "The skill [Suborn] bends a person to the Beguiler's will, making them utterly loyal. They will not willingly do anything to betray their master."

"Then we have to find them and make them confess," Gradin said. He pushed back the bench and stood. "Make them tell us where to find their master. And then I'm going to kill that Beguiler painfully."

"Sit down," Owen said, forcefully enough that Gradin sat. "We can't find the Beguiler directly, because she has a skill called [Obscure] that blocks finding magic. And we didn't have enough information about the attackers to trace them, either. But Seonn is searching for her, and she can't hide forever."

"So what does this have to do with me?" Pace asked. "You think I'm next on the list because eliminating me will give Nator a second chance? Third chance, really."

"That's exactly what we think," Owen said. "You need to take care where you go and who you're with. Stay in public places with Gradin, since Gradin is more likely to overcome any [Beguilement] and will notice if you act weird. Don't go anywhere with music."

As he said these last three words, the scraping, dissonant sound of a fiddle tuning up became audible over the many conversations filling the taproom. Owen smiled. "I realize that will be hard."

"Well, I'm sure as thunder not going to lock myself in my room until the Beguiler is caught," Pace said irritably. "I know what to look out for. I doubt I'm in as much danger as you say."

"Do not discount the power of a Beguiler," Isold warned. "She has skills you will not know to watch for. [Beguilement] and [Suborn], yes, but also the more ordinary Herald skills [Fascination] and [Charm], both of which she might use to control those around you. You might not have to withstand her direct attack, but how well can you fight off a mob? A mob which, I might add, comprises innocents who have been controlled into their actions?"

Pace grimaced. "You have a point."

"We want you to be safe," Aderyn said. "It won't be much longer, Pace. I'm sure of it. She'll be captured, and then there won't be anything to worry about."

"I hope you're right." Pace squeezed his eyes shut briefly, then relaxed. "I'm not sure I'm sold on assembling my own meal," he said, and while his words sounded weak, Aderyn could tell he was trying to bring the conversation around to lighter matters.

She ate two wedgers and drank wine rather than ale and managed to relax. Sure, they hadn't won that day, but Owen had, and so had Pace, and maybe the Wildcats would face the Hooligans again and kick their asses in a rematch. All she needed for her contentment to be complete was for Seonn's messenger to burst into the taproom, shouting that Damaris the Beguiler had been captured. Probably the news wouldn't come that way, but it was fun to imagine.

Finally, when all of them had eaten their fill, even Weston, Pace rose, prompting the others to stand as well. "Thanks," Pace said. "For letting me know about the danger."

"We weren't going to let the Beguiler have another victim," Aderyn said.

"I appreciate it. And I don't want to miss out on my chance to fight Raewyn." Pace nudged his cousin. "Since you failed to defeat her."

"She strikes like a snake with those shortstaffs," Gradin said with a grin. "I can't decide if I want family to win or if I want to see you get your ass handed to you like mine was."

"Such loyalty," Pace said. "Are you all going back to Foundation? We can walk together."

They strolled through the busy streets, passing through bubbles of light and sound created by the occasional inn or tavern along their route. Terrace One didn't have as many options for entertainment as Foundation, and most of the buildings were dark and shuttered for the night. Aderyn found herself tensing, not in the stretches of darkness, but every time they neared a place where music spilled out of the door or windows. She strained to hear the sound of a flute and relaxed every time she failed to hear it.

The crowds grew denser as they neared the edge of Terrace One, with its eight-foot-high wall. The wall's stones were rounded rather than smooth, and Aderyn idly contemplated climbing it. She couldn't think of a reason to, but it was nice to know it was a possibility.

The lift they were headed for had just arrived, and Aderyn slowed to avoid the stream of people emerging from it. She pictured what that must look like from above, like a current of warm water cutting across a river, though cold water and hot water didn't look any different, so it was a foolish notion. At any rate, their movement felt like a solid mass cutting across her path.

She bumped into someone and said, "Excuse me," just as the other woman said the same. For a moment, their eyes met, and Aderyn was struck by the woman's beauty, a pale, icy beauty of light blonde hair and wintry blue eyes. The woman's gaze passed over her indifferently, and then she moved on.

Aderyn turned to watch her go. She was part of that solid mass of people who'd gotten off the lift, but she looked like she was independent of them, like she might have floated up the side of the mountain and coincidentally joined those men and women who'd ascended a more conventional way.

Shouting broke through her reverie, the sound of Owen saying, "Somebody stop him!" and an increased randomness to the movement around her. She looked around for him and saw him forcing a way through the crowd, pointing and yelling.

Ahead, passing through the crowd as effortlessly as if he were as immaterial as the ice woman, was Pace, headed not for the lift, but for the wall.

Aderyn knew with dread certainty what he intended. She started to follow him, but the crowd pressed against her, pushing her back. More voices had taken up the shout, Weston and Livia, and after another second, she came to her senses, turned her back on Pace, and followed the Beguiler.

CHAPTER THIRTY-NINE

The crowd was just as much an obstacle going this way, but Aderyn slipped through gaps between people and shoved and kicked to make a gap when she couldn't find one. She could still see the blonde woman ahead, making her effortless way through the crowd. Common sense told Aderyn she was being stupid, that even if Pace had been Beguiled, she didn't know this woman was the Beguiler, and if she was, Aderyn could be in danger. She needed to turn around and stop Pace from doing whatever the Beguiler had convinced him to do. But in her heart she was convinced she was chasing the woman who'd sown such utter chaos and evil in Finion's Gate. And, danger or not, she couldn't bear to let the Beguiler get away.

When she reached the street, the crowds thinned, and Aderyn could run, following the Beguiler, whose pace hadn't changed. The woman didn't seem aware that someone was chasing her. Aderyn had time to wonder what in thunder she was going to do when she caught the Beguiler. She had no real weapon; Terrace One didn't like people going openly armed, so all Aderyn had was her belt knife. It would have to be enough.

Ahead, the Beguiler made a turn into an alley between a tavern and a shop selling metal pots, currently closed. Aderyn slowed as she approached the opening. She wasn't stupid enough to go racing around a blind corner into what was probably an ambush. She sidled up to the alley and peered around the edge of the metal shop.

The alley was empty.

Aderyn took another step, bringing her to where she could see the alley more clearly. Its muddy length went about thirty feet and divided in half to run behind the buildings in that row, not just the tavern and the metal shop but all the other businesses on the street. Aderyn walked quietly to the cross-alley and peered around the edge.

Something white and big flew at her face. Aderyn dropped to a crouch and drew her belt knife. Then she relaxed. It was a bird, one of the big white ones that lived on the cliffs above Finion's Gate and came into the city to scavenged dropped food. She looked both ways. Back doors lined the longer alley, but no person was visible.

Aderyn considered her options. Then she tried the nearest door, the only one the Beguiler could have reached before Aderyn came around the corner. It was locked. She looked up and down the alley again, then returned around the corner. The bird was gone, too.

Aderyn walked back to the street, her head lowered in thought. Then she stopped. She was no Pathseer, but her footprints were obvious, going into the alley. And just as obvious were the footprints of someone leaving the alley, on top of hers.

She burst out of the alley and swiftly looked both ways. No beautiful pale women were visible the whole length of the street. No white birds roosted on nearby buildings or flew across the dark night sky. Aderyn swore under her breath. Then she hurried in search of her friends.

She had to push through another crowd, this one gathered around something near the wall. With more judicious kicking and shoving, she burst through to find Pace sitting on the ground, swearing a steady stream of oaths and clutching his right arm close to his chest. Livia and Isold knelt beside him, and Weston was talking to the lift attendant. Gradin and Owen were gone.

"What happened?" Aderyn asked, dropping to her knees beside Pace.

Pace glared at her, but his eyes were glassy with pain and Aderyn didn't take the glare personally.

"Our friend laid what Owen calls 'the whammy' on Pace," Isold said in a low voice. "She convinced him life was meaningless and he should throw himself off the wall."

"No," Aderyn breathed. "But you stopped him."

"We did not," Isold said grimly. "If Livia had not acted fast with *move earth*, Pace would be dead now, shattered on the stones of Foundation."

"He still fell about ten feet," Livia said. "Broke his arm. Gradin went for a Bonemender."

"Where's Owen?"

"I assumed he was with you," Isold said. "He saw you run the other way and we thought you had been Beguiled."

"Crap," Aderyn said, rising and then standing on her toes to see past the crowd. "I wasn't Beguiled. I saw Damaris and I chased her." And now Owen was chasing *her*. He might be in terrible danger if the Beguiler hadn't gone far.

She began pushing her way back through the crowd, but saw Owen returning, his eyes on her. Better to let him come to her.

Owen came to her side immediately and put one arm around her shoulders. "Don't do that again," he said. "We don't need to split our rescue efforts."

"I didn't need rescuing. I was chasing the Beguiler. I should have said something, but everyone else was chasing after Pace and Damaris was going to get away if I waited." She sighed. "But I guess she got away after all."

"The Beguiler?"

It was a man nearby in the crowd. Aderyn's heart sank. She hadn't spoken quietly. "It's nothing," she said.

"Wait," the woman next to the first man said. "What's a Beguiler?"

"A Herald gone bad. They can control minds and emotions." The man turned back to Aderyn. "Is that why that man jumped off the wall? I thought he was crazy, but he sure doesn't look like it. Just pissed off."

"No—"

"If there's a bad Herald running around, does that mean we're all in danger?" the woman asked.

"*No*," Aderyn and Owen said together, but the murmur of "Beguiler" had started to spread.

Another woman suddenly shouted, "That's Owen the challenger! Are you friends with that man?"

"The wounded man there is a challenger, too," said someone else. "I saw him defeat Nator today."

"So why would a Beguiler go after him?" the first woman said.

"Well, shit," Owen said in a low voice. "We need to get out of here."

"This won't go farther than this crowd, will it?" Aderyn asked hopefully.

Owen gave her a look that made her add, "I know. I was trying to be optimistic."

"Get out of the way," Aderyn heard Gradin say. He had a young Bonemender in tow, a girl who looked nervous at the press of the crowd and Gradin's grim expression. As soon as she saw Pace, though, her expression changed to one of calm certainty. "It's going to be all right," she told the Lone Wolf.

"You're only level six. How good can you be?" Pace growled.

"Repairing broken bones is one of the first spells we learn," the young woman said, ignoring the insult. "Do you want to be unconscious for this? Setting the bone hurts."

"I do *not*," Pace said, but not as harshly.

"Very well." The Bonemender laid a hand on Pace's right elbow. His arm jerked, and Pace let out a sound that was very nearly a wolf's howl. The still-surrounding crowd jerked back, muttering more loudly. The Bonemender ignored the noise and put her other hand around Pace's arm, closer to his wrist than his elbow. Pace's lips peeled back in a snarl, but he was silent this time.

Eventually, the Bonemender released Pace and stood. "Good as new. That will be fifteen gold."

Gradin dug in his belt pouch and came up with a handful of coins. "Thank you so much."

"You're welcome. And so is he." The young Bonemender turned and came face to face with Aderyn. "Excuse—oh! You're Aderyn the Swift!"

"I—yes," Aderyn said, feeling as awkward as she always did when she was recognized by a stranger.

"And Owen the challenger. I didn't know you were married. That's so romantic!" The Bonemender covered her mouth with one hand like she meant to hold back more words. "Good luck, both of you!"

"It does feel like good luck," Owen murmured when the Bonemender was gone. "But let's get out of here. I want to know what happened that you ran off by yourself in a completely insane way in pursuit of someone who might still be able to Beguile you."

"It's not a long story," Aderyn said, "but I can think of someone else who needs to hear it."

"YOU SAW THE BEGUILER," SEONN SAID. HE HADN'T BEEN happy to be rousted from his bed, but his irritability had vanished when Owen told him flatly what had happened to Pace. "She got away?"

"I think she made herself look like a bird, or made me believe that's what I saw, or something," Aderyn said.

"That wasn't a criticism. I'd rather you let her get away than deal with another death related to the Games." Seonn scrubbed his hands across his eyes. "And Pace nearly died."

"Which would have advanced Nator. Again," Owen said.

"I don't need the reminder, kid, I know what the bracket looks like." Seonn tilted his head back and stared at the ceiling for a moment or two. Then he said, "Get back to wherever you're staying and don't leave until I send for you. I'm locking things down."

"Does that mean the Games are over?" Gradin exclaimed.

"It's a temporary measure while I lay my accusation against Brisa. If she's confined, she can't give orders to this Beguiler. But that, too, is temporary."

"Isn't it complicated to arrest a Councilor?" Owen asked.

"Complicated, my left butt cheek. I have to lay evidence before the other Councilors, and getting them to agree on anything is like getting a herd of cats all pointed in the same direction. Fortunately, I've got a mouse to catch their attention."

"The Councilors will be furious that someone tried to manipulate the government through the Games," Owen said.

"And they won't wait on more solid evidence to bring Brisa to trial. Until then, I want all of you competitors staying off the streets. Staying out of any public places until tomorrow morning, for that matter. In fact, I changed my mind. Go to the Green Lion Inn for tonight—it's just around the corner from the arena, and the innkeeper is used to maintaining privacy for its patrons. In the morning, I will have you escorted to the arena. You said it was harder for a Beguiler to work her skills on a lot of people at once?" he asked Isold.

"Yes. Not only does her skill become easier to resist, the influence is itself less believable," Isold replied.

"Well, that's something, anyway. Maybe we'll get lucky. Now, get going, and watch yourselves."

On the street outside Seonn's house near the arena, Owen said, "It's late enough I'm not sure his precautions are going to matter."

"I don't want to go anywhere near the edge of Terrace One until the Beguiler is caught," Gradin said. "We don't know where she ended up."

"Do you really think the Beguiler is going to try to get Pace killed again?" Weston said. "She has to know we're alert now."

"I hate to say it, but paranoia is our friend now," Owen said. "And it doesn't hurt to take precautions."

The Green Lion Inn looked more like a fortress than anywhere someone might stay for the night. The woman who met them at the door recognized Owen and Pace and nodded silently when Owen explained that they needed a secure place for the night. The room she showed Aderyn and Owen to was plainer than Aderyn expected for Terrace One, but a second look revealed the costly wood construction of the furniture and the running hot and cold water tap in the corner behind a painted screen. The woman handed Aderyn a key and nodded politely before shutting the door. Aderyn hadn't heard a single word out of her.

"I'm more afraid now than I was chasing Damaris," she said. "Being locked up like this has me considering all the possible ways she might still get at us."

"I said paranoia was our friend, but I didn't mean you should let it defeat you." Owen took her in his arms and kissed her. "Let's sleep. Tomorrow will come soon enough, and one of us has an important fight in the morning."

"You and Kendria," Aderyn said. "I'm glad it's not you and Evalyn. You might have been the one the Beguiler went after tonight."

"Yeah, arresting Brisa will help."

"You don't sound confident. Don't you think Brisa is behind the attacks?"

Owen shrugged. "This whole thing seems sort of random. I

mean, why a Beguiler? Why not hire Assassins to take out key fighters? For that matter, is Brisa so stupid she thinks no one will notice
the pattern?"

"Sometimes people are stupid that way." Aderyn buried her face
against his chest. "If it's not Brisa, then what's really going on?
Because I can't believe the attacks are completely random. Not when
everyone affected has been a Games competitor."

"I agree. And I can't think of any other explanation. Maybe I just
don't know enough yet." Owen kissed her once more and began
undressing. "If the attacks continue once Brisa is out of the way,
maybe something will become obvious."

Aderyn stripped down to her shift and drawers and climbed into
bed. "Maybe it's already obvious, and we're not looking at it from the
right angle."

"That's a much more positive attitude," Owen said.

CHAPTER FORTY

Aderyn was wakened the next morning at dawn by a soft rap on the door. When she opened it, the woman from the previous night was there, laden with packages. "For you and the gentleman, with Seonn's regards," she said in a quiet voice. "Your escort is waiting for you after your meal."

"Escort," Aderyn said, memory returning. "Thank you."

The packages contained Aderyn's Wildcats uniform and a change of clothes for Owen. "Seonn thinks of everything," Owen said. "Take a look at your potato sack."

Aderyn scowled at him and shook the blue garment out. It wasn't her uniform. This tunic was made of a much finer fabric, and embroidered on the back was the silhouette of a snarling mountain lion. "Where did he get this?"

"I might have asked Gerant to ask around for someone who could make a new uniform for you Wildcats. Something more befitting your status as second-ranked team." Owen grinned and caught Aderyn as she threw herself at him and kissed him. "Is it bad that I mostly did it for that reaction?"

"Not bad at all. Thank you. This is a lovely gift." She dressed quickly and admired how the new tunic flattered her shape.

Even Livia was in the taproom when Aderyn and Owen went downstairs. "Did you see these uniforms? They're actually stylish." She poured another cup of coffee and sipped it.

"Owen commissioned them," Aderyn said. "Are we really the second-ranked team? I haven't been paying attention."

"The final four dungeon battles are fought between teams of similar ranks," Isold said. "Lowest to highest. We will be fighting the Hooligans again tomorrow afternoon in our final match."

"Excellent," Weston said. "I'm ready for a rematch."

"I'm looking forward to fighting Raewyn," Pace said. "I've been watching her moves and I have some ideas for countering those shortstaffs. What about you, Owen?"

"Kendria is a tough opponent," Owen said. "I'm not making assumptions about her skill versus mine. She'll be harder to defeat than Jael was."

"Given that stupid Jael cheated," Aderyn said. "Kendria's at least honorable."

Owen pushed his plate away. "I shouldn't overeat. Shall we go?"

The "escort" provided by Seonn was two dozen constables, armed and armored and looking entirely serious. Aderyn, whose negative impression of the magistrates' forces had been shaped by the three who'd handled Denae's death, changed her mind. Maybe no one of them could give a real adventurer a fight, but all of them together were a serious deterrent to casual violence.

Owen left the others to enter the changing room beneath the arena, and Pace and Gradin went in the direction of their sponsor Kesslon's box, and the Wildcats took the back way into the covert. The covert was packed, with only the Scrappers and the Trailblazers not present. Aderyn settled into her seat and wished the dungeon battle was over already so Owen and Kendria could fight. She wasn't going to be able to relax until it was over.

She only paid half her attention to the dungeon, where the red tunics and the purple tunics fought over getting their respective kings up the mountain. The Scrappers had a Spellcrafter who could shut the king up, but she didn't know if the Trailblazers had a similar advantage. Aside from that idle wondering, she ignored the battle and the cheering and surveyed the Councilors' boxes. Only Raewyn was in her sponsor Raynir's box, but Aderyn recalled that Owen and Gabryl were both set to fight this morning. Pace and Gradin sat rather than stood, flanking Kesslon.

And Evalyn and Nator were alone in Brisa's box.

So Brisa had been arrested already. Aderyn didn't know why Brisa's combatants still being present surprised her. She'd sort of thought Evalyn and Nator had been in on the conspiracy, but that didn't have to be true. The Terrible Twins were too far away for her to make out their expressions or interpret their body language, but they didn't look like people who felt guilty.

A roar from the crowd startled Aderyn back to the present. "And the *Trailblazers* are the victors!" the announcer screamed. "What a great showing for their first Glory Games, huh? Give it up for the plucky underdogs!"

"I thought *we* were the plucky underdogs," Livia muttered.

"We're the dark horses that came from nowhere to upset the status quo," Weston said.

"'Plucky underdogs' rolls off the tongue better. Did you place a bet on Owen?"

"I was afraid I'd jinx him if I did." Weston leaned back to let the Trailblazers enter. The noise in the covert rose considerably as everyone congratulated the winners. The Scrappers didn't appear.

"Aderyn." Jesper raised his voice to be heard. "You should come up here."

His calmness set her heart to racing. She moved through the crowd to stand at the rail next to Jesper just as the announcer cried,

"And now we've got a match I know you've all been waiting to see! Let me hear you shout for—*Owen the Swordsworn!*"

Aderyn screamed in excitement and waved as once more Owen saluted her before going on to salute the crowd. He walked with perfect confidence. It occurred to Aderyn out of nowhere to wonder if Owen felt this was the strangest thing that had happened to him since arriving in this world. He wasn't likely to have been cheered on by screaming spectators just before fighting a duel in his own world, not unless high school history teacher was a more dramatic job than Aderyn understood.

"And now, someone who needs no introduction—*Kendria the Staffsworn!*"

The noise was a palpable pressure on Aderyn's ears, thousands of men and women chanting Kendria's name against thousands more shouting for Owen. She felt lightheaded and had to lean on the rail for support.

Owen and Kendria had reached the center of the arena, surrounded by four red-clothed adjudicators. Owen drew his sword and made a couple of passes with it before taking a ready stance. Kendria spun her staff in a complicated maneuver before doing the same.

The signal horn blew. Owen and Kendria slowly approached one another, taking each other's measure. Aderyn recalled what Owen had said about watching Kendria fight and getting a sense of her moves. It occurred to her that Kendria might have done the same with Owen. Tension filled her muscles, freezing her with her hands gripping the rail and her eyes unable to look away.

Owen struck, but in a way Aderyn would almost call tentative, as if he was still testing Kendria's responses. Kendria batted his strike away and didn't follow it up with a blow of her own. Owen struck again and followed the blow with his dagger. Kendria again parried, though it took her more effort this time.

"She wants everyone to think she's toying with him," Jesper

murmured. "But he's fast, and she knows it. If he goes after her for real, she'll be hard put to defend."

Aderyn nodded.

Though the crowd continued to cheer, the covert was silent, as if respecting the Wildcats' intense interest in this fight. Owen stepped forward to make another test of Kendria's defenses, and Kendria whipped her staff around faster even than **[See It Coming]** could respond to. Aderyn jammed a fist into her mouth to stop her screaming something potentially distracting, though there was no way Owen could hear her over the crowd. But Owen had been watching for Kendria's strike and jumped over the staff as it swept across where his legs had been. Then the two combatants were going at it for real, weapons clashing in an eerie silence as sword met staff.

"I've never understood how a staff fighter could challenge a sword fighter without their staff being chopped to pieces," Weston said in a conversational tone.

"Kendria has **[Weapon Mastery]**," Aderyn said, feeling like her words were coming from far away, as if her body was on the arena floor with Owen. "It bonds her chosen weapon to her and makes it indestructible. I don't know how any Staffsworn lower than level fifteen manages—oh!" Kendria had thwacked Owen's side, sending up a loud crack that cut across the cheering. "One to Kendria!" one of the adjudicators said.

Owen and Kendria separated and began circling. This time, it was Kendria feinting with her staff. Owen didn't even bother responding to those moves, but as Kendria struck a fourth time, Owen stepped inside her guard and thumped her lightly on the front of her leather brigandine with his dagger.

"One to Owen!"

They separated only enough to show they'd heard the call, and then they were fighting fiercely again. Owen caught Kendria's staff along the crossguard of his dagger, throwing her off balance long enough to strike her thigh with the flat of his blade. "Two to Owen!"

"I can't bear this," Aderyn said. "I'm so glad it's not to the death."

"He'd have won already if it was to the death," someone behind her said. "He's amazing. Do you know how hard it is for a trained fighter to pull his punches like that?"

Aderyn nodded. "He's very good." She swiftly Assessed him to see his **[Advanced Weapon Mastery]** skill ranks. Twenty-three. It was true, if this had been a real duel, Kendria would be dead.

In her moment of distraction, she missed Kendria's attack, the same spinning one she'd made against Raewyn. "*Two for Kendria!*" the adjudicator screamed, his voice barely audible despite whatever magic item boosted his voice.

Grateful that the announcer didn't feel the need to provide commentary, Aderyn made herself breathe deeply. The next blow was the final one.

The two combatants had gone back to testing each other, not feinting so much as striking lightly. With anyone else, Aderyn would have suspected them of playing to the crowd. Then they closed, again so rapidly **[See It Coming]** was no help. Owen parried, struck, parried again, then again caught Kendria's staff on his dagger crossguard and shoved it out of the way.

With a fillip of her wrist, Kendria disengaged and smacked Owen's wrist, making his dagger fall.

Both combatants froze. Then the call came. "*Kendria wins!*"

Discouraged, Aderyn sank into the nearest chair. Amid the cheers of the crowd, Kendria and Owen clasped wrists in acknowledgement of a well-fought match. When Owen tried to let go, Kendria held him a few seconds longer. Aderyn saw Kendria say something lengthy. Owen nodded. Then she released him, and the two of them saluted the stands. Owen's salute was short, like he thought the victor should have the lion's share of the attention, and he ran across the arena floor to the tunnel.

Aderyn rose. "I'll be back."

She hurried down the back stairs and was there when Owen came down the tunnel. "That was a great fight," she said, then felt stupid. Maybe Owen didn't think it was so great since he'd lost.

But Owen smiled. "It was a great fight. That was a slick move she made. I won't be caught by that again."

"Again? But you lost!"

"Two chances, remember? I'll fight whoever wins the final match today, and I'll go on fighting until I face Kendria again. I'm sure of it." Owen slung an arm around Aderyn's shoulders. "Will you go on rooting for me?"

"Rooting? Is that... no, I have no idea what that could mean."

He laughed. "Cheering for me, then."

"Of course," Aderyn said. "You're still the best. And losing means you'll have more fights and earn more experience!"

"There's the optimistic wife I love," Owen said.

CHAPTER FORTY-ONE

The rest of the day was anticlimactic. Aderyn's interest in the fights was mainly about discovering who Owen would fight next, though she was deeply disappointed that Jael defeated Gabryl and moderately sad about Raewyn beating Pace. "And Eirian wiped the floor with Evalyn, probably because the thing with Brisa had Evalyn rattled," she said at dinner that night. "It didn't occur to me that Eirian might be in danger because of Evalyn."

"She might still have been if Brisa hadn't been taken into custody," Isold said. "Since the Beguiler's pattern of attacks is to go after successful fighters so their defeated opponents can advance."

"I'm sure Seonn is keeping an eye on her," Owen said. "But I'm more interested in the other matchup. Raewyn and Gabryl."

"Not Kendria facing Jael?" Aderyn asked.

"That will be entertaining, sure, but I want to know if Raewyn and Gabryl are able to duel fairly if they're romantically involved." Owen drained the last drops of his ale and signaled to the serving woman for another.

"I still think it's sad that they can't be together openly," Aderyn said. "But even I can see how it would be a conflict of interest at the very least to have sweethearts or spouses fighting each other."

"I think Raynir suspects," Owen said, "but he's carefully avoiding situations where he might be forced to admit to more than suspicion. Which I don't blame him for. Gabryl and Raewyn represent a sizeable chunk of his political influence. He'd be out the door without them."

"But he'd still have you," Livia said.

"And I'm not staying one minute past that Level Fourteen system message." Owen drank again, then set his mug down. "He knows it, too. I told him as much when we first met. But—"

"What?" Weston said when Owen didn't continue immediately.

"Something strange. It didn't occur to me before, but sponsoring a champion who isn't going to be there next season weakens his position if that champion performs as well as I have." Owen chewed his lower lip in thought. "Well, maybe not. I don't know much about Finion's Gate's government, but I know the sponsors are awarded votes based on the rankings at the end of each season, and if something happens to the champion afterward, those votes aren't taken away. So he'd still get votes based on my ranking even if I'm not here next season. Maybe it's not such a weird idea." He still looked pensive.

"Raynir is still putting money into you even though you're leaving," Isold said. "I would not be surprised to learn he has another plan, possibly a more long-term one."

Weston groaned. "Politics is too much for me. First Brisa tries to game the system, then Raynir has something going on, maybe, we're not sure but we have to care because it might involve Owen. What happened to earning experience and more money than we can count in a lifetime?"

"As if anything is ever that simple, dearest," Livia said.

"AAAAAAAND THE WINNERS ARE... THE INDOMITABLES! Let's hear it for a truly stunning victory! I don't think I've ever seen a better Capture the Flag dungeon, how about you? The Rowdy Ruffians sure gave it their all!"

The announcer was in rare voice that morning, Aderyn thought. For once, it wasn't so much of an exaggeration. The dungeon battle had been exciting and tense, not least because the oncoming rain threatened to make the dungeon even more complicated. Aderyn also didn't know whose victory to hope for. She recalled Owen's strange phrase "rooting for." It still made no sense no matter which meaning of the word she considered, either implanting in the ground or digging up earth in search of something.

She leaned forward as the Indomitables and the Ruffians stormed up the stairs, laughing and joking and teasing Kathra, who'd made a hilarious mistake and nearly let Martis get away with their flag. Aderyn's attention was fixed on the tunnel opening. Owen's battle was first again today, and Aderyn was sure he could defeat Eirian. Mostly sure. Eirian had had her first defeat early and had been steadily working her way back to the top ever since. She'd defeated four champions so far, which was amazing for a first-time challenger. If she'd been up to fight anyone but Owen, Aderyn would be rooting for her, no question. She shook her head. "Rooting" was never going to make it as slang.

The announcer's voice brought her out of her reverie, and she waved at Owen when he saluted her in a now-familiar gesture. This time, she was sure she heard the tone of the cheering change, from loud shouts to oooohs of romantic sympathy. Aderyn blushed, but she kept waving.

In the trials, Eirian had wielded a longstaff, but in her Games fights, she'd switched to a sword. It was a clever reminder to the crowd that a fighter's skill was **[Advanced Weapon Proficiency]**, and that an experienced fighter was comfortable with many weapons.

"Interesting," Isold said. "I wonder why she started out with a different weapon?"

"She's level fifteen, so she has **[Weapon Mastery]**. She must be bonded to the sword instead of the longstaff, and she used the longstaff at the trials because one wooden weapon is as good as another," Aderyn said.

"Too bad no one's fooled by the difference in their levels, not at this stage of the Games," Weston said. "I could have made a killing."

"I hadn't thought about it before, but Owen and that Jael woman are both level thirteen," Livia said. "Almost everyone else is a higher level. Do you remember her weapons skill rank, Aderyn?"

"Seventeen," Aderyn said. "She definitely trained hard, I'll give her that."

The horn sounded, and Owen and Eirian clashed with a noise that echoed off the walls of the arena. Aderyn watched Eirian rather than Owen, wishing he had the **<Twinsword>** to guide her observations to his ears. Eirian was as good as expected, a careful fighter who never took risks, and Aderyn saw no openings Owen could take advantage of. He would have to be the risk-taker if he wanted to win this bout.

Owen backed away a step, surprising Eirian, who looked like she suspected a trick. She moved back herself—and Owen leaped, tagging Eirian's arm before having his weapon parried. Aderyn saw her smile. As the adjudicator called the point for Owen, Eirian lunged and turned that trick on Owen, striking his upper arm. It was Owen's turn to smile. His lips moved, and Eirian nodded.

Then the fight was on in earnest, first one, then the other driving their opponent back. Owen got in a lucky blow when Eirian incautiously lowered her guard, and then, in a surprise move, he thumped Eirian soundly across her midsection for his third blow.

**Congratulations! You have defeated [Eirian the Stalwart].
You have earned [16,000 XP]**

"What a match, friends!" the announcer shouted. "This is going to be a Glory Games to remember! Owen has guaranteed himself a place as one of this season's champions—let's show him some love!"

Owen and Eirian clasped wrists, and Owen pulled Eirian close to thump her on the back. Then the two of them raised their joined hands and saluted the crowd. Aderyn, her heart pounding rapidly, sank back into her chair. She didn't know who the chair actually belonged to, but no one looked inclined to force her out of it.

"Eirian's made herself a champion, too," Jesper said. "But they don't need the announcer to tell them that. The crowd is cheering her as well."

"Do you know what position?" Aderyn asked.

"Fifth or sixth, depending on how the rest of the matches go. A good, solid position for a challenger." Jesper sat beside Aderyn. "You know, I'm betting on Owen going all the way."

"Really? I thought you were convinced Kendria had everything sewn up."

"I was. But I'm sure Owen can take out Gabryl, and if Kendria beats Jael, Owen will have to face Jael first. That's a match I don't want to miss, Owen and Jael." Jesper shrugged. "And Owen strikes me as someone who doesn't make the same mistake twice. Both Jael and Kendria should be worried."

The announcer's voice stopped. The absence of noise caught Aderyn's attention. "What did he say?"

"I wasn't listening," Jesper said.

"He called Gabryl's name, and Gabryl didn't enter the arena," Weston said.

Aderyn turned her attention on the arena floor. Raewyn stood at the center, shortstaffs under one arm, watching the tunnel mouth. It was empty.

"Sounds like our second-place champion wants a little more encouragement," the announcer said. "Let me hear you shout for *Gabryl!*"

The noise level grew, but Gabryl didn't appear. As the seconds stretched into half a minute, a minute, the crowd's excited cheering faded until the only sound was the confused murmuring of thousands of people asking their neighbors what was going on.

"That's not good," Weston said. "You don't suppose the Beguiler got to him?"

"How?" Livia said. "And why?"

"Maybe it's not what we thought, after all," Aderyn said.

Movement at the mouth of the tunnel drew her eye, and she recognized Gabryl just as the announcer said, "And there's the man himself! Let's hear it for Gabryl!"

The cheering redoubled, but it had no effect on Gabryl, who walked rather than ran to the arena center, his head held high and his stride powerful. Aderyn's uncertainty turned into dread. Gabryl didn't look injured or drugged, but she was suddenly positive something bad was about to happen.

As if echoing that feeling, a few hard drops of rain began pattering across the arena, making dark spots on the ground. Aderyn watched in case the adjudicators meant to cancel the bout, but they were all watching Gabryl the way they would an oncoming predator.

"So is he Beguiled, or not?" Weston asked.

Isold shook his head. "I can't tell from this distance. If the Beguiler influenced him while we were watching, I'd see that. But detecting an existing effect is more difficult."

Gabryl approached Raewyn closely and leaned in as if speaking into her ear. Whatever it was he said, Raewyn reacted as if he'd punched her. Aderyn saw her lips move, and then Raewyn backed away, holding her shortstaffs folded against her forearms in readiness to battle. Gabryl drew his sword and saluted his opponent.

The horn blew. Raewyn leaped, her shortstaffs swinging out in a blinding pattern. And Gabryl flung his sword away.

Raewyn stumbled, trying to check herself before she ran over the unarmed Gabryl. One of her shortstaffs bounced off the man's shoulder. The adjudicator hesitated, glancing at her comrades for support. "One for—" she began.

Gabryl turned on the adjudicator, grabbing for her throat. Aderyn gasped and rose from her seat, though there was nothing she could do to stop Gabryl from hurting or killing the woman. "The Beguiler got to him," she gasped.

"It's true," Isold said. "I see the effect now. We have to stop him."

But Gabryl had already released the adjudicator. Something small that gleamed silver in what little light made it through the clouds dangled from his outstretched fist. He gathered it into his other hand and brought it to his lips. "I won't go on living a lie," he said. His voice boomed through the arena just like the adjudicator's had. "These Games let us test ourselves against the best, but it's at the cost of all the drives that make us human. I won't hide my emotions any longer. Raewyn, I love you, and I want the world to know what we are to each other."

Raewyn stood frozen in place, her shortstaffs dangling free in both hands. She cast a look up at Raynir's box where Owen stood beside their sponsor. Raynir was too far away for Aderyn to make out his expression, but **[Read Body Language]** told her Owen was extremely tense, as if he expected to have to stop a fight at any moment. Then Raewyn tossed her shortstaffs to the side and walked slowly to stand in front of Gabryl. The rain had increased, darkening his short hair and dampening Raewyn's light tunic. Gabryl's shoulders heaved like he'd run a mile. Raewyn gently touched his face. Then she turned her back on him and walked at that same slow, measured pace to the tunnel mouth, where she disappeared inside.

"We have to do something," Livia said.

"It's too late," Weston said. "He's already thrown everything away. And burned Raewyn's bridges, too."

"That might not be all the Beguiler did to him," Isold said, and pushed through the other teams to take the stairs leading down to the arena floor. Without another word, Aderyn and her friends followed him.

Gabryl had sat on the hard-packed earth and let the adjudicator's necklace fall to the ground. When Aderyn arrived in Isold's wake, the big Swordsworn was weeping as the rain pattered over him. "I wanted us to be free to be together," he said. "You don't know what it's like, having to sneak around, pretending we're nothing to each other."

"Look at me, Gabryl," Isold said, taking Gabryl's head in his hands.

"It's not the end of the world," Aderyn said. "Something had to change eventually, and this has to be better than separating, right? Isn't your love more important than competition?"

Gabryl jerked as if he'd been stung. He blinked, and then his eyes focused on her with a keen awareness they'd lacked just a moment before. "More important?" he said, his voice rough as usual. "More important? I just told thousands of people about that love after I swore I'd never reveal it. I've destroyed my career." He laughed bitterly. "Worse, I destroyed Raewyn's career. She's never going to forgive me. And our relationship is over."

CHAPTER FORTY-TWO

"Well," the announcer said. For the first time, his voice wasn't filled with excitement. "I guess—" His words cut off, and the dead silence that followed suggested to Aderyn that his voice amplifier had been turned off, not just that he'd stopped speaking.

Gabryl stood, weak and shaky as an old man. He cast a glance at Raynir, who from this distance looked ready to commit murder. "I'll face my destiny," Gabryl said.

"Wait," Aderyn said. "Do you remember encountering a stranger with a flute?"

"This is about that Beguiler again, isn't it?" Gabryl's voice sounded weary now. "I don't know. I don't remember music at all. I picked up my boots from the cobbler because I'd lost a nail and they needed repairing, and while I was there it all hit me at once. How stupid it was to keep this secret, how miserable it's made me. It felt like my heart was breaking and there was only one thing I could do to stop it."

"She made you feel that way," Isold said.

"No one will care that I was Beguiled to say those things. They were still true." Gabryl shook his head and trudged back the way he'd come.

Aderyn twisted around to look at Owen, who was watching Gabryl's retreating form. Then Raynir thrust away from the rail and turned on his heel to exit his box, and Owen, without looking at Aderyn, followed him.

"That was," the announcer abruptly said. "I mean, well, talk about unexpected turn-ups, right?" He didn't sound as full-voiced as usual, but his words were growing increasingly confident. "Let's turn things around, shall we? We're going to have a short break to see if this rain lets up, and then it's time for this afternoon's dungeon battle! Back for a rematch, it's the Wildcats going up against the Hooligans—this ought to be a show to remember!"

Aderyn shook herself out of the fugue Gabryl's final words had left her in. "That's us. Isn't there supposed to be a break for lunch?"

"I'm guessing someone wanted the crowd distracted from Gabryl's revelation," Weston said.

"All right, fine, but why do we have to be the distraction?" Livia said. "It's not going to stop raining soon, either. What do you want to bet they'll make us do it anyway? This dungeon is going to be miserable."

They ran back to the tunnel and made it to the room beneath the arena just as the Hooligans entered. For once, Jesper didn't look inclined to banter. "Why did you all go down there?" he asked.

Too late, Aderyn remembered no one knew about her team's involvement with the Beguiler—not to mention that the Beguiler herself was still mostly rumor. "We were worried about..." she began.

"Gabryl, as Owen's fellow combatant sponsored by Raynir, is someone we've come to call a friend," Isold lied smoothly. "We were concerned about his erratic behavior."

"Did you know Gabryl and Raewyn were involved?" Galadia said.

"They never admitted it to us, but we suspected," Isold said. "The fact that they concealed their relationship told us if Gabryl revealed it, something strange had happened."

"Strange, no kidding," Serrin drawled. "That puts them both out of the Games entirely. Raynir's got to be shitting bricks over this."

"I don't think—"

Aderyn was interrupted by Seonn barking out, "Listen up, teams! I know we're asking a lot of you, but the Games need not to be interrupted by a couple of star-crossed lovers airing their secrets to the world, right? Which means we need a distraction immediately, and you all are it."

"You're handicapping us," Jesper said. "The dungeon's going to get rained out, and all those people will leave for shelter. They won't see a blasted thing."

"It's going to stop raining, and do you know why that is, Jesper? Because I won't allow anything else." Seonn glared back at the Hooligans' captain. "We're giving you an entirely new dungeon so you Hooligans have no advantages from experience. The dungeon is called Puzzles and Passages. You'll make your way through environmental challenges manipulated by the spellslinger dungeoneers to three different puzzles. First team to succeed at the final puzzle wins."

"Environmental challenges," Jesper said, his eyes narrowing. "You mean spellslingers throwing obstacles in our way."

"You catch on quick, kid," Seonn said. "Each of the three puzzles tests your intelligence and ingenuity. You must solve the puzzle to proceed. No *fly*, *transport*, or *levitate*, and no running across the top to bypass a puzzle. No interfering with the other team—you'll win on your speed and cleverness alone. Any questions?"

"Any limitations on spells or skills otherwise?" Livia asked.

"None except what you've already agreed to." Seonn glared at Aderyn now. Aderyn scowled. He probably thought he was being funny, but she hated having her honor questioned, even in pretense.

"Five minutes for you to ready yourselves mentally," Seonn said, and left the room.

The two teams watched each other warily. Then Weston said, "It sounds like we're got a common enemy, if the—did he call them 'dungeoneers'?—are interested in screwing with us. We each do our best, and if we can turn their efforts back on them, even better."

Jesper grinned. "That is an excellent plan. To a great game, then!"

"But we're still going to keep our plans secret," Livia said. "No offense."

"I was about to say the same thing," Jesper replied.

Aderyn huddled with her friends some distance from the Hooligans, but no one said anything for a minute or so. Then Weston, who'd been tense with listening, said, "It doesn't sound like they have a plan beyond bulling through the environmental challenges. Nothing that can help us."

"We really have no choice but to ignore them, if we're not allowed to interfere with their progress," Isold said. "Move as fast as we can. And I for one am good with puzzles."

"If they're the right kind of puzzles," Livia said darkly. "Who knows what Seonn came up with?"

"Well, *I* for one would love to defeat these fellows," Weston said, "so let's keep that in mind, all right?"

The first horn sounded.

"Feel free to go first," Jesper said with a grin.

"Oh, no, after you," Weston replied, bowing elaborately.

Aderyn rolled her eyes. "Let's go together, all right? Show these people what real competition looks like."

"A true conciliator," Jesper said. "All right. Together."

The sound of cheering grew louder as they all ran up the tunnel and burst out onto the arena floor. Aderyn, waving to the crowd, felt a pang when she saw Raynir's empty box. She'd wanted Owen to see this. Probably it was better he was with Raynir, if only because he'd learn what the councilor had in mind now that two of his three champions were out of the competition.

The dungeon, a circle this time, was the biggest she'd ever seen, bigger than any of the ones preceding it, and the veil was thicker and darker, without the shimmer Aderyn was used to. She wanted to laugh at Seonn's attempt to rattle them. It was going to take more than a dark, scary obscuring field to unsettle her.

Flags waved from two poles stuck into the ground at one side of the circle, one golden brown, the other cerulean blue. Aderyn and her friends formed up near the blue pole, while the Hooligans did the same several feet away. The spacing suggested they weren't meant to get in each other's way, which suited Aderyn fine.

She wiped her sweaty hands on her trousers. Funny how her hands never sweated once she was actually in the dungeon. Beside her, Livia had her eyes closed, and her lips moved in silent conversation with herself, or something. Aderyn had never felt comfortable asking what she was saying in these moments. Weston gripped the flagpole with one enormous hand and stared at the darkness like his vision could penetrate it if he willed really, really hard. And Isold was watching the crowds with a tiny smile on his face. Aderyn knew him well enough to recognize his look of contemplative interest, as if he was considering who among all those people he might make a romantic connection with next.

The horn blasted. The veil vanished like a tablecloth being snatched away by an invisible hand. Aderyn and her friends took two rapid steps toward the dungeon and stumbled to a halt. The entire dungeon was obscured by a violent sandstorm. By the way it came right up to a certain point and didn't pass beyond that point, it looked confined by glass.

"That will blind us," Isold said. "Possibly literally."

Aderyn involuntarily glanced at the Hooligans. Jesper and Meara had already mostly disappeared into the storm, and Serrin and

Galadia were close behind them. "We need to move quickly. They're ahead."

Weston took a few steps more until he was on the edge of the sandstorm. "Everybody make a chain. I'll lead—"

"Hang on, I have an idea," Livia said. She laid a hand against the imaginary wall defined by the storm and chanted some strange syllables.

The storm in about a five-foot radius contracted, slowing until it came to a stop. The sand particles hung in the air as if frozen in place. Livia stepped into their midst, and they showered down around her. "It's *dust cloud*, inverted," she said. "Stay close to me and move fast."

With Livia chanting, the team made its way through the sandstorm raging just inches from their faces, brushing aside the sand that hung in midair so it cascaded around them. To Aderyn's surprise, the sandstorm only extended ten feet before it reached a metal wall with a door that slid open as they approached. They hurried through the doorway and came to a stop.

Before them lay a broad dais tiled with glass squares two feet on a side, five wide and five deep. Seven of the tiles were glowing with a dull light. A second, similar dais lay twenty feet to their left.

Weston ran up the three blue-painted steps to the glass tiles. "This is familiar," he said. "Quick, everyone, check for instructions, but I'm guessing I know how this goes."

They spread out through their half of the area and found no writing anywhere. "All right, here goes," Weston said. He'd been studying the tiles while they searched, and now put his foot on one of the glowing tiles.

Another door slid open, and the Hooligans came barreling through. Their faces were red and scoured-looking, but they advanced on their dais confidently. Aderyn ignored them. Instead, she watched Weston dance across the grid, turning lights on and off. This puzzle didn't look as straightforward as the one in Gamboling Coil, but Weston moved like he knew what he was doing. In less than a minute, all the glass tiles were dark, and a metal door in the opposite wall slid open. "Go, go!" Weston urged, and they ran for it.

As soon as they were all inside, the door slid shut behind them, and for a moment, they were in complete darkness. The room was stuffy and hot like the inside of an oven. Then dull lights, a sullen dark red, blossomed along a passage ahead, and Aderyn's heart sank. Cutting across the room, blocking their route forward, was a ragged-edged metal chasm that glowed with heat.

"Looks like we have to swing across," Weston said. He pointed. "There's the rope." A wrist-thick rope with a heavy knot tied at the end dangled over the middle of the chasm.

Livia gestured, and the rope swung silently toward them. "No prohibition against *telekinesis*," she said, grabbing hold of the knot. "Who's first?"

The other door slid open, and the Hooligans entered. Aderyn was only peripherally aware of them. She was sweating for real now, thanks to the heat of the room. "I'll go first," she said. "I'm worst of us at this kind of thing, and you'll want to make up time—"

"Less talking, more swinging," Livia said.

Aderyn gripped the rope with both hands and walked backward, hoping she wasn't about to make a fool of herself in front of all those people. She jumped, got her feet on the knot, and swung.

She felt herself moving faster than she thought she should based on her initial jump and hoped using *telekinesis* on teammates wasn't forbidden. She swung wildly over the dully-glowing chasm, her eyes fixed on her destination instead of the depths beneath her, and stumbled off, falling to hands and knees in her awkward descent.

The rope was already making its way back to the other side, and Livia had climbed up and was being pulled far back by Weston and Isold. Aderyn wished she'd thought of that. The two men gave Livia a push, and Livia, laughing like crazy, sailed across the gap to where Aderyn could catch her. "That was great!" Livia panted, flinging the rope back. "Too bad there's no time to do it again."

Isold, then Weston, sailed across, and a door opened in the metal wall. Aderyn's heart sank when she saw the Hooligans had beaten them across. They were gathered around a colorful set of tiles on the far wall, occasionally prodding at it.

"Aderyn! Ignore them," Weston said.

Aderyn jumped. The wall nearest them had a similarly colorful picture, and she stepped closer to look at it. Her first impression was that it was a jumbled mass of color. Then she realized the colors were regular in shape, square tiles four inches on a side. "It's a mixed-up painting," she said. "Are we supposed to put it together?"

"How do we do that?" Livia said. She tried to pry a tile off the wall, but it didn't move.

"One tile is missing," Weston said. "Let's start by looking for that."

"A moment," Isold said. He touched a tile near the empty hole where one was missing and pressed on it lightly with one long finger. The tile moved into the empty space. "I see how it works. We slide the tiles around into new configurations until it makes a complete picture."

"Well, crap," Livia said. "How long is that going to take?"

"Not long at all." Isold had begun moving tiles, slowly at first, then with increasing speed as he gained confidence. Aderyn couldn't help herself; she looked over at the Hooligans. They were removing the tiles with some effort, and as she watched, a corner of one of the tiles snapped off. Aderyn turned away as Meara cast *repair* on the broken tile.

To her astonishment, the picture was half restored. It was a painting of Finion's Gate, seen from far away, with the mountains rising to the sky above it. "How are you doing that?" she exclaimed.

"With great difficulty," Isold said. "This is extremely complex. I am trying to remain grateful that the tiles don't rotate as well as slide."

"Stay focused, and don't worry," Weston said. "There isn't anything we can do about the Hooligans."

"Thank you, that is not the kind of reminder I need," Isold said with a smile.

In seconds, the puzzle was complete. Aderyn took a second to admire it.

Then she realized the door hadn't opened.

CHAPTER FORTY-THREE

"What—it's done! Where's the door?" Livia demanded.

"We must have done something wrong," Weston said. "Maybe we were supposed to take the tiles off like the Hooligans."

Aderyn involuntarily glanced at the Hooligans. They had a pile of four-inch painted tiles on the ground and were holding some of them up and rotating them before placing them in the empty frame. "No. Seonn said we'd need to use our intelligence and cunning. This was a cunning solution. It has to be right!"

Isold stepped back, examining his work. "Something wrong, something out of place—oh, by thunder, I see it. Give me a second." Swiftly he began moving the tiles across the top of the grid. "Two of those blue sky squares are almost identical. They need to be swapped."

"Couldn't we take them off and change their position?" Aderyn asked.

"Removing the tiles is difficult and risks wasting time *repairing* broken ones," Isold said. "And I am almost—done." He switched the positions of two tiles.

A door in the metal wall slid open.

All four of them shouted in excitement and tumbled through, only to come to a stop at the edge of a platform overlooking a room as white and brilliantly lit as the heated room had been dark and hot. Below, the floor was a series of hollows and rises, all smooth and curved and extending a good thirty feet to a matching platform on the far side.

"I think I know what's up with this one," Aderyn said. She pointed at a scattering of holes on the walls to either side. "Those look exactly like they're made for shooting projectiles. And there's a lever on the far side, probably to shut them off."

"Well, that tells me who is tackling this challenge," Weston said with a grin.

"It's got to be more complicated than usual, because they know what I'm capable of," Aderyn said. "Like, the projectiles are acid bombs, or they shoot sprays of ice needles."

"They wouldn't do anything that caused permanent damage," Isold said, but he didn't sound certain.

"Bonemenders, remember?" Aderyn crouched and ran a hand over the curving surface that descended to the floor. It was rough and gritty and it gave her an idea. "Here, hold these," she said, removing her boots and thrusting them at Weston. "And wish me luck." With that, she sat on the platform and then lowered herself to the floor. Then she ran.

The first projectile whizzed past her face to splat against a curved pillar. Paint, she noted in passing, but she didn't slow to look at it. Darting, ducking, sometimes crawling, she made her way rapidly across the floor, never getting hit. It was obvious there were people manning the projectile shooters with how they were always aimed right at her. She flung herself backward to avoid two paint balls impacting on her. Instead, they struck each other with a splash that mingled red and blue to make a vivid purple.

She was grateful for her bare feet as she clambered up the wall to the platform and the lever. Despite her care, she slipped a little on paint that had struck the wall instead of her, but it didn't matter, because she was through. She grabbed the lever and yanked on it. Every hole closed over, and the next door opened. She sat, panting, on the edge of the platform until the others neared her, then grabbed her boots and put them on while Isold and Weston hauled Livia up.

To her horror, the Hooligans were already in the final room. They were covered in paint, true, but they didn't look like they'd been penalized. She felt like an arrogant fool. Her act with **[See It Coming]** was going to lose them the dungeon.

"Don't feel bad," Livia said, accurately reading her expression. "Neither team considered that *telekinesis* on the lever would have solved all our problems."

"Enough talking," Weston said. "Look at this."

The stone walls of this room were completely blank except for one largish depression in the center of the wall opposite the way they'd entered. It looked like it was made to hold a sphere the size of Weston's fist.

"No directions, no nothing," Weston said. "I'm guessing we have to find the object that goes there."

"Easy enough," Isold said. He walked to the depression and laid a hand on it, muttering to himself. When he turned back around, his eyes shimmered silver briefly, and he returned to the group. "I know where it is, but it's behind one of these walls."

"Well, I know somebody who can take care of that," Livia said. She flexed her stone fist, and with a few whispered words, it glowed with a shimmering aura.

"Wait," Aderyn said. "How thick are these walls?"

"Not thick enough," Livia replied.

"I mean, if it's going to take several blows, we'll lose time to the Hooligans." Aderyn examined the wall. "I have a skill for that. **[Spot Weakness]** shows weak spots in objects and things the way **[Discern Weakness]** does for creatures. And if there's only one object—"

"It's the wall near where we're standing," Isold said. "If there's only one object, I don't want them knowing where it is."

Aderyn Assessed the wall. She didn't have much experience with **[Spot Weakness]** and up until now hadn't really seen the point. But the moment she Assessed it, the wall gleamed with blue light outlining its contours as if traced in starlight. A row of blue circles revealed where a hidden fracture line was.

Aderyn glanced at the Hooligans once more, then stood so her back concealed her pointing and said, "Hit it there!"

Livia wound up and punched the wall. Shards of stone flew in every direction. She punched once more, and light blazed. An orb of crystal shining with blue light popped out of the crack, and Aderyn picked it up.

She turned—and saw the Hooligans racing for the depression in the wall, clutching an orb that gleamed with amber light.

"Give it here!" Weston snatched the orb from Aderyn's hand and with a smooth overarm motion threw it. It struck the rounded depression perfectly. Instead of bouncing off the wall, it sank deeper—

—and shouts and screams flooded the air, and the dungeon dissolved around them as a system message appeared in front of Aderyn's face:

Congratulations! You have defeated [Puzzles and Passages]. You have earned [10,000 XP].

Congratulations! You have received an [Ingenuity] bonus for completing [Puzzle 2] of [Puzzles and Passages]. You have been awarded a one-time bonus of [2500 XP]

Congratulations! You have achieved a perfect score in [Passage 3] of [Puzzles and Passages]. You have been awarded a one-time bonus of [3000 XP]

And then, after a pause, came the message

Welcome to Level Fourteen

Aderyn just had time to wonder about that little pause before her friends tackled her, shouting and hugging each other. "That was a tremendous risk," Isold said. "Suppose it had bounced?"

"We weren't going to outrace them," Weston said. "It's my kind of risk, the one with a tremendous payoff."

"It was beautiful," Livia said, kissing him. "Who knew [**Thrown Weapons Proficiency**] would come in handy like that?"

"Congratulations," someone said. Jesper stood nearby with his hand outstretched. A livid splotch of green paint smeared his cheek, but he was smiling. "I should have thought of that. Some Deadeye I turned out to be, eh?"

"Well, at least you didn't feel the need to show off," Aderyn said. She still felt embarrassed about the paint ball room.

"Meara doesn't have *telekinesis*, so it was this or stay behind." Jesper gestured to all of him, covered in splatters of paint. "We sure gave them a show, didn't we?"

"We did indeed," Weston agreed. "A real nail-biter." He waved at the crowd, then grabbed Jesper's hand and held their joined hands aloft as the screaming grew loud enough to press on Aderyn's eardrums.

She turned in a slow circle, waving at the spectators, but what she really wanted was to see if Owen was back. Raynir's box was still empty, to her disappointment. What could Raynir possibly still need from him?

"What a show, friends!" the announcer was shouting. "A last-minute play by the Wildcats wins them the dungeon and upsets the Hooligans' winning streak! That's a dungeon we'll want to see more of in future!"

Aderyn ran with her friends back to the covert. To her surprise,

Jesper and the other paint-covered Hooligans followed them. "We want to see whether Kendria defeats Jael," Jesper said when she asked. "These uniforms are going to take *clean* and *repair* to fix regardless of how soon we get that done. Are you going to watch?"

"I'm wondering where Owen went," Aderyn said.

"He's probably still with Raynir," Weston said, "and Raynir won't want us hanging around. Besides, I want to see Jael get her ass kicked."

"I suppose," Aderyn said, and sat beside Jesper.

The cheering was much louder for Kendria's entrance than for Jael, and this time even Aderyn could hear the boos coming from parts of the arena. She felt a twinge of compassion. It would be so hard for Jael to stay optimistic about her chances when people were audibly opposed to her. Then Aderyn shook those thoughts out of her head. Jael was mean-spirited and nasty and a lying cheat, and Aderyn's sympathy was misplaced.

But it seemed her musings about how Jael would be affected by the booing might have been accurate, because Kendria took only one hit from Jael before delivering three hits in quick succession. Aderyn cheered with the others, but her attention was already diverted to looking at the future. They'd achieved level fourteen. That was their goal. So was it really sensible for them to continue in Finion's Gate? It wasn't as if there were any dungeon battles left.

It was a stupid thing to consider, though. She knew Owen well enough to be sure he wouldn't want to stop this close to victory. Just one or two more days, and they could be on their way to the Lonely Tor and whatever awaited them there.

When they returned to the Alabaster Inn, Aderyn entered her room and, surprised, said, "Owen! What happened? Was Raynir as angry as he looked?"

Owen was stretched out on the bed, staring at the ceiling. He didn't look at Aderyn. "He was furious. Ranted and raged about traitorous champions who can't keep it in their pants, that sort of thing." He rolled over and sat up. "And I'm pretty sure it was all an act."

"An act?"

"Maybe not all of it. I don't think he knew in advance what Gabryl was going to do. But he has a plan that hasn't been derailed by losing two of his three champions. I just wish I knew what it was. I might be caught in the middle of it."

Aderyn's earlier thoughts returned. "Maybe we need to go now that we've reached level fourteen. You know, I haven't even looked at the **[Fire and Ash]** quest to see what it is now that it's unlocked? I was too worried for you."

"I'll be fine, Aderyn." He rose and put his arms around her for a kiss. "I wish I'd seen your dungeon battle. Getting the victory message isn't the same."

"It was dramatic. And fun. And a very close victory." She kissed him back. "Let's all look at the new quest and discuss it. Then it doesn't have to be just one of us making the decision."

"You're so sensible." Owen hugged her. "You really won't mind if we leave tomorrow, huh?"

"I thought I wouldn't, but then Kendria beat Jael soundly and now all I can think about is you trouncing Jael tomorrow."

Owen laughed. "I admit that idea has a lot of appeal. But suppose she defeats me?"

"You'd better laugh when you say that," Aderyn said.

CHAPTER FORTY-FOUR

Borrus joined them in their celebratory dinner, and his presence meant they didn't talk about anything but their final dungeon victory. It wasn't as if Borrus didn't know the truth about Owen, but Aderyn still felt awkward discussing anything to do with the Fated One in public. It was like Owen said: there were hundreds of wannabe Fated Ones, and there wasn't anything secret or shameful about saying you were the Fated One, but for Owen to be classed with all those posers diminished his identity as the real one.

"And it's unbelievable my stunt didn't make us lose," Aderyn moaned. "That was the kind of luck that comes once in a lifetime."

"We got three thousand experience for it," Livia said. "I don't think you should go on beating yourself up over it. Besides, like I said, I should have remembered *telekinesis*, but after using it on the rope, I guess I assumed I shouldn't repeat a spell. You know, in case it bores the spectators."

"That final throw was outstanding, Weston," Borrus said. "I was sure the orb would bounce."

"I can't believe I missed Weston's fastball," Owen said. "Did you know the orb qualified as a thrown weapon?"

"I was guessing, and I was desperate," Weston said. "On the other hand, I have done a lot of practicing with hitting targets that small or smaller, and I knew it wasn't a completely stupid thing to do. And *telekinesis* isn't as fast as that."

"Jesper said taking the tiles of that puzzle off the grid was their biggest mistake," Aderyn said. "Once they got them off the wall, they lost their orientation, so it's like we were saying about how good it was the tiles didn't rotate—they lost time figuring out which way up they went."

"You know, I'm almost sad we're leaving?" Weston said. "I'm sure I'd get tired of team battles after a while—probably after a short while—but this was fun. I'd love to pit myself against these fellows again."

"But we are leaving," Isold said.

"You don't mean you're leaving now?" Borrus exclaimed. "Not before the Games are over?"

His words silenced the others. To Aderyn, they felt like the reminder of hovering doom. "We should talk about that," she said.

"Aderyn." Borrus fell silent. "I can't make your decision for you," he finally went on. "And I'm sure compared to the Fated One quest, these Games are frivolous. But there are a lot of people counting on you, and I hope you'll consider that."

Aderyn hugged him. "Thank you for not demanding I do as you want."

"That worked exactly once in our whole lives," Borrus said, hugging her back. "And you never let me forget about the consequences, so I'm not sure that's a smart option in any case."

After Borrus left, they gathered in Owen and Aderyn's room, which as usual when they were all present felt crowded. None of them cared. Each of them silently opened their Codex and read the entry for **[Fated One's Destiny: Fire and Ash]**.

A threat from the Lonely Tor puts the surrounding

communities in danger. Find and eliminate the threat to proceed. This quest is automatically activated upon acceptance. Recommended minimum adventurer level for this quest is 16. WARNING: A solution that puts the communities in danger from a different threat is not considered a success. Reward: [50,000 XP] plus any XP gained through actions taken to complete the quest.

"I don't remember that warning being there before," Weston said.

"Neither do I," Isold said. "It makes no sense. Or I suppose it's the kind of warning that makes sense in the moment."

"I'm concerned about the quest activation," Owen said. "It sounds like that means whatever the threat is, it isn't a threat until we trigger it by accepting the quest. Which we did by reaching level fourteen a few hours ago."

"You mean, because those communities are in danger now where they weren't before?" Aderyn said. "Maybe that means we should go immediately."

"Yeah. Because I have visions of a dormant volcano working its way toward eruption, or a lost dungeon opening and spilling out monsters." Owen looked like those were the least of his imaginings.

"We've earned a lot through dungeon battles, but it's not enough to pay for *world door* for all of us," Weston said. "We're going to be on foot whether we leave tomorrow morning or in three days when the Glory Games are over. I say we stay long enough to see Owen earn us a good chunk of experience and then head out. Two days won't make a difference."

"Despite my forebodings, I was thinking the same," Owen said. "Though for me it's also that I feel I owe Raynir something. If I left, he'd be completely without champions and be booted from the Council."

"I'm in favor of staying, too," Livia said. "I don't care about

Raynir's political position, but he might feel generous toward the champion who rescued him. Financially generous, in particular."

"I guess that makes sense." Aderyn frowned. "We need to maintain our honor, and I think that means staying."

"Then we're in agreement," Isold said. "Two more days, two more victories—"

"Three," Owen said. "I have to fight Kendria twice because she's undefeated now."

"All right, three more victories and we'll be back on our quest path." Isold unfolded himself from where he sat cross-legged on the floor and dusted off his posterior. "But it occurs to me that we haven't discussed our other problem. What about Damaris the Beguiler?"

Aderyn felt ill as the memory of chasing Damaris returned. "What about her? Is there anything we can do?"

"I hate to say it, but I don't think so," Owen said. "Seonn's people are still hunting her, and with Gabryl's admittedly scanty information, they claim to be closing in on her. All we can do is stay alert in case she attacks one of us. You're not going out alone, Isold?"

"Sadly, no," Isold said. "As a Herald, I have a few more protections against her than the average adventurer, but I am not immune, and if she were to Beguile me, we would be in serious trouble. And it is raining quite hard. So I intend to stay in tonight, cursing Damaris's name."

"It's better than being Beguiled into praising her name instead," Owen said.

"GOOOOOOOOD MORNING, FRIENDS!" THE ANNOUNCER sounded more enthusiastic than ever. "This is it—the final battles of the 47th semi-annual Glory Games! This has been a season to remember, hasn't it? Let me hear you shout!"

Aderyn, seated in the covert, didn't feel capable of shouting with the spectators or her friends in the nearby seats. Her throat was dry, and she didn't know if her palms were sweaty because they gripped the rail tightly enough to ache. She didn't know why she was so anxious. This battle didn't matter, and Owen would defeat Jael regardless. But between the announcer warming up the crowd and the cheering spectators, an atmosphere of anticipation filled the arena.

"Let's get started, all right?" the announcer said. "Our first fight is between two challengers who tested each other through the preliminary trials and who fought their way to where they stand today. Facing each other for the first time since the trials, *Owen and Jael!*"

The crowd had been noisy before, but now their shouting and screaming sounded like wild animals challenging each other. Aderyn resisted the juvenile urge to put her hands over her ears.

Owen and Jael walked out onto the arena floor, neither running, both waving at the crowd. Owen crossed to beneath the covert and saluted Aderyn with a smile. All her anxieties vanished in the rush of love that swept over her. It would be all right, no matter what happened in the fight.

Jael, on the opposite side, didn't act like she cared about the occasional boo. Her arrogant stride annoyed Aderyn, but, again, none of this mattered, except that Owen was sure to win. Aderyn secretly hoped he'd make Jael look like a fool doing it.

The combatants met in the center of the arena, and the adjudicators moved into place surrounding them. Owen and Jael drew their swords and both leaned in to tap their blades against each other.

"He sure looks like he doesn't want to get any closer to Jael than he has to," Livia commented.

"I can't blame him," Weston said. "Not with the way she cheats."

Sure enough, the moment the horn blew, almost before their blades had disengaged, Jael leapt for Owen's chest, thrusting her sword at the center of his brigandine. Owen dodged the blow and, taking advantage of her overextension, delivered a blow of his own to her shoulder blades. The cries of the spectators drowned out the adjudicator's call.

Jael stepped back, rotating her shoulder. Owen held his sword at the ready, waiting for her to move. Again, Jael lunged, but this time it was a feint, one Owen didn't fall for. Swiftly, he drew his dagger and used it to block Jael's next swing, shoving the blade up and away so he could strike her armored stomach. Jael lunged for him, but Owen stepped away as one of the adjudicators, who in Aderyn's opinion were extremely brave to get in the way of edged weapons when they weren't armored, pushed Jael back with a warning audible to the crowd via the [Amplify Voice] magic item. "Combatants retreat after a solid hit is announced," she said. "Don't make me warn you again."

Jael's sneer was visible even at that distance, but she backed away. In another second, she went after Owen, and this time Owen returned blow for blow, both their swords flashing in the dull pewter light that came through the storm clouds. Aderyn watched Jael anxiously, wishing more than ever that Owen had the <Twinsword>—but that would be cheating, and she knew Owen wouldn't want to win that way.

But after all these fights, Jael's strengths and weaknesses were clear to her Warmaster's vision, and she had told Owen about some of them, like how Jael flourished her sword an extra time after a full lunge, like she needed to regain her balance. She'd already done it once, and if Owen remembered and noticed—

Owen once more caught Jael's sword with his dagger and lifted it for an opening, but Jael was ready for the trick and disengaged. And there was the lunge, and the flourish—and as her sword was out of position, Owen pushed it aside with his sword, stepped into the opening, and thrust his dagger at her undefended midsection.

Congratulations! You have defeated [Jael the Swordsworn].

You have earned [10,000 XP]

"*Owen wins!*" the adjudicator's voice boomed.

Aderyn found she was on her feet screaming with the crowd. Owen stepped away from Jael and saluted her with crossed sword and dagger, though **[Read Body Language]** told Aderyn his gesture was meant to be like his strange upraised middle finger gesture he called "flipping the bird." That didn't mean anything in this world, but Aderyn had taken to using it and hoped she could start a trend.

Jael, her shoulders heaving, didn't move. Her sword hung at her side, that beautiful weapon Aderyn wished was Owen's. Owen turned his back on her and saluted the spectators, all of whom were jumping and waving and sometimes hugging their neighbors. He paused to sheathe his dagger, then waved at the crowd again. Now **[Read Body Language]** said he was uncomfortable with the praise and wished he could leave, but he wasn't going to disappoint his supporters.

"Something's wrong," Isold said.

Aderyn turned to look at him. He was standing just as everyone else was, but his body was rigid and his head was tipped up as if he was a dog catching a scent. "What is it?"

"Jael," Isold said. "Damaris is here. Jael's been Beguiled."

Aderyn whipped around. Jael still stood with her head bowed and her sword dragging in the dirt. "Beguiled? To do what?"

"I don't know, but we need to get down there," Isold said.

Jael raised her head. Her sword fell from her hand to clatter onto the hard earth. With a few swift strides, she was behind Owen, reaching for his dagger. She snatched it from its sheath and in one quick motion drew it across Owen's throat.

CHAPTER FORTY-FIVE

The world froze. Aderyn watched the ruby spray of blood spatter the earth without comprehending it. Red drops, darkening the hard-packed floor—surely rain wasn't red? Owen's eyes were wide with surprise. His hand slowly rose to clasp his throat. Someone was screaming nearby, a high-pitched, horrified sound Aderyn thought she might never forget.

Then she realized she was the one screaming.

Everything jerked back into motion. Jael backed away from Owen, lowering the dagger. Both Owen's hands were bloody as he tried to stop the flow from the terrible gaping wound. He dropped to his knees, then collapsed sideways.

Someone had hold of her arm and was dragging her away. She fought the person, feeling if she lost sight of Owen, he would die, but then she realized it was Weston lifting her and bodily hauling her down the covert stairs. At the base of the stairs, she got her feet under her and ran.

She almost beat the Bonemender, who had reacted more quickly than anyone else. Panicking, she fell to her knees and tried stupidly to push the Bonemender away. Again, Weston's hands restrained her. She was breathing so hard her chest hurt.

The Bonemender knelt beside Owen and put his hand over the gash. Blood continued to flow, staining the spellslinger's hand. "It's good, right?" Aderyn babbled. "His heart is still beating, so it's good, isn't it?"

The Bonemender ignored her. He put his other hand at the center of Owen's chest, atop the blood covering the front of his brigandine, and bowed his head.

Aderyn waited. The Bonemender didn't appear to be doing anything. Her impatience grew until she shouted, "Stop it! Stop sitting there doing nothing! Heal him!"

"Aderyn," Weston said. "He's doing his best."

"He is *not* doing his best! He's just—he's sitting there covered in Owen's blood—" Her words cut off with a choked gurgle, and a single sob tore out of her.

The Bonemender stood and wiped his hands on his clothes without seeming to care about the bloodstains. "I'm sorry," he said. "I wasn't fast enough. It's too late."

"*No!*" Aderyn screamed, and wrenched free of one of Weston's hands. "No, damn you, it can't be too late, it can't—" More sobs choked her, and she sagged, not fighting Weston as he kept her from falling.

She heard a sound like the chime of breaking glass, a tiny sound that nevertheless cut across the murmurs of the crowd and her own weeping. The strangeness of it caught her attention, and she blinked away tears to see a red light centered on Owen's left hand, expanding outward in all directions until it became a hemisphere overlapping his body and including Aderyn and Weston and Jael and the adjudicator holding Jael.

Aderyn held her breath. The <**Ring of the Cat**>. Gamboling Coil had said it could save Owen's life, but Aderyn had thought that meant moving him out of harm's way, or deflecting a lethal blow.

Now the red light deepened until it was a few shades paler than Owen's own blood and pulsed like a beating heart.

Owen's left hand twitched. Slowly, he raised it to touch his throat. It was still bloody, but the gash was gone without a mark to show where it had been. The red light faded to nothing, not even the spark of red that had been the ruby in Owen's ring. All that was left was an empty socket next to the emerald and sapphire.

Aderyn let out her breath. Feeling dizzy from more than just lack of air, she flung herself on Owen and worked her arms around his shoulders to hold him tightly. She couldn't think of anything to say, just held him and felt overjoyed when his arms encircled her.

"I guess Gamboling Coil was more generous than I thought," he murmured. "What a strange experience."

"What was it like?"

"You know, I'm not sure I can describe it. But it will have to wait, anyway." Owen detached Aderyn from himself and got heavily to his feet. "Killing me won't change anything," he told Jael coldly.

Jael looked terrified and, for once, fully human without a trace of arrogance. "I didn't," she stammered. "I don't know what I was thinking. I needed you dead—except I swear to you I didn't, I really didn't!"

"You were Beguiled," Isold said.

"Convenient excuse," Seonn said, startling Aderyn in his sudden arrival on the scene. "Claim it wasn't your fault, use these other Beguilements to cover your desire for revenge."

"It's true, though," Isold said. "Jael was definitely Beguiled. I've removed the effect, but—*shit*."

Isold swore so rarely it startled Aderyn. "What's wrong?"

"I saw the moment the Beguiler worked her skill on Jael. She was here." Isold sounded furious. "She was here somewhere and we let her escape."

"No," Aderyn heard herself say. She felt distant from her body again, but this time it was rage that fueled her—sheer fury at how close she'd come to losing Owen, at how Damaris saw nothing wrong with playing with people's lives. "No. I refuse to let her get away."

"We can't track her," Weston said. "Remember **[Obscure]**? She'll misdirect us."

Aderyn shook her head. "I've seen her face now. And touched her, if she was behind the illusion of the white bird before. **[Obscure]** isn't perfect. It conceals, but it doesn't make Damaris invisible. I'm certain the **<Wayfinder>** won't be fooled a second time. We are going to find her."

"Excuse me," said the adjudicator holding Jael's arm. "What are you all talking about? A Beguiler? Is Jael guilty of murder—of attempted murder—sir, what in thunder happened?"

He addressed this to Owen, but it was Seonn who answered. "Hold Jael pending inquiry. Beguiler or no, we can't have challengers or champions thinking they can boost their ratings through murder. You—" He pointed at Isold. "You said the Beguiler was here? I'll summon enforcement—"

"There's no time," Aderyn said. "We have to go *now*." She reached into her belt pouch and pulled out the **<Wayfinder>**.

Seonn eyed it skeptically. "You have a **<Wayfinder>**? How long have you had it?"

"Do I have to answer?" Aderyn asked.

With a scowl, Seonn said, "I choose to pretend you didn't take that thing into my dungeons. Go on. Once I've got enough enforcement, I'll be on your trail. Good luck."

"Thank you," Owen said.

Seonn stared at him in silence. Then he turned away and ran for the tunnel.

Aderyn was barely conscious of the murmurs from the spectators, but nothing could have distracted her from her goal. "Damaris the Beguiler," she whispered, and the largest spike lit a pale pink. She rotated until she was facing the tunnel—that was natural; the **<Wayfinder>** always directed her down a navigable path, not through walls. The glow of the spike brightened and turned a deeper pink, reassuring her. Without watching it further, she ran, surrounded by her friends.

On the street outside the arena, Aderyn turned rapidly in a semi-circle and said, "She went right."

"Everyone surround Aderyn," Owen said. "Weston, you break the crowd. Isold and I will guide her. Livia—"

"I'll stand ready to smack the bitch when we see her," Livia said, sounding deeply pleased at the prospect. "Is it a problem if we kill her?"

"We still need to know what her plan is," Owen said. "If she was hired by someone, discovering that person's identity is crucial. But if it's our lives or hers—"

"Come on," Aderyn said.

They'd done this before, following the <**Wayfinder**> at speed through a spriggans' stronghold, but that had been mostly empty. Now they made their way through the streets of Terrace One, dodging or pushing aside anyone who didn't get out of their way fast enough. Aderyn was conscious of nothing but willing the orb to go on tracking her prey. She stared at the glowing steel spike, alert to the smallest change in color or intensity. The heat of the thing warmed her hands, something she was grateful for in the cold afternoon air.

She called out direction changes, right, right, left, ahead, as the spike gradually heated and its color went from pale pink to the blush of a girl's cheek to the deep red of a blooming rose. At some point, rain began falling, lightly at first and then in hard, hammering drops Aderyn shook out of her eyes and hair.

When the orb pulsed once and then went instantly dark, Aderyn stumbled and was supported by Isold and Owen's hands. She looked around, finally conscious of her surroundings.

They had come to a dead-end street, except Aderyn had never seen one like this before. It was more of a courtyard than a dead-end, a round extension of the street around which buildings were arranged like cards fanned out in someone's hand. There were five buildings, all of them tall and elegantly faced with marble. Porticos shielded each of the doorways, narrow and pillared with gilding along their roofs. Unlike the main streets of Terrace One, this dead end was empty of pedestrians. Lights blazed at the windows of three of the five buildings, and Aderyn heard music.

"That's the one," she said, swiping tendrils of wet hair from her eyes. "That tavern."

"I think it's an inn," Weston said. "Not that it matters."

"But it's not like the places the <**Wayfinder**> led us to last time," Owen said.

The sound of a flute skirled high above the rest of the music. Owen cursed. "We have to go in now. Who knows what she's Beguiling them to do?"

They burst through the door and kept going. Aderyn had enough time to register that if this was a taproom, it was the most upscale taproom she'd ever seen, with white tablecloths and sparkling crystal glasses and shining silverware, but then she saw Damaris and everything else faded away.

The Beguiler sat with a group of musicians dressed all in somber, dark clothes. Unlike them, she wore an ice-blue gown that sparkled here and there with crystal beads. Her pale blonde hair was piled atop her head with a couple of ringlets trailing artfully down on one side. For a moment, Aderyn was struck by her unearthly beauty, not because she admired it but because she saw the woman not as a human being, but as a monster to be defeated.

Damaris saw them immediately. The sound of the flute cut off. In the Beguiler's moment of hesitation, Aderyn Assessed her class skills, wanting every edge [**Improved Assess 2**] could give her.

Name: Damaris
Class: Beguiler
Level: 15
Class Skills: Perform (flute) (15); Knowledge: Magic (14);

Knowledge: Monsters (5); Knowledge: History (7); Knowledge: Social (14); Knowledge: World Lore (13); Identify Magic Items (12); Charm (12); Obscure (12); Map Access (12); Cause Fear (8); Fascination (8); Persuasion (7); Perform (singing) (5); Suborn (5); Resist Magic (4); Illusion (6); Hypnosis (6); Seduce (5); Beguilement (6); Break Enchantment (3); Perform (lute) (1)

   <u>**Skill Alert**</u>**: Cause Fear (8), Illusion (6), Beguilement (6)**

Damaris lowered her flute. The other musicians stopped playing, a few at a time so the music came to a ragged stop. All through the taproom, patrons were murmuring to their companions as if they hoped someone could explain this intrusion.

"Excuse me. Excuse me." A willowy man approached them. He was dressed all in black like the musicians, but the cut of his coat and trousers suggested he was of a higher class, at least to Aderyn. "This is a private eating establishment. I'm afraid I have to ask you to leave." He stared at Owen's bloody condition, which wasn't as bad as it had been before the rain but still looked as though he'd had his throat slit.

Owen ignored both his words and his appraisal. "We're here for Damaris," he said, nodding at the Beguiler. "She will come with us to answer some questions before the magistrates."

"This is a misunderstanding," Damaris said. Her voice was unexpectedly rich and throaty, like melted chocolate mixed with heavy cream. "They have the wrong person. You're not going to—"

"She's Beguiling him," Aderyn said, lunging forward.

All the musicians stood as one and formed a barrier between the room and Damaris. They reached behind their instruments and drew knives, most of them short-bladed but all of them deadly-looking. Owen grabbed Aderyn and put her behind him. "Give up, Damaris. It's over."

Damaris smiled and raised the flute to her lips. She played a single note before Aderyn snatched up a heavy glass candlestick from the nearest table and hurled it at her. It struck the flute and sent it spin-

ning away, making Damaris gasp in pain as the tumbling flute
scratched her face.

The four musicians moved forward, knives raised. Owen
shouted, "Don't kill them! It's not their fault!" and met the nearest
musician with a punch to the jaw that dropped him like a stone.
Weston joined him in the fight.

Damaris backed away, still protected by their bodies, and sang a
sweet, sultry melody with no words. Its beauty touched Aderyn's
heart briefly, and then someone grabbed her from behind, breaking
the spell. It was the willowy man, whose eyes were glazed over and
whose jaw was slack. Beside her, tentacles of earth burst through the
floor and restrained a patron who'd risen from his table intent on
attacking her.

Then another song joined Damaris's melody, weaving through it
so the two sounded like counterpoints to one another. Aderyn
stomped on her captor's shoe with her sturdy boot and elbowed him
sharply in the face. He screamed and let her go. Aderyn caught sight
of Isold, his head lifted in song, his whole body tense with effort. She
brushed past more patrons who looked confused, like they thought
they should stop her but didn't know why. She skirted Owen and
Weston's fight and slammed into Damaris, shoving her head against
the wall before taking both of them down.

Half the song ceased. Damaris looked up at Aderyn groggily.
"You," she said, her voice still beautiful. "You were my best work."

Hot rage flooded Aderyn, the memory of having been Beguiled,
and she punched Damaris in the face, knocking her head back again.
Blood trickled from the woman's nose, and she sagged in uncon-
sciousness.

**Congratulations! You have defeated [Damaris the Beguiler].
You have earned [17,000 XP]**

CHAPTER FORTY-SIX

Hands pulled her away from the Beguiler. "You stopped her," Owen said in her ear.

"I want her dead," Aderyn seethed. "Dead. She's never going to stop hurting people."

"We've won, Aderyn. She can't hurt us anymore." Owen held her close. "It's up to Finion's Gate how they deal with her, but I'm guessing execution is where that leads."

Aderyn closed her eyes tightly and nodded. Owen smelled of rainwater and blood, nothing like himself, and suddenly she felt very tired. "Let's take her in."

"Isold is still countering her [Charm]." Owen kissed her once before hugging her again. "She tried to raise all these people against us, but it must have been too much of a challenge even for her, because only about half of them tried to attack. Since almost everyone here is non-classed, that makes it easy to remove the [Charm], but we don't want any lingering influences."

"These fellows were more difficult," Weston said, nodding at the musicians. He was gagging and binding the Beguiler, who was regaining consciousness. "I think they were under a true Beguilement, not like the others."

Aderyn lifted her head from Owen's shoulder and surveyed the taproom. It wasn't as full as before, and the door hanging open to the chilly rain told her why. Most of the remaining patrons huddled in small groups well away from Aderyn's friends. The willowy man was mopping his face with a now-bloody handkerchief. "I will have you know I am on good terms with the magistrates!" he said in a somewhat nasal, clogged tone. "They will see you prosecuted for this... this *invasion!*"

"You can tell them you hired a Beguiler to entertain your patrons," Livia said. She tapped some of the earthen tentacles, making them crumble into loose soil. "I'm sure they'll be understanding."

"A Beguiler? Of course not!" But the man's demeanor became uncertain. "That is—she chose to sit with our musicians, and that's... actually, I don't know why I allowed it. It's against the musician's guild code. Really, a Beguiler?"

Isold's song came to an end, and the Herald approached the distraught man. "We will remove her, and ensure she receives justice. We apologize for our part in the fight, but we acted with authority from the magistrates to apprehend the Beguiler. I am certain you understand."

Aderyn recognized when Isold was deploying elegant language to overwhelm someone. It wasn't even a skill, just his own natural ability, but it always worked.

"Understand," the willowy man said. He stared at Damaris, who Weston was pulling to her feet. "Of course. A Beguiler. How dreadful."

"Sorry about the mess," Livia said. She didn't sound sorry.

The man ignored her. His attention was still on Damaris, who with her bloody nose could have been his twin in inflicted injuries. "What else has she done?"

"Nothing you need to worry about," Owen said. "Let's go."

Weston guided Damaris through the door, preceded by Owen. Aderyn brought up the rear. With Livia and Isold flanking the Beguiler, it was unlikely she was going to escape, but Aderyn intended to make sure that didn't happen. Never mind what Owen said; Aderyn wasn't going to be satisfied until Damaris was permanently unable to hurt anyone, ever again.

This time, she noticed the attention they got from passersby. The rain had stopped, and there were many people out on the streets again, probably interested in an early supper like those people at the exclusive inn had had. All of them stopped and stared at the bound and gagged woman escorted through the streets by a handful of adventurers who all looked like they'd been in a fight. Owen in particular got more than his share of notice, but Aderyn didn't start worrying until she overheard the conversations.

"...Wildcats..."

"...doing here, and who is..."

"...the challenger Owen, looks like he was knifed!"

"...allowed to capture beautiful women..."

"I think we might be in trouble," she murmured.

"I hear it," Weston said. "This isn't going to do our reputations any good, at least not until rumor spreads the truth. But don't worry. Nobody's planning to attack us. They just think it's strange that we're acting like constables."

Something whistled past Aderyn's ear. Damaris jerked and sagged. Aderyn saw the bloody crossbow bolt emerging from the Beguiler's left shoulder just as Owen said, "We're under attack!"

Another bolt flew past, missing everyone. Weston and Owen hustled Damaris into the shelter formed where two buildings met at a narrow alley between them. Aderyn, crouching low to make herself a worse target, scuttled to join the others just as several more bolts flew at them. One struck Livia in the fleshy part of her upper arm, the one that was stone below. She grunted in pain. "Push it through," she said through gritted teeth. Aderyn whipped her tunic off and pushed the bolt out of Livia's arm, then wrapped her tunic around the wound.

"That's it. Now I'm pissed off," Livia said. She stood, not seeming to care how her body was silhouetted against the alley, and with a few curtly-murmured words she stomped the ground in front of them. Violent ripples passed through the paving stones, and cries of alarm turned to cries of pain as *thunderstomp* sent them sprawling.

"We have to go," Weston said. "There are at least three of them, and they're concealing themselves well. I think they're Assassins."

"Assassins? After us?" Aderyn said.

"After Damaris," Owen said.

The Beguiler's breathing was heavy, making the crossbow bolt jerk wildly with every breath, and her eyes were glassy with pain. Owen looked her over with indifference. "I think—"

Damaris convulsed. Then she shook with a powerful seizure. With an oath, Weston removed the gag. "If she vomits—"

Livia sat down hard on the dirty paving stones. "Poison," she said thickly, and her eyes rolled up in her head.

Aderyn instinctively checked their team roster. Livia's health bar was green instead of blue and was about two-thirds its usual length and shrinking. "What do we do?" She unwrapped her tunic from around Livia's arm and stared at the two still-bleeding wounds as if that would solve the problem.

Isold fumbled in his clothes for the **<Healing Stone>**. "I don't know how well this works on poison, but it's worth trying." He palmed the round stone and pressed it against Livia's wounded arm. Instantly, Livia's health bar stopped shrinking, but it remained that same vile green color. Her breathing became shallow, and her whole body was rigid as if she was fighting the poison with her will alone.

"Damaris is dying," Owen said.

Isold removed the **<Healing Stone>**. "No, don't!" Aderyn said.

"Her health drops when she's not being healed. She might die before the poison runs its course."

"I can't heal them both," Isold said. Without hesitation, he laid the stone against Livia's arm again.

Owen abruptly leaned over Damaris, who had stopped convulsing and lay so still Aderyn thought she was already dead. "What did you say?" Owen said.

This time, Aderyn saw Damaris's lips move, but her speech was too soft for Aderyn to hear. Then Damaris sagged, and Aderyn didn't know how she could have thought Damaris was dead before, because the profound stillness in which she now lay could never be mistaken for anything but death.

The crossbow bolts had stopped, and the street was full of people rushing away from the scene of violence. The friends all sat in silence, watching Livia and her status in their team roster. Isold said once, "This is the deadliest poison I've ever heard of. It might drain the <**Healing Stone**> before she's healed fully."

"Those Assassins are gone," Owen said. "One of us could go for a Bonemender."

"I'm staying here," Weston said. "And what if the Assassins were actually after us and not Damaris? We can't separate and risk anyone else."

"I don't think they were after us," Owen said. "Damaris, right before she died, said something that surprised me. She said, 'The votes don't matter.'"

Aderyn blinked. "What does that mean?"

"I don't know. She had to have been talking about the Glory Games and the votes each champion earns for their sponsor, but all the votes? Or just the votes one person has?" Owen swept his damp hair back from his face. "I think something else is going on. Damaris went on acting after Brisa was taken into custody, so either she was acting on her own out of pure spitefulness, or Brisa wasn't the one paying her."

"Doesn't that mean it was one of the other Councilors?" Aderyn squeezed water out of her ponytail and wiped her bloodstained hands on her tunic. "Who else cares about the Glory Games? We've already learned that there's no way to make a fortune at wagering on the matches unless you can fix them, and Weston says that's virtually impossible."

"Impossible to do without being detected," Weston corrected. He held Livia's stone hand and was intently running his thumb over its curves. "It's the way they have things set up... and none of us care about that."

"Brisa's champions climbed higher in the rankings thanks to the Beguiler's meddling," Owen said. "Not much higher thanks to *our* meddling. She had twelve votes going in, and if nothing else changes —and if she's still eligible—she has thirteen now. So it was a stupid plan."

Weston leaned forward, interested. "What about the other councilors? Did any of them gain votes?"

"Most of the existing ones lost votes, actually." Owen's voice had the distant sound of someone counting mentally. "Sabetta, Balan. Raynir, obviously. Emmalia gained a few. The real winner is Kesslon, the new guy. He sponsored both Pace and Gradin and they give him sixteen votes."

"So he could be the one," Aderyn said, "except several of those attacks were directed at stopping Pace, not advancing him, and if Kesslon's plan was to divert attention from himself, that's a stupid plan, too."

"Except Damaris said it's not about the votes." Owen shook his head. "Damn it, why couldn't her dying words have been the name of her employer, or something useful like who sent those Assassins after us?"

Livia's shallow breathing stopped.

Weston grabbed her shoulder, saying, "No—"

Livia drew in a deep, natural breath and relaxed. Weston shook her, but she didn't move.

"The poison is gone," Isold said. "But the <Healing Stone> is drained. We'll need to buy another one.

"You can't recharge it?" Aderyn asked.

"Any healing item requires at least a sliver of magical energy for a new charge to latch onto. I'm afraid this is an ordinary rock now."

"I'm so glad it was enough." Aderyn straightened Livia's tunic, though she wasn't in a position to care about modesty. "What a wonderful coincidence!"

"Actually, it ran out of charges several seconds before the poison stopped its effect," Isold said. "I chose to hold onto hope."

They stared at him. Weston said, "We could have..."

"A Bonemender couldn't have reached us in time, as I think you realize," Isold said gently. "She survives. We move on."

"As Owen survived," Aderyn said. "I wish we could find Gamboling Coil so I could thank it again."

"I couldn't have been entirely dead, because we're still married," Owen said, taking her hand.

"We are! But that Bonemender said it was too late!" She clutched Owen's hand, seeing again in memory's eye that spray of arterial blood.

"I don't have an answer for that, and I'm not sure I want to investigate too closely." Owen touched his throat with his free hand. "But if you're thinking I'm now going to be careless with my life because I have two more Get Out of Death Free cards, think again."

It was another five minutes before Livia blinked and sat up. "Poison," she spat. "Blasted Assassins. What did I miss?"

"Damaris is dead, and her last words were a cryptic message that has us rethinking everything we thought we knew about this mystery," Weston said, drawing her to sit close against him.

"Dead, huh? Guess it couldn't have happened to a worse

person." Livia leaned back against Weston and sighed. "So, now what do we do?"

Owen rose. "I'm going to the arena to get Seonn's enforcement. They can take charge of the Beguiler's body. Then we're all going back to the inn to get cleaned up, fed, and rested. And while that's happening, I'm going to figure out what Damaris meant that the votes don't matter."

It took practically no time for Owen to return with a passel of constables and three inquirers, because they were already on the way to investigate reports of people with crossbows shooting into the crowds of Terrace One. Aderyn stared at Damaris's contorted features as the constables carried her away and felt not a trace of remorse. Apparently her famous compassion had its limits.

Owen's plan was disrupted by Seonn, following in the enforcers' wake. He insisted on hearing the whole story, up to Damaris's death. Owen didn't mention the woman's dying words, and neither did anyone else. Aderyn wasn't sure why she was convinced Owen was right to keep that quiet, especially since she didn't think Seonn was complicit in manipulating the Games. He cared too much about their integrity to ever go along with a plan that could destroy them. But she stayed silent as Owen explained why they couldn't save Damaris and once more felt a remote lack of pity.

Back at the Inn, Aderyn changed out of her uniform and into ordinary clothes while she waited for Owen to use the bathhouse. When he returned to their room, the first thing he said was, "Didn't you want a bath, too? You looked like a drowned rat when we captured Damaris."

"In the morning, maybe. It's just my hair that was wet, and that will dry soon enough." Aderyn wrapped her arms around him and held him close, resting her head on his shoulder. Now he smelled of soap and clean linen, not horribly of blood. "I'm so glad you're alive."

"It was so strange," Owen said. "Being dead. I was dizzy, and I couldn't see anything—you know, how it feels when you lose a lot of blood? And I couldn't feel my body. But then I was completely free of pain. Not just the pain of the wound, but all the little pains we live with all the time and never pay attention to. Like I was perfectly healthy in a way no human ever is. And I heard a voice, a woman's voice, but I couldn't understand what she said. Then I was conscious, and you were there, and it was all over."

"I didn't even think to look at my Codex. Our union should have been nullified." The thought of that made her feel sick.

"I don't know what it means that it wasn't, either." Owen ran a gentle hand over her damp hair. "I was serious about not being cavalier with my life. I don't want to go through that terror again."

"You didn't say you were afraid."

"I knew I was dying, and the only thing I was aware of was that dying meant leaving you behind." Owen kissed her. "There isn't a lot I'm afraid of, but that tops the list."

She returned his kiss wholeheartedly. "We don't need dinner, do we?"

Owen tugged her shirt free and slipped it off over her head. "Eating is overrated."

CHAPTER FORTY-SEVEN

Aderyn sat on the end of the bed the next morning and watched Owen don his newly-clean armor. "I don't want you to fight today," she blurted out.

Owen paused, startled. "What brought that on? You don't think I'm in danger, do you?"

She shook her head. "It's just that after yesterday I've lost my taste for the Games. Fighting other people isn't the same as fighting monsters who might kill us, or kill innocent people. Now the idea of you battling Kendria seems pointless."

Owen sat beside her and took her hand. "Do you think we should leave? Because we could. There's nothing keeping us here."

"Nothing but our honor," Aderyn said. "You leaving would mean Raynir would lose his Councilor position. I don't feel comfortable doing that to him."

"Hmmm." Owen stared at nothing. "It would ruin him, that's true. But if something happened—like, if we found out our delaying was costing the communities of the Lonely Tor their safety or their lives—we'd leave. Finion's Gate politics aren't our business."

"And I don't know that that's true. That the Lonely Tor people are in danger, I mean. Besides, Weston was right that a day or two's delay in starting the journey makes no real difference." She rested her head on his shoulder. "I'm just being silly. Of course you should fight. I want Kendria to lose."

Owen slid his arm around her waist and kissed the top of her head. "Because of how she treats Borrus?"

"I know it's petty of me, but I don't like how arrogant she is. Like she knows she's the best and everyone else is inferior. I want her to find out she's not the greatest. Maybe then she'll do something that will make Borrus realize what she's really like." She hugged Owen for a moment and then rose to find her hairbrush. "Let's do this."

Owen chuckled and finished fastening his brigandine before sliding his vambraces on and securing the straps. "I admit to feeling petty myself. I haven't spoken to her since our first fight, but I got the feeling she was unsettled by how close she came to losing."

"Good. That's going to work in your favor," Aderyn said.

They walked together to the arena, Owen in his armor, the Wildcats in their uniforms though they wouldn't compete again. It struck Aderyn that they likely wouldn't compete in the Glory Games again ever. It was a strange feeling. She'd loved the little dungeons and the challenges they posed, but the idea of doing that over and over again for years—the Hooligans had been at this going on three years, the Indomitables almost as long!—felt as pointless as she'd told Owen the solo battles felt. All these months they'd been grinding to reach level fourteen had felt like forever, like they'd abandoned their quest to achieve the **[Fated One's Destiny]** even though they hadn't had a choice.

The grind was over, though. Two more days, three at the most, they could start the journey to the Lonely Tor. And maybe they'd find someone who could cast *world door* for a price they could afford that would get them... well, all the way to the Lonely Tor was probably out of the question, but Guerdon Deep or the sanctuary cities were possible. The thought of seeing her parents again, introducing Owen as her husband, cheered her out of her funk. Focus on the now, she told herself. Let Owen beat Kendria. The rest could wait.

They separated at the room beneath the arena. Aderyn kissed Owen and said, "Good luck. Keep an eye on her off hand so she doesn't catch you with that twist and disarm trick again."

"I will remember. I love you." Owen kissed her in return and waved to the others.

"He looks confident," Weston said as they climbed the stairs to the covert.

"He should be. He's going to kick Kendria's ass," Livia said.

"That's more certain than you ever are," Isold said. "Indulging in optimism?"

"Owen learns from defeat, and he's never made the same mistake twice," Livia declared. "This isn't optimism. It's conviction."

"I feel the same," Aderyn said.

To her surprise, the covert was packed with men and women in colored tunics. "This is it for the season," Jesper said when Aderyn exclaimed in pleasure at seeing all of them. "None of us have ever had a personal investment in the solo fights before, even if it's one step removed. And this is the first time in several seasons Kendria's had a real challenge."

"I still say she's going to win," Martis said.

"You want to put hard money on that?" Weston said.

Martis grinned. "I'm not *that* certain. I love my money and I like it to stay close."

Weston groaned. "You people are all so conservative when it comes to wagering. I should have been able to make a killing on Owen's prospects."

"*You* are conservative when it comes to wagering," Livia reminded him.

"Yes, but I'm unusual. Most people who like wagering don't care about how bad the odds are. I was hoping to capitalize on that."

Weston shook his head, smiling in resignation. "I guess I'll have to settle for the three thousand gold I've won so far."

Livia gasped and punched him with her flesh-and-blood fist. "Three thousand? You've been acting like a child deprived of a trip to the candy store."

"It would have been four times that if anyone had taken that first wager. Ten to one odds." With a sigh, Weston sank into his chair. "The money you don't make is the saddest loss."

"Goooooood morning, friends!" the announcer shouted. "Who's ready for the final battle!"

The crowd's murmur surged to a roar. Out of nowhere, Aderyn wondered what the announcer looked like. Based on his enthusiasm, she pictured him as a Herald, a good-looking, lean, agile-fingered man with a mobile face who was quick with a joke. She hoped she never saw the man, because her imagination suited her and she'd hate to learn he was balding and short.

"We won't keep you waiting any longer! As challenger, we have someone who's fought his way to the top as you've all watched. Those of you who were here yesterday saw his miraculous recovery from a vicious, unprovoked attack—let's hear it for *Owen!*"

Aderyn shouted and waved her hands as Owen entered, not at a run but at a measured pace that made him look confident. The bright sun gleamed off his blond hair as if it also wanted him to win. Owen saluted Aderyn, pausing for a few seconds longer than usual as the crowd's screams grew to a fever pitch, then strode fearlessly to the center where the red-suited adjudicators already waited.

"And defending her position as number one champion, the woman who's won your hearts over several seasons of fierce competition—*Kendria!*"

Kendria walked as confidently as Owen had, but unlike him, she didn't acknowledge the crowds. Aderyn wanted to believe that meant she didn't care about their support, but it looked more like Kendria's attention was fully on Owen. Aderyn hoped Kendria had been as rattled as she believed by her near loss to Owen last time.

Kendria reached the center. Rather than taking her position opposite Owen, she walked to one of the adjudicators and said something at length. The adjudicator put a hand over her voice amplifier and replied. Kendria shook her head and said something else that had the other adjudicators drifting over. Owen remained where he was, though **[Read Body Language]** told Aderyn he was only doing it out of courtesy and was extremely curious about what was going on.

The conversation went on for half a minute before Kendria held up a hand, demanding silence. Then she crossed to where Owen stood and again spoke at length. Whatever she said made Owen tense up with suspicion.

"What's going on?" Weston said.

"Kendria wants something unusual," Aderyn said. "At least, Owen's skeptical of whatever it is she's saying."

"You can hear that?" Jesper asked.

"No, it's a Warmaster skill shared with her partner—wait, they've agreed on something." As she said this, Owen and Kendria shook hands, and Kendria took her place opposite him.

The first adjudicator Kendria had spoken to released her voice amplifier and said, "We have a request from the champion. Should Owen defeat Kendria, he would be required to defeat her a second time to achieve a final victory because Kendria is currently undefeated. The champion has chosen to forfeit her right to a second fight should she be defeated in the first one. This combat alone will determine who is the first-ranked champion of the Glory Games."

The murmurs of the crowd increased. Aderyn gasped. "Why would she do that?"

"Because she's Kendria," Martis said. "She's not going to lose."

"She almost did lose last time," Jesper pointed out. "This is the kind of arrogance that gets you defeated."

"It's not arrogance if she knows she can win," Martis said.

"Shhh," Aderyn said. "They're starting." It didn't matter if they stopped arguing, given how noisy the arena was, but all her attention was focused on Owen and she didn't want distractions.

Staff tapped sword. The signal sounded, and Owen and Kendria began circling, looking for an opening. Owen feinted, Kendria ignored it. Kendria made a move that never came close to Owen. Owen ignored that one. The noise of the crowd diminished, as if they were listening hard for the sound of wood or metal striking armor.

Kendria's move was so fast Aderyn would have missed it if she hadn't been counting the woman's paces. Every time she'd seen Kendria fight, Kendria had struck after exactly fifteen paces, regardless of what direction those paces had been in. She'd told Owen, but said, "Don't count on it. If she's going to vary her attack, that would be an easy way to do it."

But Kendria hadn't changed anything this time. Her staff came swinging in, moving rapidly up high to catch her opponent's attention before she made the actual hit from below. The staff swung up—

—and Owen's dagger caught it from below and lifted so it swung past his thigh. For the briefest moment, Kendria was off balance, and in that moment Owen struck her upper arm just at the edge of her armor's sleeve.

"One to Owen!" the adjudicator shouted, his amplified voice bellowing over the arena.

Aderyn let out a relieved hiss. Owen had been paying attention before. He wasn't going to be caught by the same move twice. A new move, on the other hand...

The two disengaged and went back to circling. This time, it was Owen's turn to lunge forward, his sword and dagger weaving a complicated pattern Kendria deflected, though not with ease. Neither found an opening, and Owen was stepping back when Kendria changed her grip on her staff and brought it around hard and fast. In the moment before it struck Owen's side, Aderyn thought of Owen's description of a baseball bat that wasn't the kind of bat she imagined, but was a fat stick for striking a ball. The staff cracked against Owen's armor, making him wince.

"One to Kendria!" two adjudicators cried at once.

Aderyn wiped her palms on her tunic and clutched the rail so they'd stop sweating. The combatants had separated for only a second and were now exchanging blows rapidly, striking and parrying and striking again. Owen deflected the staff and reversed the sword's strike to hit Kendria's thigh. "Two," Aderyn breathed, echoing the adjudicators.

"Just one more," Livia said in the same low voice. "One more."

Circling again, Kendria and Owen feinted, neither taking the bait. The crowd quieted to a dull roar, waiting to see who would strike first. The rail was rough against Aderyn's palms where the varnish had worn off. She imagined dozens of others gripping the rail as she had done. She doubted any of them had been as tense and anxious as she was now.

"No," she breathed. Owen had moved in, his sword raised, his dagger hanging forgotten in his left hand. Kendria snapped her staff around, blocking the sword's slash and then whipping up to crack against Owen's hand, disarming him—

—except his hand wasn't there.

The staff swished through empty air as Owen avoided Kendria's blow, continuing the dagger's swooping arc to strike its blade against Kendria's armored abdomen.

There was a moment of perfect silence. Then the announcer shouted, "*Owen wins!*" and the arena erupted with shouts and screams and chanting of Owen's name.

Congratulations! You have defeated [Kendria the Staffsworn].
You have earned [21,000 XP]

Aderyn found herself on her feet, hugging Jesper and shouting with excitement, then hugging Martis, who was laughing a bit ruefully, then clutching her friends and dancing a four-person jig. She peeled away from the group to watch Owen, who was standing next to Kendria. He was saying something, and in the middle of his elation he also felt an unexpected desire to act honorably.

Kendria extended her hand to clasp his wrist. She spoke, shaking her head, and Owen suddenly felt smug as well as happy and determined. They clasped one another in a warrior's salute, and then Owen turned and raised both hands above his head, saluting the crowd, then his sponsor Raynir, and finally the covert.

"Raynir doesn't look as happy as I thought he would," Aderyn mused.

"Owen's waving at you. Be a good wife and show how proud you are," Livia said, nudging her.

Aderyn laughed and waved back at Owen. He saluted her a final time and then followed Kendria into the tunnel.

"That was history made right here in front of our eyes!" the announcer shouted. "I don't know about you, but I need a break. In ten minutes, we'll present the winners of the forty-seventh semi-annual Glory Games!"

"Is that it, then?" Weston asked.

"Oh, there's another big bash tonight," Jesper said. "All the Councilors being not very subtle about how high their rankings are now, or pretending to be gracious losers. We go because it's good visibility for next season."

"You're determined to leave, though, right?" Kathra asked.

"We have business down south," Aderyn said.

"The Fated One quest," Jesper said.

Aderyn drew an incautious breath and coughed on spit that went down the wrong way. "What do you—"

"It's not a secret that Owen is the Fated One," Jesper said.

"Everyone saw it. The system brought him back from the dead, and why would it do that if he wasn't important?"

"It wasn't the system—" Weston began.

"Yes, he's the Fated One," Isold said. "We didn't want to make a fuss, because aside from that, he's really an ordinary man."

Kathra and Martis laughed. Jesper chuckled with them and added, "Sure he's ordinary. He beat the undefeated champion in a three to one victory without breaking a sweat. He's got enough charisma to sway a legion of followers. And he came back from the dead. Those are all ordinary things."

"Jesper," Aderyn began.

"Look, I for one always assumed the Fated One stories were faked by people who wanted fame and casual sex," Jesper said, resting a hand on Aderyn's arm. "The idea that there might actually be a Fated One is exciting. And comforting, in a way. Like the system is looking out for us. So don't feel like you need to protect Owen. Nobody here is upset about him concealing his identity."

Aderyn gave up. "Thanks, Jesper."

"And you're off on another quest," Kathra said with a grin. "I can see how Glory Games dungeons might lack enough excitement."

Aderyn remembered the terror of fighting the Sarnok and the fear of being trapped in Sorrowvale forever. "Excitement isn't all it's cracked up to be," she said.

CHAPTER FORTY-EIGHT

I t felt like much longer than ten minutes before the announcer said, "This is it, friends—the culmination of the forty-seventh semi-annual Glory Games! There have been a number of upsets over the last week, so I won't keep you in suspense any longer. Ranked tenth among your new champions, Caprissa the Swordsworn!"

Aderyn gasped. "I thought she was eliminated!"

"Yes, didn't the Beguiler's attack make her incapable of continuing?" Weston leaned forward to stare as Caprissa ran forward, her blonde ponytail bouncing around her shoulders. She wasn't armed, though she wore the light armor Aderyn remembered from her battles.

"A lot of fighters were eliminated, not least Gabryl and Raewyn," Jesper said, though he sounded as surprised as the others.

"And I doubt Jael is still in contention after murdering Owen," Livia added.

Aderyn hadn't considered that. If Jael hadn't been Beguiled to attack Owen, she would be third ranked now. Seonn had sounded grim when he'd said he wasn't going to let anyone think hurting or killing opponents would benefit any competitor. Aderyn hoped that meant Jael was gone.

"And ranked ninth, Nator the Swordsworn!"

"Whatever happened to them? About Brisa?" Kathra asked.

"Brisa was cleared of complicity with the Beguiler Damaris," Isold said. "As far as I know, nothing happened to her or her champions' rankings."

Aderyn was almost certain **[Read Body Language]** now extended to people who weren't Owen, because Nator didn't look happy. Of course, he had dropped several positions in the rankings, so maybe it didn't take a special skill to realize how he felt.

"In the eighth rank, Quillon the Swordsworn!"

"Aww," Livia said, "he left his awesomely intimidating sword behind."

Weston nudged her. "Maybe it's a family heirloom."

"And maybe he's compensating for all those physical shortcomings." Livia shrugged. "Really, does he expect anyone to take him seriously when they're looking at his sword and wondering about the size of his—"

"Next up, Rhidius the Stalwart in the seventh rank!"

Aderyn watched Rhidius jog toward the growing line of champions. "He is the kind of physical specimen Quillon wishes he was, no question," she said.

"And Sabetta lost power. A lot of power. Rhidius dropped from third rank," Weston said.

Aderyn remembered how Sabetta had looked at Owen like he was a prime stallion she wanted to add to her herd. Was Sabetta regretting her loss now? She surveyed the rows of boxes and spotted Sabetta all the way to the left. Sabetta was applauding coolly and showed no sign of discontent, but she wouldn't, would she? Aderyn was grateful politics had nothing to do with her.

"In the sixth rank, another newcomer, Gradin the Swordsworn!"

Aderyn cheered loudly for the personable young man. He wasn't terribly bright, but he was loyal and kindhearted and maybe that was more important. Plus, he had his cousin—

"And in the fifth rank, Pace the Lone Wolf!"

Pace looked good for someone who'd jumped off Terrace One nearly to his death. He slapped his cousin on the back cheerfully as he acknowledged the cheering.

"I wonder why they let cousins compete?" Weston mused. "If sweethearts can't, and spouses can't."

"I've heard," said Martis, "they consider sibling rivalry an interesting spice. Probably that extends to cousinly rivalry."

"I'd still love to see them fight each other someday," Aderyn said before recalling that her team wasn't likely to be here when they did.

"And now, in fourth rank, Evalyn the Swordsworn!"

Aderyn had been searching the boxes for Kesslon, Gradin and Pace's sponsor, so she happened to see Brisa just as Evalyn ran onto the arena floor. Brisa looked angry, and she wasn't clapping. That, Aderyn didn't understand. Brisa had been exonerated, and she'd even gained one vote, which gave her a good deal of power in the Council. "The votes don't matter," the dying Damaris had said. Was this what she'd meant—that Brisa's votes were irrelevant to how the Council worked?

"And here are our top three champions," the announcer cried. "In third rank, a woman who fought her way back from early defeat —Eirian the Stalwart!"

Aderyn cheered for Eirian, but her heart wasn't in it. Not because she disliked her, because she liked Eirian a lot. No, it was the mystery of Brisa's reaction that drew her attention away from the arena floor. Aderyn hated politics for the same reason she hated riddles—they meant you had to look at things at least three different ways, and Aderyn preferred a straightforward approach. But at the moment, she wished she understood what in thunder was going on in Finion's Gate's government.

"In second rank—" The announcer paused like he had never

expected to say these words. "In second rank, Kendria the Staffsworn!"

The cheering for Kendria was as loud as ever, but to Aderyn it sounded like the crowd was waiting for something.

The announcer waited for Kendria to reach her position in the line the champions formed. After another few seconds' pause in which the crowd fell nearly silent, he said, "And the winner, and first-ranked champion of the forty-seventh semi-annual Glory Games —*Owen the Swordsworn!*"

Congratulations! You have been ranked first among all challengers and champions of the 47th semi-annual Glory Games!
You have received [30,000 XP]

Aderyn smiled as the cheering began. *That* was what they'd been waiting for.

She leaned on the rail, not cheering or clapping or shouting, just watching as her husband ran to join the other champions. Again, she thought how strange this must all be to him. She'd never been gladder that the system had for whatever reason dragged him out of his world and into hers.

"He looks like a hero," Isold murmured in her ear.

"Because he *is* a hero," Aderyn replied. "And it has nothing to do with these games, either."

"But that's not all we have to celebrate!" The announcer sounded, if anything, more cheerful than before, which meant he was practically manic. "Let's again honor your Glory Games teams!"

There was some frantic scrambling as teams who'd been scattered through the covert came together and then clattered down the stairs as their names were called. When the Hooligans and the Wildcats were the only ones left, Jesper said, "It's an honor to have competed against you all."

"Likewise," Weston said.

"I get what you meant about testing yourself against the best," Aderyn said. "Thanks for the opportunity."

Jesper's smile was wicked. "Too bad you're not staying. We won't be beaten again." With that, he followed the announcer's shout of "The Hooligans!" out of the covert and across the arena floor.

"This was pretty exciting," Aderyn said.

"No more nerves about being stared at?" Livia elbowed her lightly in the ribs.

"None. Well, maybe a—"

"And finally—*The Wildcats!*"

The others picked Aderyn up and carried her down the stairs as she laughed and pretended to struggle. Then they ran to where the Hooligans waited near Owen. Owen clasped Aderyn's hand. "You're not made for fame, are you?" he asked.

The cheering pressed down on her, increasing her extreme self-consciousness about being stared at. "I can handle it, I guess. But I don't love it."

"Then you're going to hate this," Owen said, and swept her into his arms for a long, satisfying kiss that made her forget the crowd, the arena, the whole world.

When he released her, she said breathlessly, "I bet some people passed out watching that."

"Only some?" Owen said, his eyebrows raising. "Then I didn't do it right."

Aderyn laughed. "Oh, you definitely did," she said, "but let me give you a reminder," and she drew him close and kissed him in return.

When the cheering subsided, the announcer said, "Let's show some respect to the Councilors of Finion's Gate, everyone." A circle of light that came from nowhere focused on Raynir's box. "Councilor Raynir." The announcer's voice was subdued, respectful, like he knew that to the Councilors the Games were deadly serious. Raynir came to the front of the box and raised one hand in salute. No one cheered, and the murmur of voices died even more.

The circle of light vanished only to reappear elsewhere, highlighting another box. "Councilor Balan." Balan repeated Raynir's movements, down to the salute.

"So Balan isn't the top dog anymore," Livia said.

"He doesn't look like someone who's lost," Weston said.

The light bounced from box to box as the announcer read off names: Kesslon, Emmalia, Brisa, Sabetta, Camlon, Yvona. The elderly woman he named last smiled and waved vigorously as if this was the best entertainment she'd had in years. She was the only one of the Councilors who didn't look glum.

"Well, friends, on behalf of everyone who makes the Glory Games run smoothly, thank you for making us part of your lives for these few days, and we'll see you next season!" The announcer sounded weary for the first time, which made sense to Aderyn, because staying that unrelentingly enthusiastic about anything had to get old after a while.

With Owen's arm around her shoulder, she and their friends strolled through the crowd of champions and teams to the tunnel entrance. Aderyn realized someone was calling her name. She stopped and waited for Jesper to join them. "After an hour at the Council bash," he said, "the teams get together at the Stonehaven Tavern down in Foundation, and we party all night, so if you still have energy after you've been with the Council a while, you all are welcome to join us."

"Thanks, we'd like that," Aderyn said.

"You're a lucky man," Jesper said to Owen. "If she hadn't been so obviously attached to you, I'd have made a play for Aderyn's heart."

"I hear that doesn't make a difference so long as the lady isn't married," Owen said.

Jesper shrugged. "I know futility when I see it. And you are a lucky woman," he added, gripping Aderyn's hand briefly. "I hope you have a wonderful life together, though the Fated One isn't likely to see much peace."

His words sent a chill through Aderyn, as if he was prophesying the future. "We can face anything together," she declared, willing it to be true.

"I believe it." Jesper clapped Owen on the shoulder. "I really do."

Once the team was in the room beneath the arena, Owen said, "Let's wait here a while. I don't want any of us mobbed, and I'm sure those spectators are still thronging the streets."

"Good plan," Weston said. "We can wait over there."

Aderyn noticed Kendria talking to her father, with Borrus nearby as usual, and irritation flooded through her. "What did you say to Kendria after the fight?" she asked Owen.

"I told her if she wanted a rematch, I wouldn't hold her to her earlier decision." Owen leaned against the wall and yawned. "I'm afraid she thought I was taunting her, though I was polite. And I was serious. I didn't want there to be any question about my victory, and I would gladly have fought her again. But she said she didn't go back on her word, though it was clear she wanted to. I respect that."

"It's better than I expect from her," Aderyn said. The room was empty now except for their team and Kendria, Javath, and Borrus.

Weston assumed the casual pose that meant he was eavesdropping. "That is some argument," he murmured.

Though Aderyn couldn't make out words, she could hear the tone of the murmurs, and Weston was right—Kendria and Javath were arguing in low voices. Immediately, Aderyn looked at Borrus. He had the look of someone torn between two terrible options.

Javath's voice was growing louder, and Kendria had started pitching her voice to be heard above him. Javath looked ready for a fight. "What about that farce?" he said. "That—why did you give up your right to a second fight?"

"I should have beaten him," Kendria said. "It was more dramatic, putting my victory on a single fight. I knew I could beat that upstart."

"Kendria," Borrus began.

Javath overrode him. "You were arrogant, and it cost you your position, you fool. What did you think? That you were invincible?"

"*You* always said I was," Kendria shot back. "Following in Mama's footsteps, wasn't it? Whose career did you really care about, Father?"

"Look, this really isn't—" Borrus tried again.

"Stay out of this, Borrus," Kendria said, not looking away from Javath. "I'm not interested in your opinion. I want to hear from my father. Was this ever about me, or was it only about my reflected glory shining on you?"

Aderyn was watching Borrus instead of the quarreling pair. The pain that crossed his face when Kendria dismissed his opinion as worthless made her take three rapid steps toward the little group. Weston grabbed one of her arms, Owen grabbed the other, and together they towed her back. "Didn't you hear what she said?" she demanded.

"Yes. More importantly, Borrus heard it. Just wait, Aderyn," Owen said.

"I've had enough of your backtalk, Kendria." Javath made a cutting-off gesture. "I suppose second rank isn't the end of the world. And the upstart is leaving, so next season, you'll be positioned to take the top rank again. Now, you'll go to the Council party tonight—"

"And what if I don't?" Kendria said. "What will you do? Nothing. Because you're powerless without me. And I'm leaving. Borrus, come with me."

Borrus stared at her impassively. "No," he said, as if coming to a realization, "no, I don't think so."

"What are you talking about?" Kendria said. "I want you to come with me. Isn't that enough for you?"

"Hmm," Borrus said, tapping his finger against his lips. "You know, I don't think it is. Not so long as I'm always going to be second rate. Which is what I'll be to you, now and forever."

Kendria's eyes widened. "Borrus. What are you saying?"

"Something I should have said a while ago. We're done—or rather, whatever this twisted thing between us is is done. Sorry." Borrus extended a hand to Javath. "I've enjoyed working with you, sir, but I'm ready to leave your employ. I hope there are no hard feelings."

Javath shook Borrus's hand distractedly. "No, of course not, if you're sure—"

"I'm sure. Goodbye, Kendria."

"Goodbye?" Kendria sneered. "It's not like you're going to find another woman like me who'd be willing to put up with how ridiculous you are."

Aderyn sucked in an outraged breath. "Owen, kick her ass again," she demanded.

Owen laughed. "Just... wait."

"I certainly hope I'll never find another woman like you," Borrus said calmly. "And that 'upstart' is my sister's husband, and a true hero who would defeat you a thousand times over if that's what it took to convince you you're a loser."

Kendria gasped. "A loser? How dare you!"

Borrus saluted her briefly. "Good luck in future. You're going to need it." He turned on his heel and walked toward Aderyn.

Aderyn waited until he was close enough for speech, then said, "I'm so glad."

"So am I. I'm sorry I didn't see it sooner. I guess I really was ridiculous." Borrus smiled, but his shoulders slumped.

Aderyn hugged him. "It doesn't matter what you were so much as who you're going to be, Father always says."

"I agree," Owen said. "What will you do now?" He glanced at the others, then added, "There's an open space on our team if you're interested in joining an upstart Glory Games champion and a ragtag bunch of misfit dungeon battle veterans."

Aderyn sucked in a breath. "Yes! Borrus, we would so love you to join us, wouldn't we?"

"If you're willing to endure the trouble we seem to find," Isold said. Livia and Weston just nodded.

Borrus hugged Aderyn hard, then released her. "I would love that, but honestly, I think I'm ready to retire."

Aderyn gasped. "Borrus, you can't let that woman get to you! She's awful and a complete loser. You know that."

Borrus smiled. "It's not Kendria. For the past week I've been evaluating what I've done, how I put my adventuring career on hold to work with Javath, and I realized I've lost the drive. What I want is to return home. See if Pia or Nollan are back. Meet our grandfather. Buy a tavern, maybe, and introduce Finion's Gate cuisine to Far Haven. But I'm honored by the offer."

"I'll miss you," Aderyn said, blinking back tears.

"And I'll miss you, little sister. But with the way you're advancing, it won't be long before you find your destiny and come back home as well." Borrus squeezed her shoulder.

"We'll be traveling south in a few days. Maybe we can go together as far as Far Haven," Owen suggested. "That assumes we can't find faster transportation."

"I'd like that," Borrus said.

CHAPTER FORTY-NINE

The midnight-blue dress shimmered like an aurora when Aderyn moved, its fall of silken skirts whispering like jealous women as she turned. She looked at as much of herself as she could in the half-mirror on the wall of her room and sighed with satisfaction. She hadn't managed anything elaborate with her hair, and the tendrils escaping the bun were more by accident than by design, but she looked good.

The door opened, and Owen said, "I forgot—oh." He stood frozen in the doorway, staring. His wide-eyed, astonished expression filled Aderyn with mingled self-consciousness and pleasure.

She turned slowly, running a hand over her hip to smooth the fabric. "What do you think?"

"I think I forgot my own name there for a second. Aderyn, you look amazing. How did you find a dress that fits you so perfectly in only eight hours?"

"Gerant introduced me to a retired Spellcrafter who makes and alters women's clothing. He has many clothing-related magic items— some of them sew by themselves, even—and he makes what appeals to him and then alters it to fit the buyer." She walked slowly toward him, putting a little shimmy in her step. "So, you like it, then?"

Owen's eyebrows rose nearly to his hairline. "Do I like it? You know I think you're beautiful whatever you wear, but this makes you look extraordinary. Am I allowed to feel smug at having captured the Swift's heart? Because I guarantee, married or not, you'll have a hundred men wishing me safely dead tonight. Even though they know death doesn't stop me."

Aderyn laughed and put her arms around his shoulders. "Smugness is reasonable. And we make a very attractive couple." She'd chosen the color of her dress with an eye to matching Owen's blue and gold vest, and for not having had the vest on hand, she'd guessed well.

Owen kissed her lightly. "I forgot I shouldn't go armed to the Council party. I've gotten so used to wearing a weapon I didn't even remember I had it until Weston said something." He unstrapped the sword Raynir's money had paid for and propped it in its sheath in a corner. "But now I'm glad I did, because I want to escort you and make everyone we meet wish they were us."

"You're far more motivated by making people jealous than I believed," Aderyn teased.

"Maybe it's a guy thing, feeling it reflects well on me that a beautiful, amazing woman chose me over everyone else. You think a guy like me would have had a chance with a woman like you in my world?" Owen ran a hand down her back and kissed her again, more deeply.

"A guy like you. You mean, handsome, a powerful fighter, winner of the Glory Games, and a hero with a fantastic destiny?" She kissed him in return. "You're angling for compliments, dearest."

"Well, when you put it like that..." He brushed a tendril of hair away from her face. "And if we don't get out of here immediately, I'm going to forget there's somewhere else we need to be."

"So sensible," Aderyn said.

They once more rode in Raynir's carriages, from the inn to the lifts and from the lifts to one of Terrace Two's elegant mansions, not the one they'd been to at the beginning of the Games. It was like most of the other houses on the street, if you could call such elaborate structures something as ordinary as "houses." It wasn't wide, but it was five stories tall, with lights blazing from the man-sized windows of the first three stories above ground level. Carriages waited in a line to disgorge their occupants, but Raynir's carriage bypassed the line and took the five friends directly to the front door with its marble portico, no waiting.

"This is Raynir's personal residence," Owen said, extending a hand to Aderyn to steady her while she lifted her skirts out of the way to descend from the carriage. "The Chief Councilor is expected to host the final gathering."

"That seems risky," Livia said. "Nobody knew whether that would be Raynir or Balan until the final combat. Maybe Balan has a lot of food and some unemployed musicians sitting at his house."

"Yeah," Owen said distantly. "That's true."

"What are you thinking?" Aderyn said. "Is something strange about that?"

"Only what Livia suggested, that Raynir threw this together fast for someone who didn't know he'd be a host tonight." Owen stopped and looked far up at the distant upper stories of the mansion. "Well, he's been in politics for a while. Maybe it's normal to have this kind of uncertainty going into the final rounds."

"It's cold out here," Livia said. "Let's go in and leave the worrying about how strange Finion's Gate politics are to the people who actually care." She looked remarkably like herself despite her gown of old gold satin and a necklace of amber chunks. Aderyn had half expected, given Livia's distaste for dancing, that she would have disdained fancy dresses as well. But Livia had been as pleased with the

Spellcrafter's work as Aderyn, and held herself as confidently as she always did. Weston, who looked like a well-groomed mountain in his dress clothes, gave her fond, admiring looks whenever she caught his eye. And Isold, in an eye-catching vest of maroon and rose-patterned velvet, had the look of someone ready to make a conquest or three.

The ground floor was quiet, with music and voices drifting down the stairs and growing louder as the friends ascended. At the top of the stairs, Aderyn hesitated. The staircase led to an enormous ball-room that looked like it filled the entire first floor. Enormous windows like mirrors lined the walls, golden chandeliers filled with <Everburning Candles> hung overhead, and dozens of pillars held up the ceiling and still left room for dancing. The friends hadn't arrived late, but people already thronged the room, standing in small groups and talking in low voices that made quite a din given how many guests were present. No one stared, but Aderyn felt in her gut it was only a matter of time until they did.

"This way," Owen said in her ear, and hooked his arm around hers. Aderyn was grateful for him steering her around. All her earlier confidence in her appearance faded. Sure, she was beautiful, but that only meant *more* people were going to stare.

"Excuse me," a man said. Owen stopped. "Congratulations on your victory, Owen. It was remarkable. I would never have believed a level thirteen adventurer could defeat someone of level sixteen. Truly astonishing."

"Thank you," Owen replied. "It was a challenging combat."

"I suppose with you being the Fated One, it's reasonable. What is that like?" the man continued.

Aderyn felt Owen's arm tense. "Um," Owen said, "it's—"

"Owen the Swordsworn!" another man said. "Congratulations! And this must be the famous Swift. Lots of victories all around, eh? I suppose being the Fated One rubs off on your teammates—you are a team, yes? Not just husband and wife?"

To her horror, Aderyn heard mutterings of "the Swift" and "the

Fated One" from the growing crowd surrounding them. She told herself to stiffen her spine. These people weren't a threat, and it was stupid of her to be so uncomfortable with being stared at. She caught a glimpse of Livia and Weston a short distance away, at the center of their own crowd, and wished she could be as confident as they were.

"Aderyn, what makes you impossible to hit?" asked a nearby woman who leaned in as if asking Aderyn to share a great secret. "It's a Warmaster thing, isn't it? How is it no one else knows what Warmasters are good for?"

"Well," Aderyn said, "it's a skill called **[See It Coming]** that shows me a glimpse of whatever is trying to hit me, a second or two before it does, so I can move out of the way. And Warmasters—"

"Yes, tell us your secret," a tall, gangly man said. "My daughter is a Warmaster and we were so disappointed for her, but if you've made it work, there must be hope for her after all."

That cleared her head. "She needs a partner, a fighter who can make use of her tactical skills. I hope she finds someone. I hate to think of any Warmaster believing they're useless, when all it takes—"

"And Owen is your partner," someone else said. "Did your tactical skills help him cheat? Is that how he was able to defeat Kendria?"

Irritated, Aderyn said, "We don't cheat. Owen didn't have the advantage of any of my skills in the arena, not the way he does when we fight monsters. And if you doubt my honor, you should take Seonn's word for it, because he won't allow cheating and I think you know that."

Owen tugged on her arm. "Excuse us," Owen said to those addressing Aderyn, "we have to go." Aderyn gratefully followed where he led, out of the crowd and rapidly around the ballroom to where a man dressed all in white held a serving tray of drinks in tall flutes. Owen handed one to Aderyn and took another for himself. "I didn't think we'd be mobbed here," he said.

"I can't believe all those people have heard about the Fated One already. It's only been a day since Jael's attack." Aderyn sipped her wine and wished it was beer she could gulp down by the mugful. "That does make me wonder what happened to her."

"I asked Seonn this afternoon while you were at the dress shop," Owen said. "Jael was eliminated from the competition for this year."

"Meaning she can compete next year? How is that fair?"

"It's not her fault she was Beguiled, though it was her hatred of me that made that Beguilement stick." Owen drank half his glass. "And I asked him to give her a second chance."

Aderyn gasped. "Owen!"

"Aderyn, what happened probably humbled Jael in a way nothing else would. And it gives me pleasure to be magnanimous to the woman who killed me. Besides, it's not like we'll ever meet again, so this doesn't hurt me." He drained his glass. "Let's keep moving so the jackals don't have time to descend."

Aderyn giggled. "That's a good word for them, given how many probably want a sensational story to tell their friends later. Just like jackals wanting a piece of the kill."

They circled the ballroom. Aderyn wished they hadn't left Livia and her pocket watch behind, because with how overly attentive everyone was, she was looking forward to the moment when they'd been at the party long enough they could escape to a better party at the Stonehaven Tavern. She smiled and chatted with people only as long as Owen wanted to stand still, then moved again. After only a little while, she realized she was answering the same questions repeatedly, and it became harder to remain civil.

So when she ran into an elderly woman with a familiar face, and the woman said, "Aderyn. Are you enjoying yourself?" Aderyn said, frankly, "Not really."

The woman laughed, and that made Aderyn recognize her. Yvona, the new Councilor who was Caprissa's sponsor. "I imagine I understand how you feel. This is rather overwhelming a gathering, isn't it?"

"It is, and it's not awful, I just don't like being stared at." Owen had moved a few steps away, but Aderyn found she didn't feel lost, not with how matter of fact Yvona was.

"With as lovely as you are, you probably can't get away from that, and when you add your personal fame, and your husband's fame..." Yvona shrugged gracefully. "But I understand you're leaving Finion's Gate."

"Yes."

"Such a pity. I would have liked to see my combatants fight Owen, but I suppose we can't have everything we want, or there'd be no point to living, would there?"

"Your combatants? Someone other than Caprissa?"

"Indeed. I'm sponsoring Raewyn as well."

Stunned, Aderyn said, "Raewyn? Wasn't she eliminated?"

"She was, for this season. Now that she and Gabryl are no longer together, and in fact I understand Gabryl has retired as an adventurer, she's eligible again. As a challenger, of course, starting at the bottom, but eligible. And I believe in the power of second chances." Yvona waved. "Raewyn, over here."

Aderyn turned involuntarily. Raewyn wore a dress as elegant as Aderyn's own, but she looked uncomfortable in it—or maybe it was just that people were staring at her just as much as they were at Aderyn. Aderyn felt a rush of sympathy for the Swifthands. At least Aderyn's notoriety came from something positive.

Raewyn joined them and said, "Hello, Aderyn. I like your dress," in a tone so flat Aderyn knew the woman was miserable from more than just being stared at.

"Thank you," Aderyn said. "Raewyn—"

"Yes?"

This was probably all wrong, but no one else in this room except Owen could tell Raewyn what she needed to hear. "I was Beguiled to hate Owen. I said horrible, cruel things to him because of [**Beguilement**]. He could have hated me, but he didn't. Raewyn, you need to be compassionate or you're going to lose the most important person in your life."

Raewyn froze. "You don't—" She swallowed. "This isn't about love. He ruined me. And he never apologized."

"Because he feels so guilty he's afraid he deserves your hatred. You have to be the one who acts. Please, Raewyn. You both spent so long pretending, and now that you can be together openly, do you really want to lose that?"

Aderyn was aware of Yvona watching this in silence, but most of her attention was on Raewyn. Raewyn's eyes shone with unshed tears. Then she said, "Will you excuse me, Yvona? There's something I need to do."

Yvona nodded. Raewyn cast one long look on Aderyn before walking away. By the time she reached the exit, she was almost running.

Aderyn took in a deep breath of warm air scented with a hundred clashing perfumes and the smell of human bodies all crammed together in too small a space. "Maybe," she said.

"Maybe, what?"

Aderyn had almost forgotten Yvona. "Maybe they'll deny the Beguiler one of her victories, I guess."

"You understand compassion well," Yvona said.

"That's what Owen always says. I hope he's right."

The sound of a deep-voiced bell rang out, silencing the crowd as they searched for its source. "Greetings, all," Raynir said. He stood a few steps up on the stairs that led to the second floor, impeccably garbed in a silk shirt and trousers and brocade vest and with a dignity that suited his physique. Despite the warmth of the room, his face wasn't flushed. "Thank you for attending our gathering. At this time, it's traditional for the Chief Councilor to say a few words of thanks, in recognition of everyone who made the Glory Games a success, and to speak briefly about the coming six months and what Finion's Gate will accomplish."

He paused just long enough that Aderyn had to control a fidget. "However," Raynir continued, "I'm afraid I must break with tradition. As of two hours ago, the government of Finion's Gate has been disbanded. We will no longer determine its rule by way of the Glory Games."

CHAPTER FIFTY

For a few seconds, the room was perfectly silent. Then murmurs began and grew into a roar punctuated by shouting. Aderyn stepped closer to Owen. "Did he give any hint that this would happen?" she said in his ear.

Owen shook his head. His gaze was firmly fixed on Raynir, who stood still, his chin held high, ignoring those who shouted his name. "The votes don't matter," Owen murmured. "How did Damaris know?"

Aderyn drew in a startled breath. "So that's what she meant! But —if Raynir and the Councilors were planning this, why go through with the Games?"

Raynir plucked something small from beneath his collar and raised it to his lips. "That's quite enough," he said, his voice booming out over the noise. "Be silent, and I will reveal more."

The crowd quieted, though there were still murmurs here and there. Aderyn cast a quick glance at Yvona, who looked as placid as ever. So this wasn't a surprise by Raynir—unless Yvona was extremely self-controlled, which Aderyn would believe.

"Damaris the Beguiler interfered with the Games in an effort to upset the balance of power in Finion's Gate," Raynir went on. "Her disruption revealed a hitherto unrecognized weakness of our method of distributing power, namely that an attack on a champion is an indirect attack on a Councilor. While my colleagues and I stand by our system, in which recognizing and promoting talent shows the influence and understanding of a man or woman that extends to their ability to govern, the system has always been rigorously guarded by the integrity of those participating. The idea of an outsider interfering was, we believed, unthinkable."

Owen had taken Aderyn's hand as Raynir spoke and was holding it tightly. He was worried about something, but Aderyn didn't know what. Again, she wished she understood politics to know if Raynir's explanation was reasonable.

"After much deliberation, my fellow Councilors and I have made a decision." Raynir leveled a cool gaze at Balan, then at Kesslon. Both men, who Aderyn had previously observed to be bold and brash, stood stoically calm, expressionless and unmoving. "We have calculated the votes as assigned by the most recent Games and determined that the Councilor holding the most votes will be Chief Councilor until we have carried out an evaluation of new options for the governance of Finion's Gate. That is, of course, myself. All other Councilors will obviously remain as advisors to the Chief Councilor for the same term."

Owen muttered something under his breath.

"What was that?" Aderyn whispered.

Owen shook his head. His gaze stayed fixed on Raynir, and his jaw was tight like he was suppressing an outburst. Aderyn looked at Raynir then. He still looked perfectly calm and dignified. It wasn't at all hard to see him as Chief Councilor.

"However," Raynir said, and now he smiled like someone presenting a wonderful gift, "the Glory Games are a part of Finion's Gate history and tradition, and losing them would mean losing a part of what gives our great city its identity. Therefore, the Games will continue exactly as they are now, though the top ten champions will no longer earn votes for their sponsors. We hope they will continue to be a draw for citizens and visitors alike."

The shouting began again almost immediately, men and women clamoring to be heard. One voice pitched above the general noise said, "Does that mean you're going to be Chief Councilor for life? How does that—"

"Of course not." Raynir smoothly cut the speaker off. "We will evaluate a number of options for governance, in search of one that best befits the needs of the city. I hope you are not suggesting anything underhanded. It is pure luck, and the gift of the Fated One, that I was not deprived of all my votes."

"But how is anyone to enter government if they can't sponsor a champion?" a woman demanded. "The Council has always been open to anyone."

"Anyone with enough money," Owen muttered.

"I assure you, we will keep the representation of the people foremost in our minds," Raynir said. "Enough questions. Please, enjoy yourselves. There will be music shortly, and you are free to stay as long as you like." He turned his back on the room and climbed the stairs out of sight before anyone could stop him with more words.

Aderyn turned to Yvona. "What was that? Did you know—"

"Of course, dear. Don't worry about it." Yvona smiled pleasantly.

"But—"

The noise grew unbearably loud as men and women argued with one another over what Raynir's announcement meant. Owen continued to stare at the place where the Chief Councilor had been. Aderyn watched Owen. "What part of that are you angry about?"

"Pick one," Owen said. "Come on."

He drew Aderyn along after him to the stairs, breaking the crowds without pausing anywhere long enough to be drawn into conversation. They ran up the stairs to a landing where the stairs turned on themselves, finally ending at a T-junction of three hallways leading left, right, and ahead. Owen continued straight ahead without pause. His left hand hovered over the hilt of an imaginary sword as if he anticipated a fight. That worried Aderyn because she hated not understanding things, and not understanding this situation might, she felt, be harmful to one or both of them.

Owen stopped at a door that looked like all the other doors lining the hall and let go of Aderyn's hand. He drew in a deep breath and turned the knob, thrusting the door open as if he wanted to startle whoever was in the room.

But Raynir didn't act surprised. He stood with his back to them, looking out one of the many tall windows behind an enormous mahogany desk. Lights burned low in sconces along the walls, and Aderyn could see Raynir's faint reflection in the glass. His gaze never wavered. "Good evening, Owen, and to you, Aderyn. Won't you sit?"

"I don't think so," Owen said. "This isn't going to be a polite conversation."

Raynir inclined his head. "That's up to you. I for one believe polite discourse is always possible between civilized people."

"And you're civilized," Owen retorted. "You manipulated the system to gain power."

"And what else is civilization but the manipulation of others for the sake of power?" Raynir turned. His dark eyes were fathomless in the low light. "That such manipulations provide benefits to everyone do not, I'm sure, matter to you on your high horse."

"I almost died because of your power struggle, so forget about morality. You made this personal." Owen sounded so bitter Aderyn forgot for the moment that she had no idea what either of them were talking about.

"So you know," Raynir said. "How did you find out?"

"I'm not that clever. It only all fell together when you made your little announcement," Owen said. "You were the one who hired Damaris the Beguiler."

Aderyn's mouth fell open. She stared at Owen, then at Raynir.

"How—" she began, then shut up. She probably shouldn't have given away to Raynir that she was confused. Too late now.

But Raynir was smiling. "I'm glad it took you that long. I'm not a fool. You would have interfered if you'd known what I was doing."

"Damaris's last words were 'the votes don't matter.'" Owen was regaining some of his calm. "You were manipulating things so you would lose all your votes. Raewyn and Gabryl through elimination, me through death. Bet you were shocked as hell when I didn't die."

"I meant Gabryl to kill Raewyn in the arena," Raynir said calmly. "Damaris used her own initiative there. She always did prefer to make people suffer. And yes, your inconvenient resurrection ruined my original plan."

"But you said you would stay Chief Councilor because you had the most votes," Aderyn blurted out. "And you only had that because of Owen winning. Why would you want to lose all your votes instead?"

She immediately regretted speaking when Raynir turned his attention on her. His eyes were cold like a predator's. "Losing all my votes would put me in a moral position—you should appreciate that, Owen—to demand a change in government, as someone whose position had been eliminated by outside interference. I had to scramble for an alternative justification. But I succeeded, and now I no longer need to humiliate myself by participating in this ridiculous show every six months."

"Unless we tell the world what we've learned," Owen said.

"Who will listen to you?" Raynir shrugged. "Fated One or no, you're still a stranger to Finion's Gate, and I have been a part of this city's government for thirty years. Don't think I haven't laid plans for consolidating my power. If you speak, you'll find yourself having a fatal accident."

"You couldn't kill me before. What makes you think you can do it now?"

"True." Raynir looked at Aderyn. "But you're not the only one vulnerable—"

Owen drew in a furious breath. Aderyn strode forward and shoved Raynir up against the windows by his collar. "Don't you *dare*," she said, her earlier confusion gone. "Try making me a target, and you'll find out what else a Warmaster is capable of. I've already identified half a dozen weak points in this house's defenses, and I have a friend who can sneak in through those weak points and put an end to you and make it look natural. That's if our other companion doesn't level this house with you in it. And if you think we won't dare act so overtly, well, you know what a Beguiler is capable of, so try imagining how much damage a Herald acting on behalf of his friends can do."

Raynir's eyes were wide, and his chest heaved. He said nothing.

"Aderyn, let him go," Owen said. "He gets the point."

Aderyn snarled at Raynir once more and then released him forcefully. Raynir remained where he was, his breathing subsiding. He stared, not at Aderyn, but at Owen.

Owen stepped closer. "We have the power here, Raynir. So why shouldn't I go out there and tell everyone the truth?"

Raynir swallowed. When he spoke, he'd regained his calm. "This form of government, this shuffling around of power twice a year, is unstable. If we are at all threatened by our neighbors, Finion's Gate will fall. Think what you like of me, but I have spent most of my life making this city powerful, because that is what keeps its citizens safe."

"You think that justifies ruining several people's lives and at least two murders?" Owen said.

"As compared to what, Owen?" Raynir said forcefully. "Would you prefer anarchy? The decay of social order and the rise in violence as the government collapses—a collapse we've skirted numerous times in my thirty years on this Council? You may not want to face facts, but I spared the lives of thousands, maybe tens of thousands, by my actions, and I consider some minor disruption and a couple of deaths a small price to pay." He stepped closer to the window. "Kill me if that will satisfy the demands of your shortsighted sense of justice."

Owen took a step closer. Raynir didn't flinch.

"Owen," Aderyn said, "is he right?"

Owen shook his head. "No," he said. "But he's not wrong, either." He gazed at Raynir for a few seconds before saying, "I find your manner of gaining power repulsive. Disregard for human life makes you the bad guy as far as I'm concerned. But it sounds you've been a powerful influence in Finion's Gate all those years, mostly for the good of the city."

Raynir didn't move. His jaw worked as if he was suppressing speech.

Owen watched him in silence for a moment, waiting to see if he would say anything. When he didn't, Owen continued, "So—yeah, I hate that you got away with at least two murders, but the one thing you and I agree on is that sometimes the greater good is what matters." He sounded calm, but Aderyn could see by the stiffness of his shoulders and the tension all down his back that he hated himself for saying those words.

"Very well." Raynir straightened his collar. He'd mostly regained his poise, but his eyes kept darting to Aderyn in a nervous way. "Very well. But you'll leave Finion's Gate immediately. I won't take the chance you won't change your mind, and I doubt you have any interest in remaining here."

"We'll leave tomorrow," Owen said. "And you'll pay for someone to send us where we're going. Someone of *our* choosing."

"Of course. A gesture of goodwill."

Aderyn snorted. Raynir almost controlled a flinch.

"I'll return the things you paid for," Owen added. "I'd prefer not to be beholden to you in any way."

"In that case, I'll buy them back from you, if you're so interested in fairness and equity." Raynir gripped the back of the chair behind the desk. "After all, one way or another, you did contribute to putting me in the position I hold now."

"That's not something you want to remind me of," Owen said coldly, and turned his back on Raynir to walk to the door. Aderyn glared at Raynir a moment longer before following Owen.

On the stairs, she said, "We should get out of here. All of us."

"I think I might break something if we don't," Owen replied. "Were you serious about what you said? Knowing half a dozen weak spots?"

"No."

"I see."

"It was a dozen."

Owen laughed and put his arm around Aderyn's waist as they stepped off the stairs. "Raynir needed Borrus's warning about how good you are at getting revenge."

"He did, didn't he? Well, I think I convinced him anyway. Level fourteen, remember? **[Improved Assess 3]**. This house has more holes in its defenses than a sieve."

Owen laughed harder. "I wish you'd said that."

"Still, Owen, don't you think we should warn someone? Yvona, maybe? The Councilors ought to know what Raynir did."

"What makes you think they didn't?" Owen's jaw tightened again. "I'm sure the change in power structure wasn't as clean and amicable as Raynir made it sound during that public announcement. But letting Yvona know isn't a bad idea. Then we'd be sure someone is watching Raynir closely."

"I'll tell her—look, she's over there, near Isold."

"For about half a second," Owen said as they followed the sounds of Isold's singing, "I was afraid of what Raynir might do to you to get at me. And then you reminded me you're not a helpless maiden. You're never going to wait around to be rescued, are you?"

"Certainly not if you need me to rescue you," Aderyn said with a smile.

CHAPTER FIFTY-ONE

The party at the Stonehaven Tavern was much more fun than Raynir's elegant but soulless gala. Nobody who'd been to that one bothered to change, and the gathering at the tavern was a wild mix of people dressed in sparkling gowns and brocade vests next to men and women wearing ordinary adventurer's garb. Aderyn danced, and drank too much, and teased her new friends with how they'd never know whether the Wildcats really could be beaten. It was after three a.m. when she and Owen returned to their inn, Weston and Livia having left half an hour before and Isold having vanished with a couple of giggling women close to midnight.

Despite all that, Aderyn woke clear-eyed and refreshed just after dawn. She stretched and thought about ways to convince herself to fall back asleep. Experience told her she'd be in need of a long nap come midafternoon. But experience also said she was wide awake now, and sleep wasn't going to happen.

She reached for Owen, but stopped herself before she could wake him with a touch. Just because she was wakeful didn't mean he couldn't use a rest, especially if they were traveling to the Lonely Tor later that day. The idea invigorated her further. Finally, back on track to fulfil the Fated One quest!

To distract herself, she called up her Codex and whispered "Advancement."

Name: Aderyn

∞ Jacob Owen Lindberg

Level: 14

Class: Warmaster

<u>Skills</u>: **Bluff (13), Climb (11), Conversation (13), Intimidate (10), Sense Truth (14), Survival (8), Swim (1), Knowledge: Monsters (10), Knowledge: World Lore (5), Knowledge: Demons (1), Unite**

<u>Class Skills</u>: **Improved Assess 3 (23), Awareness (17), Knowledge: Geography (10), Spot (14), Discern Weakness (23), Dodge (14), Improvised Distraction (14), Outflank (17), Draw Fire (10), Keep Pace (16), Amplify Voice (13), See It Coming (18), Basic Weapon Proficiency (Swords) (12), Read Body Language (11), Basic Map Access (4), Compel (8), Spot Weakness (3), Secret Message (2), Bonded Mind (0)**

[**Bonded Mind**]. Owen had it too, so it was a paired Warmaster skill. It didn't make them instantly able to hear each other's thoughts, which Aderyn thought would be awful if it happened constantly. She loved Owen, and he loved her, but people needed privacy even from their loved ones. There hadn't been any time to experiment, either, what with Owen being resurrected and the terror of dealing with Damaris and finding out what Raynir's plot was. Well, she and Owen had survived all this time without that skill, so it wasn't like it meant life or death. She hoped.

She carefully rolled out of bed and dressed, then went downstairs to the taproom. Davith emerged from the kitchen with a covered platter as she entered. "Hey, Aderyn, you want some of this?" He removed the silver lid from the platter, revealing piles of steaming, aromatic sausages. "Go ahead and sit, I'll bring you a plate and a fork.

You want new beer with that or apple juice? The apple juice is really good this time of year."

Armed with a fork and knife, Aderyn dug in to sausages, fried apple slices drizzled with honey, and a pile of roasted potatoes, washing it down with the best apple juice she'd ever tasted. Weston joined her about halfway through her meal. "I never thought anyone would beat me to the breakfast table," he said. His eyes were bleary like he'd forgotten to drink antitoxin after overindulging.

"Sometimes I wake extra early," Aderyn said. "I'm going to miss this when we're gone."

Davith paused in the act of scooping potatoes onto a plate for Weston. "You're leaving? Aren't you going to stay for the next Games?" He tipped his head back and said, "Oh, right, because Owen's the Fated One. I guess that's more important." His expression of reluctant resignation made both Aderyn and Weston laugh.

"Everyone's talking about Owen, though," Davith said. "And I know people tried to bribe Pa to give them access to him, like let them in at dinnertime so they could try to eat with the Fated One and make themselves important. Of course Pa would never, because that's the sort of thing that gets around and next thing you know nobody wants to do business with you on account of you're a double-dealer."

"We appreciate that," Weston said.

"In fact, we needed to ask your pa for something, if he's available," Aderyn said.

Davith nodded. "Anything for you lot, Pa says, since having the Fated One stay here is worth more than he's making off you in rent." He ran back to the kitchen.

Weston and Aderyn exchanged amused glances. "We're a novelty," Aderyn said.

"Maybe we can get Gerant to give us a discount," Weston replied.

Gerant appeared a few minutes later, straightening the apron he wore while helping in the kitchen in the early mornings. "What can I do for my favorite patrons?" he said with a wink and a grin.

"We need to speak to a spellslinger who can cast *world door* and can get us as close as possible to the Lonely Tor," Aderyn said. "By preference, someone Councilor Raynir doesn't know." They'd discussed this the night before, on their way to the party at Stonehaven Tavern, but that last bit was Owen's contribution.

"It's probably paranoia, and maybe *world door* doesn't work this way, but I'd just as soon not give Raynir the chance to double-cross us," he'd said, "and I do not want to end up south of the sanctuary cities in who knows what kind of territory." Nobody could argue with that.

Gerant didn't even blink. "I know three who meet most of that description, and I can inquire about which of them can work the spell so you'll end up closest to the Lonely Tor. Should I have the individual meet you here, or would you prefer to go to them?"

"If they could meet us here this afternoon, that would be best," Weston said.

"Not a problem. I'll let you know who to expect." Gerant nodded amiably and strode away.

"*That* is what I'm going to miss about this place," Weston said. "If not for Raynir, I'd want to settle here for good when we give up adventuring."

"Doesn't Livia want to stay near her family?"

Weston shook his head. "We'll go back so I can get to know them, but Livia isn't close to her parents and she says her family always gets into a fight eventually, any time more than three of them are together. So we're free to choose wherever. I never realized the possibilities of a really big city."

Aderyn nodded. There were definitely advantages, but she still hadn't changed her mind about returning to Far Haven. The idea of living surrounded by her family, of having children who could grow up beside their cousins, excited her.

The thought reminded her of something else. "I'm going to say goodbye to Borrus. He'll need to know our change in plans. I am sad about not traveling with him, but it's hard to turn down a free trip directly to our destination."

"Now that we're finally back on track, the idea of walking for another two or three months has lost its appeal," Weston agreed.

Aderyn strolled through the streets to the lift, enjoying her anonymity. Very few people recognized the Swift without her uniform, and she was jostled by passersby just as if she was anyone else. She waited in line at the lift without making a fuss—Borrus was likely not awake yet anyway—and then walked the mile to Borrus's hostel, nodding and smiling at the servants bustling to their places of employment. She wasn't sure that was something she liked about city life, the divide between wealthy and poor, but for all she knew, the wealthy were kind and generous and the poor didn't feel subservient.

The hostel's equivalent of Gerant met her at the door. "Miss?"

"I'm here to see my brother, Borrus," Aderyn said. "Is he awake yet?"

"Your brother." The man connected the dots, and his eyes widened, but he controlled himself. "Miss, Borrus moved out last night. I can direct you to his new residence—actually, permit me to provide you with a guide."

Aderyn remembered then that Borrus had been sharing quarters with Javath and Kendria. No wonder he'd moved. "I would appreciate that."

Borrus's new quarters weren't as nice as the hostel, but if he was leaving soon, he probably didn't care about quality. The innkeeper showed her to the taproom, which was full of patrons eating a substantial breakfast. *That* was the sort of thing Borrus cared about.

Borrus pushed back his chair when Aderyn approached and hugged her. "Sit! Do you want something to eat?"

"I ate already. Go ahead with your meal, don't mind me."

Borrus returned to eating. "So, have you settled on a plan?"

"Councilor Raynir is paying for *world door* to send us to the Lonely Tor directly. I'm sorry we won't be able to travel with you."

Borrus lowered his fork. "That's generous of him, considering—well, except he no longer gains power based on his champions. It's still a huge expenditure. Sounds like he's hurrying you out the door!"

Aderyn laughed and hoped it didn't sound forced. "He was grateful to Owen, and I think he felt guilty about Owen being killed. On account of how Owen wouldn't have been in that position if he hadn't been fighting on Raynir's behalf." She wished so badly she could tell her brother the truth, but again, even if he was leaving Finion's Gate as well, he couldn't keep a secret well and this was a secret with devastating consequences.

"I suppose that's true." Borrus, to her relief, didn't sound suspicious. "Are you leaving today, then?"

"This afternoon. How about you?"

"Tomorrow morning. I have business to wrap up here. I was tempted to hire someone to send me directly to Far Haven, but I'm going to need all my savings to buy that tavern I mentioned. So I'll continue adventuring until I reach home, and then I'll retire." He pushed his empty plate away. "You know, I'm happy to tell our parents anything you want, but you really ought to write them a letter."

Aderyn nodded, embarrassed that this hadn't occurred to her. "Can I get pen and paper somewhere? I want to spend as much time as possible with you."

"Upstairs," Borrus said. "Let me read it over your shoulder. I'm sure you've had adventures you've failed to tell me."

"You don't know the half of it," Aderyn said.

"So," Aderyn asked, "how does *world door* work?" She was the only one of her team who hadn't experienced it before, and she was both curious and nervous at the thought of being almost instantly transported across the world.

"It takes about a minute per casting," the Windwarden Lyrista said. She was tall and willowy and dressed in gauzy robes that fluttered lightly even though they were in the Alabaster Inn's private parlor and the air was perfectly still. "It appears as a portal, but when you step into it, it expands into a tunnel. Remember to keep walking, no matter what you see."

"Why? Does something awful happen if you stop?" Livia asked, somewhat belligerently. She hadn't been thrilled about depending on a Windwarden, because, as she said, "Windwardens are all flighty and scattered. Like as not she'll send us into the ocean."

"No, but it does give me a headache." Lyrista smiled sweetly at Livia. The Windwarden didn't strike Aderyn as flighty at all, maybe a little distracted, but certainly not to the point of casting a spell incorrectly.

Livia muttered something under her breath, but made no more audible complaints.

"I'll go first," Owen said. "Then Aderyn, Isold, Weston, and finally Livia. You said this would put us within ten miles of the mountain's base, right, Lyrista?"

"No farther than ten miles away," Lyrista said. "But no closer than five, I'm afraid."

"That's fine. Thank you." Owen faced the others. "Are we ready?"

They nodded. For once, Aderyn's palms were dry. This was a completely different kind of nerve-wracking than being stared at by thousands of people.

Owen nodded. "Go ahead, please."

From her waistband, Lyrista drew a couple of short sticks about as long as the batons used in the dungeon relays. Filmy cloths in pale blue and white and gauzy purple were attached to their ends. Lyrista raised the sticks above her head and began speaking words that almost made sense. As she spoke, she lowered the sticks while waving them back and forth so the fabric rippled. Aderyn glared at Livia, who wore a look of utter disdain. Livia kept quiet.

Then, through the rippling fabric, something else became clear: a broad yellow plain with tall grasses that waved in a strong wind, and in the middle of the plain, a single mountain without foothills or other peaks. Aderyn couldn't tell how far away it was because nothing in the image gave the mountain perspective.

With a snap, an oval frame that looked carved of cherry wood blinked into existence around the image of the plain and the mountain. Owen immediately walked through it. As soon as both his feet passed the portal, his image flattened so he appeared to be a two-dimensional painting framed by the oval, though Aderyn couldn't imagine anyone wanting a portrait of someone's back. She drew in a sharp breath. Suppose this was Raynir's doing? Suppose he'd gotten to Lyrista and paid her to cast a spell that killed them all and only looked like *world door*?

"Time passes differently in *world door*," Lyrista said calmly. "You'll see."

Abruptly, Owen vanished. Lyrista drew a deep breath. "One moment, please, this is so tiring."

Aderyn waited impatiently for the Windwarden to regain her composure and repeat the thing with the sticks. As soon as the wooden frame appeared, she stepped through. If Owen was dead, she intended to join him.

She found herself in an oval passage whose walls and ceiling fit the wooden frame exactly. The walls shimmered like they were made of water and only an invisible force contained them. When she took another step, the floor squished beneath her feet. It was an unsettling experience, but she made herself walk at a steady pace with her arms flung out low for balance. She really didn't want to touch the walls. Ahead, the scene of the plain and the mountain didn't change, and she couldn't see Owen. Frustrated, she walked faster, but the end of the tunnel didn't get any nearer.

And then, in a blink, she was through.

She looked around and found Owen standing a short distance to the right. He'd shielded his eyes against the setting sun and was staring at the distant mountain west of where they stood. When she turned, the tunnel was gone.

"I can't see anything strange about the Lonely Tor," Owen murmured. "I thought for sure we were talking about a volcano, from all that fire and ash business. But there's no lava and no earthquakes."

Aderyn stood by his side. "I've never heard of the Lonely Tor being a volcano. There are some on a ring of islands off to the east, or so my father's books say."

"Well, I know nothing about volcanoes or mountains, but I'm not sure this one is natural. Not all by itself like that."

"Very little is known about the Lonely Tor," Isold said, coming up beside Owen. "It might well be a dormant volcano, or a giant dungeon, or some construction of the system for reasons unknown. Though if the [Fated One's Destiny] quest directed us here, I'd lean toward the last."

"A giant dungeon," Aderyn breathed. "Imagine that! Suppose the [Fire and Ash] quest means we have to search the interior of the mountain for a magic item that will... I don't know what it might do, but something amazing!"

"That could mean a long search," Owen said. "That's a damn big mountain."

Aderyn looked over her shoulder to where Weston had just appeared. "Weston, tell Owen that huge dungeons are exciting!"

"They can be, or so I've heard," Weston said. "Though in my opinion they're more exciting if several teams are trying to defeat them at the same time, like in that one book."

"*Seven Teams For the Win*, I read that too. See, Owen?"

"I have visions of an endless passage lined with doors, each with a creature waiting patiently for adventurers to attack with no regard for monster ecology," Owen said sourly.

"It's never like that," Aderyn scoffed.

"Never like what?" Livia said. "Wow, that thing is huge. Do you think it's a dungeon?"

"I guess we're going to find out," Owen said. "Let's get closer and see what else happens. I haven't seen any of the surrounding communities the quest referred to."

They walked westward together, surveying the territory. It did look empty. There were no signs of roads, no smoke rising from unseen chimneys, just miles and miles of yellow grasses surrounding the sullen charcoal-brown mountain upon which nothing grew. Aderyn still wasn't sure she appreciated its full size, though it did seem taller than the peaks of the Welterwall to the north.

The sun was nearly directly in her eyes now, hovering about a finger's breadth above the distant horizon. She squinted, blinked tears from her eyes, and focused higher on the peak. She stopped and grabbed Owen's arm. "I just saw movement about a quarter of the way from the top. Does anyone else see that?"

"There's something there," Weston said. He shielded his eyes and added, "Something lighter than the rocks. Moving fast."

Aderyn could see it more clearly now—something the size of her fist that appeared to crawl across the surface of the mountain. For one mad moment, she had the illusion she was looking at a roach on a wall. Then the creature detached itself from the side of the mountain, spreading wings that caught the light of the setting sun and glowed warm bronze.

They all froze. Great wings beat in huge, lazy flaps as the creature rose, higher and higher. Then the wings snapped open, and it glided in a long, slow descent, growing larger as it flew toward them. Fleeing was impossible. There wasn't anywhere to go.

Aderyn stared in horror, her mind too numb to think, as the

thing swept nearer and nearer and then soared overhead and continued eastward.

She turned with the others to watch it go. No one spoke for nearly a minute, until it was out of sight. Then Livia said, "Well, crap."

Weston blew out his breath. "Now what?"

"Maybe it was just visiting," Aderyn said, and felt instantly foolish. But no one laughed.

"That possibility never occurred to me," Isold said. "They're semi-mythical."

"Nothing mythical about that," Owen said. "That was definitely a dragon."

Appendix: Character Sheets

NOTE: These character sheets represent the status of the companions at the end of the book, which means it reveals everything the companions learn about their skills throughout the story. If you haven't finished the book, don't read this unless you don't mind spoilers!

Name: Aderyn

∞ Jacob Owen Lindberg

Level: 14

Class: Warmaster

Skills: Bluff (13), Climb (11), Conversation (13), Intimidate (10), Sense Truth (14), Survival (8), Swim (1), Knowledge: Monsters (10), Knowledge: World Lore (5), Knowledge: Demons (1), Unite

Class Skills: Improved Assess 3 (23), Awareness (17), Knowledge: Geography (10), Spot (14), *Discern Weakness* (23), Dodge (14), Improvised Distraction (14), *Outflank* (17), Draw Fire (10), *Keep Pace* (16), Amplify Voice (13), See It Coming (18), Basic Weapon Proficiency (Swords) (12), *Read Body*

Language (11), Basic Map Access (4), Compel (8), Spot Weakness (3), Secret Message (2), *Bonded Mind* (0)

*italics are paired skills with partner

Name: Jacob Owen Lindberg

∞ Aderyn

Class: Swordsworn

Level: 14

Skills: Assess (11), Awareness (13), Climb (10), Conversation (13), Sense Truth (12), Spot (11), Survival (5), Swim (10), Knowledge: Demons (1), Unite

Class Skills: Advanced Weapon Proficiency (24), Advanced Armor Proficiency (17), Knowledge: Monsters (11), *Exploit Weakness* (23), Dodge (15), Parry (15), Improved Bluff (13), *Outflank* (17), Trip (5), *Keep Pace* (16), Disarm (6), Intimidate (11), Charge (6), Two-Weapon Fighting (7), *Read Body Language* (11), Basic Map Access (4), Overrun (5), Demoralize (5), Sunder (2), Shatter Confidence (1), *Bonded Mind* (0)

*italics are paired skills with Warmaster

Name: Weston

Class: Moonlighter

Level: 14

Skills: Assess (12), Climb (14), Conversation (12), Intimidate (10), Sense Truth (12), Survival (4), Swim (3), Knowledge: Social (13), Knowledge: Demons (1)

Class Skills: Pick Locks (13), Advanced Sneak Attack (13), Advanced Weapon Proficiency (12), Advanced Armor Proficiency (11), Improved Detect Traps (15), Disable Traps (12), Improved Spot (17), Awareness (14), Dodge (14), Stealth (15), Improved Bluff (13), Dirty Fighting (9), To the Heart (13), Hide (9), Improved Thrown Weapons Proficiency (8), Disguise

(1), Hide in Plain Sight (5), Evasion (6), Basic Map Access (4), Escape Artist (3), Unarmed Combat (2), Improvised Weapon (1)

Name: Isold
> Class: Herald
> Level: 14
> Skills: Assess (10), Awareness (13), Bluff (10), Climb (7), Conversation (7), Intimidate (4), Sense Truth (15), Spot (13), Survival (4), Swim (2) Knowledge: Demons (2)
> Class Skills: Perform (singing) (15); Knowledge: Magic (12); Knowledge: Monsters (12); Knowledge: History (9); Knowledge: Social (10); Knowledge: World Lore (13); Identify Magic Items (13); Charm (15); Distraction (11); Map Access (14); Inspire Courage (11); Fascination (9); Persuasion (9); Perform (drum) (10); Suggestion (7); Resist Magic (6); Shout (3); Hypnotize (7); Find Object (3); Coercion (2); Break Enchantment (4); Perform (flute) (1)

Name: Livia
> Class: Earthbreaker
> Level: 14
> Skills: Assess (6), Awareness (8), Bluff (7), Climb (3), Conversation (9), Intimidate (13), Sense Truth (10), Spot (10), Survival (4), Swim (3), Knowledge: Demons (1)
> Elemental Powers: Earth, stone
> Class Skills: Knowledge: Magic (14), Elemental Blast (earth spray, shower of small stones, rain of large stones, stone sphere shrapnel) (13), Earth to Mud/Mud to Earth (8), Mage Armor (shifting stone slabs) (8), Excavate (7), Summon Elemental Hammer (3), Basic Map Access (4), Tremorsense (3), Sculpt Earth/Stone (3), Speak with Stone (0)

Spell List

0-level spells: Daze; Drench; Light; Telekinesis, minor; Mending; Freezing Ray, minor; Root, Spark

1st Level spells

Air Bubble; Break; Force Shield; Grease; Heat Metal (slow); Loose Bonds; Mudball; Sunder Weapon; Thunder Punch

2nd Level spells

Create Pit; Dust Cloud; Earth's Endurance; Thunderstomp; Mirror Image; Mud Minion; Improved Mending; Protection from Fire, Mass (big earth dome); Skip

3rd Level spells

Iron Spike Attack; Thunderstomp, Greater (directed); Clairvoyance; Dispel Magic; Immobilize; Telekinesis, Greater; Daylight

4th Level spells

Stone Ladder; Stone Sphere; Transport, Minor; Invisibility (self); Earth Glide; Stone Fist; Daze, Mass

5th Level spells

Hungry Pit; Dismissal of Demons; Scry; Lighten Object; Darkvision; Passwall; Burrow

6th Level spells

Move earth, major; Stoneskin, Mass; Invisibility, Mass; Dispel Magic, greater

7th Level spells

Immobilize, greater; Sunburst

AND NOW A SPECIAL MESSAGE...

Did you enjoy this book? Want more LitRPG adventure goodness? Then the LitRPG Books Facebook group is for you! Find new recommendations, connect with fellow readers, and more!

ABOUT THE AUTHOR

In addition to the Warmaster series, Melissa McShane is the author of many fantasy novels, including the novels of Tremontane, the first of which is *Servant of the Crown;* The Extraordinaries series, beginning with *Burning Bright;* and *The Book of Secrets,* first book in The Last Oracle series.

While her home remains in the mountains out West, she currently lives in Kerala, India, with her husband and two rambunctious Persian kittens. She wrote reviews and critical essays for many years before turning to fiction, which is much more fun than anyone ought to be allowed to have.

You can visit her at her website
www.melissamcshanewrites.com
for more information on other books and upcoming releases.

To subscribe to her newsletter, which is published monthly, visit
www.melissamcshanewrites.com/contact-me-2/join-my-mailing-list

ALSO BY MELISSA McSHANE

WARMASTER

Warmaster 1: Dungeon Spiteful

Warmaster 2: Winter's Peril

Warmaster 3: Gamboling Coil

Warmaster 4: Sorrowvale

Warmaster 5: The Glory Games

Warmaster 6: The Lonely Tor (forthcoming)

THE BOOKS OF THE DARK GODDESS

Silver and Shadow

Missing by Moonlight

Shades of the Past

Path of the Paladin

Bright Moon Deception (forthcoming 2024)

THE LAST ORACLE

The Book of Secrets

The Book of Peril

The Book of Mayhem

The Book of Lies

The Book of Betrayal

The Book of Havoc

The Book of Harmony

The Book of War

The Book of Destiny

THE LIVING ORACLE
Hidden Realm

Hidden Enemy

Hidden Pursuit

THE EXTRAORDINARIES
Burning Bright

Wondering Sight

Abounding Might

Whispering Twilight

Liberating Fight

Beguiling Birthright

Soaring Flight

Discerning Insight

THE NOVELS OF TREMONTANE
Pretender to the Crown

Guardian of the Crown

Champion of the Crown

Ally of the Crown

Stranger to the Crown

Scholar of the Crown

Servant of the Crown

Exile of the Crown

Emissary

Warts and All: The Deluxe Expanded Edition

The View from Castle Always

Winter Across Worlds: A Holiday Collection

www.ingramcontent.com/pod-product-compliance
Lightning Source LLC
Chambersburg PA
CBHW071633260626
47170CB00001B/88